CW00507240

ALL-AMERICAN WEREWOLF

ANTONIO RICARDO SCOZZE

This book is dedicated to my Nameless Ones; you know who you are.

PROLOGUE

Are you ready? Are you, my Dear Friend, ready to delve once again into this world of horror, into this twisted hellscape we've only just started to explore – this, the Atrocissimus? We scratched the surface of this perverse space and began to expand your awareness in my first book, *The House on Blackstone Hill*. There I revealed to you some horrifying truths of the world around you, and now, with every step we take together in this journey you grow ever closer to knowing the truth – stark, clear, and unadulterated.

But once again, my Dear Friend, I must ask you: Do you *really* want to know? Do you truly want to know the unvarnished truth, to peel back the curtain that's been draped over the Atrocissimus for all these millennia, to fully see and understand what lurks beneath you? I would understand if you didn't; knowing the truth, the absolute truth with no embellishments, can be a terrible burden to bear. I would understand if you wanted to turn aside from this journey even now.

The secrets we're going to unveil together are shocking and

realizing that you've been lied to your entire life can be overwhelming. Not only that, but learning you are part of an endless supernatural war, that you are the plaything for evil entities can deeply disturb some people. Discovering that there is an entire hidden world ruled over by foul, twisted demons can be well-nigh traumatizing.

However, what I'm about to show you in this next part of my slowly unfolding series might haunt you. Realizing there are people, regular humans who willingly, even happily, traffic with these evil beings for their own enrichment and power, and the ends to which they'll go to secure that power... well, my Dear Friend, that might be just too much.

If you're disturbed by this level of awareness, perhaps you should turn aside. If learning the uttermost truth, if having all the workings of this massive cosmic system plainly revealed to you is knowledge you'd rather not have, then, by all means, Dear Friend, lay aside this book and continue floating in a stream of blissful ignorance. But if not, let's begin exploring some more of the dark, dank corners of the Atrocissimus.

So, again I ask you... are you ready?

CHAPTER ONE

Lenny Stevens sat on the front porch of his small rural house in the brutal early July heat, slowly swaying on a two-person swing as the odor of fireworks still hung in the moist air. The slight, gentle movement he made as he swung through the humid night was the closest thing he'd get to a breeze; the heat wave that had gripped Maryland for the entire summer continued to hold the region in its grasp.

If the heat this summer weren't bad enough, the humidity made it even worse. As Lenny lit a cigarette and breathed in the late-night air, he could smell the damp hanging in it. It felt like being wrapped in a wet blanket. The bedroom he shared with his wife was like an oven, and since they couldn't afford to replace their air conditioner, he'd come to the porch to cool down rather than spend one more sleepless minute lying in a pool of his own sweat.

To cool down, and to think.

Lenny worried about the future. Ever since graduating high school, he'd worked at one of the factories just over the county border in Pocomoke City, the past seven of which he'd been first shift foreman. Although he and his wife, Cindy, had never had much in the way of riches, Lenny's factory job had afforded them the comfortable little house in which they lived with their two rambunctious boys – both of whom were, thankfully, visiting his parents for the week. His job allowed for the bills to be paid and put food on the table, and enough acres of land so Lenny could pursue his side-business as a small farmer. Overall, things were good.

But that rock-solid foundation on which Lenny *thought* he'd built his life was starting to crumble. He realized the mistake he'd made by thinking life would be predictable, assuming it would follow his plan when he was promoted to shift foreman. Lenny figured he'd stay in that job for the next decade or so, then move into the shop foreman position. Finally, after many long years of loyal service to the company, he'd retire to Florida with a nice pension to live out his days fishing and growing fat.

It was a good plan until the manufacturing jobs started to disappear. For the past five years Lenny had watched as one factory in Pocomoke City after another grew ever more anemic until, after having moved most of the operations elsewhere, each factory finally closed. Lenny had prayed his own factory could avoid that fate, but in the last two years, he'd seen the same process starting there. He'd watched with growing angst as first one division was closed and everyone working there got laid off, then another division was moved overseas, as everyone there likewise got pink-slipped, and so on. Lenny feared he had a target on his back, and it was only a matter of time before he, too, lost his job.

Lenny felt like he was trapped on a slowly sinking ship, knowing what the inevitable outcome would be but fearing he might drown if he jumped overboard. He took a long drag of his cigarette and looked down at this dog, curled comfortably at his feet.

"What would you do, Max?" he asked, patting the dog's head as he did. "What would you suggest I do?"

If Max had any wisdom to offer, he kept it to himself.

Lenny let out the smoke in a long, discontented sigh, and as he did, he thought he heard rustling in his cornfield a few yards away from the porch. Max suddenly became interested in that spot as well, but at the same moment he heard Cindy open the screen door. Thoughts of whatever the sound might have been immediately left his mind when he looked at his wife, her skin glistening with sweat, her hair sleep-tousled, wearing a sheer negligée that hid very little of her nude body under it. Max, however, fixed his stare at the same spot in the cornfield.

"Can't sleep again?" Cindy asked softly in the quiet night, lighting her own cigarette as she joined him on the swing.

"Nope," Lenny answered, putting his arm around Cindy, and pulling her close to him, though her skin was warm and sweaty. "Too damn hot up there."

"Not much better out here, though."

Lenny nodded his head in agreement, taking a long drag off his cigarette. "No, not much better, but at least it don't feel so damn stuffy out here."

After a moment of silence, Cindy said, "But I assume it ain't just the heat that got you up. Worried 'bout work?"

"Yeah, I am," Lenny said, flicking the cigarette butt out towards the driveway. "I'm worried, but I'm also stuck, you know? Like, I can see what's gonna happen. The writing's on the wall, everyone can see it coming. So, I should leave, get another job." Lenny paused to light another cigarette, taking a long first drag as he did. "But problem is, factory work is all I ever done, all I know how to do. I'm thirty-five, a little too old to learn a trade, no way

I'm going back to school. And honestly, I don't want to start over in another factory. I worked my ass off to get where I am now, and I really don't want to go back to working on the line."

Holding Cindy close to him, Lenny could feel the soft swell of her breast pressing into his chest, and he found her slick, sweaty skin to be wonderfully distracting.

"We need to come up with something," Cindy said, her head leaning against her husband's bare chest.

"I know."

"I heard people talking at the restaurant of maybe there being oil or natural gas or something in the western part of the state, maybe up in Pennsylvania. They say that pays real good money."

"Yeah, I could do that. I'd probably like that. I think that'd have me out in the field a lot, though," Lenny said, gently massaging his wife's hot shoulder with his fingertips as he drank in the image of her body. "We'd be separated for weeks at a time, I think. You okay with that?"

She thought for a moment, her hand resting on his thigh. "Hmm... I don't think so. I'd miss you too much. Maybe one of them crabbers that work out of Crisfield?"

"Well, babe, then I'd be out for weeks at a time. I'd be gone more than if I were in the oil fields."

A silent moment as the two thought about their very limited options, coming up with nothing.

"So, what do you suggest?" Cindy asked at last, lifting her head from Lenny's chest to look into his eyes. "You don't make enough from farming to cover the bills, even with what I bring in. We'll need to do something else."

"I know, I know," Lenny said, no longer focused on the discussion and dismissing it from his mind. He'd gone over it a million times before and found no obvious answers. He was tired, and the more he looked at his wife's all but naked body, the hornier he became. "For now, let's just enjoy having the house to ourselves for once," he said, as he leaned in to start kissing his wife's neck.

But just as Lenny was about to move his hand to Cindy's breast, he again heard the rustling sound in his cornfield. Lenny and Cindy both looked that way, half-expecting to see someone watching them, as Max got on his feet and started barking loudly. As they did, they caught the faint odor of rotten eggs.

"What is that?" Cindy said in a harsh whisper.

"I don't know," Lenny said, as he started to walk towards the cornfield, Max joining him. "Stay here," he said to Cindy.

Lenny walked slowly, carefully, the way he would while out hunting, like he was trying to sneak up on whatever might be in the corn even though he was exposed on his lawn. He scanned the field, hoping to catch sight of what might be lurking in the waist-high corn. The dim lamp over his driveway only illuminated a few rows into the field, so there could be something hiding in the dark beyond the light. Max barked aggressively the whole time as he approached next to Lenny, eyes on the cornfield.

Lenny paused, coiled and ready to move in an instant, if need be, trying to see or hear anything. He couldn't, though he knew there was something out there in his fields as the rotten egg smell became worse.

"Max!" Lenny yelled as the dog suddenly ran headlong into the field, disappearing into the darkness. Lenny took two quick steps to follow him, then stopped when he heard Max yelp once in pain, followed by an immediate end to his barking. "MAX! *MAAAX!!*"

Lenny stood in the abrupt silence, trying desperately to hear or see anything. He saw nothing but his darkened cornfield and heard nothing but blood flowing in his ears as his heart pounded in unexpected terror.

"Lenny," Cindy whimpered from the porch behind him, "what's going on?"

"I don't know," he said. "I think Max got hurt. Get the—" Lenny stopped speaking abruptly, as he caught swift movement to his left and the odor of sulfur became overwhelming. He pivoted and whipped his head around to see what it was but only had time to catch a glimpse of his own death approaching.

Lenny shrieked once in abject, overpowering horror. A shaggy creature with a gigantic paw swiped down at him, the long, curved claws slicing easily and deeply into his face, tearing off his cheek and ripping out his lower jaw, then continuing down to pull open his neck. As Lenny's bloody corpse fell to the ground, the creature sank its fangs into his chest and, clutching his body with its talons, ripped his upper body wide open with a deep growl.

When Lenny was attacked by this huge, hairy beast, Cindy threw herself back against the screen door, frozen in terror, her eyes shocked wide open, unable to breathe let alone scream. But when it ripped open Lenny's chest cavity, his blood pouring everywhere and pink organs falling out of his body with wet *plops*, she could no longer contain the shock of watching her husband being killed and mutilated; she screamed loudly, piteously, and until her throat hurt.

The creature stood looking at her, blood and gore dripping off its claws, red irises glowing in the dark night. It roared once in answer to her screams, an unearthly cry, one unlike any animal on Earth. Running with impossible speed on two legs, the beast ended Cindy's life as savagely as it had Lenny's, then took the time to destroy her remains.

Then, its fur caked and matted with bits of flesh, clotted blood, and shards of bone, the creature threw back its head and howled triumphantly into the dark night.

CHAPTER TWO

As his personal chauffeur passed the iron gate and turned onto the long gravel driveway leading to Raven Hill Manor, Louis Garrou finished reading a small story buried deep in the pages of *The Washington Post* Sunday edition about a spate of bizarre animal attacks in the past week all throughout rural Somerset County, Maryland. According to the article, conservation officers were on the hunt for a rabid bear that had apparently killed no less than seven people in the days following the Fourth of July. All the bodies, the report noted, were ripped and shredded beyond recognition.

"Well, I'll be damned," Garrou said. "Carlos, did you see that story in the *Post* about those animal attacks?"

Carlos, his driver, glanced in the rear-view mirror a moment to look at Garrou, then said, "No, sir, but I saw a report on the news about it. That's horrible."

"Damn right it is. I was going to all those town hall meetings on the Delmarva and never once realized this was happening. How terrible."

"Yes, sir. It is that."

Garrou looked again at the headline that read *Thompson Closing Poll Numbers with Garrou in Senate Race*, then tossed the paper aside with a grunt. He watched as the gigantic Gilded Age mansion loomed in front of him with all its imposing Italianate revival opulence, surrounded by flocks of crows as it was always. He'd grown up in that mansion with his parents, his siblings, the servants, and the memory of the entire Garrou family history, something that had been drilled into the children from an early age. He and his siblings all knew that they weren't so much living their own lives as they were furthering the glorious history of the Garrou family and fulfilling its destiny.

His six siblings were scattered all around the world working as leaders in industry, banking, the media, and education. His generation was doing their duty to live up to the family name, furthering their agenda on a massive scale. But he, as the eldest and living so close to the family estate, had the additional duty of visiting his mother on a regular basis.

As Garrou walked into the grand foyer, he breathed in the familiar odor of his childhood home: Old leather, fresh-cut flowers, and tangy burnt incense. He paused to check himself in an enormous, gilded mirror that had once belonged to a king of France. His Bill Blass suit was impeccable as always, as was his strawberry blond hair, though he did adjust his tie to perfect the knot dimple. Though only meeting his mother for their weekly Sunday brunch, his appearance mattered.

He thought of the cold, hard woman that was his mother as he picked a small piece of lint off his suit coat. Mariette Garrou, matriarch of the family and incessant driver of her children's success. She was ancient and unyielding and had been his entire life.

He knew she'd be sitting on the private family patio reading the *Post* as she waited for him because Sunday brunch is served on the patio during summer, and she always read the newspaper. If it were raining, the table and chairs would be moved to the portico, but brunch was *always* served outside. She would never consider an alteration to her ways, nor would the thought enter her mind that it is unrelentingly hot outside and perhaps not the ideal environment for eating.

He knew she was unbending, obdurate, and implacable, and always would be.

Garrou smiled to himself as he walked onto the patio; the picture he'd created in his mind perfectly matched the reality he saw. There sat his mother, stiff and straight as always, her half-moon glasses perched on her nose, reading the *Post*. She, as always, wore an archaic black dress that seemed as if it was original to the one hundred ten-year-old family mansion, with her hair tied into a severe bun atop her head. Servants in sharp white Eton jackets and matching white cloth gloves on their crossed hands stood a respectful distance away, awaiting an order from either Garrou.

"Good morning, Mother," Garrou said as he crossed the patio to kiss her. She presented her cheek to him, but never once did her eyes stop reading the story.

"Did you have a pleasant hunting trip?" she asked.

"I did indeed. I downed seven of them."

"Well done. That was a fine speech you gave about how workers need the full backing of the government, and so it should support them everywhere," Mariette said, without making eye contact. "Very inspiring, and no doubt uplifting for the poor and working classes."

"Thank you," said Garrou, glancing at one of the servants and snapping his fingers. The young man rushed to the table, laid Garrou's napkin on his lap, poured him a cup of coffee from the silver carafe, then served him a croissant and some fruit before retreating with similar alacrity to his original spot.

"You do know how deeply I care for the plight of the working man."

"Of course," she said, as what passed for a smile briefly teased up the ends of Mariette's thin lips.

Garrou regarded his mother closely and noted that, although he remembered her as always being old, she looked even more aged of late. Her always pale skin was now nearly translucent and was so pallid it seemed almost to glow in the glaring sun; if he weren't wearing his Ray-Bans, Garrou doubted he could look right at her. Her wrinkled skin seemed to have become more deeply etched of late, and her slight tremor appeared worse. Her hair, which up until recently had always been her natural red color, was now streaked with long wisps of pure white, making her bun look almost like the swirl of a candy cane.

Though Mariette had surrendered none of her intensity or vitality, and she moved with the grace she'd always shown, Garrou believed his mother looked somehow older. He'd once thought she was immortal, but, no, she could age just like everyone else.

"How are you, Mother?" he asked. "Is everything well?"

Mariette looked up from the newspaper at her son with unflinching ice blue eyes, one eyebrow raised.

"Am I well?" she said, her voice strong and fierce. "Am *I* well? Louis, may I remind you that I'm not the one running for the open Senate seat and not the one who should be leading the polls by double digits – especially given our connections – but who is *not!* I'm not the one who is being upstaged by some country bumpkin farmer and being made to look foolish. You are!"

Louis sat back in his chair and sighed. *Fuck*, he thought to himself. *Politics. Always politics. And now here comes the lecture.*

Mariette pointed to the folded newspaper she was reading. "Have you seen these latest poll numbers, hmm? Are you reading what the opinion pieces are saying?"

"Yes, Mother, of course," Garrou said. "I'm a United State Congressman, I know enough to check the poll numbers and opinion pieces. My election staff is keeping me updated on all of this."

"Uh-huh," she said dismissively. "Sim Thompson is gaining on you in the polls. They are writing about him now like he is a viable alternative, that he is the leader the state needs and not you. Earlier in the year, after the sudden and *tragic* death of Senator Wilkes, Thompson was being written off as an 'also-ran,' as an opposition candidate just for the sake of opposition, but now he is becoming a serious threat to you... to all of us."

"I know, Mother. I know."

She swept her thin, bony hand into the air as if pushing aside his defense. "You know, you know," she said contemptuously, "but I don't see any *action*, Louis. I don't see you taking on an enemy and annihilating him, the way you were taught."

He looked at his mother as the realization of what she was saying dawned on him. "You want me to... again? Like Wilkes?"

"Nothing and no one can be allowed to stand in your way," she said, and then in a whisper, "in our way."

Garrou slowly chewed a small piece of croissant as he thought. "I need some time to plan it. I want it to look like an accident, like with Wilkes."

"Time?" Mariette asked, speaking softly. "What time do you think you have? Might I remind you it was long ago decided by the High Commission itself that you would be president? Your duty, your singular mission to our coven, and to the Coven Universal, is to become president so you can establish policies to further our rule. The national covens will, of course, assist you to win the presidential race, but if you lose *this* race then all these plans will have been for naught – and, let me also remind you, this was the entire reason you were given the Gift of the Wolf."

The Gift of the Wolf. The ability to change into a huge, wolflike beast at will, one granted through demonic power to only select members of the Coven Universal. It was a most convenient power to have when one wanted to eliminate political rivals in a clandestine way, or just to kill just for the sport of it.

Garrou thought back twenty-seven years to the night of his sixteenth birthday, the night he was given the Gift.

He'd been raised in the regional coven. He'd been saturated in its beliefs, aware of its awesome powers, and dedicated to its goals from an early age. Having a High Priestess as his mother made that inevitable. Garrou had become a full member three years earlier when he'd sacrificed a child on the bloody altar, and in that time, he'd been preparing himself to be worthy enough to deserve the Gift.

Garrou had been given a list of challenges to accomplish, of goals to achieve in something of a Satanic agoge. In addition to reading and analyzing some dark grimoires, Garrou had been given a list of heinous acts to commit. As a student at the Fairmont Preparatory Academy in California, Louis not only had many potential victims within easy reach but an even larger pool of victims waiting in the surrounding community, a community that would never believe a Fairmount student could be guilty of these crimes.

The first task on Garrou's list was a simple one: Kill a random person, anywhere, at any time of day, with any weapon. That was easy enough and he was able to check it off within a few days. The tasks, however, grew in complexity and danger, as any good agoge should. It took him the entire three years to accomplish them all.

One of the later tasks he struggled with was to kill someone in public with nothing but a screwdriver and without being arrested. Garrou puzzled over that for a time but eventually found an elegant solution. He ground down the end of a large screwdriver until it was nothing but a giant shank, then went to an adult movie theater. Taking a seat directly behind a man who was too focused on the action on the screen, Louis waited until he was distracted by pleasuring himself and shoved the screwdriver into the base of the man's brain in one swift movement. Garrou twisted and turned the screwdriver a few times to make certain the man was dead, and then simply walked away, leaving him there with a screwdriver sticking out the back of his head.

Garrou's final task was a challenging one, but one that, like all the others, he accomplished with aplomb and ability. He was to rape and murder a married woman in her house during the day while her husband was home, but to do it without his ever being aware. Garrou pulled off this most difficult of all agoge tasks with planning, daring, and a little bit of luck: He pulled the front door closed behind him even as the husband walked in through the back after having finished his yard work.

And so it was that Garrou had proven his worth, his ability, and his willingness to kill, maim, and rape in Satan's name. Due to completing his agoge, he was finally allowed to have his Gifting ceremony when he turned sixteen. He recalled how on that night so long ago he'd stood naked before the altar as several masked priestesses in black robes anointed him with aromatic oils and painted his body with potent runes and sigils.

As they did so, Mariette, wearing a horned animal skull mask, chanted powerful ancient words of magic while she sacrificed seven choice young virgins, slitting their throats, and collecting the blood in a large, gilded basin. After killing them, she eviscerated each one in turn and collected their entrails to chop into the base of a chunky salve, which she smeared all over his body after the priestesses had finished, still chanting her spells.

Mariette had taken the athame she'd used to sacrifice the girls and sliced a sigil into Garrou's back, and then finally called upon the demon Marchosias to grant him the Gift as she poured the virgins' blood over his head. From that moment, Garrou could take werewolf form whenever he wanted, towering over ten feet tall when he did, having supernatural strength and speed.

The very next night he went hunting for the first time, whispering the words that turned him into a werewolf, and killed a farmer who lived not far from their mansion in Poolesville. The transformation process turning into the Wolf was agonizing, and while not as long or drawn out as depicted in the stories, it took nearly a full minute for Louis' bones to be broken and knitted back together, for his muscles to swell into their massive proportions, and for his tendons and ligaments to stretch so he could reach his full inhuman height. As he endured the pain of becoming the Wolf that first night, the words his mother often said to her children echoed in his head: *There is no power without sacrifice, and there is no sacrifice without pain.*

Garrou had loved the feeling of unbridled power that first kill afforded him and lusted after the feeling with every subsequent kill. The power that came with limitless wealth was magnificent, and the power that was attached to being a congressman delightful, but Garrou found there was no power like that of taking another person's life, especially in the form of a demonically empowered beast.

He sipped his coffee, meeting his mother's unwavering blue eyes. "I'll take care of it, Mother," he said. "One way or another I'll take care of that up-jumped hick farmer."

CHAPTER THREE

P eter Brunnen loved watching the deliberations in the House Chamber from the galleries above. Though others might think them unbearably dry and boring, he found the processes that ran the American government to be fascinating. Every little procedure, every tradition, every symbol of American democracy built into the Chamber itself was exciting for Peter.

He glanced around the galleries. Built to accommodate hundreds, there was a mere handful of people watching that day, most of whom were Congressional staffers like himself. Stretching his long legs out to have more space and rubbing his smooth, cleft chin, he could never understand how the galleries weren't packed every day with people watching their government do its work.

Peter returned his attention to the speaker, a congresswoman from California: "... was arrested and subjected to a secret, hooded military tribunal in which she was denied due process, according to the State Department, human rights groups and the United Nations Commission on Human

Rights..." Today the House was considering, among other things, what actions to take to secure the freedom of an American convicted of terrorism held prisoner in Peru. Peter found it amazing that the government of the most powerful nation on earth would take time to even discuss helping a citizen convicted of a crime in another country. He ran his hand through the mop of unruly, sand-colored lazy curls atop his head as he considered the marvel of it.

How could people not be riveted by this? he thought. *How could they just not care? I'll never understand people.*

As the proceedings went on, Peter looked around the Chamber, thinking about the meanings of the symbols in it. There were, of course, stars and cornucopia and bas relief busts, but his favorite was always the illuminated skylight above. A bald eagle, wings outstretched, seemed ever to float serenely above the Chamber as if watching the decisions made there and judging their worth. But to Peter, the eagle always seemed more than just a passive observer and judge – as Peter believed were too many of the American electorate – but more of a protector, as if it soared above the deliberations with its wings spread wide to shield those in the Chamber from evil influences.

He brought his attention back to the congresswoman for a bit as she continued. "... She has been held under horrendous prison conditions in the Peruvian Andes and we are all very concerned with her failing health. Lori has been subjected to long periods of isolation which have been cited by Amnesty International as cruel, inhumane and degrading treatment, in violation of..."

His eyes lifted from the lectern where the congresswoman spoke to the two great fasces flanking the large flag behind the Speaker's podium. Peter had always been a fan of that Roman symbol and the meaning behind it. He appreciated how it meant an individual thin rod could easily be shattered, yet when bundled together, a group of such rods is both flexible and strong, strong enough to weather many blows.

It'd been pointed out before to Peter that he was an idealist, but he truly believed if enough people were to act in concert to create change, then change could happen, regardless of how poor or disconnected or otherwise powerless they might be as individuals. He believed it was only a matter of the willingness to *fight* and to stand together against what people thought was wrong.

That was the entire reason he'd taken a job on Congressman Sim Thompson's staff after graduating college the previous year. Peter had been born and raised in a little Maryland town called Mountain Lake Park, and he'd spent the last several years watching as all the businesses seemed to slowly evaporate. Never much of a thriving metropolis to begin with, Mountain Lake Park had turned into a husk of its former self and was now just a scattered collection of houses. It was the same in the nearby town of Oakland just as it seemed to be all throughout Garrett County.

And he believed the reason was entirely because of terrible decisions made in Washington, decisions that favored the powerful at the expense of everyone else, ones designed to line the pockets of those who needed it the least by taking it from those who had the least. So, idealistic or not, Peter came to Washington to help change things.

The congresswoman finally finished her remarks as Peter again attended to her words, "... has given the President the authority, short of war, to gain the release of a U.S. citizen who has been wrongly incarcerated abroad, then we must do all that we can do to bring Lori home."

"Hey," Peter heard a hushed voice say next to him. He could smell her distinctive lilac odor just before she spoke as a lightness settled on his heart and a thrilling tingle went down his spine. "I thought I might find you here."

He turned and smiled broadly at Angie Fontaine, a fellow staffer working for a congressman from Alabama.

"Hey, babe," Peter said, kissing her quickly as she sat next to him. "How is your day going?"

"Pretty well, thanks," Angie said in a southern accent he thought would sound musical, even if she were reciting tax code. "It's been a fairly straightforward day. How about you, honey?"

Peter paused a moment before answering, realizing he was again getting lost in Angie's brilliant green eyes, the way her long, brown hair framed her lovely face, and the way little dimples formed every time she smiled. He'd been doing that a great deal lately, noticing with excited amusement that he'd spent much of the past several months staring into her eyes, especially at their dinner dates. Pete would listen to Angie's lilting voice as she talked about politics, getting lost in the depths of her eyes, finding it adorable the way she kept pushing her glasses up her little nose.

Peter had been driven by idealistic goals to come work in Washington, preparing for a future in Congress himself; he had also, unexpectedly, fallen in love.

Peter still found it amazing that this smart and ambitious woman, who was also lusciously curvaceous, had somehow found a tall, lanky policy nerd was a catch worth dating. Peter loved her sharp mind and her sense of humor, the way she'd put a pen to her lips when thinking, and even her habit of bouncing a leg when she was nervous. Though an unbiased observer might note that Angie was perhaps a bit too plump or that she had an overbite, Peter noticed none of that. To his eyes, Angie was perfection and beauty personified.

"It's been pretty busy, actually," Peter said, noting that it was now Angie who seemed to be lost in his hazel eyes. "We had a meeting earlier today, Thompson's voting on the Bilbray amendment now, another meeting in a little while, and then maybe some committee stuff. I'll eat, I guess, at some point. It's not easy juggling a full-time Congressional schedule with an election."

"No, I guess not," Angie said, gently stroking his hand as she spoke. "Okay, so... who's your favorite poet?" This was something the pair had been doing since they started dating. They'd been together now for several months but hadn't known each other the previous twenty-five years of their lives. They were trying to find out these little details and so would randomly ask such questions.

"My favorite poet?" Peter asked. He liked reading but wasn't much of a poetry guy. "Umm... Poe, I guess."

"Poe?" Angie asked incredulously.

"Yes, Poe," he said. "C'mon, 'Nevermore, quoth the Raven,' and all that. That's classic stuff."

"Actually, it's 'Quoth the Raven, Nevermore,' but whatever."

Peter looked at Angie and waggled his finger at her, yet she continued smiling a toothy grin at him, nonetheless. "Listen, Little Miss Smarty Pants..."

"Uh-huh." Peter's threats were unimpressive.

"Okay, fine... what's your worst personality trait?"

"Hmm..." Angie said, putting a finger to her cleft chin. "I guess it's that I can get so lost in a good book, I don't hear if people are talking to me and forget what I need to do. I can't tell you how many times mamma had to come get me from my room because I didn't hear her yelling my name for dinner."

"Ooh, damn," Peter said. "You don't want mamma mad at you."

Angie chuckled. "Definitely not *my* mamma. What about you? Your worst trait?"

"That's hard to answer since I'm so awesome, but—"

"I can provide some suggestions, if that'd help," Angie said smiling.

Peter looked at Angie with mouth wide open, hand on heart, as if crushed. "Hmpf. Fine, now I guess I know where you stand... I suppose it's that I'm too stubborn. When I get something in my mind, I'm like a bulldog with a bone. I just can't let go."

"Sometimes that can be a good thing," said Angie.

"Yeah, sometimes it can be, but I can also drive people crazy with it. Okay, favorite genre of writing?"

Angie giggled as she covered her face, then said, "Horror."

"Horror?!" Peter asked. A few of the other gallery attendants turned to look at the sudden outburst as the couple shrunk into their seats, again speaking softly.

"I know, I know, it doesn't go with poetry so much but, you know—"

"You kidding me? I love horror. Want to guess whose work first got me into it?"

"If you say Poe then that's another thing we have in common," Angie said, the pair clutching hands in their whispered excitement for the genre. "I read *The Tell-Tale Heart* in middle school and got addicted to horror right away."

"Me too!" said Peter. "Man, the dead vulture eye of the old guy always gave me the creeps. Do you like – shit, wait, what time is it?" he asked, now looking at this watch. "Shit. I need to get going."

"Okay. Dinner tonight, my place?" Angie asked with a smile that flashed her dimples and brightened her already lovely face.

"Yeah, absolutely. Hey, that *Blair Witch Project* movie comes out next Friday. You want to go see it?"

Angie scrunched up her face, then said, "Well, I like horror books a lot more than I do horror movies, but we can give it a try. Wait – what's your favorite horror movie?"

Peter chuckled a little, then said, "It's definitely *Fright Night*. A little campy, I know, but I just love that movie. Okay, babe, I gotta go!"

Peter gave Angie another kiss then headed out. He grabbed a quick lunch and returned to Thompson's office as the team was assembling for their afternoon meeting, then took a seat at the large conference table near his friend, Rick Johnson.

"Hey, Rick," Peter said. "How's it going?"

Rick shook his head and rolled his eyes, then said, "I'm just about going crazy keeping up with all these media requests. I mean, it's good that the boss is getting national attention now, but damn it! My head is spinning."

"I hear you, man," Peter said as he nodded solemnly. "I think we're all just about crazy at this point. All I know is I'm really looking forward to the recess. At least it'll get us out of here."

"Mmhmm... hey, how are things going with Angie?"

Peter smiled reflexively at the mention of her name. "It's going good, man. It's going real good. I think she's the one for me."

"That's awesome, Peter. I'm happy for you." Rick patted his friend on the shoulder and smiled as Thompson rapped his knuckles on his desk to get the meeting started.

Thompson, as he always did during these staff meetings, sat at his desk, suit jacket off, tie loosened and collar open, sleeves rolled up, leaning back in his chair with his hands cradling his head. His chief of staff, legislative director, and press secretary sat in the chairs in front of his desk while the remaining staff sat at the conference table off to the side.

"Alright, Jimmy," Thompson said to his chief of staff after he'd gotten everyone's attention, "take it away. What do we got?"

"Well, to begin with," Jimmy said, "we've made some of the language in the speech you're going to give on the floor about keeping manufacturing in-country crisper and more succinct, but we do need to discuss some of the verbiage..."

Peter tried desperately to follow the thread of the discussion and take notes on what was assigned to him, but ever since he started dating Angie, his mind wandered away in meetings with surprising ease. Try as he might to pay attention, somehow his thoughts seemed to quickly drift back to her. As the team discussed prioritizing legislative initiatives for the upcoming fall – and as he pretended to be attentively taking notes – Peter found himself thinking about how good Angie always smelled of flowers when he hugged her. As the meeting changed focus to what Thompson could expect during his appearance on *Face the Nation* that Sunday, Peter seemed almost stuck on how smooth her skin was when he'd rub her arms – Angie could somehow feel chilly in an oven, apparently! – or how soft her lips were when they kissed. As the team started to debate the best tactics to leverage advantage against Garrou, Peter found himself wondering how edible she might look nude – a delight he had yet to experience.

Nearly an hour later, Peter was jolted back to the meeting when Jimmy, the chief of staff, and Drew, the legislative director, began to loudly disagree on some important point. As they did, Lana, the press secretary, aligned herself with Jimmy and the disagreement looked like it was about to become a two-on-one fight.

"All right, all right, *all right!*" Thompson yelled even

louder, taking control of the meeting back. "That's enough. Killing each other isn't going to help us win an election against big bad Lou Garrou. That's got to be our focus here, not whose idea might be better."

Thompson stood and sighed heavily, running his hand through his salt-and-pepper hair as he walked out from behind the desk. The weight of his schedule was showing on him.

"You know, I never quite feel comfortable in this town," he said. "Everyone's too fake, everything's too fake. I always feel we're all on some damn Hollywood set and I can't stand it. I don't know about you guys, but it makes me cranky. Makes me antsy." The nodding heads, Peter's included, indicated Thompson was not alone in that. He sighed again heavily, then said, "We need to get out of here for a spell, go on something like a retreat. We got a lot to work on and we can't do it here, not without killing each other."

The staff members looked at one another, murmuring their assent, then Jimmy, as chief of staff, spoke on their behalf as usual. "Hey, sounds good. What do you have in mind, Sim?"

Thompson walked back to his desk to check the calendar. "Let's see, today is the... twenty-first of July. Our summer recess begins August ninth. Let's just table everything we can for the next two weeks. In that time, I want all of you coming up with as many ideas, proposals, new perspectives, whatever, as you can. From the eighth to the thirteenth, we'll take a retreat at my hunting lodge up there in the mountains. It'll be cooler than this damn place, it's smack dab in the middle of a hundred acres of woods so no one will be around, nice and quiet. What do you say, folks?"

Everyone agreed this would be an excellent idea, and Peter was especially thrilled to be once again in the woods of Garrett County, where he'd spent most of his youth. Plus, he'd heard about the hunting lodge before, a great sprawling building made out of huge oak beams built at the turn of the century by Thompson's grandfather and he was eager to spend a week in it, even if it was to work.

The team was suddenly rejuvenated and energized, ready to begin what they were certain was going to be a memorable retreat.

CHAPTER FOUR

1

G arrou's home was right on the Chesapeake Bay in Crisfield, a sprawling glass and steel modern house separated by acres of marshy fields from his neighbors, and he also owned a stylish brownstone house he lived in while working in Washington. He'd regularly entertain guests at both these locations, but when he wanted to have a large, formal dinner party set to show off his wealth and prestige, nowhere was better suited than Raven Hill Manor.

He sat now at the head of an immense dinner table in the mansion's ballroom. The table, though oversized and easily capable of accommodating the twenty dinner guests that sat there now, was still dwarfed by the size of this ballroom in which Garrou's great-grandfather had once held dances for hundreds at a time.

Cream colored, with a painting of blue sky on the ceiling and architectural details gilded in actual gold leaf, and an intricate parquet design in the hardwood floor with a gaping fireplace behind Garrou, it was a gigantic room in which to hold a dinner party. He felt the empty space was fine, though, because not only did it give the servants plenty of room to attend to the dinner guests it also seemed to focus the entire room on him, which he always enjoyed.

Garrou and his mother sat at either head of the table, and between them were some of the most powerful and influential people from seven important spheres: The news media, entertainment industry, government, education, banking, manufacturing, and the military. These important facets of modern American life were carefully chosen since these, more than any others, influenced what people were allowed to know, how they were taught to think, and how they spent their money. The individuals who represented each were chosen with even more care based upon their ability or willingness to support Garrou, as well as the overarching goals of the Coven Universal. Although only three of the dinner guests belonged to and knew the occult power of the Coven, all of them were receptive to its goals to one degree or another.

This was an extremely important dinner party for Garrou. He always used every interaction with a person as an opportunity to gain advantage, but tonight was a rare chance to gather a collection of influential people and then develop some power over them. Every detail of the dinner had been thoughtfully planned. The finest foods were being served after having been prepared by chefs flown in from Michelin three-star restaurants just for this evening, the best wines from their well-stocked cellar were offered along with the meals, and then whiskey, cigars, and other treats for a select group later, after dessert. A professional string quartet was hired to provide soft, pleasant live music during dinner. The entire mansion smelled of the delicious feast being prepared.

All their guests' appetites had to be fully satisfied, and Garrou wanted everything to be perfect, regardless of expense.

As Garrou watched his guests slice their filet mignon and saw the blood-tinged juices ooze out of each cut, he was reminded of the fresh young girl they'd sacrificed earlier at a Black Mass in their hidden sacrarium just before dinner. He and Mariette had wanted to ensure their demonic companions were all well pleased, so they created evil spiritual energy for the evening to feed from. Having a steady stream of lost, homeless waifs at Garrou's disposal was one of the benefits he enjoyed by volunteering as a director on the board of a national foster care agency.

"So, Congressman Garrou," Nick Arnolds, the corpulent president of a large manufacturing conglomerate said, "what do you hear about a possible trade deal with China? Do you think that's likely?"

Garrou chewed his mignon slowly as he thought, then, pausing with his wine glass half-raised to his mouth for effect said, "What I can tell you is that there will be a deal signed between our two countries by the end of the year." To finish the dramatic scene, Garrou took a sip of his fine red as he looked at the industrialist through his wine glass.

The man lowered his fork, regarding Garrou slack-mouthed, his second chin wobbling heavily. "Are you serious? I mean, you are absolutely confident in this information?"

"Nick, I can guarantee it."

The man's face twisted into a hungry grin as he glanced at his wife, and he seemed almost to drool in anticipation. "This is the most perfect news I could imagine, Congressman. This means that market will finally be open to our products, and hopefully soon we can move production there, too. That'll save us millions while we earn *billions*. The only thing better than more is even more. Do you have any details you can share?"

"Well," Garrou said, taking another sip of his wine, "obviously not everything is agreed upon yet, but it now looks like China is willing to slash their tariff rates for the United States, and to open all the various markets to our businesses. We'll definitely come out on top in the agreement, though it's a winner for everyone."

"I understand labor is pushing back," said Sam Cain, a high-ranking official in the Department of Defense. Cain represented a small but powerful cabal within the department, one that made most military decisions. Should America go to war it would be because Cain and his associates believed it profitable, not because of any decision the president made. "Any worries about that?"

"Actually," said Mick O'Callaghan, a congressman representing the Boston area and long-time supporter of the Garrou family, "they're not so much pushing back as they've expressed some concerns about industries moving overseas. They're worried about potential job losses."

"So, what will we do about them?" Arnolds asked through a large bite of steak.

"Same thing as always," Mick said. "Assure them American manufacturing will remain strong. We'll make sure the union leaders benefit financially if they only make a show of pushing back, and then offer them a hand in making some domestic laws. Something different, something high-profile and not related to labor laws, maybe something like the environment. Let them stick it back to the activists. Their blue collars will show, they'll get a kick out of that."

"Sounds like a reasonable plan," Cain said flatly. "Garrou, are you worried about how something like this will play out with voters, what 'Main Street' will think about it?"

Garrou felt a sudden flare of anger and gave Cain a hard

look for not using his title, something he felt he'd earned. He knew it was a deliberate slight on Cain's part. It was a subtle way for the proud government official to remind the congressman that he was there before Garrou was elected and would probably be there long after.

If I didn't want tonight to go smoothly, you'd already have your throat ripped out, dickhead.

The anger passed just as quickly as it arrived, as did the hard look, replaced by Garrou's charming smile. "Well, Sam, to be honest," he said, "I don't really care. Oh, I'm sure there'll be some people that complain, grassroot activism, action committees, so on and so forth, but I'm not worried about that. We'll lose a few votes here and there as factories close, but it won't affect enough people for it to really matter. And, honestly, people won't care at all after a while because they can get their stuff for cheap, which is all most folks are really interested in."

Arnolds raised his wine glass, and said, "Here's to consumerism. Long may it reign." He then took a large swig of his drink.

"Bottom line," Garrou went on, "is that I don't care about factory workers enough to worry about their votes. I'm certain they'll still vote for us regardless because that's what they do. Honestly, this is what they get for working in factories to begin with. Besides," Garrou said, looking at two other dinner guests, "if our friends in the media play their parts right, we'll be able to convince people this will benefit them in the long run."

"As for my part," said Hugh Pettibone, an influential Hollywood movie producer with a reputation for a perverse sexual hunger that started during his years with Garrou at Fairmont, "I'm eager as fuck to break into that market. It's fucking huge. We're already developing scripts that take place in China or feature Chinese characters as the good guys and shit like that.

It's going to be huge, fucking huge, so I don't want to do anything to threaten it. You can bet your ass we'll add messages into some of the TV shows our subsidiaries control that present this in a positive light."

"Excellent," Garrou said. Then, turning to Emma Oscuro, a woman in an emerald-green business suit who ran a news media corporation with newspapers, cable news programs, and news magazines under its control, he said, "Em? What will the news have to say about this?"

"Oh, don't you worry, Lou," she said. "This deal will be heralded as being the greatest boon to the American economy since the Square Deal, the envy of the entire free market world. It'll be written up as starting the new millennium in a whole different, and lucrative, reality." She then popped a cherry tomato into her mouth, smiling at Garrou.

"Thank you, dear," he said, raising his glass to her and winking. They had a long and passionate history together, having come of age in the coven at the same time.

"How are you feeling about Sim Thompson?" Mick asked, his timing perfect and just as they had rehearsed it earlier. He didn't know about the existence of the Coven, but he'd unwittingly spent his long career in Congress working towards many of its goals, nonetheless. The older congressman had always been a supporter of Garrou's despite the age difference due to a debt of gratitude he owed his grandfather; the elder Garrou had gotten Mick out of serious trouble when he was much younger.

"I'm glad you brought that up, Mick," Garrou said, standing at the head of the table to give his practiced speech. "I appreciate all of your help with this important China initiative and having the chance to coordinate our message. Now, I'm going to ask for this same support and coordination for me personally. As you all know, I'm currently engaged in a *killer* campaign against Thompson, and so I could use all of your help, and the help of your colleagues to assist me to claim the Senate seat come the special election. So," Garrou said, raising his wine glass for all to join him, "here's to victory in the Senate... and to everything that comes after."

"Hear, hear," they all said in unison, his mother's voice raising above the others.

"And what does come after, congressman?" asked Abiku Ogbanje, a professor, dean, and popular writer from Howard University, with a knowing smirk.

Garrou sat again, his most disarming smile in play. "Well, Dr. Ogbanje, you know our mother raised us all in the Episcopalian Church to be good and faithful servants, so I'm just going to answer that question by deferring it over to the will of God."

"Amen to that!" said Mariette.

2

Later, after dessert and coffee had been served, Garrou took a select group into what was once called the men's smoking room while his mother escorted the remaining guests to continue entertaining them in the drawing room. Together with Garrou were Mick, Hugh, Nick, Sam, Jerry Black, and Raymond Leonard. Black held a position of power and influence like that of Emma in news media, whereas Leonard was highly placed in the Federal Reserve. Of the six additional men in the room with Garrou, only Nick and Leonard were also part of the Coven Universal, although they conducted their rites at different covens.

The men sat on comfortable hunter green leather furniture original to the house, leather than had been oiled daily for over a hundred years and so was still as soft, supple, and squeaky as the day on which it was purchased. They sat smoking Cuban cigars and drinking a twenty-year-old bottle of Glenrothes whiskey in a room with coffered walnut walls, trophy elk racks, and an antique pool table beyond the setting on which they sat. At one end was a large fireplace, and at the other were French doors, currently obscured by dark red, velvet drapes.

"Well, gentleman," Garrou said, loosening his tie, "as you all no doubt already know I will be running for president in 2000. Some might think it narcissistic to be a Senator for such a short amount of time before running for president, but I'm doing it. The support I mentioned out there, about the Senate race, I will really need next year, when I go after the White House. Are you men with me?"

Each man nodded his head as he either took a sip of smooth whiskey or puffed on his cigar.

"Absolutely," said Nick, to which Black added, "Yes, absolutely."

"Of course, I am," agreed Leonard.

"You know I'll always support you, Lou," said Mick, slapping Garrou's knee.

"Good," said Garrou said with a smile, "because... I believe I'm looking at the core of my cabinet right here in this room." Each man's chest puffed out a little bit with pride, especially Sam's, no doubt imagining themselves running the department of his choice and enjoying the benefits that come with such power, just as Garrou knew they would.

"One thing I can tell you for damn sure, Lou," Mick said, "Is that I'll be able to assure Massachusetts goes to you when you run for president, and I'm confident I can bring *all* of New England to you."

"Good," Garrou said. "And I assume we can count on the base coming out to vote?"

"Yeah, obviously," Mick said with a chuckle. "That's a lock. Look, bottom line, all you have to do is keep saying the right things, win the Senate, keep looking like older Brad Pitt, and I can guarantee you the presidency next year. Well, all that, and don't completely fuck up on *Meet the Press* tomorrow."

Garrou clapped his friend on the shoulder and, "Thank you, Mick. I've always appreciated your wisdom and support. And, yes, I'll try not to fuck up too bad. Russert's a fair guy, though. Should be fine."

"Yeah," Mick agreed, "it should be."

Then standing, Garrou said, "But enough work for tonight. Enough talk of politics, gents! Let's have some entertainment, shall we?" and clapped his hands twice.

As soon as he did, a middle-aged woman accompanied by three young girls, scampered out from behind the drapes and starting lighting large candelabras full of long, black candles that had been positioned all throughout the smoking room. Once they were all lit, the woman turned off the lights, so the room was bathed in the soft orange glow of the many flickering candle flames.

"Lou," Hugh whispered harshly, his excitement choking his voice, "what do you have planned, you ol' bastard, you?"

"Shut up and watch, Hugh," Garrou answered, then, turning to the woman, he said, "You may begin, Mrs. Tarma."

She nodded to one of the girls, who pressed the play button on a portable stereo CD player, which started playing loud dance music. As soon as the music started, another girl, older than the other three, came out from the curtains and began dancing. Each man, enthralled by her shaking and gyrating and rhythmic grinding, slowly put their drinks and cigars down to watch her. Their placid faces hid the growing lust Garrou could see was gripping each in turn.

Garrou knew the girl dancing was only eleven, though she was far more developed than one would expect for that age. With how scantily clad she was, her heavy makeup, her long dark hair, and the provocative ways in which she sexually moved her body to the music, she easily could have passed for sixteen or seventeen.

As she inched her way closer and closer to the men themselves, her dancing became even more suggestive, until she was within reach of them. Once there, she pressed her body against each of them – except Garrou – in turn, bending over to grind herself against each, grabbing their crotches, rubbing their erections through their suit pants. The music grew more fevered in speed and tempo, as did her movements.

The girl's dancing became ever more frenzied and lustful, as did her audience. Garrou watched his future cabinet with interest as he saw them loosening or taking off their ties, rolling up sleeves, and licking their lips. He could feel the energy and intensity in the room growing even as it became hotter and hotter from the many candles burning. He knew the growing tension would soon break, and it did.

Hugh Pettibone stood with a low growl and grabbed the girl by her upper arms, pinning them to her body as he kissed her violently on the lips, then moved to biting her neck and shoulders. He ripped off the small cloth she had covering her breasts, pulled down her tiny shorts, then bent her over the antique pool table and began to rape her. The other men, as if coming to after being in a trance, stood and began pawing and playing with her as they awaited their turn.

Though very young, Garrou knew the girl was no virgin. She'd been instructed to expect this very thing and to silently accept whatever the men did to her because it glorified her coven. Garrou watched as the girl, trying to keep back tears, raised her head from the pool table and looked at her foster mother. Mrs. Tarma merely nodded to her, as if letting her know she was doing everything right. Sitting back in his comfortable leather chair, Garrou laced his fingers behind his head, smoked his cigar, and enjoyed the entertainment.

CHAPTER FIVE

"Oh, my goodness..." Peter said, exhaling a long tendril of smoke. It was a bad habit he was trying to quit, but he found it hard to relinquish when either extremely relaxed or excited. "Someone call the police because this guy's getting murdered."

Peter was sitting up in bed as Angie snuggled close to him, his arm resting lazily around her shoulders. They were both still naked as they enjoyed a lazy Sunday morning following their first night of lovemaking, one that Peter was certain he would never forget. At various points throughout the preceding night, each had expressed undying, passionate love for the other, and Peter was seriously now thinking about finding the perfect diamond ring to ask Angie to marry him.

As if last night hadn't been glorious enough, Peter was starting his day off with a treat by watching Garrou make a fool of himself on *Meet the Press*. Russert had started predictably enough, tossing him softballs about the race against Thompson, allowing Garrou to focus on his favorite campaign theme of restructuring the economy to favor the working class.

After the first commercial break, however, the tone of the interview changed, with Russert really pressing Garrou. He pointed out that Garrou spoke like he was an ally of the working class, as if he were a populist, painting an image of himself toiling in a factory or mine prior to getting elected to Congress, whereas the only work he'd ever done since getting his Stanford law degree was for the Garrou Foundation.

"My family, like a great many other American families, has been wonderfully blessed by this country and the opportunities to be found here," Garrou said. "Tim, my goals, my initiatives, my entire platform is trying to make certain that every family in America has the same opportunities mine did, and so everyone can share the wealth."

That's when Russert dropped the bomb that made Peter react so. He asked Garrou if, just the night before, he'd had a dinner party for a select group of friends. Garrou confirmed he did, noting it was a small event for associates he hoped to lean on for support in the Senate campaign.

"Congressman Garrou," Russert said. "An audiotape was anonymously provided to the producers of this television program, one that seems to be a recording of you speaking very disrespectfully of the American electorate. Here, let's take a listen."

Though there was a low hiss throughout the recording and overwhelmed at times by the sound of a cello playing, a voice very much like Garrou's could be heard saying, *"I don't really care... there'll be some people that complain... but I'm not worried about that. We'll lose a few votes... but it won't affect enough people for it to really matter... people won't care at all after a while because they can get their stuff for cheap, which is all most folks are really interested in... I don't care about factory workers... I'm certain they'll still vote for us regardless... that's what they do... this is what they get for working in factories to begin with.*"

"Oh, shit," Peter exclaimed. "His goose is cooked!"

"What's going on?" Angie murmured sleepily next to him.

"Well, good morning, sleepyhead," Peter said, kissing her gently atop her head. "How'd you sleep?"

"Hardly at all, and I'm happy for it," she said, smiling up at Peter. "What's going on? What are you watching?"

"*Meet the Press,* and Garrou is getting killed by Russert."

"Really?" she said, popping up excitedly, squinting to see the television without her glasses. "What's happening?"

Peter clued her in very quickly, then said, "Watch... or listen, as the case may be."

"Congressman Garrou, do you care to comment?" Russert asked.

Peter noted there was the slightest flicker of something on Garrou's well-practiced neutral look, though he couldn't quite place it – was it fear? Anger? Contempt? All three at once? Peter couldn't tell.

Garrou then smiled, though rather than his normally charming smile this looked more like a pained grimace, and said, "Tim, I have no idea where that tape came from or where it was recorded, but I can categorically deny that's me on it. It's fake."

"A fake?" Russert repeated.

"Absolutely," Garrou said. "I can completely deny saying that, and I'm sure my dinner guests will all attest to the fact that I never said those words. In fact, Tim, I wouldn't be at all surprised if this weren't some nasty political trick by my opposition to make me look bad."

Oh, he's good, Peter thought. *No one will believe that crap, but he sure as shit can think on his feet. He's good.*

"Congressman, are you accusing the Thompson campaign

of making a fake recording of you to make you look bad?" Russert asked.

"Tim," Garrou said, trying to sound sincere but failing, "I don't think for one minute Congressman Thompson had anything to do with this. We disagree on a great many points, but I know he's a good man, a fair man, and he'd never condone such a low political maneuver as this. However, that doesn't mean there aren't some rogue elements in his campaign, or staff, or even within the party itself. There is documented evidence of the national party establishment doing highly unethical things to advance their candidates."

Angie turned to Peter with her pointer finger out, a suspicious look on her face. "Did you do this? Are you the evil mastermind behind this wicked plot?"

Peter looked down in phony shame, whispered, "Yes," and then began tickling Angie. As both were still naked and in bed, the tickling led to kissing, which led to groping, which led to natural and expected physical reactions.

"You wanna... breakfast... out after?" Peter asked in between kisses.

"Mmm..." Angie moaned in response. "But first... I want... you."

Peter's last fully formed thought before being pulled down into the sensual delights of sex with a woman whom he deeply loved was, *I sure hope Sim does better in his interview today than Garrou did!*

CHAPTER SIX

1

"Are you fucking kidding me?" Garrou screamed angrily. "Seriously?! Are you *fucking* kidding me, Mother?!"

Garrou had been having several terrible days. It started with the debacle on *Meet the Press*, since which time the recording had been almost the sole focus on all the twenty-four-hour network news channels, the lead in the network evening news programs, and the subject of numerous newspaper editorials. Garrou's campaign cleaved to the claim it was a forgery, but even with the assistance of Emma Oscuro and Jerry Black painting him as the victim, the tenor in the opinion pieces was often suspicious of that assertion.

Many editorials described Garrou as elitist, arrogant, pompous, and – his personal favorite – "burdened with an over-arching sense of smug self-superiority." Though most stories danced around whether Garrou was lying about the tape, they also seemed to dispense the need to have that confirmed: whether the tape was accurate or not, they implicitly accused

Garrou of being duplicitous and contemptuous of the American voter based upon his stated goals compared to his lifestyle.

Garrou had been angry since the interview because he'd felt ambushed, and his name was now being smeared by some media outlets. Even though he certainly *was* contemptuous of the American electorate, he didn't want that fact discussed in news stories for days on end. News items like that are terrible for one's likability polls.

Which was another reason for his current dark mood. Garrou's poll numbers had nosedived ever since he appeared on *Meet the Press* and the tapes had been made public. Whereas he was well ahead of Thompson with a comfortable double-digit lead just a few days earlier, the two were now approaching a tie as he'd plunged precipitously while Thompson's numbers had surged. The gnawing, mind-numbing frustration of watching as all his plans turned to ash in his hands and crumbled to dust right before his eyes, was almost too much to bear. A murderous rage had been building within him for days.

2

This wasn't even the worst of it. Yesterday he'd had a meeting with Ted McManus, the founder of a private, for-profit prison company that had facilities all across the country. McManus had worked with Garrou in the past when crafting the 1994 Crime Bill, making certain the law would be written to guarantee there'd be a massive influx of incarcerated Americans, which there were. This had, in turn, made his company massively profitable. The following year McManus submitted notes on NAFTA because he'd have less competition as an employer and could offer his workers fewer benefits if factories were to shut down. This made the company even more profitable. McManus had recently secured a lucrative contract with the federal government, and all these things combined had made him into a reliable financial contributor to Garrou.

Until the meeting yesterday.

"My goodness," McManus had drawled in his rich South Carolina accent, using his Panama hat to fan his fat face, "I do believe it's hotter than blue blazes out there."

"Well, luckily the air-conditioning works pretty well here in the Capitol," said Garrou, watching as the sweat dripped from McManus' pasty face onto his light blue, seersucker suit. His office had already begun to smell of the man's perspiration. "What can I do for you, Ted?"

That was a polite contrivance. They both knew full well why McManus was visiting him. He was a regular contributor to Garrou's campaigns, and the expectation was that McManus would continue donating generously to buy access to the policy-making process to steer it towards his own interests. This was the simple reality of American politics, and everyone knew it. However, that didn't mean there couldn't be polite contrivances to cover those uglier realities.

"Well, Louis, I wanted to talk to you about that. You know... face-to-face, man-to-man," McManus drawled slowly.

"Oh?" Garrou said. "I didn't know there was anything *to* discuss."

McManus chuckled, and said, "Well, there is. In case you hadn't noticed you didn't exactly acquit yourself the other day on *Meet the Press*."

Garrou felt another sudden flare of rage as he had at the dinner party with Sam Cain, gritting his teeth angrily. "Yes, Ted," he said coolly. "I'm well aware."

"See, the thing is," McManus went on, "I'm afraid your

entire campaign has gone cattywampus now and has gotten so ugly it'd make a freight train take a dirt road. I believe donating more money at this point would be like putting lipstick on a pig."

"Ted," Garrou said, "we've hit a bump. Bumps always happen in campaigns; you know that as well as I do. I can guarantee you I'm going to win the Senate seat, no worries there."

"I'm just not certain I agree with your rosy interpretation, Louis," said McManus. "I hear tell your plans are you're going to run for president next year. You ain't even won the Senate yet and here you are measuring the drapes for the Oval Office. No, sir. I'm sorry but you've gotten too big for your britches."

Growing impatient with McManus and his southernisms, Garrou leaned back in his plush desk chair, crossed his arms, and said, "Enough bullshit, Ted. Get to it. What are we talking about?"

"Bottom line," McManus said, the hard-driving businessman in him coming out, "I ain't giving you another dime of my money, Louis, until I believe you can be a winner again. But I just don't think you can. Thompson is coming up behind you faster than a knife fight in a phone booth, and after you screwed the pooch on TV the other day, well, I do believe your political days are all over."

McManus stood, putting his hat back on his head and saluted Garrou with a flick of the brim, then said, "I am sorry, Louis, but I just don't back losers," and walked out of the office.

3

And so it was that Garrou had suffered through a terrible week only to find himself now screaming angrily as he sat in his

BMW M3 as his string of bad days continued to get worse. Garrou returned home to his brownstone in Capitol Hill yesterday after the meeting with McManus to find one of his mother's crows waiting for him on his stoop. It hopped around as he approached, and when their eyes met the spirit disguised as a crow spoke to him in his mind, telling Garrou he'd been summoned to Raven Hill Manor the following day to explain himself to his mother.

Summoned. It had actually used the word *summoned*, repeating what Mariette had told it to say. He'd been summoned by his mother as if he were some kind of servant that needed to be disciplined. His slowly burning internal rage was exceeding even his trained capabilities to contain.

He'd been summoned... only to find the intricate iron gates across the drive that led to the mansion closed and locked, barring his way.

"*For fuck's sake!*" Garrou screamed, then, after composing himself, recited the couplet spell he knew would release them. The gates groaned as they slowly swung open to allow him in. Garrou knew Mariette hadn't intended to block his access by having the gates closed, but rather to send him a subtle message: Get yourself together or find yourself on the outside.

He took in a deep breath and closed his eyes for a moment, then released it slowly to relax. Even though Garrou had been in a wicked mood these past few days because of everything going on, he'd noted a persistent, low-level anger growing within him the past several weeks. He smoothed his hair before proceeding down the long driveway, dispensing any concern about his mood. It must be the result of the intense stress he'd been under for months, he thought.

Garrou saw the flocks of crows that always kept watch on the property and did his mother's bidding seemed agitated, cawing loudly, flying in tight circles above the mansion, landing to perch only to then take flight again. He'd long ago learned that he could judge his mother's mood based upon how her crows were behaving.

Walking into the mansion, he went straight to his mother's morning room. There, sitting upright as always and perched on the edge of a rich burgundy leather wing chair, Garrou found his mother surrounded by several days' worth of discarded newspapers. He could see that Mariette had read *The Washington Post, The Baltimore Sun, The Los Angeles Times,* and *USA Today,* as well as others he couldn't identify. She was currently reading a copy of *The New York Times,* folding it into quarters as she always did.

Mariette didn't acknowledge his presence as she continued reading the newspaper, and Garrou suddenly felt very much like a peasant coming before his high and mighty queen to beg for mercy. That subservient feeling grew as Mariette continued to neither acknowledge her son nor even offer him a seat, as did his gnawing anger.

Growing impatient with the awkward silence, he at last quipped, "Doing some research, Mother?"

She finally lowered the newspaper and said, "Yes, actually. I'm reading about how my fool of a son somehow managed to squander his chance to win the presidency despite having the power of the Coven Universal behind him."

Garrou sighed and squeezed the bridge of his nose between his eyes as a stabbing headache took him. "Mother, it's not as bad as all that—"

"Not as bad?!" Mariette now yelled at him like he was a child. "*Not as bad?!* If you believe that then you really are a fool, or you just haven't been following the news."

Garrou was no fool, but it was true he hadn't been reading the papers or watching much news since the first day after. Thanks to his friends in the media a shift in reporting had begun in which the possibility of the tape being a forgery was now being considered. Earlier that day on *Morning Edition* he was pleased to hear a reporter query the Thompson campaign if it had been involved in creating the tape; Garrou delighted in how quickly political myth became reality with just a few select keystrokes. However, many of the editorials remained critical of him, so these Garrou chose to ignore.

"You obviously have not read these editorials, because if you had then you'd know they're flaying you alive," Mariette continued. She read from the *New York Times*: "'Regardless of the origins of the allegedly counterfeit voice recording, it should be obvious Garrou shows a fair amount of duplicity in his politics. His vast wealth and lavish homes notwithstanding, he claims, in theory, to always support the working poor and to be willing to retool the entire economy to benefit them, yet all of his policy initiates in practice seem only to favor the wealthy.'"

Mariette picked up several of the discarded papers, then again read from them. "This is what the *Los Angeles Times* has to say, and I quote, 'Though Congressman Garrou certainly has all the appearances of a leader – handsome face, well-built, always exquisitely tailored – it is the editorial board's opinion that he may, in fact, be lacking in actual leadership qualities. If the recording is authentic, then his attitude captured on it alone should disqualify him for office, to say nothing of his ability to casually lie so easily to a member of the press.' Oh, Louis, very impressive, very impressive indeed!"

Mariette tossed the paper aside, then picked up another. "And this, Louis, this is from the *Sun*, which you might consider your hometown paper. 'In the upcoming special Senate election, this state has two very different candidates, and their recent appearances on Sunday morning programs – Garrou on *Meet the Press* and Thompson on *Face the Nation* –

acts as a perfect metric by which to show how different they are. Whereas Garrou appeared arrogant, snobby, and pretentious, Thompson appeared as a true man of the people, a natural leader, and perhaps far better Senator material.'" Mariette dropped the paper and hissed at Louis, "There are more, but most say the same thing. What do you have to say for yourself?"

Garrou, feeling puckish and already irritated, was not in the mood to beg his mother for forgiveness.

"Well," he said, "Mother, I agree... I am incredibly handsome and well-built." If he were trying to elicit a response from his mother, Garrou was disappointed as she continued to stare at him with her pale eyes.

"Joke all you want, Louis," Mariette said, "but your foolishness and arrogance have nearly cost you this race, *and* the presidency. Yet despite that, Thompson is still in this race. How can that be, Louis? You're letting everyone down and here you are doing nothing. What are you going to do about this?!"

Garrou sighed, his anger growing right along with his headache, and said, "Mother, I already told you—"

"No, I don't want any more excuses, Louis. You're letting down the coven and mocking your family name. I want to hear what you're going to do! What will you do about this enemy that still lives, that scorns you simply by breathing?!"

"He will be taken care of," Garrou said, trying to remain calm as his anger grew now into a throbbing rage.

"No!" Mariette again yelled. "I don't believe you! You're failing and I fear will keep failing. Tell me what you're going to do and when you're going to do it!"

"Mother, I—"

"What will you do?!"

He clenched his teeth and squeezed his eyes shut for one

moment, his hands balling up into tights fists as he tried to dull the rage taking over his brain.

"Mother—"

"No!" she said, slamming her fist against the armchair. *"What are you going to do?!"*

"I'M GOING TO FUCKING KILL HIM!!" Garrou roared, his voice becoming intensified and augmented by the deep growl of the Wolf. At that moment, that brief moment between allowing his rage to rush forward and getting himself back under control, Garrou felt almost like he wasn't in command of his mind. He had a fleeting image of himself in wolf form, running free and wild in a primal green forest, chasing down his prey, tearing it to shreds, and glorying in his own destructive capabilities. It was a brief though enticing picture of pure release for Garrou.

Mariette sat regarding her son for a moment after his outburst, then softly said, "And there it is at last."

Garrou swallowed hard, his heart racing after his eruption, blinking quickly as he tried to get grounded again. He ran a hand through his thick hair and fixed his tie as he came back down, then said in a harsh whisper, "I'll take care of it, Mother. I told you I would, and I will."

Mariette nodded and smiled. "Yes," she said. "I now believe you will, Louis." She stood and came to him, then placed her hand on his arm. "This is of the utmost importance. You know that. I had to be certain you had the mettle to do what needs to be done, and I can see now that you do." Gently touching his cheek as any mother might, she added, "I *am* proud of you, Louis. We all are."

Then, just as quickly as it arrived, that tender mothering side of Mariette retreated again and she swept past Garrou, saying, "Come join me for lunch in the solarium."

Mariette walked out of the morning room without another

word, leaving Garrou in there alone with the leather furniture and scattered newspapers. He looked around, dazed, and confused by what just occurred as he thought about what all this meant.

Why did I get so angry like that? Why did I have that image? Why did Mother react like she did? What the fuck just happened?

Garrou followed his mother to the solarium for lunch and thought about what had occurred in that room and what came next. While he might not know the answers about his outburst, he did know that there was some killing to be done. Garrou also knew who the first person would be he was going to shred.

CHAPTER SEVEN

"I'm going to miss you so much," Peter said softly to Angie, holding her short body close to his lanky one as they lay together in bed. With the upcoming Thompson staff retreat in a week, Peter and Angie had wanted to get some alone time away. They both took the day off work on this Friday and drove from Washington across the state to the Brunner's small hunting cabin tucked away in the West Virginia mountains. Though hardly a vacation resort, the plan was for the couple to disconnect from their busy schedules for a long weekend and spend the whole time together hiking the rugged trails, swimming in the nearby lake, just enjoying nature and each other's company.

They'd been at the cabin for several hours at that point, but all they'd accomplished on that list so far was to enjoy each other's company by having sex several times.

Angie gently rubbed Peter's face as she looked into his eyes, then whispered, "I'm going to miss you a lot more. You'll be tied up every day with brainstorming and strategy planning and shit like that, distracted by your team. You'll be too busy to even think about me much. I'll be stuck in DC alone for a week during recess in an empty office thinking about you."

They kissed, then Angie said, "You know, I came to DC because it was a great opportunity. Maybe give me the chance to meet up with some lobbyists, get to know them, start a career in lobbying eventually. I never thought I'd meet the man I'd fall in love with."

"Me neither," Peter said. "I never thought I'd meet the man of my dreams, either, but that Henrique *es muy caliente!*"

Angie laughed, lightly smacking Peter's chest. "Shut up, you big dork."

Peter chuckled at his joke and rolled onto his back, lacing his fingers under his head, then stared at the rough-hewn beamed ceiling above. As this was a crude, one-room hunting cabin with only a small loft above for sleeping, the peaked ceiling was only a few feet away. He very much wanted a cigarette, especially after that delightful morning of marathon sex, but since he was trying to quit, Peter decided to distract himself by talking instead.

"You know," Peter said, "I pretty much lived here during the summers when I was a kid."

Angie raised up on her elbow to look at Peter. "You did?"

"Yeah – well, not strictly in this cabin, but with my grand-parents over in Dellslow," he said, crooking his thumb behind where they lay. "Every year, pretty much as soon as school was over, my parents would send me to be with my grandparents for the summer. I've already told you about my brother Danny, and when he died in that accident, I just think a part of my parents died with him, you know?"

"Yeah, I know, hon," Angie said, laying her head on his shoulder.

"They're good parents, I know they tried their best. It was hard growing up in that house, living under the shadow of a brother I never knew. I just think dealing with me all summer was too much for them after he died. So... off to Grammy and Granddaddy I went!"

Peter felt a touch of melancholy as he thought about the older brother he could remember only in grainy images, the sadness always etched onto his parents' faces, even when they were smiling, and how that wound never quite seemed to heal. However, his mind quickly turned to the many happy days he and his grandfather spent at the cabin. They would sometimes sleep over, sometimes not, but they'd always explore the outdoors, and the young Peter learned to love being in the woods. Peter often longed for the quiet simplicity of those days.

"What were they like?" Angie asked. "Your grandparents, I mean."

"Oh, they were great," Peter said. "Really great. Kind, caring, hardworking... eh, kind of simple. They grew up here in West Virginia. My Granddaddy was a coal miner his whole life. He was lucky and retired just before all the mines started shutting down. I don't know if Grammy ever traveled past the county line, to be honest. She did make a great rhubarb pie, though."

Peter thought about how one decision, often made far away from where it impacts people, can unknowingly determine the course of lives for many generations to come. The Brunners were lucky because Peter's grandfather had just retired and his father had enough time to shift gears, even though following his own father into coal mines had always been his intention. When it became obvious what was happening, Peter's father moved his young family to Mountain Lake Park to take a job in facilities at the nearby hospital, the town where his brother would die in a drowning accident.

One pebble truly can start an avalanche.

"So, anyway," said Peter, "me and Granddaddy would

spend a lot of time here, sometimes fixing the place up a little or cutting wood, sometimes playing checkers on the porch, sometimes hunting. Sometimes we'd just sit and listen to the crickets."

Angie smiled as she thought of that, then said, "Mmm... that sounds sweet."

"Yeah, it was. During the school year back in Maryland I'd still spend as much time outside in the woods as I could but being here with my grandfather was the best. A lot of the time we'd sit there just chatting about whatever. Sometimes he'd tell me scary stories of the creatures that are supposed to be around in these mountains," Peter thought for a moment, then said with a chuckle, "Hmm... maybe it wasn't Poe that got me hooked on horror, maybe it was Granddaddy."

Angie giggled at that. "What kind of creatures are supposed to be around here?" she asked.

"Oh, well, there's Mothman. You've heard of him, right?"

"Him I've heard of."

"Right, okay. There's also Snarly Yow... the White Thing... the Grafton Monster... yeah, we have quite a few supposed weird things up in these mountains."

After a moment, Angie again got up on her elbow so she could look at Peter and said, "Okay, so, let me ask you this: There are lots of stories from around here of weird creatures and stuff. Have you ever seen anything out here in the woods?"

Shocked by a memory that poured back into Peter's mind like a torrent of raging flood waters, he turned away from Angie as if startled and again stared at the ceiling. He tried to find words but instead, all that happened was his lips moved with no intelligible sounds coming out. It was a memory he'd tried hard to forget.

"Oh, my... Peter, I'm so sorry... I didn't mean to..." Angie said, stunned to see him reacting in such a way. "I'm... I didn't mean to..."

He put up a hand. "No, babe, it's okay," he said. "You didn't do anything. It's okay, it's just... something *did* happen out there, in the woods not far from here, and it scared the hell out of me when I was a kid. I just... you know, I haven't thought about it since then. I guess I tried not to."

"Honey, I'm so sorry," Angie said. "We don't have to talk about it if you don't want to."

Peter rolled over to face her, taking her hand in his. "No, it's okay. It's been... what? I was around eleven, so it's been fourteen some years. I'm okay to talk about it."

Despite his reassurances, Peter still paused to take a deep breath and to compose his words. He was a little concerned about how this beautiful woman lying next to him with whom he was now hopelessly in love would react to his story. She might be a fan of horror, but some things only went so far.

I sure hope she doesn't think I'm off my rocker! Well, Granddaddy always said, "No way through it but to do it."

"Okay, so," Peter began, "I was around eleven, maybe twelve. We were out hunting deer, and it was freezing, I can remember that. It was early December, and it was cold and damp, but there was no snow. Just a miserable frozen mix falling all morning."

He paused, the details of that morning now as vivid in his mind as the day it happened. Peter could recall the damp, woodsy odor of the frigid air and the soft tinkling sounds of the falling ice crystals. He remembered the feel of the cold ground as he sat on it, leaning against a tree, looking down at the carpet of brown leaves. They were covered in a thin layer of ice that reflected the dim, mist-shrouded light that morning, the edges of each leaf wreathed in a chunky ring of white frost.

"I was sitting against a tree," Peter said, so immersed in that remembered environment he could now feel it almost more than he could the real world. Though the loft was warm, Peter felt a chill run down his spine as he recalled the numbing cold of that day. "I was waiting for my grandfather to come back from doing some scouting or something. So, there I was, all alone in the woods when I heard the sound of footsteps approaching."

Peter paused again and, glancing down, was surprised to see that his hand was shaking slightly as it held Angie's. She noticed this too and pressed her other hand against his.

"Are you okay to go on?" she asked, with a tone of concern in her voice.

Peter again took a deep breath and said, "Yeah, I'm okay. I'm just surprised how much fear this is bringing back up." He swallowed hard, then went on. "So, I heard these footsteps approaching, and at first, I thought it was Granddaddy, but then the more I listen the more I'm not certain. People and animals sound different in the woods, but what I heard sounded like almost a combination of the two."

Peter stopped a moment to gather his words, then said, "I was a little confused and was just about to call out to what was making the sound, thinking maybe Granddaddy was missing where I was, but something told me not to say anything, not to make a sound because that *wasn't* my grandfather I heard. I keep listening and looking real careful, trying to see anything through the mist. Then... then I see movement through the fog, and I could tell it wasn't my grandfather. It looked about the size of a person, maybe a little bit smaller..."

Angie was entranced by Peter's story, her eyes widening, leaning in slightly as he spoke.

Peter went on, saying, "I thought maybe it was a big coyote or something like that, so I brought up my rifle to shoot it if it came at me. I looked at it through the scope, but the mist was still too thick for me to clearly make it what it was, and I could only make out its movement. I could hear the sounds it was making now, like, this grunting, choking, hacking, growling sound. But then this little breeze came up and blew away enough of the mist that I could make it out clearly. That's when... that's when I saw..."

His mouth again moved without making words, and he blinked hard as the complete vision he'd seen that day returned to him. Peter's entire body was gently shaking now despite the warmth of the loft. It was as if the cold of that day so long ago was now deep within him, but he knew this wasn't a recollected temperature he was reacting to but rather the mind-numbing fear and dread he'd felt then.

"What was it, Peter?" Angie whispered tautly, her curiosity overwhelming her concern. "What was it you saw?"

"I saw..." Peter said. "I don't even know how to explain what I saw. It looked like a naked, gaunt person, or at least something that might once have been human, but like it'd been tortured and mutilated. It was so thin I could see its ribs and hip bones sticking out, and its arms were like toothpicks. The skin was a sickly whitish-gray color. This... thing was crawling on its hands and feet the way a person would, but the arms and legs were, like, lengthened and they'd been split in half, so it had four skinny arms and legs. It almost looked like a spider. The fingers and toes were unnaturally long and twisted into claws. The back was arched like a cat when it gets scared, but it looked like the spine was exposed, and so were the bones of the neck."

"You're... you're..." Angie stammered. "You're kidding, right?"

He looked at her with all the earnestness a person could express with their eyes. "No, I'm not. I wish I were, but I'm not."

She nodded and said, "Okay. Go on."

"But the worst thing of all, the thing that terrified me the most, was its head. Its head looked like a jawless human skull, with long fangs for its upper teeth. There was no bottom jaw, but instead, there was this other hand that seemed to come out of its chest with the same long, sharp claws, and it just kept opening and snapping shut. But even though it was a skull head, it had normal eyes. There was just enough skin around its eyes for it to have eyelids and a brow, and it looked like it was in agony, in pain. Physical and emotional. It looked like it wanted to die."

Angie put her hand to her mouth, shocked by what Peter had just described to her. "What did you do?" she whispered.

"I froze," he said. "I was so terrified there was nothing else for me to do. I started shaking I was so scared, the rifle rattling in my hands. If it had charged me, I probably would've been too terrified to even shoot. Luckily, it slowly made its way away from me. I'm convinced it would've killed me had it known I was there. A few minutes later Granddaddy came back, and we moved to a new location. He said I looked pale when he saw me, so I just told him I saw a coyote and I was scared. That was the end of it."

Angie lay back, putting her hands on her head. "Wow..." she said. "That's just... wow."

"You don't... you don't think I'm crazy, do you?" Peter asked her.

"No, not at all," she said, turning back towards Peter. "I mean, I have no idea what happened to you out there. I have no idea what it was, I don't know whether that was a hallucination or maybe some ill wild animal that looked like what you saw, but I totally believe that you saw what you say you did."

"But... you don't believe anything weird like that could

really be out there, like something from the old stories? Do you?"

"Honey," Angie said, "I love horror stories, and I guess maybe ghosts could possibly exist, maybe, but no, I'm sorry. I just don't believe there are any weird creatures like that stalking our forests or caves or whatever. I heard similar stories before from... well, from other people, but... I never put much faith in them. I believe your story; I just don't think it was what you believe it was."

"Does this make you nervous?"

"No, of course not," Angie said. "Why do you ask?"

"Because you're making the mattress move, you're shaking your leg so hard," said Peter. "You always tap your leg when you're nervous."

"No, I don't," she said, grabbing her leg to keep it still.

"M'kay... you say so."

"I'm not nervous, and I just think you were mistaken. Like I said, I just don't think you saw what you do."

"Okay," Peter said, nodding. "I get that, that's fine. I don't know what it was, either, and I really don't know what I believe about all those weird creature stories. All I know is I saw something horrifying that day. I guess there could be more out there than any of us realize."

They lay together in comfortable silence for a bit, until Peter said, "Well, look, I don't know about you, but I'm starving."

"I can't imagine why," Angie said with a playful wink.

"Mmhmmm..." said Peter, giving Angie a quick kiss. "And we're going to need our strength for later, so I'll get the fire going, and let's put those steaks on."

The pair finally got themselves out of bed, Angie throwing on Peter's T-shirt and him just his boxers. As they cooked their dinner around a roaring campfire in the cooling evening air, they joked and laughed, talked about what the plans for tomorrow would be, and relished their time together.

But after telling Angie his story a grim darkness and a dread had entered Peter's mind like a shadow, making him now look at the dense surrounding woods with trepidation. He wondered what horrors lurked in them, what terrors prowled about in the night. What other nightmare creatures were there in the world?

Very soon, Peter would find out.

CHAPTER EIGHT

1

On the same night Peter fearfully peered into the West Virginia woods wondering what foul creatures might be hiding there, Garrou lurked in a Maryland thicket keeping watch for his prey.

It was Friday evening, and Garrou knew when Ted McManus was conducting business in Washington, he would drive into the countryside every Friday to visit an unremarkable farmhouse nestled in the rolling hills of Maryland. The otherwise innocuous-looking house was a brothel that catered to the sexual needs of powerful men from the city, ones with unique tastes. All the young women employed in this house had been trafficked and now were sex slaves held there to be used as harshly as the clients wished. The people running this establishment preferred the safety of hiding it in the country rather than the convenience of having it in the city, and so it was that McManus made his way through the woods to meet a recent arrival still chained in the basement.

Garrou knew all this because he'd clandestinely made certain McManus became aware of this house's existence some years earlier. He'd long ago found it useful to know the weaknesses of his friends and enemies alike, information that was useful when former friends became his enemies.

Garrou, in his massive werewolf form, crouched in the underbrush as he waited for McManus to drive by. The grinding rage that had exploded out of him a few days earlier with his mother had abated, and in that time, he'd been his typical cool and calculating self. However, now that he was again the Wolf, Garrou found the fury to have returned in a raw, primal way. It wasn't so much a rage as it was an animalistic lust to run down prey, rip apart living flesh, to splash himself with the hot blood of his kill. Whereas Louis had always been able to think just as he would normally as the Wolf, tonight, for the first time, he noted his thoughts were more animal like than ever before.

Garrou rather liked that feeling of wild blood lust.

As the gloaming had grown darker and became night, Garrou's red-glowing eyes could make out every detail in his environment. It was not long before he could hear McManus' Lincoln Town Car approaching. He stood and watched, waiting for McManus to exit the small woods he was in and cross over several knolls towards the wooded hill where Garrou awaited him. When he did, Garrou unconsciously began to drool in anticipation of the salty blood he would soon feel spurt into his mouth, and his heart began to pound. It was an urge almost sexual in its raw, primal nature.

Garrou watched as the car, moving swiftly due to McManus' own lustful desires, cleared the far wood and crested the first small knoll before disappearing again for a moment behind the ridge. As McManus crested the next hillock, Garrou's breathing increased to match his racing heart, and his powerful muscles tensed, growing taunt to prepare himself for what he was about to do. Garrou always loved these moments just before the attack, when the stalking was done and the killing was about to begin; the Wolf, however, just loved the killing, the destroying, the rending and ripping and tearing. It just wanted to obliterate.

McManus' car dipped once again out of sight as he followed the curvy, meandering road, then again crested the final knoll nearest the hilltop where Garrou awaited. As he watched, Garrou heard the engine roar into high gear to clear the hill. He growled, thinking of how his fat former donor must be imagining the young flesh he was soon going to torture, accelerating his car to get there as fast as he could.

Too bad, fucker, Garrou thought.

As McManus' car continued to accelerate up the hill, Garrou timed his steps and rushed out, running with unnatural speed to come alongside the car. Using the demonic strength of the Wolf, he slammed into McManus' car with all his impressive power. He believed McManus would panic after getting hit, lurching the wheel too far to the left – which is exactly what he did. The force of Garrou's attack made the car veer far off the road towards the woods, McManus yanking on the wheel and stomping on the brakes in a desperate attempt to avoid hitting them. All he accomplished was to lose control of the car. The laws of physics are unyielding, and by turning the bulky Town Car so abruptly McManus forced it to flip into a series of barrel rolls, smashing glass and twisting metal as it bounded several times before it came to rest with a final crash on its battered roof.

Garrou had watched the entire thing unfold and was delighted by the way it played out. He could see McManus hanging upside down, trapped by his seatbelt, blood pouring along his plump face. As wonderful as all this was, Garrou was even more delighted when he heard a high-pitched screeching come from McManus' car.

"Nnggghhhhhhhhhh!" McManus wailed wordlessly in pain, then, "Help me! Anybody?! *Heeeeelp meeeeeeee!! Heeeeeeeeelp!!!*"

Garrou had no intention of leaving things to fate or dumb luck and had already planned to make certain this was finished but being able to do so while McManus was still alive only made it even better. He slowly walked towards McManus' smashed car, stretching out the man's dread and seasoning his delicious revenge.

McManus had at first continued to yell for help mechanically, repeating the same refrain but sounding fatigued, his voice slurred by injury. All the sounds McManus was making stopped as soon as Garrou growled to make his presence known. He was at first hidden in the shadows cast by the thicket, but when Garrou stepped out into the bright light of the almost full moon McManus saw a hairy, hulking, growling creature that smelled of sulfur approaching him. His languid and mechanical yells were replaced with shrieks of pure panic.

"OH MY GOD!" he screamed, "WHAT IS THAT? HELP ME! HEEEELP MEEEEE!! *HEEEEEEEEELP MEEEEEEEEEE!!!*" Garrou watched as McManus' panic took complete hold of him and he began to flail wildly, trying to free himself of his restraints and get away from the creature stalking him. Garrou reveled in his panic as he smelled the pungent odor of fresh urine coming from McManus' car. This was turning into a lovely evening.

As Garrou walked closer and closer to McManus, the pleading screams for help were replaced with tears and panicked, piglike squeals, wordless cries of animalistic terror. Garrou had heard those same cries so many times before, when his prey realized there was no escaping death, no avoiding his long claws or his sharp teeth. No matter how well educated, powerful, or wise, every human facing imminent bloody death would always devolve into a mere shrieking animal insane with terror.

To Garrou, it was the beautiful sound of true power, unrestrained and unrestricted.

Squeezing out every exquisite drop of revenge he could, Garrou paused at McManus' car as he looked down at him to whip the man's panic into a frenzy. It did, as he continued to thrash about uselessly, trying to get free even as his screams and wails sounded more and more beast-like. Garrou smashed through the windshield and tore apart the seatbelt, freeing McManus to fall on his head. He then reached for McManus' lower legs and pulled him out of the car, holding him aloft upside down.

Garrou regarded McManus, seeing the look of wild fear on his face. He'd stopped screaming, his face frozen in an anguished grimace of pain, fear, and loathing as he breathed heavily, his eyes wide, bulging from his head, his entire body shaking. Sweat mixed with the blood and streamed down off him, pooling on the road below.

"W-w-w-w-w-w-," McManus stuttered, trying to speak, "w-w-what are you?"

Garrou brought up his foreclaw to McManus' eyes as if he were pointing at him, then gently stroked his face with its cold, hard curve. Tracing the sharp tip of it down McManus' thick neck, Garrou slid it along his chest towards his swollen belly, to the man's crotch, and then back to his face. The fear too much to bear, McManus again wet himself.

Garrou then yanked McManus up hard so he could look directly into his eyes, and in a deep, growling tone that sounded more animal than human, he said, "I don't support losers, either."

A sudden look of shock and confusion briefly touched upon McManus' face for a second before Garrou sunk his talons deep into McManus' gut, then ripped his entire ponderous belly open with one swift, sloppy tear. His entrails fell to the ground with a loud wet *splosh!* as thick, bloody tendrils remained still connected to his gaping wound. McManus didn't even have time to scream before he was eviscerated.

Garrou held him up like that for some time, inspecting McManus' gutted body and rejoicing in his ability to annihilate. He then tossed the body aside like a broken rag doll beyond the crash site, flinging his guts everywhere. He knew McManus' death would be ruled an accident, the massive damage to his body caused by the twisted metal and sharp shards of glass. Satisfied with his work, Garrou threw back his head and howled proudly as he always did after a successful – and quite enjoyable – kill.

2

His work for the night done, Garrou now walked to the woods where he had his clothes hidden in a small bag not far from where his BMW was parked. He'd learned long ago he needed to strip before becoming the Wolf, having destroyed his clothing the very first night he'd transformed into the beast. Being forced to sneak naked back into Raven Hill Manor was bad enough; getting caught by his sister and teased endlessly was far worse.

Garrou found the spot where he'd hidden his bag, then whisper-growled the words to transform him back into a human – and nothing happened. He looked around dumbfounded for a moment, even looking at his clawed hands to confirm what was obvious. He hadn't changed back. Garrou again said the words, and again nothing happened, fear quickly overtaking his calm demeanor. His heart raced with a nervous uncertainty that was edging towards panic when he once again said the words and began the minute-long, agonizing transformation back to normal as he always had before.

Plunged into the darkness of woods seen through normal human eyes after he recovered from the pain, Garrou felt around inside his bag until he found a small towel, then wiped off his bloody hands. He found his clothes and tossed on his light shirt and shorts as quickly as possible. Making his way along a small trail by the light of the moon, Garrou reached the car and then sat in it for some time without leaving as he wondered what the trouble transforming back into a human might mean.

Nothing like this had ever happened before. He didn't even know how it could; this was black magic, after all, not some machine in which the gears could rust and the belts fray. Magic was supposed to work reliably with no warranty required. Bewildered and concerned, Garrou reluctantly took out his Nokia cell phone from the glove compartment and called his mother. He needed answers and was certain she'd have them for him.

One of the servants answered the phone with Victorian-like formality, then took what felt like an eternity to bring it to his mother. Once Garrou had her on the line he skipped any niceties and launched into a detailed account of the attack on McManus and his difficulty transforming back into human form.

"Why did that happen, Mother?" he asked. "What's going on?"

"That's the true Gift of the Wolf," she said.

Garrou was confused. "Gift of the Wolf? What do you

mean? I've had the Gift since I was sixteen and never once had an issue transforming back."

"Well," Mariette said, "it takes time for its full effect to be realized, but eventually, based upon how often someone accesses the Wolf, the powers become permanent, and you will become almost indestructible. The Gift, the *true* Gift, is that in time you will get to remain in Wolf form, hunting and killing and serving the coven, and will live almost forever. There is no power given to us humans without sacrifice, and there is no sacrifice without pain, after all."

Garrou was stricken speechless. Sacrifices? Did she think he hadn't made sacrifices? Did those three years of work before his ceremony not count as sacrifices? Did the hours perfecting his craft not count? Was the sigil carved into his back not a sacrifice?

This had conveniently never been mentioned to him before, not while he was being raised to see the Wolf as the greatest thing a person could aspire to become, not while he completed his agoge, and never in the many years following. His mother's words echoed in his mind: "... *the powers become permanent... you will become almost indestructible... you get to remain in Wolf form... and will live almost forever.*"

His dumbfounded speechlessness was quickly replaced with a searing anger. "You knew?!" he yelled at his mother. "You knew and you never fucking told me this would happen?! How could you have kept this from me?!!"

"I couldn't tell you," Mariette said. "Everyone who has been given the Gift has to find this out for themselves. These are ancient mandates that must be obeyed."

Garrou now better understood some of the things that had been happening to him. This explained that seething rage he'd been feeling just prior to the meeting with his mother and why the Wolf seemed to have taken over for a moment. It explained why, while waiting for McManus, Garrou had felt more beast like than he ever had before. It also occurred to him that this didn't explain everything.

"Wait, just wait," he said. "You've always told me I was supposed to be president, that I was selected by the High Council itself to be president. How the fuck is a fucking were-wolf supposed to be the president?!"

Mariette spoke as if explaining a simple concept to a not overly bright child. "This transformation usually takes many years, though it does depend upon how often one changes. Once president you will obviously not need to change at all in those eight years – there will be others who can do that work for you. Afterward... well, when it becomes obvious the Wolf will soon become permanent, something will be arranged. You'll have the rare opportunity of watching your own funeral as the nation mourns its fallen former president."

Garrou sighed as he rubbed between his eyes, irritated by this development but not surprised. He knew there were always hidden agreements, some additional duty ordered, secret strings attached, to anything associated with power that comes from the Coven Universal.

I should have known better.

Something his mother had said occurred to him. "What do you mean, I'll be indestructible? I'll live forever?"

"That's the awesome reward you get for willingly sacri-ficing your normal life for the good of the Coven," Mariette said. "When fully taken by the Wolf, you will start to become impervious to all forms of weapons. First your chest, and then your head, then it will later spread to your arms and legs. If someone should stab you or shoot you it won't matter. You'll be protected by Marchosias' Gift."

Though still annoyed, this intrigued Garrou as he raised an eyebrow thinking about the implications. Though the Wolf was a massively powerful primal killing machine with long teeth and sharp claws, he'd always known how vulnerable he was to gunfire. Garrou would stalk his prey for as long as he needed to, surveying the area to make certain there was no one else around he couldn't see, someone who might come out with guns blazing. He was especially careful when hunting rural prey with the way those people clung to their guns.

"But," Mariette said, interrupting his reverie, "don't be careless. You're still vulnerable as the Wolf and will be for some time. Also, you're not protected from *everything*. Holy water, of course, will always burn you as an acid would when you're the Wolf. A fire that's hot enough and burns long enough would kill you. Drowning will kill you, as would explosives. So, Louis, please do try your best not to get blown up."

His mother showed a sense of humor, that rarest of all her sides. Garrou chuckled almost more from it being so unexpected as he did the joke itself. "Yes, okay. I will try to do my best to avoid bombs."

Far off, Garrou could hear the high-pitched peal of emergency sirens approaching. Someone must have come upon McManus' car and called it in, meaning that shortly emergency personnel, including police, would be swarming the area. He didn't want to be there when they arrived, so Garrou ended the call with his mother and drove off, heading back to his Washington brownstone.

As he drove to the city, Garrou thought of everything his mother had said. He was irritated at being duped, but that was subsiding as he thought more and more of what the true Gift entailed. In time, he would remain as the Wolf forever and have all but eternal life. Garrou found that strangely enticing. There were some luxuries of human life Garrou was certain he'd miss, but overall, he felt attracted to the wild freedom that existence promised him.

He knew he'd be bored as a former president, giving speeches, raising money, shaking hands, but deprived of the power he lusted after. He'd be forced to engage in all the aspects of politics he most loathed with none of the delicious power to go with it. Why bother? Garrou would much rather remain in wolf form and stalk a verdant forest somewhere, chasing down and destroying his prey.

More to the point, though, is that he would now be protected on his hunts, something that Garrou very much appreciated. From what his mother said in time his entire body would be clad in an unbreakable armor when taken by the Wolf, though for now he still needed to be careful. He'd have to remember that on his next hunt, one that was far more important than any other he'd ever gone on.

And a kill that would be so much more satisfying.

CHAPTER NINE

The afternoon after Peter and his colleagues left for their week-long retreat at Thompson's hunting cabin, Angie sat in her small apartment thinking.

She'd given Peter a lift in his Toyota Avalon to the Capitol, from where the staff was going to drive to the retreat in two SUVs, then returned to her place to spend the afternoon watching some videos she'd rented at Blockbuster. After dinner, Angie wanted to read a horror novel. This was the beginning of the August recess, and Angie wanted to get her calm week off to a good start since she'd been assigned to stay back to manage the Washington office.

Despite her intentions, Angie found herself too distracted to get into the plot of the movie. Her mind kept going back to the conversation she'd had with Peter at the cabin about his childhood terror as her leg bounced without her being aware of it. She'd been busy helping get her office ready for the recess and hadn't thought about his story much in the past week, but now that things were quiet, she found herself ruminating on it.

Angie found Peter's story of seeing some nightmarish creature lurking in the West Virginia woods to be disturbing beyond measure. She cared for him deeply, and it hurt her to think he might have had such a horrible experience as a young boy. It also disturbed her because she didn't quite believe it, as she had said to him that day; however, what bothered her the most about his story was that she'd heard similar ones before.

Just like West Virginia – or every other state, she assumed – Alabama also had its share of stories about horrible creatures stalking its dark, quiet corners. She'd never seen anything like that, but her brother, Nate, had told Angie a story when they were kids that sounded uncomfortably similar to the one Peter had.

In this case, he'd been fishing out at a secluded spot in the woods near their home when he'd nodded off due to the sultry July heat. Nate had awakened with a start when he'd heard a choking, growling noise and the sound of something approaching. He'd seen a woman, or at least what looked like what was left of a woman, one whom he said had been disfigured.

Disfigured. That was the only way he was willing to describe it. Nate refused to give any more detail about what he'd meant by that because he said it was too horrible to explain. At the time, Angie had expected her brother to make it obvious he was pulling her chain by laughing, teasing her in the way typical of an older sibling. But he didn't. Instead, he stared at her with eyes too wide, eyes that seemed to bore through her with a look of wild desperation. Nate's eyes seemed suddenly to have seen too much, too many horrors.

They didn't talk about it after that first time, but she noted as the years passed her brother never went fishing again.

Angie sat there ignoring the movie, thinking about what her brother had seen and the conversation she'd had with Peter. She'd never known her brother to make up something when he wasn't picking on her, and the fact he'd given up fishing – something he'd loved when they were younger – had always struck her as odd. Angie had grown to love Peter and didn't think he was the kind of man to lie pathologically, nor was he one to have delusions.

Angie had meant what she she'd told Peter at the cabin that, while she believed his tale, she just couldn't get behind the existence of unknown evils wandering through the dark places of the world. She didn't... or at least she hadn't. Angie knew something had happened to Nate that day so long ago, so if it wasn't what he'd told her, then it was something else. She'd also heard similar stories from other, older family members, but these always seemed to be a second-hand retelling of a recollection someone else had, so she'd always dismissed those. Angie couldn't dismiss Nate's experience, just as she couldn't Peter's story. She'd seen the horror in his eyes as well and knew he was being honest. He, too, had seen something terrifying that day, something that'd had affected him profoundly.

As she sat there thinking, Angie became discomfited the more she considered there might be horrible things out there of which she had no idea, a deep-seated fear of hers. It gave her an icy chill to consider an entire universe of terror just under her everyday existence. Angie had an uncomfortable feeling like she was watching as curtains were peeled back just enough to allow her a peek of the darkness beyond, and what she saw behind them was horrifying to consider. The traumas of the regular world were bad enough, but at least she could meet those head on in the light of day; the thought of nightmarish things crawling about that, not only could she not see, but not even comprehend, was far worse.

Angie remembered a book she had on the one small set of shelves her apartment had space for, *The Encyclopedia of Myths and Legends*, a gift she'd received from her mother a few years earlier. She'd never looked at it before since reading encyclopedias wasn't enjoyable and her mother had missed the mark in trying to get a book that would satisfy her interest in horror. Nonetheless, Angie took it out now and began to lazily flip through its pages.

She really had no idea what she was looking for and wasn't even certain if she was looking for anything at all. Angie just felt confused and a little uneasy, and, as was her typical habit, the thought of finding answers in a book seemed like her best possible move.

The book was exactly as the title suggested: A detailed encyclopedic listing of myths and legends from all over the world. In its many articles, Angie found every terrifying creature she could think of, as well as many she'd never even dreamed of before. Disturbingly, she found several articles about creatures that could have been what either Peter or her brother had seen. Though this wasn't confirmation their stories were true, it was at least suggestive.

She sat, lost in thought. The movie had long since ended, plunging her apartment into a deep silence she was too absorbed by her thinking to notice until the phone rang, startling her. She crossed her living room to pick up the cordless phone in the kitchen.

"Hello?"

"Hey, girl," said her friend, Malcolm, a fellow-congressional staffer who served under a congresswoman from New York City. "How are you doing?"

"Oh, I'm fine. Peter left for that staff retreat today and so I was just... doing some reading."

"Mmm... okay," Malcolm said. "I was wondering if you wanted to come get some dinner with me and Freddie tonight? We're going out anyway, but since you're alone and we're both marooned here while the rest of our staffs are back home, I figured we'd give you an invite."

Dinner? Angie thought to herself, surprised Malcolm and his boyfriend would be going out so early. She glanced at the microwave and saw it was already well past five o'clock in the afternoon. *Holy shit. I've been thinking about this for hours!*

"Yeah, you know what, that'd be great," she said. "I think I could use to get out of here tonight. Can you give me... ten minutes to get changed?"

"Absolutely," Malcolm said. "We'll be over in a few."

They both lived in the Cardozo neighborhood of Washington and so would often walk to visit each other, or to stroll in the evenings, or to get meals together. Angie's mind still raced with a general sense of vague dread as she quickly threw on more appropriate clothes to get dinner, but by the time she walked out of her apartment building to meet Malcolm and Freddie she was looking forward to a meal out.

She hugged and kissed both on their cheeks, but as she pulled back from Freddie, she had an electric shiver tingle down her spine. As she did, Angie saw across the broad street a young woman standing there watching her. Angie might not have noticed her at all if not for the woman's bright red hair contrasted against her pale white skin. Plain-faced and wearing a black dress that seemed somehow anachronistic, she reminded Angie of women in their novitiates she'd sometimes see while visiting the Basilica, though this woman's dress looked less uniform-like and more like an old-fashioned, plain black dress.

As the trio walked away, Angie glanced behind her and saw that, though the woman hadn't moved at all, she was watching them closely. That nebulous sense of unease she'd been feeling all day came back now harder than before, though it had dissipated while distracting herself with thoughts of dinner out. She pulled her eyes away from the strange young woman when she realized Malcolm was speaking to her.

"Hello... Angie?" he said. "Girl, what is wrong with you? You look even whiter than normal."

Angie shook her head a little to clear her thoughts, running her hand through her long hair, then said, "Did you guys see that woman back there?"

"Who?" Freddie asked, and they all turned to see the woman standing there, unmoved yet staring at her still. They turned back away from the woman as if getting caught peeking at something they should not have been, none of them wanting to meet her unyielding stare. "That creepy-looking redhead there?"

"Yeah, her," Angie answered.

"I see her now," said Malcolm. "Who is she?"

"I don't know. Just some woman I saw staring at us when I came down."

"At us?" Freddie asked, "Or at you? I mean, she was waiting outside your apartment building."

"Yeah," Angie whispered, "I don't... I don't know, really."

As if of one mind, the trio looked back to where the red-haired woman had been, only to see her now gone. Though it was a hot and humid August day, Angie felt another chill race down her spine.

"Well..." Malcolm said. "That was some weird shit."

A brief moment of silence as Angie thought about how that strange woman, though completely random and unrelated to the stories she'd been thinking about earlier, seemed like just another small crack in what she had thought was a secure paradigm of the world.

Into this silence Freddie said, "I don't know about you guys, but I'm starving. Where are we going to eat?"

Angie and Malcolm looked at each other, smiled, and at the same time declared, "Ben's."

"Awesome," said Freddie. "I am dying for some chili cheese fries!"

"You're always dying for something from Ben's, who are you kidding?" Malcolm teased.

The trio walked the several blocks it took to get to the Washington landmark, then sat at a booth. The restaurant was busy as always, with people coming and going, constant chatter, and an energy Angie found quite soothing considering how twisted her thoughts had been that day. She talked and laughed with Malcolm and Freddie, discussing politics with her colleague and music with his boyfriend. Their meals arrived and Angie was able for a time to get lost in the delicious flavors before her.

And yet there was a creeping, dark sense in her mind, one that seemed to teeter in the shadowy fringe right between conscious awareness and the subconscious. It felt to Angie that somehow the jigsaw puzzle she'd made in her mind long ago to create an understandable picture of the world wasn't quite fitting together anymore. The sides of her pieces no longer seemed to meet flush, the corners were now off, and there were cracks everywhere.

Angie would attend to the conversation she was having with Malcolm and Freddie, then feel herself being dragged into the darkness again, and then once more be able to attend. Angie finally blurted out, "Do you guys ever feel like... like things don't make sense sometimes? Like... there's something else going on out there and we don't ever get the full picture?"

The pair stopped chewing to look at her for a moment, mystified by her sudden question unrelated to what they were talking about.

"Ummm..." Malcolm said. "Things don't make sense? Like... how?"

"Like," said Angie as she searched for the right words,

feeling frustrated by having only the vaguest concept of the question herself, and not knowing how best to express the problem. "Like... ah, shit, I don't know. I've just been having this weird sense today like there's more to the world than we could possibly know, like there are things going on, maybe right under our noses, that we don't know about."

"I know the government is into some shady shit," Malcolm said. "I know it has secrets on top of secrets. There are things going on none of us will ever know about."

"No," said Angie, feeling more frustrated, like she was trying to convey important technical information to someone who barely spoke English. "I'm not talking about the government. I'm talking about... life. The big picture. Almost like... like you live in an apartment, but you think it's a house, so you don't know you live in an entire apartment building and can't figure out what's going on, why you hear other people and why the water pressure changes and things like that."

Angie looked at their puzzled faces staring back at her, half-eaten hot dogs in their hands poised almost to their mouths.

"Am I making any sense?"

"No," the pair answered in unison.

Angie sighed, feeling increasingly exasperated. "Like you realize you've been floating in a mist but never realized you were before. Like everything you thought about the world wasn't what you thought it was and that there were things out there you could never even dream of. That maybe you've been lied to."

"I could never dream of polka music existing, yet it does," said Freddie.

"Which *is* horrifying," added Malcolm.

"Guys," Angie said, looking around, trying to find the right words, "that's not quite what I'm talking—"

She stopped mid-sentence as her eyes, wandering around

the restaurant as she searched for a different way to phrase her question, seized upon a flash of color when she happened to glance outside. There, between people in line and coming and going from the restaurant, she caught a glimpse of bright red hair. Looking now more carefully, Angie was able to see brief flashes of the plain-faced woman from before, again standing on the other side of the street staring at her.

Angie sucked in her breath as she realized what she was seeing, and harshly whispered to the pair, "Guys, it's her. It's the woman."

"What?" Malcolm exclaimed, trying to pivot in his seat to look out the window. "Where?!"

"She's there," Angie said, pointing out the window as a primal fear grew inside her, "she's right... there." But now as she looked, Angie realized the woman was gone, lost in between the people moving inside the restaurant and the traffic outside.

"What the hell?" Freddie asked. "What's going on?" But Angie had no answer for him, being just as confused as he was.

Angie was quite upset from this strange event and wanted to leave the restaurant right away. Rather than walking the several blocks to her apartment they called a taxi, and then Malcolm and Freddie saw her safely back to her place before leaving. She asked Malcolm to call when they returned home because of that woman lurking somewhere out there; he did, but said he saw nothing at all.

Angie felt agitated and upset for the remainder of that day, peering out her window several times to see if the strange woman was out there. She wasn't, yet still Angie felt disturbed. She realized that, in the overall scheme of things, what happened to her wasn't the most bizarre. Angie reminded herself there are always strange people in the world, many of whom live in a big city. People stare, sometimes intensely, that just happens. It's just a few blocks from her apartment building to Ben's, she reasoned, so the woman could have walked there herself.

But put together with her thoughts earlier, with that gnawing sense the world was skewed, off kilter even as others insisted it was fine, seeing the strange woman twice made her feel uneasy. It was a sense that was only going to grow as the week went on.

CHAPTER TEN

1

The week spent at Sim Thompson's hunting cabin had proven to be an effective retreat for the team, and Peter felt proud of the work he and the others had done in that short time.

They started every morning with a hearty breakfast cooked by Thompson himself, which also acted as an informal team meeting to decide what the objectives for the day were. Then they'd break off into smaller groups, sometimes working together and sometimes individually, with lunch being another informal check-in meeting. Thompson insisted on a daily siesta in the early afternoon for people to relax, nap, hike outside, or whatever they needed to do to keep their minds fresh.

During these siestas, Peter would often rest in his bed and read, but the thumping coming from neighboring bedrooms suggested the retreat had given rise to several office romances. While he felt somewhat amused by these developments, overhearing those afternoon liaisons always made him ache for Angie more than he already was.

The team would have a formal meeting at three o'clock to nail down whatever else needed to be accomplished, finally breaking in the late afternoon for a different staff member each day to make dinner for the team. Peter enjoyed cooking, so when it was his turn, he made steaks on the grill he'd been marinating in a special sauce of his own concoction, together with cheesy garlic mashed potatoes and green beans amandine. He felt proud of the results with not a scrap of food leftover.

The evenings were given over to relaxation and socializing, although things on this last night of the retreat had devolved into an unabashed party. Music blared from the stereo system, everyone had a drink in their hand, and the team was gathered together in the open great room of the cabin, dancing and singing and chatting as they celebrated what had been a superb week of work together.

Everyone, that is, except Peter. Although he felt pleased with what they'd accomplished that week and was pleasantly numb as he drank his third beer of the night, Peter wasn't much in the mood to party. The team was leaving the next morning and he was thrilled to get back to see Angie.

2

Seeing Angie, however, was not the only reason Peter was ready to get out of this forest. He was also eager to head back because he'd had a distant dread gnawing at him the entire time the staff had been secluded in the wilderness.

Peter had felt uneasy ever since that bizarre childhood memory resurfaced while at the cabin talking to Angie, and so the entire week he'd felt like there was something in the foliage lurking, watching them, waiting. This foreboding had grown darker all week, so he was especially anxious to leave on this final night of the retreat and didn't feel like partying.

So instead, he sat near the cold fieldstone fireplace, slumped low in his chair with his long, lanky legs stretched out crossed at the ankle before him, some distance removed from the raucous revelry. From there, Peter watched his co-workers' antics and took in Thompson's hunting cabin. *Cabin* is how Thompson referred to it, but Peter thought it was more of a rustic mansion in the woods and nothing like what his family would call a hunting cabin.

The high vaulted ceiling of the great room was supported by huge oaken timbers aloft together with several mammoth beams acting as pillars. All the walls were covered with knotty pine, which in the seventy-odd years since it'd been built had taken on a deep honey tone. Two wagon wheel style rustic chandeliers hung from the ceiling, both of which were needed to adequately light this huge room. Peter sat on rustic-looking furniture made from hewn oak limbs, but which was also refined enough to have hunter green leather cushions, which matched the furniture gathered by the television, and a reading nook in the corner. Peter believed his family's entire cabin could fit inside this great room alone.

Peter finished his beer and considered getting up to grab another one, but that would require him walking through the throng of dancing, laughing, screaming people in the middle of the great room. The fireplace where he sat was on the far side of the room and the coolers were near the door opposite him on the other side of it, so instead he contented himself to sit and watch his drunk coworkers some more.

He saw that Thompson made sure to interact with every-one, but not for too long, and he also noted the congressman was only drinking a Coke. *Very smart*, he thought. Peter also remarked that Drew, the legislative director, was getting way too comfortable with the intern they recently took on for the fall semester. *That's not so smart.* Peter then realized the chief of staff and press secretary had disappeared from the party altogether, and he was willing to bet they were upstairs right now thumping loudly in a bedroom near his. *I just hope they're done by the time I go to bed.*

Peter was just about to get up and weave his way through the group to get another beer when Drew turned down the music and yelled, "Everyone! Everyone! Can I have your attention, please?! Everyone, hello!!"

The group eventually settled down and turned to face Drew, who was standing with this arm around Thompson. "Since Jimmy is currently, uh... indisposed at the moment, I figured I'd say a few words here before everyone got too shitfaced to care—"

"Too late," several voices said at once, all noticeably slurred.

"Alright, ya heathens, settle down," Drew said. He raised a red plastic cup, and went on, saying, "Here's to the best damn congressional staff in all of Washington!"

The team cheered loudly throwing back their drinks. Peter joining in by raising his empty can of beer and saying, "Woo," to himself.

"And here's to a kick-ass week of hard work that's going to have us win in November over that smug, elitist bastard Garrou!"

Another cheer from the team, this time louder and more animated. Peter again participated with a half-hearted, "Woo."

"And here's to our boss, the very-soon-to-be Senator... Simuel... Thompson!"

The staff now cheered even louder than before, cheers that

turned into a celebratory *whoot-whoot-whoot* chorus. Peter clapped lazily a few times for his boss.

Thompson stepped forward during the cheers, his hands raised as he tried to silence his staff. "Thank you, thank you. Alright, settle down, folks. I want to thank you all for such a great week of hard work, for your dedication, and for your belief in me personally. You know when I first got into politics—"

His impromptu speech was cut short when the entire hunting cabin was plunged into darkness. Someone from the staff gaggle screamed, replaced a moment later by a nervous, drunk giggle. Peter stood up at the unexpected dark, that dull sense of loathing growing stronger in his mind as it pushed out his pleasant buzz.

He stood but didn't move so profound was the blackness. They were in the middle of the woods, miles from the nearest small town, and the outdoor lighting on the property had gone out, too. The moon that night was a mere fingernail of a crescent, so there wasn't even its pale light to help illuminate the room. Several people spoke at once, some joking, some concerned.

"Anyone have a flashlight on them?" a voice asked in the dark.

"Who carries a flashlight with them?" another retorted.

"What the hell, why'd the lights go out? It's not storming," said a third.

"Was there maybe a crash somewhere?" asked someone else, or perhaps it was the first person Peter had heard. It was hard for him to tell who was who in the dark and over all the chattering voices speaking at once.

"How about this?" asked Drew, as he flicked his cigarette lighter, bathing the great room in a weak orange light. "That helps a little."

The handful of staff members that had lighters also joined him in using their small flames to illuminate the room, which collectively gave it an orange hue that swam and jumped as the flames flickered, making the shadows cast in deepest black wobble in a way Peter found unsettling. He felt the flickering light cast by the lighters was almost dizzying, though it was better than the utter darkness.

"I think there's still a light over here on the mantel," Thompson said as he walked towards the fireplace where Peter sat. "Oh, hi, Peter. I didn't see you there at first. Do you see a red emergency lantern with a handle – ah, here it is."

Thompson had just turned on the blinding white lantern when there was a sudden crashing sound at the front door so loud and violent that, for a moment, Peter thought there had been an explosion. The thick oak door burst apart as if a bomb had gone off, showering the room with chunks of splintered wood flying through it. One piece the size of two fingers twirled through the air and hit Drew in the throat with a loud *thwok!*, lodging there deeply. Another piece came whirling past Peter's head, almost killing him.

A half-second later, before anyone had the chance to react or say anything or even grasp what was happening, a gigantic animal, a beast, a hairy nightmare creature, came rushing in through the shattered doors just behind the shower of splinters. It had burst the door apart, sundering it into pieces, and dashed in, then paused a moment to survey the petrified staff members. They all stood rooted in place, too horrified to move, the people with lighters still holding them high. The creature roared at them, a ghastly cry like nothing Peter had ever heard before, terrifying in part due to its primal rage but also because it was impossibly loud. It then began to slash, rip, and tear away at the team in a frenzied rage.

The creature first ripped off the arms that were still holding the lighters up, limbs flying as the splinters had, blood splashing everywhere, the cabin now illuminated only by the single white beam of Thompson's emergency lantern. That was enough to break the horrifying spell their terror had cast on them, the remaining uninjured staffers now running away in the dark as fast as they could. The creature, taking long strides with every step, kept up an unending frenetic attack on the staff, slashing at them with its gigantic claws again and again and again. It tore open backs, ripped off scalps, and for one unlucky co-worker of Peter's, lopped off his head with one quick slash of its curved talons.

Peter, just as terrified as his co-workers, stood rooted where he was, remaining so even after the others had broken because of the fireplace pressing at his back. But, even through his fear, Peter saw what appeared to be... was it *intention?* Was it *purpose?* Despite the limited light and being as terrified as he was, a calm part of Peter's brain recognized the creature knew what it was doing. Even as it slashed remorselessly at the remaining staffers it scanned the room and seemed to be searching, as if looking for one particular person.

Then, it stopped as its gaze clutched hold of Thompson with eyes that had red glowing irises.

Peter saw those two crimson glowing orbs in the dark, and afterward, when he doubted what happened, when he questioned his own memory, he reminded himself that he *saw* it and he *knew* the creature paused when its red eyes locked on Thompson. It was there for a purpose, for a person, and that person was Sim Thompson.

Having found its target, the creature roared once again in unearthly rage and loudness, then pushed past several staffers and closed on Sim with such speed that it seemed almost instantaneous. Peter watched, helpless and paralyzed with horror, as the creature fell upon Thompson with one gigantic paw raised. Thompson, dumb with terror, simply stood there slack-jawed, looking up dumbfounded as he shone the bright light on the hirsute bringer of his own death.

And a swift death it was. The creature slashed down with its upraised paw with all its force, ripping open Thompson's body from his left shoulder to his right hip. Peter watched numbly as blood and bone shards and scraps of bloody torn cloth splattered everywhere, Thompson's pink intestines pushing through the slashes across his belly. He sank and dropped the emergency lantern and it landed, illuminating the violent scene with an unsettling light from below.

Thompson slumped after the attack, but before he could fall, the creature grabbed him and held him high above its head with both paws. Then, the creature twisted his body one way, bones snapping like a string of firecrackers and flesh rending with a wet sound, twisted his body the other way, then finally ripped him in half with a great bloody tear, splashing Peter with his boss' blood and viscera.

The beast threw Thompson's body parts to the ground in front of it, and then looked down at what remained of the congressman. Later, when Peter would recall this horrifying event, he would explain how the creature appeared to be staring at the corpse as if it was gloating victoriously.

Splattered with Thompson's blood, close enough to the creature that he could smell its pungent, rotten egg odor, Peter now feared he was going to be the next to die. He had noticed an ax leaning up against the fireplace earlier and lunged to grab it while he had the chance. The creature, still staring at Thompson's wrecked body, saw his sudden movement and stepped towards Peter as it raised a bloody paw.

Without thinking, without planning what he was doing, without any real hope for success, Peter lashed out at the beast with the ax, swinging it with all his force. It bit into the creature's face as it stepped forward, landing diagonally from brow to jaw, taking out its right eye. Although Peter had swung with every bit of adrenaline-driven strength he had, the ax only dug into the creature's skull a bit, as if its skull were made of steel.

Despite that, the creature lurched back, howling in intense pain. It stumbled back several steps, stopping at one of the massive oak pillars with its left paw covering its now dead eye while its right one supported itself on the wooden column. Peter, still wild with fear, lashed out again at the creature with the ax. Though he aimed for the creature's head, this time he missed and hit its paw instead, slicing into it deeply. He cut so far that Peter saw half the paw fall to the floor.

The creature again howled angrily in pain as it cradled its ruined right paw in its left one and glared at him with a look of hatred in its remaining red-glowing eye. It growled at Peter, as if considering its options, then pivoted and sprinted back out through the shattered remains of the door.

From beginning to end, the furious attack took around one full minute.

Peter stood there for a moment staring vacantly at the dark doorway after the creature had fled, then let the ax slip from his hands. Shocked by what had just happened, he looked around with unblinking eyes surveying the damage. Bathed in the pale light from the lantern, Peter could make out splinters from the ruined door were scattered everywhere. He saw the walls were spattered with blood, and as he scanned the room, he could see arms lying on the floor, the tattered shreds of flesh and clothing, the bodies of his dead team members, and the injured staffers writhing in pain. He could hear the groans and screams of his wounded fellow staffers. Peter glanced up at a swaying rustic chandelier as it made a gentle creaking sound, and there he saw the head of his co-worker looking down at him through blood-flecked glasses. The coppery odor of blood hung thickly in the air.

As if recalling an all but forgotten dream, Peter thought of Sim Thompson. Slowly turning to look – dreading what he was about to see, hoping he was wrong, but knowing the truth – Peter saw the bisected body of Thompson lying crumpled on the floor. Wheeling back around and squeezing his eyes shut against all the terror he'd been witness to, Peter remembered that he'd been splashed with Thompson's blood and now tried to wipe it away as if it were acid burning his skin. As he did, Peter began to tremble violently as all the horrors of the night crushed down upon him. Feeling like he was grinding the blood into his skin rather than wiping it away, he fell to his knees and screamed until his throat was raw.

The weight of witnessing such violence was just too much for him to bear.

3

A few hours later, Peter sat in the back of an ambulance as he chain-smoked cigarettes with a still trembling hand. He stared blankly in front of him as paramedics, police, and people from the coroner's office bustled about the scene talking to witnesses, caring for the wounded, and taking out the dead. The whole area was bathed in flashing red and blue lights from the many emergency vehicles. Peter saw none of it. He was re-watching the bloody end of Thompson on a continual loop, an image he felt unable to shake from his mind.

As he did, though, his mind also replayed what he'd seen of the beast – or the bear, which he'd overheard is how the police were already framing this attack. Though the staff member's descriptions varied widely because of the dark, and though Peter specified the creature's irises glowed red, the consistent description was of a huge, hairy beast that moved on two legs, had sharp claws and teeth, and attacked with wild violence. Bears often stood on their rear legs to attack, and since there were already active investigations of a rabid bear on the Delmarva that had attacked several people earlier in the summer, Peter had heard it was assumed this was the same animal.

Peter thought differently.

CHAPTER ELEVEN

T he next day, the crows flew in agitated circles high above
Raven Hill Manor reflecting the upset of the resident
within.

Mariette Garrou sat perched on a leather wing chair in the
parlor of her mansion listening to that evening's edition of *All
Things Considered.* Her pale face looked even tighter than it
did normally, her thin lips all but disappeared due to the
tension etched on her face. Though she always comported
herself in a stiff, formal way, her current rigidity was the result
of a terrible internal pressure. She absentmindedly worried a
lace handkerchief she held as she listened to the report.

"Tragic news coming out of Washington today," the newsreader said, "as we gather more details on the shocking death of
Congressman Simuel A. Thompson, killed last night in a
bizarre bear attack during a staff retreat at his hunting lodge in
Maryland. Thompson, who had represented the state's Ninth
Congressional District in Washington since 1990, has been
described as popular among his colleagues and with voters. The
congressman's unexpected death has shaken the capital as well

as his home state. Thompson was running against Congressman Louis P. Garrou for the open Senate seat and was gaining significantly on Garrou in the polls. His sudden death this late into the election process has thrown the entire Senate race into a tailspin. Though there has been no official announcement yet from Governor Glendening, it is assumed Thompson's wife, Catherine, will be offered the chance to serve out the remaining time in his term. Three of Thompson's staff were also killed with an additional five wounded."

While the newsreader spoke, Mariette poured herself water from a crystal decanter on the small table next to her chair, took a sip of it, then let out a long, breathy sigh. The look of tense anxiety engraved on her wrinkled face never once altered as she braced herself for what the next news item would be.

"Meanwhile," the newsreader continued, "it was reported early this morning that Congressman Garrou was involved in a motor vehicle accident. Details of the accident are still sketchy, but Garrou was apparently returning to Washington after visiting his mother in Poolesville, Maryland, when he swerved to avoid a deer and lost control of his car. He is currently recovering in the hospital and is listed in stable condition. In a statement provided by the campaign, Garrou says, 'Though I've been injured in the crash and need to take a leave of absence for a few weeks, I will return to the Capitol as soon as possible to continue working for the people of Maryland and the United States.' He also added that his thoughts and prayers are with the Thompson family. In other news..."

Mariette sat still as a marble statue. She was no longer listening to the radio as the news continued, her mind lost to a maze of dark thoughts. As she did, the handkerchief she held was crushed as her hand collapsed into a shaking fist, her typically placid face twisting into an enraged mask. With an angry shriek, she lashed out at the decanter and glass on the table next to her, shattering the crystal to pieces. Mariette sliced her hand in several places as she did but was oblivious to the pain and blood trickling down her arm.

She almost immediately regained her icy composure as her thoughts returned to the full implications of Louis' injuries. Mariette had been informed there were already messages being sent, meetings held, whispered conversations had. She knew irreversible processes had now been set in motion, ones that could have dire consequences for her family, for her coven, and for the Coven Universal. The High Council was unforgiving; failure was intolerable, and it *always* had a price.

"There is no power without sacrifice," Mariette whispered sadly, "and there is no sacrifice without pain."

CHAPTER TWELVE

1

Angie was awaked in the early hours of the morning when Peter sat up and shrieked in horror, then screamed, *"THEY'RE ALL DEAD!!"* just as he had more often than not in the two weeks since returning home from the staff retreat massacre.

"It's okay, honey, it's okay," she said in a soft, soothing tone as she put her arms around his thin body. Every time she'd repeated this same routine in the days since his return, Angie could feel his heart pounding in his chest and his body still trembling from the terrifying nightmare from which he'd escaped, his naked flesh covered in a thin sheen of sweat. Peter sat up in the bed, shaking and staring into the dark room with unseeing eyes for perhaps a minute, until his heart rate calmed, and his breathing evened, as the awareness of what was happening returned to him.

He looked and met Angie's eyes, swallowed hard, then

licked his dry lips. He said, "I'm sorry... I had another nightmare."

"Yeah," she whispered, still holding him close, "I know."

He lay back down in bed, rubbing his eyes as if trying to scrub away the horrors he'd just seen in his dream. Angie thought this might have been the ninth, perhaps tenth, night that Peter had a horrifying nightmare so terrible it drove him out of his sleep in a panic.

"What time is it?" Peter asked, still rubbing his eyes.

Angie squinted to see without her glasses. "It's half-past four in the morning."

"Yeah," he whispered. "Okay. Not as early as they used to be." Then, after lying in the pale gray light of the bedroom for a few minutes, he said, "I won't be able to sleep after that, so I'll just get up now. Go back to sleep, babe. I love you." He kissed her on the forehead, then slipped out of bed as quietly as he could.

As she watched his shadowy form walk out of the dark bedroom, Angie thought, *They seem to be getting better. That's good.*

<hr />

2

Peter had called Angie after the attack to tell her what had happened, and though it was the middle of the night when he did so, she had driven across the state to pick him up. All Peter did during that long drive home was to smoke one cigarette after another and stare into the distance, lost to his thoughts. He responded to Angie's many questions with terse, one-word answers. He spent that first day home staring, smoking, his right leg bouncing nervously.

They agreed that it would be best if Peter stayed with Angie rather than returning to his own apartment and made plans for him to move his stuff into her place when he felt better, then went to bed early because of how exhausted he felt. Later that night, Peter had his first and, Angie believed, his worst nightmare.

She'd been awakened by Peter thrashing in his sleep as he mumbled, "No. No. No... no... no... please, God... no." He'd then screamed, *"THEY'RE ALL DEAD!!"* as he sat up, panting, sweating, eyes bulging in fear, looking but not seeing anything but the fading images he'd just been forced to witness. Angie had wrapped her arms around him then just as she had done this night and soothed him, reminding him that he was safe, and it was only a nightmare.

"What was the dream about?" Angie had asked that first time.

Rubbing his eyes, Peter had whispered haltingly, "It was like reliving the attack again... except this time... the creature ripped apart everyone in its way rather than some getting to safety. As it approached me and Thompson... he kept saying, 'Do something, Peter, do something, you need to do something.' Then, it..." Peter shook at the recollection, holding himself as if chilled to his core, "... it picked him up, and... and... you know... it killed him. But when it did, this rain of blood... just started pouring down... covering everything, covering me and the corpses and the creature... and then it slowly started to approach me, arms out, just getting closer and closer and closer... and then I screamed myself awake."

Angie had continued to hold him afterward in the dark of their bedroom until she fell back asleep, though Peter lay there for hours tossing and turning, unable to get any more rest that night. When Angie found him the next morning, sitting cigarette in hand, staring at the blackness of a turned-off television set, Peter told her he'd surrendered even trying to sleep and got up at around three o'clock.

The nightmares were becoming less intense and happening later in the night, so Peter was at last getting some rest. This was good news, because even though the remaining Thompson staff had been allowed time off during the recess, his return to work in early September was approaching. Still, Angie was worried about him, so she groggily got up and joined him in the living room.

There was a conversation she'd been putting off they needed to have.

<hr />

3

She found him sitting on the couch, thinking, still smoking, but no longer with the vacant, staring eyes he'd had in the days right after the attack. His mood had improved since coming home, as had his ability to plug into his environment and not just float through it in a daze, adrift in a sea of traumatic images.

"Those things are going to kill you," she declared, walking out into a cloud of pungent mist. "I wish you'd quit again."

"I know," Peter said, exhaling a long tendril of smoke as Angie sat on the couch and snuggled up to him. "I wish I could, too, but at least for right now they're helping to keep me calm."

"Hmm," said Angie. "I suppose. Maybe we should get you some lollipops or something."

Peter shrugged. "Maybe."

They sat like that in silence for several minutes as Peter finished his cigarette and Angie sat, left hand splayed out as she admired the light sparkling off her very new diamond engagement ring. On their way home that first day Peter had asked her to stop at a local mall and told her he'd be right back. When he returned, he opened the ring box, saying he'd come to realize after the attack how things can change in an instant and how precious life is. He couldn't waste another second not having Angie as his wife and he desperately wanted to marry her. She said yes.

"Why are you up?" Peter asked. "You don't have to be at work for hours. You hardly have to be there at all right now."

"I just didn't feel like I'd fall back to sleep," Angie answered, lying a little.

"Sorry I woke you. These nightmares just keep on happening."

"Yeah, but they seem to be getting better, right?"

Peter nodded in agreement. "Yeah, they are. Thank God. I felt like I was losing my mind there for a while."

"Since we're up..." Angie began, not quite certain how to proceed, "umm... let's talk about what you were saying just after you gave me the ring. Do you remember?" Peter had remained quiet on their drive home, talking the most as he proposed to Angie. He showed a flash of honest happiness when she said yes, and the newly engaged couple hugged.

But when they pulled apart Angie had seen Peter's eyes were filling with tears, and for a moment she thought he was just overwhelmed by emotion because of everything that had happened. Instead, he'd started to hyperventilate and sob as he rambled incoherently about the bear not being a bear and there being a mystery hand somewhere and about how he had to burn his clothes because they were soaked with Thompson's gore and how none of this made any sense. Angie hugged him again until he stopped crying and suggested they talk about things later.

It was now well past later.

Peter looked down, then whispered with downcast eyes, "Yeah, I remember."

"It's nothing to be embarrassed about, Peter," Angie assured him. "You survived something traumatizing, something horrifying. It's okay that you had a little breakdown not even a full day after it happened."

Peter nodded.

"But what you were saying at the time," Angie said, "I couldn't make it out. Not entirely. You were saying something about the bear, but it's not the bear. You said there was a hand somewhere. What were you talking about?"

Peter lit another cigarette, then, after a long silence, said, "That's what I've been thinking about all this time. I've been thinking about it since the night it happened. Nothing makes any damn sense, and I can't figure it out."

"What can't you figure out?"

"You know the police and all the reporters said this was some bear attack, like a rabid bear running wild, right?"

"Yeah," Angie answered as she nodded. "That's what they were reporting even the morning after it happened."

"Right," Peter said, growing more animated. "See, but here's the thing. That *wasn't* a bear I saw. No way in hell that was a bear."

"Then what was it?"

"That's what I can't figure out. I've been wracking my brain for two damn weeks, and I can't figure that out."

"Well, what makes you think it wasn't a bear?" Angie asked.

"I grew up in the woods. I've seen bears, I've hunted bears. That was no bear. I watched as it moved... almost elegantly, running on two legs, not the unbalanced shuffle bears do when they're forced to stand upright. No way that was a bear."

"Okay... I'm not arguing, I'm just playing Devil's advocate

here, but everything happened so quickly, and you said it was dark. Could your memory be wrong?"

"Yeah... but that's not all," Peter said, appearing excited the more he talked about it. "I saw it searching even as it attacked, trying to find Thompson. I know it was there specifically to kill him like it was a hit or something. Bears don't do that. It had red glowing eyes. Even if it were rabid its eyes wouldn't glow red. And even though it was dark, I could tell that thing was built like no bear I've ever seen before. Then, I saw it cradle its wounded paw in its good one and stare at me almost... *hatefully* is the only word I can think of."

"Hmm..." Angie grunted, thinking. "That certainly is all very odd."

"And you haven't heard everything yet," said Peter. "First of all, there's the door. Bears almost never come into houses through the door since for them a door just looks like part of the wall. But the rare times they do break in through the door, they'll just push it in, not burst it apart. There is no bear alive that could burst a door apart like that, especially not a thick, solid oak door like the one at the cabin. Bears are strong, but they're not *that* strong. That door burst to pieces like a bomb went off."

"Hmm..." Angie again said, confused.

"But here's the biggest reason. I cut into a paw tipped with long claws, but what I saw on the floor was half a human hand."

Angie stared at him for a moment and then cocked her head to the side as she tried to work out what Peter had just said.

"What?" she asked. "You saw... half a hand?"

"Yeah, as real as you see me now, I saw it there, lying on the ground," Peter said. "The thumb, pointer, and middle fingers, and the palm part in between. After I'd finished shaking and screaming and I'd calmed down, I noticed it lying there in a small pool of blood where the paw should have been. I looked at it carefully, and it was definitely a human hand with long, slender fingers. The nails looked manicured."

Angie stared at Peter, shocked, confused, and incredulous at the same time. "No... I mean... no, it couldn't... that can't... what? Wait, wait. Couldn't it... have come from one of the other staffers? You said things got pretty... messy."

"Yeah, it sure did," Peter said. "But I heard some of the police discussing it as I sat in the ambulance. There were body parts scattered all around the cabin, though all the severed pieces could be connected to the person they came from. Not the hand. Not one of my co-workers lost part of their hand, and I *know* it came from the beast."

"What did the police say when you told them about beating off the bear and about the hand."

Peter, looking sheepish, glanced down at the floor a moment, before raising his eyes to meet Angie's and said, "I never told them."

Angie shook her head and blinked twice quickly, then said, "You never told them?"

"No. I knew they'd never believe me, and I was in no mood to try to explain that after I'd mentioned about it having red eyes. They all but laughed at me, and one prick of a cop said, 'Bears don't have red eyes, sonny, and this was a bear attack.' No use trying to convince them when they'd already made up their minds, you know?"

"Yeah," Angie agreed. "I guess so."

"But listen," Peter said, putting his hand on Angie's knee, "I'm telling you... that hand fell from the beast when I cut it."

Angie, still trying to process everything Peter had just told her, looked at him slack-jawed and confused.

"Bottom line is that whatever attacked us, it was no bear."

"Then what was it?" Angie whispered, again feeling a vague, inchoate horror lurking in the back of her mind.

Peter rubbed his eyes, then scratched his head. "That I don't know. I know it wasn't a bear. What it was, though... I have no idea."

Angie thought for a moment. "It's like those stories we talked about at the cabin, the Snarly Yow and the White Thing and all that."

Peter looked at her with eyes askance. "I thought you said you didn't believe in weird things crawling around out there in the wilds."

"Well, I..." Angie said, unsure how to go on. "I'm not really certain anymore, to be honest."

Peter, with a questioning look on his face, asked, "Why? What happened?"

Angie sighed, then explained to Peter about the story her brother had told her so many years earlier and how it much resembled his own experience. She showed him her book and how there were many entries in it that could be what either of them saw, and she finally told him about her bizarre experiences with that strange, plain-faced woman in black.

"Babe, are you okay?!" he asked. "Did she come back? Did you call the police?"

"I'm fine, and she didn't do anything illegal so nothing to call about. It was just a really weird experience, you know?"

"Yeah," Peter said, "I know all about those."

"So, anyway... it's not like I'm saying I believe in these things, but I am saying there's something going on we don't know about."

"Yeah, there is," Peter said. "I'm beginning to think there's a whole world chugging away right under our feet we know nothing about."

"And I agree with you," said Angie, "about this so-called

bear. That was no bear. Hands don't magically appear. What it was, though, I also have no idea."

They chatted about the strange incident with the hand and how Peter was moving on from that horrifying night. Angie was very pleased to hear him talking more and more about it, and to do so without that anguished look etched on his face. She was happy to see his smile return, the bright look in his eyes, and his usual zest for life coming back. Angie had been worried about Peter and feared he might never rebound from this, like some older great-uncles of hers who had never quite recovered from their experiences in World War Two.

Though Angie feared the reality that the world was far stranger than she ever considered, she now thought there might still be room for hope in this bizarre new world.

CHAPTER THIRTEEN

1

"All right, everyone," Jimmy said once the much-depleted staff was assembled for the meeting, "let's get this started. We have a lot of work to do to continue Sim's legislative vision, and this is going to be like switching horses midstream: hard, but not impossible. We've had a horrible loss, yes, but I want us to build off that incredible energy we had at the retreat before... well, before we left. Before we begin the meeting itself, though, Catherine has a few things she'd like to share with everyone. Catherine?"

"Thank you very much, Jimmy," Catherine Thompson said on this first day back after the August recess to the surviving staff members in what used to be her husband's Capitol office. She stood at the desk as she spoke. "To begin with, I want to thank you all for your loyalty to Sim. For your dedication. For your hard work. He knew how hard you all worked for him and how much you believed in him. I know he appreciated it very much, and so do I."

Catherine looked gaunt, ravaged by a grief that had tormented her and ground her down an inch at a time since Thompson's horrible death. Peter had only met her a few times before, but each time she had been spirited and lively. Now, she appeared as a shell of a woman. Her skin was pale, her eyes outlined in red from the many hours of crying she'd done since the attack. She spoke softly, and Peter felt even that stretched the limits of her energy. The night Thompson was killed, Peter realized, Catherine had died as well.

At Thompson's closed-casket funeral, Catherine had wailed loudly, making sounds of such profound anguish and pain Peter prayed he never suffered like that. She looked almost insane with heartache, one that he knew wasn't just because her husband had been killed but the violent, horrific manner in which he died.

Later, at the reception in the Thompsons' sprawling farmhouse following his burial, Peter saw Catherine take a handful of pills, then walk unsteadily up the stairs not long after to disappear into her room for the rest of the day. The hurt of losing Thompson, and losing him in that violent way, was just too much for her to handle.

"Sim loved being a congressman," Catherine said, "and serving the people of our state... though he did complain about Washington an awful lot." There were a few gentle chuckles scattered throughout the room, and Peter saw the ends of Catherine's mouth twitch upward in what might have been a smile, but it dissolved like smoke in a breeze. Tears swelled in her eyes. "He loved... he loved you all and loved doing this work."

Catherine paused to dab her eyes with the handkerchief she now always kept with her, one with an *ST* embroidered on it in red cloth. She pressed it to her face a moment before continuing, breathing in the scent of her deceased husband.

"I also want to thank you all for your tremendous sacrifice," she said. "I know all of you have suffered terribly, whether because of your own injuries, or from the loss of friends and colleagues, or just because you witnessed such a horrifying event. I want you all to know that I know that pain far too well, and if you ever need to talk about how you're feeling, I'm always available. Talking might be good for both of us."

The loss of so many staffers was obvious in this wide-open office. Whereas these meetings would have previously had the room full of team members and every seat occupied, there was an obvious void now caused by those who'd been killed and the injured who were still recovering from the attack. Peter was pleased to see that Drew, having survived the wood shard to the throat, had returned to work today, though he still had a large bandage over his wound and his voice would likely never rise above a harsh whisper.

Peter reflected on his own recovery following the attack, and he wondered how far he would have gotten if it were not for Angie. Every time he had a nightmare – which he had not for several days in a row! – she would hold and soothe him, helping him to get grounded back in reality.

Angie told him she'd read up on traumatic experiences and shared with him what she found out. She encouraged Peter to talk about what had happened and how he felt, and Peter found the more he confronted those events by discussing them the less horrific they became in his mind.

Though his term of endearment for her was still Babe, he'd started to think about Angie as being his Angel, a rescuing angel that saved him from drowning in his own trauma. Asking her to marry him was doubtless the best decision he'd ever made.

Catherine paused, seeming to search for the right words before going on. "However," she said, "I need you all to realize something very important about this appointment from Governor Glendening."

Peter glanced at Rick, who, with the space available at the conference table, was now sitting on the other side of it, and nodded to him knowingly. They'd spoken after the funeral about how they expected Catherine to manage her new responsibilities.

Rick, who at the time was still walking carefully as the hundreds of stitches in his wounds across his claw-ravaged back healed, thought she was going to be a figurehead, serving the remaining time in her husband's term but not pushing anything new, or anything at all. Peter, however, felt that since she was a vigorous woman, she'd take up Sim's causes and push them as far as she could, possibly even running for election afterward. Seeing her now, however, he suspected his friend had called it right.

"He offered this to me because it's an old tradition," Catherine said, fresh tears beginning to well up in her eyes, "and I accepted it to honor Sim's memory, to honor his sacrifice. To honor him. But I have no interest in politics, and I don't actually want to be a congresswoman. So, I need you all to know that I'm going to serve out his term, but I'm just going to vote on committees and on the floor, but nothing else."

Jimmy looked at her confused. "What? Catherine, that's not what we talked about before."

"I know, Jimmy, I know. But... I wasn't really thinking clearly then. It was right after the funeral, and I thought that's what Sim would want me to do. But I can't Jimmy. I can't. I'm sorry... I'm sorry to all of you."

"No, I... I get it," Jimmy said unconvincingly. "We all get it."

"I'm going to show up as much as I need to until his term ends next year," Catherine announced. "I'll vote as needed. I'll do my duty. But that's it. No legislative initiative. No bills written in my name. Nothing. I will just be serving time. And I won't be running for election. After the elections next year, I just want to go home and be left alone."

Peter looked around while she spoke. Rick appeared passive, having anticipated this response, but everyone else in the room had a shocked and dismayed look on their faces. They had honestly believed they'd be able to pick things up where they'd left them before the retreat, that life would go on as normal. Peter now realized they'd all gone through a gate on the night of the attack that had closed and locked behind them. There was no going back now, no return to normalcy. Everything was forever changed.

All the energy, all the enthusiasm and the belief they were working towards some noble goal had been ripped from their hearts. Jimmy sat with his head in his hands, and some staff members were wiping away tears. They'd all worked so hard for Thompson and what he believed in that, to have it end now, like this, was almost as hard to accept as his death itself. The remaining staff listened to her deflated, looking defeated.

"And as for the Senate race," Catherine said shrugging, "well, I suppose Louis Garrou is guaranteed a win. I don't really know, nor do I really care. Either way, it won't be me running for that seat."

That was perhaps the worst side effect of Thompson's cruel death. The team had made tremendous strides to mount a serious challenge to Garrou, something that earlier in the year no one thought possible. Although Garrou's campaign had halted at the same time of the attack due to his own injuries from the car accident he'd been in – which Peter had heard were serious, though he'd also heard Garrou had returned to the House today – that was hardly relevant now, and frustrating because the team had gotten so close. They'd exploited chink after chink in his armor to come within striking distance of Garrou in the polls. The team believed they'd soon be changing sides of the Capitol as Thompson would get elevated to the Senate. Knowing that Garrou benefitted from Thompson's death wasn't just tragic, it was heartbreaking for Peter and his colleagues.

Peter had volunteered for a congressional campaign while a freshman in college for a woman very much like Thompson as his interest in politics grew. Her victory seemed like a foregone conclusion, with every poll suggesting she would win. Come election night, however, her opponent had somehow eked out a slim victory. The gut-wrenching feeling he had that night of a victory stolen away at the last moment was exactly how he, and everyone else on staff, felt after the staff meeting.

But more to the point, it was a painful reality for Peter and everyone on the Thompson team because they loathed Garrou. Politics can get gritty and sometimes dirty, but there was typically a professional distance maintained between what was said about an opponent and the person themselves. This allowed politicians to run successful campaigns, to disagree on most every issue, and yet still maintain the level of collegiality needed to meet in the middle, compromise, and get things done for the people. Things can get heated, but they rarely became personal.

In this case, it *was* personal. Garrou represented everything that Thompson, as a populist, hated and worked against. He was rich, privileged, and used his many connections to other stratospheric elites to gather even more power and wealth to himself. Those benefits always seemed to come on the backs of regular, everyday working people, whom he clearly held in contempt.

Peter knew that for Garrou, the value of a person was the degree to which they could be used for his own enrichment, and the average American offered ample opportunities for him. He was the kind of person who loved complex rules because he got to make the rules, and they always benefitted him and his cohorts. Thompson thought Garrou's legislative past proved the point, and his staff reflected that view. Peter thought Garrou was smug, so obnoxiously smug, and everyone on staff agreed with that assessment.

Having this arrogant elitist waltz into the Senate based upon Thompson's violent death was maddening for Peter and the rest of the staff. It was an insult to their sense of decency and everything they believed in. Peter felt like if they had put together the best campaign they could and Thompson still lost, then at least everyone on staff would be able to feel pride in giving it their best and would accept the choice of the voters. This was a sentiment he shared with his colleagues since everyone involved in politics knew sometimes you won, sometimes you lost.

But this? This was something entirely different.

"Now, if you would all please excuse me," Catherine said, at last sitting at her desk, looking wan and exhausted, "I'd like some time alone before I have to meet with the Speaker. He and Sim grew close while serving in Congress together since they both grew up on farms..."

Surprised by the abrupt dismissal, the staff members glanced around at each other without moving for a few moments, unsure what do to under these strange circumstances. Jimmy took control as usual, and said, "Alright, everyone, you heard Catherine. Everyone go and... I don't know... get some work done."

2

Peter gathered up the papers and legal pad and pens he'd had ready to go for the normal staff meeting he'd anticipated and put them back in his Stebco briefcase. He then caught up with Rick, who was waiting at the door for him.

"Well," Rick said, as they strolled past the offices of other congresspeople. "That was all kinds of weird."

"It sure was," said Peter. "But you nailed it. She did exactly what you thought she would."

"Yeah, I did, but I wish I'd been wrong on this one. I so wanted her to pick up where Sim had left off, and I'd really wanted to go after Garrou."

"Mmm," Peter agreed. "So, what are you going to do with your afternoon?"

"Well," he said, "we're still getting all kinds of media requests. We have this one guy over at *The Washington Post* who keeps nagging us. It's kind of insulting that Sim is more popular now that he's dead than he ever was when alive, but I guess that's the media there for you. I'd better get with Lana to see how she wants us to handle the press. I don't know, though. After that train wreck back there, I might just find a quiet spot outside and read a good book."

"Seems reasonable."

"What about you?" asked Rick.

Peter glanced around, not quite certain what he was going to do. There was a rhythm to work, a comforting predictability to knowing what was expected, what to do, when things were going to happen, and so on. That staff meeting, or whatever it was, proved to Peter there would be no stability in the new Thompson office for quite some time.

"I'm not really certain," Peter said with a sigh. "I need to go back to the office to drop my briefcase off, then I think maybe I'll stretch my legs, go for a walk. I need to clear my head a bit, I think."

"All right," Rick said. "Take it easy. I'll see you tomorrow."

Peter continued along the halls, passing offices of other congresspeople and their staffers. As he did, Peter could sometimes catch snatches of meetings going on, conversations about the initiatives they were working on, of orders given and plans being made. He passed staffers trotting out on an important errand, and he knew from personal experience while they might be tired, they also felt exhilarated because they were doing something important, something vital. Regardless of which side of the aisle they worked from, they believed they were doing work that mattered.

He no longer did. As deflated as the rest of his co-workers might have been at this turn of events, Peter was even more so. He felt crushed and demoralized. He was an idealist and had felt all the hard work he did was worth it because it counted, it made a difference in the big picture. Peter had believed he and the others were engaged in the good fight, pushing back against a rolling tide that could crush everyday people. Idealistic or not, he'd felt a little like a knight of old slaying dragons.

Peter feared serving as a staffer to Catherine Thompson until the 2000 elections was going to be very difficult, and that the end of her term would take a painfully long time to get here. It now was obvious to him the dragons were going to win, at least in that office.

What would he do, Peter wondered, if he now couldn't slay dragons?

* * *

3

Peter had been plodding along, eyes downcast, one hand deep in his pocket, not really paying attention to his surroundings.

He'd made his way to the Capitol Rotunda, busy as it always was with people coming and going, the neo-classical brilliance of that space lost on him. He didn't have a particular goal in mind as he made his way to the Rotunda, rather being led there by the aimless wandering amongst his dejected thoughts.

With so many busy people coming and going, Peter lifted his eyes to avoid running into anyone. As he did, he caught sight of Garrou on the Senate side of the Rotunda, talking with his chief of staff, as she jotted down notes on what he was saying. He was walking towards where Peter now stood, who had stopped dead in his tracks.

He was shocked by the sight of the congressman. Garrou looked *almost* altogether normal. His hair was perfectly coifed, as always, his double-breasted suit the best available, and his confident strides gave the suggestion Garrou owned whatever space it was in which he walked, as usual.

But his face. His face, Peter could see even from his view across the Rotunda, was noticeably damaged, twisted in such a way that he couldn't help but suck his breath in one quick gasp and stare wide-eyed at Garrou.

The congressman had an angry red scar going across his well-tanned face. The scar was deeply furrowed into his once Hollywood-beautiful face, creating a ripple in his skin that made the damage look even worse. The scar started from above his left brow, stretched across his now white, deadened right eye, and then continued down his cheek at an angle to his jaw. His jawline was lumpy on the right side and asymmetrical like there was some harm done to the bone and his teeth. Garrou's mouth was turned downward at an angle on the right side, pulled down by the injury done to his face.

As Peter stood staring at Garrou, he noticed the congressman spoke nonchalantly to his chief of staff as she scampered to keep up with his long strides. His left hand was in his suit pants pocket, but he gestured with his right hand as he spoke – or more appropriately, what remained of his right hand. Peter at first thought his hand was deformed until he realized Garrou only had half a hand left. He still had his ring and pinky finger, the remainder of the hand missing down to his wrist.

He looked back to Garrou's face and realized with a sickening shock the congressman had seen him and was staring at him hatefully.

Peter sucked in his breath again, feeling like he'd been caught peeking at a secret that wasn't his to behold. He glanced away, averting his eyes as he started to walk, trying to look casual though he could feel the blood drain from his face so horrifying was it to have that dead eye boring into him.

Peter, for no logical reason, felt exposed and vulnerable in that wide-open space, like an animal alone on the savannah. The baleful glare coming from Garrou was so intense that Peter could almost feel the look drilling a hole through him. He hesitated as Garrou strode closer, not knowing if he should turn to the left or the right, and if it would appear too obvious that Peter was trying to avoid him if he did. If he didn't, he'd have to pass Garrou and that awful, dead eye staring at him.

Not knowing what else to do, Peter continued to walk forward as he tried to appear casual, yet still glanced at Garrou. He would see Garrou staring with all possible malice, then glance away again, unable to bear that white eye staring at him. He felt awkward as he did so but couldn't help looking back at Garrou and then quickly away again. Time seemed to slow down, the entire universe contracted to the diminishing space between him and Garrou, between Peter and that loathsome, evil-looking eye. Peter could feel his heart pounding in his chest and hear his own uneven breathing as a wild, unreasonable fear took him.

Peter looked up, saw the hatred in Garrou's eye, then glanced away. Taking a few more timid steps, he'd again cut his eyes upward quickly, feeling a tingle of fear race down his spine, and then again turn his eyes away, unable to bear the loathing in Garrou's intense stare. After what felt like an eon to Peter, the two passed mid-Rotunda, Garrou slowly pivoting his head to continue glaring at him for as long as he could. Garrou then passed behind Peter, returning to the conversation he was having with his chief of staff as if that had never happened.

Feeling overwhelmed with a rolling wave of nausea, Peter turned to get outside as quickly as he could. He burst through the doors to the great plaza there, feeling shaky, sitting on the stone steps, and filling his lungs with the still, humid air. He sat there for some minutes with his eyes closed, taking deep breaths, until he fought back the urge to vomit. Peter looked around, dazed and confused, feeling like he'd just awakened from one of his nightmares.

What the fuck? he thought. *What the fuck was that? Why was he looking at me, like he wanted to kill me? What the fuck?!*

The image of Garrou's hateful look, especially that chilling, milky dead eye glaring at him, struck Peter like a slap, and he shivered at the malevolence captured in that stare. As he did, though, he thought of the wounds Garrou had and realized they seemed strangely familiar. A deep, diagonal scar slicing down across his face that had ruined his right eye to the point of blindness. Half a right hand, with only two fingers remaining, the rest seeming to have been cut off. The exact same damage, he now recognized, as the creature that had attacked the staff retreat.

What the fuck?!! he again asked himself, stunned and confused by everything that had just happened.

CHAPTER FOURTEEN

1

O*h, no!* Angie thought as she returned home and saw Peter once again sitting in their living room, eyes wide, smoking nervously. *What happened?!*

"Honey?" she asked, fearing he might have been triggered by something and had a relapse. Peter had been doing so well the past week or so, with his good mood back to normal and no nightmares for several nights. He'd been preparing himself to go back to work and to see the surviving staff members. Angie had feared there might be something about seeing his colleagues again that could bring back all his horrific memories. When she walked in and saw those wide-open, unseeing eyes, Angie thought her worst fears had come true, especially because Peter had called her midafternoon to say he was heading home early.

She let out a long sigh of relief and felt the tension melt away when he lifted his head, looked at her, and flashed her that broad smile she loved so much.

"Hey, babe," he said tiredly. "How are you? How was your day?"

"Busy," Angie said, "busy-busy-busy. Things apparently didn't go so well back home over the recess, so we have a lot of holes to fix... and some spinning to do. Lots of balls in the air we need to juggle right now. How about you? How was your day?"

"How was my day?" Peter said, reflecting her question as he took a last drag on his cigarette before butting in out. "It was... weird. Really, really weird."

"Oh, how so? What happened that you came home early?"

Peter stood and wrapped his long arms around Angie, bending down low to kiss his much shorter fiancée.

"I don't want to think about it right now," he said. "I've been thinking about things all day since I got back, and I'm tapped for now. C'mon, let's make some dinner. You hungry?"

"Starving!"

<hr />

2

A love of cooking was one of the many things they shared, and so dinner prep was a way for them to connect after a long day as well as an evening duty. The pair liked to put on music, pour some wine, and then spend the time it took to make dinner in Angie's small kitchen touching every time they passed; sometimes just gentle, accidental sweeps and other times very deliberate grabs that had occasionally led to the table there being used in some inventive ways. Regardless, it was a fun period after their workday that both enjoyed very much.

Come the weekend they wanted to experiment with a French-themed menu, with chicken fricassee served with potatoes lyonnaise and salad Niçoise, then crepes for dessert planned. Since that'd be too complicated and labor intensive for after work, tonight they were making gamberi alla busara, prawns cooked in a fresh tomato sauce. As Peter started to fry the minced garlic and diced onions, Angie prepared the prawns, enjoying the nightly dance around each other as they made the different elements and talked about their day.

Angie explained how Jenkins, the congressman on whose staff she served, had made a few votes the last term that were unpopular in their mostly rural district, ones that were seen as favoring urban areas more than the countryside. He'd had several town-meeting style get-togethers all around his area for the recess, and the voters didn't hold back on their opinion about reneging on his campaign promises.

"So," Angie said as she and Peter danced to an upbeat tune playing on the radio now that the white wine had been added to the frying prawns, "we have a whole lot of bridges we need to mend. Jenkins is going to have to do all kinds of acrobatics to get himself in their good graces again. People were apparently *pissed* at him and gave him both barrels at these meetings."

"Well, that's what happens when politicians go back on their words. In some countries people like that literally get both barrels. Here, all they need to deal with are angry – oops, bring it in," Peter said, as a slow-moving love song replaced the lively one. He pulled Angie close to him and they now danced slow circles in the kitchen, then kissed her gently.

Angie wondered if that electric tingle she experienced every time Peter kissed or touched her would ever dissipate, ever diminish over the years. Would his presence just fade into the background over a long lifetime shared together, she wondered. It seemed impossible that the touch of her tall, lanky fiancé could ever be anything other than exciting. Angie had never expected to fall in love when she came to Washington to work for Jenkins, but even in this short time together Angie couldn't imagine her life without Peter in it.

I don't even want to think about that!

It had pained her to watch Peter suffering as he had in the days after the attack. Angie had feared for his stability, indeed his very sanity, as he would repeatedly wake from those nightmares screaming and staring with wild-eyed panic, his chest heaving, his sweat-slicked body shaking. Watching Peter struggle all those nights had been almost as traumatic for her as it had been for him, but those days seemed to be behind them now and Angie could focus on them beginning their lives together.

She was eager to see what the future held for them. They'd talked about staying in Washington for several more years to get additional experience and make connections with influential people, then moving to Alabama so Angie could begin a career in politics herself. Peter would be her obvious campaign manager, then chief of staff, helping her to stay focused on the needs of average people – what they both believed being a congressperson is supposed to be about. This was a change of their individual plans, but both agreed their shared one was far better.

For right this moment, however, Angie wasn't worried about the future and wasn't thinking about the past. At this moment she felt like she had everything she needed as she slowly danced with Peter in her kitchen, thick with the odors of cooking.

Looking up at Peter's hazel eyes, she said, "So... what about your day? What happened that made it so weird you had to come home early?"

Peter groaned. "Well, a few things, really. Let me tell you about this so-called staff meeting we had today..."

He then went into detail about the staff meeting with Catherine Thompson, and how devastating it was. Peter shared with her his experience of volunteering for a candidate in whom he believed, one whom he thought would win, only to have election night turn into a soul-crushing defeat. He explained how everyone looked devastated after the meeting and must have been feeling that same terrible sense of loss after Catherine made it clear she'd be keeping the seat warm for whoever won in 2000 and nothing else.

"Wow," said Angie, mixing the prawns back in with the tomato sauce and covering it with the lid. "That must've been weird."

"Yeah, it was. Weird, and totally heartbreaking."

"I bet. And basically, conceding to Garrou has to make things even worse."

As he gathered things for the dinner table, Angie noticed Peter paused when she said that, looking away for a moment as he sighed. She knitted her brow in some confusion at Peter's response, thinking perhaps the stress of going back to work and the strange day he'd had there made him more emotional than usual.

That's odd, she thought.

"Yeah, well..." said Peter as he got the wine, crusty bread, and balsamic vinegar on the table, "that's another weird thing that happened today. Did you happen to see Garrou at all?"

"I caught a glimpse of him, from a distance. He looked... horrible."

"More like horrifying, actually. Did you see his eye?"

Angie shook her head. "No, not really. I was too far away."

"I did. Up close and personal. His eye is dead and, like, milky white. It's really terrible to look at."

As Peter spoke, Angie served their meal, then sat at the table where they gently tapped wine glasses.

"Buon apettito," she said.

"Amen," Peter answered.

"Why isn't he wearing an eye patch, do you think?"

Peter paused his chewing a moment and thought about her question, then said, "I think because... it's intimidating. It's scary and he knows it, and he gets off on scaring people. He's a beast, it's his nature. That's what beasts do. It's a power trip kind of thing... you know?"

"Maybe," Angie said, not certain what Peter meant.

Peter chewed slowly, with that far-away look in his eye again, until he at last said, "I saw his injuries. Up close. We happened to... to pass in the Rotunda. He looked at me, babe, with... with this look of absolute hatred, that one dead eye boring into me. You know what that eye was like?"

"No, what?"

"It was like the Old Man's 'vulture eye' in *The Tell-Tale Heart*. That's what looking into his eye, with all that... *loathing*... was like."

"Oh, shit," Angie said. "That is creepy."

"Yeah," said Peter, distant again, as he tore off a chunk of bread. "I saw his injuries. He has this terrible scar going down his face, from above the left lid to his jaw, right across the eye."

"Yeah, I guess the car crash was pretty bad," Angie noted.

"Car crash, yeah..." Peter said. "That's what they say it was, anyway."

Angie stopped, fork-speared prawn halfway to her mouth. "What do you mean, 'that's what they say'? You don't think he was in an accident?"

Peter took a large gulp of white wine, then gave Angie an intense look before he spoke again. "Alright, listen," he said, "this is going to sound bizarre, but listen. Hear me out. Okay?"

"Umm... okay."

Peter took a deep breath. "Okay, he has a giant scar going down his face, and his eye is dead, right?"

"Right."

"This accident he was supposedly in happened on the same night as the attack at the cabin, correct?" Peter asked.

"Correct," Angie agreed.

"His hand is missing the thumb, pointer, and middle finger, and it looked like they'd been... cut off."

It then occurred to Angie where Peter was heading with this, her eyes growing wide as the shock of realization hit her. "Cut off... like with an ax?"

Peter shook his head emphatically. "*Exactly* like with an ax! He has the exact same injuries the creature that attacked us had, and he looked at me when we passed like he wanted to kill me. It was so intense I felt sick after. There was no reason for that, babe. Unless... he had a reason to want to kill me."

Angie also took a large gulp of her wine, then shook her head. "Okay... What are you actually saying here?"

Peter stared at her, a pained look of desperation washing across his face as he struggled to verbalize the words that had been in his mind since the incident at the Rotunda. "I think... I think... he's a... werewolf."

Angie met Peter's wordless stare for many seconds, her mind reeling with what her future husband just said, shook her head, and then poured herself another large glass of wine. She drank almost all of it in three large draughts.

"Honey," she said softly, trying hard to not sound like she thought Peter had lost his mind but failing, "that makes no sense. None at all."

"None at all?" Peter retorted. "You were the one who not long ago agreed with me that the so-called bear attack wasn't a bear, and the half-hand that magically appeared there was weird. That's what makes no sense at all."

Angie slumped back in her seat, then said, "Yeah, but that's different."

Peter stretched out his arms in a questioning way. "How? How is that any different?"

"Because there obviously shouldn't be a hand there," she said. "That's just common sense. It's a given. But what you're talking about is making a solution out of nothing. Accusing Garrou of being a werewolf makes no sense. This is... werewolves aren't real. They can't be real!"

Angie thought of the reason she hated horror movies, a film called *An American Werewolf in London*. She was seven years old in 1981 when it came out, and far too young to see it in the movie theaters even if she'd wanted to. But the following year, Nate had gotten a video tape of it from a friend of his who'd recorded it off HBO. After their parents had gone to their room for the evening one Friday night in late October, he'd told her she also had to go to bed because he wanted to watch it.

Even as an eight-year-old Angie was feisty and headstrong, so she refused, saying she wanted to watch it with him. Nate warned her this was a *horror movie* – he'd emphasized the "horror movie" part, as if she was stupid and had never heard of such a thing before – and that it was too scary for a little kid like her. Since Nate was only two years older than Angie, being called a "little kid" by him made her bristle and she became even more obstinate, so she refused to budge. Nate warned her she'd regret it, but Angie laughed him off.

She regretted it. Watching that movie was horrifying for her, between the gore and the slowly decomposing best friend and the family-killing wolf Nazis. The absolute most terrifying part for Angie, though, was watching the transformation into a werewolf. Watching the main character's agony as his limbs extended over several long minutes was chilling, and she'd had nightmares for several days afterward.

Angie found what Peter was suggesting intolerable because it reached a fear that had rested undisturbed, nestled deep inside her psyche for years. The fear of a shadowy unknown, the dread of some horrendous monster lurking in the dark well of her mind, of something that appears human but is in fact a nightmare monstrosity and watching as it takes its true form. Her dread of this inchoate darkness went far beyond a movie and had grown into a deep-seated loathing of some horrible unfamiliar. This was a dark dread that had lingered in her mind for years, one that had been challenged by all the bizarre things going on in her life.

"Why can't they be real?" he asked. "We just talked about how there's a whole world of things we don't know anything about. You said you could believe that there are things in the world that make no sense, that there are things going on we'll never know about. Nate saw something out there, I saw something. You had that weird experience with the woman."

"Peter, that could have been coincidence," Angie said, seizing upon cold logic as a way to push back the vague sense of dread growing in her mind. "How many redheads are there in Washington? Thousands? Hundreds of thousands? So, there was some weird random woman staring at me, and then later I saw another one who just happened to look like her. Coincidence."

Even as Angie spoke, she recognized the hollowness of her words and how unlikely her own scenario sounded.

"Coincidence?" Peter asked. "Do you seriously believe it's just a coincidence that Garrou has the exact wounds that I gave the creature, and that his accident happened the same night we were attacked, and that he looked like he hated me, *and* that Thompson's death benefits him? Is all that a coincidence?"

Angie had no answer for Peter, so instead she just retreated to her previous objection. "But this makes no sense!"

"No, no it doesn't, babe," Peter said softly, looking at Angie as he shook his head. "It makes no sense at all. But that doesn't mean it's wrong."

The pair sat in silence chewing their food as they thought, the sipping of their wine the only sound interrupting the silence. Although she could admit the circumstances were odd, even bizarre, Angie just couldn't bring herself to believe that the creatures lurking in her childhood nightmares might be real. She refused to accept the darkness that prowled in the deepest corners of her mind might exist in the real world. Accepting that as reality was something she couldn't do.

Clear thinking prevailed as it always did for Angie. She'd learned much about trauma while reading up on it after the attack, and she knew it was common for people who have been through something as horrible as Peter had to make connections that weren't realistic. While not delusional, she knew traumatic events could encourage outrageous, sometimes even paranoid, links in survivors' minds between given people and the events that'd had happened, especially if there was an emotional component involved.

It was obvious to Angie this had been an emotional day for Peter, just from the fact of returning to work and seeing his surviving colleagues, but then also the bombshell of Catherine's decision dumped on him. Added to that was the crushing realization that Garrou, whom the entire team despised, was going to benefit from Thompson's death, which had made his mind focus on the unfairness of it all. Then, seeing his twisted face – a face that Peter interpreted as being hateful because of his emotions about Garrou – made Peter create a nonexistent explanation to tie everything together.

Angie decided what she had to do was allow Peter to convince himself this was wrong. She could offer counter points forever, but unless he truly cleaved to the fact that

Garrou wasn't a werewolf and that they don't exist, then he'd always have a bit of lingering doubt in his mind about it. She had a plan.

"So," she said. "What do you want to do about this? Not like you can call the police on him."

"No," he said, shaking his head. "No, I certainly can't. No one would believe me. Hell, you don't even believe me, and you love me."

Angie reached out and put her hand on his, then said, "No, but luckily I don't need to believe you to support you. But I have an idea about what we can do."

Peter raised his eyebrows. "Oh? Okay, what is it?"

"Well," she said, "right now, what we need is information, data. Guidance. Not like we can visit the resident werewolf expert at the university, you know? But it just so happens we work literally across the street from the world's largest library. If there's something about Garrou or his family that would suggest he's a werewolf, then surely, we'd find it in the Library of Congress, right?"

Peter rubbed his smooth chin as he thought, then said, "Yeah, you're right."

"Okay, then. You're going to have a lot of time on your hands, and I can find some research to do for Jenkins to come over as often as I can to help. Let's give this some time, dig in deep, find out everything we can about him, his family, their history, whatever. Maybe there'll be something there that proves what you're saying, and we can take it from there. Sound like a plan?"

"Sounds like a good plan," Peter said. "Better than anything I was coming up with. I was thinking... well, never mind what I was thinking. It was stupid. I like your idea more."

Angie held out her wine glass, which Peter tapped as sign of their agreement. They continued with their meal, having far more normal conversation as they discussed the everyday interests they shared in politics, news, and upcoming books they wanted to read. Later, as they settled into bed for the night, Angie felt proud for having handled this bizarre situation elegantly.

CHAPTER FIFTEEN

1

At the very moment Peter and Angie discussed things over dinner, Garrou knelt, naked, spattered in the blood of a dead drug-addicted prostitute. The body now lay across the altar in the hidden sub-basement sacrarium he'd had built under his Crisfield home. Her skin had already turned an ashen gray as long, bright red rivulets of her still-warm blood oozed down from her neck.

As he knelt, Garrou stared into a brazen basin filled with water, to which had been added an aromatic oil and the blood of the prostitute. Through an act of magic, Garrou was able to scry using the liquid, learning things of which he'd otherwise remain ignorant.

Although he attended the covenstead at Raven Hill Manor for major Satanic ceremonies, he used this private altar for his personal sacrifices and small acts of black magic. Garrou's rage had been almost impossible to contain as he passed *him* in the Rotunda, that worthless staffer of Thompson's who had injured him during the attack, the one who'd caused him so much pain and trouble. Garrou had ached to transform right there, to let go of all his constraints and inhibitions and whisper the words to become the Wolf, to finish what he'd started at Thompson's cabin.

He knew he couldn't give in to such luscious temptations, regardless of how much he longed to do it. Nonetheless, Garrou had almost been able to taste the staffer's hot, salty blood squirting deliciously into his mouth as he tore open this man's neck.

Instead of giving in to his murderous lust, Garrou knew what needed to be done. He made a few inquiries regarding the staffer and discovered his name was Peter Brunnen. That was all he needed to find out through official lines; everything else could be discovered through more clandestine methods.

Garrou had then canceled the rest of his day after returning to the office, claiming he felt overwhelmed with lingering pain, and left for his Crisfield home. There was a collection of people the coven associated with who provided snatched gifts for sacrifices – some were members of the coven and dedicated Satanists, some freelancers, some who just enjoyed kidnapping and torturing people – so Garrou had ordered one delivered to his home later that evening.

The prostitute had been picked up with the promise of a lucrative overnight job with plenty of drugs, so she'd happily allowed herself to be driven from Baltimore to Crisfield. It was with delight that, after having her strip, put on a blindfold, and bend over the altar, Garrou then slit her throat with one swift slice, collecting her spurting blood in the waiting basin.

After laying her body on the altar, Garrou had reached into her opened neck, then smeared her blood over his face and used it to write the appropriate sigils on his body. He then chanted the words to turn this mixture into a magical elixir. As the blood, water, and oil mixture swirled, it turned pitch black, glowed, and then finally unfolded, revealing an image in the center of the basin. As it did, Garrou joined a faraway conversation.

A short, curvy woman with whom Peter was having dinner was already speaking: "... what we need is information, data. Guidance. Not like we can visit the resident werewolf expert at the university, you know..."

So, he thought. *You've pieced it together. Clever little impudent bastard, aren't you? Not that it'll matter. You'll be dead soon regardless.*

"But it just so happens," the young woman continued, "we work literally across the street from the world's largest library. If there's something about Garrou or his family that would suggest he's a werewolf, then surely, we'd find it in the Library of Congress, right?"

Clever idea, whoever you are. I presume you're his girlfriend, right? You're very clever, aren't you? It's a useless move, but clever, nonetheless.

"Yeah, you're right," said Peter, and Garrou sneered at the mere sound of his voice. Though he was not aware of it, he let out a low, hate-filled growl.

His mind flashed to an image so suddenly that he flinched as if slapped, a powerful one that in the half-second it lasted he could hear, smell, and feel everything as if he were there, almost as if he'd been transported to the place he saw. Garrou saw himself as the Wolf in another verdant wood, one that looked like an ancient, overgrown forest with enormous, moss-covered sequoias. It was a wilderness that looked like it hadn't seen humans for hundreds of years if it had seen them at all.

Garrou knew he was chasing Peter through these woods and had already injured him. He was toying with Peter the way a cat would with a mouse, slashing him, bleeding him, making him suffer the way he'd suffered. Garrou was chasing him but holding back, making him have a small glimmer of hope he might escape this ravening nightmare creature that was bearing down upon him.

But after chasing Peter a bit longer and slashing his back and his legs a few more times, Garrou made it clear there was no escaping him, there never had been, and all hope must be abandoned wherever the Wolf chose to prowl.

The Wolf leapt onto the limping, panting Peter, sinking his teeth deep into his right shoulder and knocking him to the ground. Peter shrieked in pain as the Wolf's long fangs sunk through flesh, muscle, and bone, then tore his arm and shoulder from his body with one brutal yank. His blood streamed down the Wolf's throat and tasting the hot liquid pour into him only ignited his lust for destruction even more. While Peter still barely clung to life, the Wolf set upon mutilating his body, ripping his chest open, tearing off limbs, smashing his head into a bloody pulp.

All this Garrou saw in a fraction of a second. He licked his lips expecting to taste fresh blood and shook his head as he nervously glanced around to remind himself where he was. As he did, Garrou could hear the woman in his scrying basin speaking: "Okay, then," she said. "You're going to have a lot of time on your hands, and I can find some research to do for Jenkins to come over as often as I can to help…"

Okay, he thought, *she's a staffer for Jenkins, that good ol' boy hick. I need to find out who she is, learn more about her, too. Knowing that will be useful.*

An idea was forming in Garrou's mind, one that would allow him to taunt and torture Peter as he exacted his revenge. Perhaps not in the primal, brutal way the Wolf lusted to, but one that would rend Peter's heart in two emotionally before he did so literally.

"Let's give this some time," said the woman, "dig in deep, find out everything we can about him, his family, their history, whatever. Maybe there'll be something there that proves what you're saying, and we can take it from there. Sound like a plan?"

My family? My history? That's an interesting angle. Garrou thought for a moment about his plan, his eyes narrowing and his mouth curving up into a cruel smile as he did. *Oh... I can definitely use that to tease the bastard even more. If he wants to learn about my family then I'll just help him a little.*

"Sounds like a good plan," Peter said. "Better than anything I was coming up with. I was thinking... well, never mind what I was thinking. It was stupid. I like your idea more."

What were you thinking, Peter? Will you share your mind with me? No? Guess I'll just have to pull apart your skull and take a look to find out for myself.

Garrou watched and listened for several additional minutes but learned nothing of importance, so he recited the spell couplet to deactivate the liquid, leaving it a black, viscous substance that steamed like hot tar and smelled like putrefaction. He remained on his knees, thinking about what he should do next and what the progression of steps should be.

His thoughts lingered on how best to exact revenge yet at the same time remain safe. Although he was daily growing more invulnerable, and the true gift had saved his life by dulling the ax blow to his head, he could still be hurt – the scar across his face was a testament to that as was his mangled hand. Garrou assumed his arms and legs were still at risk and he needed to be careful. He'd attacked impulsively when killing Thompson, in part due to his own rage and partly to prove he could eliminate an enemy to his mother, but regardless of the reasons he'd acted without a well thought out plan and now suffered the consequences. He had no wish to make a similar mistake again.

It was obvious Peter and his girlfriend warranted close watching, so he'd have to scry on a regular basis to keep an eye on them. That meant frequent trips back from Washington to his house to make the proper sacrifices. Garrou looked at the corpse splayed out across his altar even as a fly landed on her slit throat, rubbed its forelegs together as if anticipating a feast, then crawled into her gaping neck wound.

I'm going to need a lot more of them.

He'd thought long enough, and now it was time to clean up. The woman's sticky blood had long since dried to his skin and the coppery odor was thick in his nostrils, so Garrou was eager to wash her sacrifice off. He'd leave the body to his demonic familiar to dispose of. Whereas Garrou's mother had the constant murder of crows circling her house, he had what to the world appeared as a simple black cat named Felix.

"Felix?" he called once he'd gone upstairs after locking up his sacrarium. "Felix? Where are you?" Although the demonic spirit merely took the shape of a cat, it still enjoyed prowling about outside to hunt mice and small birds, so Garrou would often have to wait on it to return to carry out assignments.

When I'm president I'd better get a whole team of high-ranking demons working under me, he thought as he got in the hot shower. *Having some nothing soldier as my familiar is just insulting.*

Garrou dried off, then put on comfortable clothes for the nearly three-hour drive back to Washington. He checked his Rolex and saw it was almost seven o'clock. If he didn't run into traffic or an accident, he'd be back to his brownstone with a little time to review notes and consider his meeting schedule before bed. He had looked forward to returning to his normal routine and wanted to get back to his house in Washington as quickly as he could; Garrou's mind had already turned to the legislative issues he was working on and what he wanted to accomplish at the meetings over the next two days.

As he put a few things he wanted to take with him into a small duffle bag and walked out to his living room, Garrou was shocked to see a man standing there.

2

A momentary flash of terror was replaced just as fast with surprise when he recognized the black suit, dark gray turtle-neck sweater, and olive-toned skin of Mr. Poneros, the regional coven's demonic overseer. The odor of sweet burnt spices hung in the air.

"Mr. Poneros!" Garrou exclaimed. "I didn't expect to see you here."

"Good evening, Mr. Garrou," the demon said formally in an affected Greek accent, his cold, pale gray eyes locked onto Garrou's.

Such a private visit from a demonic overseer was uncommon – so uncommon that Garrou had never heard of such a thing – and he should have been warned of this visit by Felix. He looked around, expecting to see his familiar.

"Where's Felix?" he asked Mr. Poneros. "Why isn't he here?"

"I've sent him away for a bit," Poneros said, "so that we might speak privately. He does so enjoy playing the part of a cat, after all."

Garrou was confused and a little worried, his mind racing with the possibilities of what this visit could mean. Demonic over-seers acted as a direct link between Hell and the ruling structures of the major covens, known collectively as The Commission, that together comprised the Coven Universal to make sure everything was being done to satisfy their Satanic master's overarching plans. Since these plans took centuries to unfold, an immortal overseer who could direct the machinations was required to see them.

Such a demon would typically only ever commune with the highest-ranking levels in a major coven, and even then, with specific instructions. He felt anxious as there was no reason he could think of for such a visit.

Why would I get a visit from such a powerful demon? I don't even know his real name. What could we have to discuss privately? What the fuck is going on here?

"Don't worry, Mr. Garrou," Poneros said, holding up his hand. "All your questions will soon be answered."

Garrou felt a flash of anger at himself for becoming emotional and not shielding his thoughts in the presence of a demon. He'd been instructed from an early age that all his thoughts and feelings could be read, and possibly manipulated, by such an entity. While the coven might consort with demons and worship their master, leaving oneself so exposed was still a foolish idea. Garrou stood there, meeting Poneros' gray eyes, and cleared his mind of any thought. Poneros smiled at him as he did, the silence in his mind clear to the demon.

"I understand my sudden visit may be causing you some discomfort," Poneros said. "I can respect that. But I at least helped clean up your mess. Since Felix is indisposed at the moment outside chasing mice, I felt like it was the least I could do."

Garrou knitted his brow, an inquiring look on his face because of what Poneros said. The demon pointed outside, and there in the growing dark, he saw the reanimated corpse of the prostitute walking through the weeds in the marshy ground towards Dougherty Creek and the Chesapeake Bay just beyond. Garrou watched as she walked steadily into the water, walking deeper and deeper until she was submerged.

"She will keep walking until she's miles out," Poneros said. "What's left of her body will wash up in a few weeks far away from here. I do believe that's what Felix does with them if I'm not mistaken. Correct?"

Garrou nodded. "Yes, it is," he said, still trying to keep his mind blank.

"Ah, there. You see? Now I've done my good deed for the day," Poneros said, mockingly pressing his hands together and looking upward as if in prayer.

"Mr. Poneros," Garrou said after a moment, "why are you here?"

"Yes," said the demon, "we come to that at last. You have been summoned to a meeting of the Supreme Tribunal and I've been asked to fetch you as quickly as possible."

Poneros' words struck Garrou like a hammer blow to the head. He felt the blood drain from his face and his knees wobble. Although he was rich and powerful, the son of a high priestess, possessing the Gift of the Wolf, and many other attributes that normally made him feel above everyday concerns, being called before the Supreme Tribunal was reason to feel crushing fear.

Every individual coven had its own Tribunal for lesser infractions, and the regional coven had the Great Tribunal for more serious ones. Rarely was anyone ordered to go before the Supreme Tribunal. This was reserved for the most serious infractions against the High Council itself, and the punishments were always severe.

And painful.

"I've been... been called," Garrou said, stammering uncharacteristically, "... before the Supreme Tribunal? Why?! I haven't done anything wrong!"

Poneros put up his hands as if trying to calm Garrou.

"Relax," the demon said with a chuckle, seeming to be amused by Garrou's reaction. "This is an informal meeting, not an official conclave. You're not charged with anything and they're not standing in judgment of you. However, as the overseers of Coven discipline, they just want to have a few words with you to ensure they don't *need* to stand in judgment of you. Consider this an honor because of your family's long, dedicated service. Not many are given such a chance."

Garrou took a deep breath, then let it out in a long string. He felt relieved. While it was good to know he hadn't been charged with anything, being summoned before the Supreme Tribunal was still ominous, even if it was only for a few words.

"Are you ready, Mr. Garrou?" Poneros asked.

He nodded. "Yes, I am."

Poneros walked to the closet in Garrou's living room, which, like any other closet, was full of mundane items. Poneros tapped on the door three times at three different spots, used his finger to draw some unseen figure on it, then opened it. The closet door now led to a subterranean corridor illuminated by a long line of iron candelabras, each holding many burning candles. Garrou could smell the wet, earthy odor, and heard drips of falling water echoing along the rock passageway.

"This hall will lead you to the Supreme Tribunal," said Poneros, sweeping his hand invitingly towards the opening. "They await your arrival in the Great Hall, which will be to your right."

Garrou hesitated, uneasy about proceeding but unable to refuse. He took a quick breath, then steeled himself, straightening up to appear confident, and walked forward. He might be terrified, Garrou decided, but he would at the very least appear assertive and empowered as normal.

"Good luck," Poneros said as Garrou passed by, then stepped in and closed the door behind them. The sound echoed down the stone hallway like thunder. He turned, and as his eyes adjusted to the orange glow provided by the numerous candles, he saw Poneros waiting there. The door behind him was massive and ancient-looking, with oversized, swirling hinge decorations nailed to the thick oaken beams. To his eye, Garrou thought it looked like the kind of door one would find in a medieval castle.

He walked slowly down the hall, touching the cold black stone of the corridor as he did. Garrou could see that, rather than being a natural passageway in a cave, the walls had long ago been carved out of the rock by hand. As he passed a candelabra, the illumination revealed faded paintings on the wall done in the medieval style.

The first portrayed demons sharing their knowledge with people through a book of spells, and then those same people doing acts of magic, tormenting their enemies. Further down the corridor, he saw a mural of prancing demons torturing naked people in Hell, while a select few, guided by some other demons, looked on in clothed comfort. Garrou walked on, then saw a painting showing a blood red Satan with seven curved horns on his head arrayed like a crown sitting on a throne, stuffing humans into his fanged mouth, as kings, bishops, and even the pope knelt and bowed in worship. Standing behind the throne on either side were crimson-robed, hooded figures.

Garrou suddenly recalled seeing murals like these before and recognized where he was. He was on the Isle of Skye deep under the rocky pinnacles of The Storr. He'd been shown this place during one of the many trips to Europe his family took when he was younger. While his father was conducting business, Garrou's mother, always interested in impressing her children with the need to honor the Coven Universal and its past, made certain to visit places rich in Satanic history.

This was once a Black Academy, one of the string of clandestine schools hidden underground across Europe in remote places during the Middle Ages. These prestigious colleges, the headmaster of which was always a powerful demon, taught their arts to promising Satanists and helped to keep the Coven Universal together during the medieval period. This academy, once a thriving school teaching Black Magic and honoring Satan through ritual sacrifices, had closed when the demon possessing The Storr vanished during the Renaissance. It was now long since forgotten about, save for a few Coven members – and, apparently, was the meeting place of the Supreme Tribunal.

The mural of a triumphant Satan marked the end of the hall. As Garrou turned to his right, he saw the Supreme Tribunal sitting in a vast, high-ceilinged chamber that had also been cut out of the solid rock. The room was filled with hundreds of candles, while burning incense filled the space with a spicy odor and a lazily floating haze that stung Garrou's eyes. Through the wispy smoke, he could see seven figures seated in a semicircle, watching him as he approached.

Sitting on an ornately carved stone throne was a hooded, red-robed Master Mage, the black sash that indicated his rank tied at the waist. The white mask he wore gleamed in the candlelight, and Garrou saw there was, as always, a Luciferian sigil etched on the mask's forehead. The raised dais on which his throne sat was several steps higher than the elevated platform on which three Mages sat on either side of him, their faces covered in similar masks. Their hooded robes were also bright scarlet, a constant reminder of the blood a Mage must always be willing to spill to further the Coven's goals.

Garrou walked to the center of the room and stood before the Supreme Tribunal, where he could see carved on the ground a large circle wreathed by many sigils and symbols. It appeared the stone floor had been charred and cracked in the circle, Garrou knew due to brutal Satanic justice being meted out swiftly through Black Magic.

"Kneel," said the Master Mage in a deep, German-accented voice.

Garrou obediently took a knee, though he looked at the impassive masked face of the Master Mage, meeting his eyes unflinchingly. The fear he'd felt earlier was being replaced with his typical haughty spite, the arrogance that had propelled him, and his entire family, into such high levels of power. It's what made him a Garrou.

I might be forced to kneel, but I refuse to grovel.

"Louis Pierre Garrou, do you know why you have been called before the Supreme Tribunal?" asked the Master Mage.

"No, I don't"

"We called you here so we could speak to you and warn you against what happens when Coven members betray the High Council," said the Master Mage. "We do this only because of your family's service to the Coven Universal."

"Crimes?" Garrou asked. "I'm no traitor! What crimes? I've committed no crimes against the Coven."

"Not yet," said a British female Mage to Garrou's right. "Perhaps."

"Not yet?" he said. "What does that mean?"

"It means," said a male American Mage to his left, "that you were given an assignment by the High Council itself, an assignment of great importance, and that you are failing in that assignment. In our opinion, that *is* a crime against the Coven Universal."

Anger blossomed deep inside Garrou, a burning, primal

anger. The anger of a captured wolf being taunted by fools. An image flashed through his mind of becoming the Wolf, of tearing these Mages to shreds, of painting the black walls of the chamber red with their blood, but Garrou knew better than that. He stuffed the violent image back down deep into his psyche. He knew there were demons here in this chamber listening to his every word, spoken or not, and watching every move he made. Garrou knew he'd be the one torn to pieces before he uttered the first syllable of the spell to become the Wolf, so instead, he pushed the anger down.

"How am I failing?" Garrou asked. "I killed Thompson, I eliminated an enemy and a rival. Now my way to the Senate is open, and then the White House, as I was ordered."

"You did so foolishly, sloppily," said the Master Mage, his voice becoming angry. "You had every opportunity to kill him with no witnesses and without getting injured, yet you failed to seize those opportunities. So now, here you are, disfigured and with a crippled hand. How juvenile you've been!"

Garrou looked from one masked face to another, feeling confused. "I don't see what that has to do with things, or why it matters at all to you. I'm the one who is suffering, not you."

"It matters," said a female American Mage to his right, "because Americans are shallow and stupid. They don't care about policy, they don't pay attention, they're numb and just want to be told what to do. All they care about is that their leaders are charismatic, charming, and good-looking. You used to be all three. Now you're ugly, repulsive to look at it, so all the charm in the world won't matter. We believe you've ruined your chances to be president."

Now Garrou hung his head. He'd never considered how his injuries, how his new appearance, might affect his chances to win the presidency. After the attack he'd just wanted to heal, get back to the plan, to move forward. It had never occurred to him that a shallow electorate might reject him because of a scarred face and missing fingers. Garrou didn't want to admit the Mage might be right, but he wasn't completely convinced she was wrong.

"So, you see," said the Master Mage, "on what a knife's edge you lie. Your injuries are your own fault because you acted rashly, and because of these injuries, you might not achieve the task assigned you. That failure would be unacceptable to us and would, if it came to pass, be considered a crime."

Garrou knelt there, head down, for some time as the Supreme Tribunal wordlessly looked on.

"No," he said, lifting and shaking his head. "No. You're wrong. You're all wrong. I know politics. You don't. Even if I am repulsive to look at, I can turn that to my advantage. I can pull on their heartstrings, make overcoming my struggle part of the campaign. It'll make me more approachable, more like them and their little lives. I can win this. I can. I *will* win this."

"We do not have the same unshakable faith in your abilities as you do," said a Mexican-accented Mage. "You are going to have to do something to prove to us you're worthy of trust. If not, then the High Council may withdraw its support for you, and then... well, then you'd be named a traitor to the Coven."

"Proof?" Garrou said, almost yelling. "How am I supposed to prove this to you? The Senate election is in two months. When I win, isn't that proof enough?"

"And the presidential election is next year," said the Master Mage. "We are unwilling to wait for either. We need a demonstration of your abilities, your planning, your cunning. Your *ruthlessness*. We must know you still have what it takes. We must have something positive to report back to the High Council."

Garrou thought, then shared with the Supreme Tribunal his nascent plan about how he wanted to exact revenge against

Peter for having injured him. The Mages liked his thinking but added several details and made some demands of their own to make Peter's pain even more exquisite and to, as they said, "salt the meat" of his vengeance. Garrou also recognized that their demands made the plan far more challenging because they were making it a test of his worthiness.

Once they were done discussing his plan, Garrou said, "And then after all this is over with, I can guarantee you I will be elected president next year. Then we can usher in a new era of power and glory for the Coven Universal."

"Enthusiasm and confidence are not the same as a guarantee," said the Master Mage. "But for now, Louis Pierre Garrou, we will trust you in this matter. This was a warning. This is the only warning you will receive from us. Do not fail the High Council or the consequences will be severe."

"I won't," Garrou said. "I will fulfill my mission."

"You may stand," said the Master Mage. Then, pointing at Garrou and speaking sternly, he added, "Don't become overconfident. Remember, you were given this task, but you're not the only one who could do it for the Coven. You are not unique. You are not indispensable. If you fail, we will simply select another and wait. We can be endlessly patient. Now go. Mr. Poneros will conduct you home."

3

Garrou pivoted and strode out of the chamber, again pushing down furious images of slaughtering the Mages. As he walked down the hallway, he could hear the Mages speaking amongst themselves, though Garrou couldn't make out what was being said. He walked past the demonic murals paying them no mind this time and arrived where Mr. Poneros had been awaiting him.

"Hello, Mr. Garrou," Poneros said. "Are you ready to go home?"

"Yes, I am," said Garrou, feeling very tired.

Poneros nodded, then tapped three times on the oak door and drew another figure as he had at Garrou's closet. The demon opened the door, which Garrou was surprised to see now led to the well-appointed living room of his Washington brownstone.

"I saved you the drive home," Poneros said, again sweeping his arm forward, inviting Garrou to pass through the open door. "There was an accident on the Chesapeake Bay Bridge, and you wouldn't have gotten home until early in the morning. We want you fresh tomorrow, so... here you are."

Garrou walked forward into his other home, then turned to Poneros and said, "Thank you."

The demon again nodded. "Goodnight, Mr. Garrou. Good luck with fulfilling your task." He then closed the door and was gone.

Garrou stood in his living room for several minutes, dazed and confused as his head spun with everything that had happened since he passed Peter in the Rotunda. The events of this day were almost too much for him to fathom. It was not the first day back to the House he'd expected to have. It wasn't like any day he'd ever expected to have.

I had no idea this was so serious, that the High Council was so concerned, he thought. Garrou rubbed his eyes, the fatigue crushing now. He was physically exhausted because of pushing himself to return and was still healing from his wounds, but also tired of feeling like a marionette on a string, being pulled this way and yanked that way on the whim of the Coven. This hearing at the Supreme Tribunal was only the most egregious example of feeling like nothing but a pawn for its insatiable lust for power, but it was not the only one.

The wish to find an isolated wilderness somewhere, transform into the Wolf, and just be wild and free was almost overwhelming at that moment. Sometimes he longed to give in to the primal beast that lurked inside him – perhaps actually *was* him, more than this suited and suave politician – and just live free.

But as much as he wanted to, Garrou knew he couldn't do that. Not yet. He had a duty to the Coven to fulfill, and it was now obvious what would happen if he failed. Besides, even though he might be a pawn for the Coven's power grab, he enjoyed having part of that power. If this was the price he had to pay for it, Garrou figured, then he'd be a marionette for a time.

Shaking his head, Garrou poured himself some Woodford Reserve, drank it like the bourbon were water, then poured himself another. He then took his drink and sat by the fireplace to think about everything as he now sipped his whiskey.

CHAPTER SIXTEEN

1

Every time Angela walked into the Library of Congress, she couldn't help but pause to take in the sheer size and ornate beauty of the Jefferson building, then smile as she deeply breathed in its bookish odor. She'd already wasted many hours in the reading room when she was supposed to have been doing research for Jenkins because she'd stumbled across some unexpected book, and long been drawn into its pages. Angela had always joked she should just move her office to Jefferson and would in a heartbeat if given the opportunity.

"I spent a lot of time in libraries as a kid, you know," she said to Peter as their gaze lingered on the lobby's opulence. "I could happily get lost in a place like this."

"Yeah, you told me. That's because you had no friends as a kid."

Angela nudged him with her elbow for that quip, then said, "No, I just... well, okay, I didn't have *many* friends, but I've always loved getting dragged into a good book for hours and hours. I guess I'm just a nerd."

"Well, you're the prettiest nerd I've ever seen," said Peter, giving her a quick kiss on her cheek. "So... where do you think we should begin?"

Angie had been giving thought to this question since she'd suggested to Peter the day before they find information about Garrou. "I think we should start with him, right?" she said, whispering as they entered the hushed working interior of the building. "Start with his own history, learn everything we can about him, the whole nine yards. Maybe that'll tell us something interesting."

"Alright, that's what I was thinking, too."

The pair only had a few hours that first day to spend in the library as duties back at the Capitol drew them away. During that time, Angie could tell Peter believed they might find something of importance right away by the enthusiasm he showed taking notes from books and newspaper articles on microfiche. But, other than basic, dry biographical information available anywhere, they found nothing at all.

Angie and Peter were unable to get back to the library until the following week, so they made copies of articles to take home over the weekend. Rather than joining Angie to prepare meals those days, she watched as Peter sat at their table hunched over the pages of the copied materials they'd taken back. He'd read and re-read them, scribbling notes, sitting back at times to stretch his length out and to stare at the pages, as if trying to will information to appear.

"Come on," Angie eventually said, taking the pen and papers out of his hand and offering hers in return, "come help me with dinner. You need to put this aside until Monday."

"But, babe..." Peter said.

"No, now come on. You've been obsessing over this for days

and you need a break. Plus, I like making dinner with you. It's no fun on my own."

Peter sighed, rubbed his face, but then smiled and took Angie's hand to be led into the kitchen. "You're right. I have been getting a little crazy about this... what are we making?"

Angie turned on the radio and the pair danced between cooking tasks, chatting, joking, and laughing, but even as they did, she could tell Peter wasn't quite present in their usual kitchen antics. She hoped that, once this was settled and they found nothing to suggest Garrou was a werewolf, that he could get out of his own head once and for all.

That following week, they were able to spend far more time at the Library of Congress, since Angie had been given several items to research and Peter had time on his hands now that Catherine Thompson had taken over.

"Hmm..." Peter said three days into their investigations as he sat at a microfiche machine, "this is interesting. Very interesting."

Angie pulled her chair next to his and said, "What? What are you reading?"

"This is a newspaper from California," Peter said, pointing at the screen. "I was reading it because there's an article on page six about Garrou's time at the private boarding school he went to. He apparently had won an award for his performance on the debate team. Of course."

"Okay."

Peter moved the microfiche knobs to bring up another article, buried further in the paper. "This story, however, is about a spike of unsolved murders in Anaheim, where the school is located, that had been happening the past few years."

"Oh," Angie said, "What kind of murders?"

"Well... looks like there was a shooting of a homeless man, a hooker was slashed and gutted, some guy was killed while wanking off in a porn theater, it looks like someone in a drug house was doused with gas and burned. There are several more, but you get the point."

Angie looked at Peter for a long moment. "Umm... I don't get it. What does that have to do with Garrou?"

"All of these murders happened when he was there at the school. The spike started when he was about thirteen years old and ended after he left. The article said some people suspected there was a link to the school."

"Why did they think that?"

"Ah," Peter said, raising his pointer finger. "They thought that after an underclassman killed himself. Apparently, some investigators figured if a kid would kill himself at the school, then maybe there was, like, a gang of murderous teenagers there."

"But, Peter," Angie said, whispering even more than she had been, "none of this has anything to do with him being a... you know."

"Yeah, but it at least proves he's a murderer."

"No, it doesn't," she said. "Not at all. It proves there were a bunch of unsolved killings while he was there, that's all. I mean, it doesn't look like there was anything weird about the ways these people were killed, right?"

Peter sighed. "No, it doesn't. They were all shot, stabbed, slashed. Typical stuff."

"And were there ever any suspects?" she asked, leaning in towards the screen.

"Well," Peter said, as he readjusted the article, "There's this guy. An addict who was found nodding off in the alley behind the house where the woman inside was raped and killed. He was convicted for the murder, though there were a lot of people who said he couldn't have done it and only got sent to prison because of his race and because he was an addict."

"Okay, then. Doesn't that seem more reasonable?"

After a long moment of silence, Peter said, "Yeah. I suppose so."

"I agree he's a bastard," said Angie, "and a creep. He's even a dickhead. But I don't think he's a killer. Nothing here would prove otherwise. Okay?"

Peter again sighed. "Yeah. Alright."

The remainder of that week proceeded much the same way, with Angie and Peter finding troves of information about Garrou's life. They found dozens of stories about his youth, his years at Stanford, serving on the board of his family's foundation, and especially about his career in politics. Both pointed out that many of the articles about him made it seem like he'd been destined for the government, almost being groomed for leadership by his parents from a young age. A student newspaper article from Stanford even referred to him as a possible future president.

The following week again found them pouring through all the information the pair could find on Garrou, and now, on this first day of autumn, they had started to branch out into his family's history. They discovered that Jacques Garrou, the youngest son of a great noble family from the Gevaudan region of France, had relocated to Louisiana in 1788 to establish himself in the New World as he never could back in Europe. Since then, the family had always enjoyed an abundance of wealth and power, reaching new heights under Garrou's great-grandfather, Giles, who had moved the family from Louisiana to Maryland to better influence the Washington politicians he'd purchased.

In two weeks of almost daily research, the only thing even approaching salacious that Angie and Peter found about the family was a suggestion Guillaume Garrou, the congressman's grandfather, had multiplied his already impressive wealth by getting involved in bootlegging during Prohibition. They learned nothing about the Garrous that suggested they were anything other than a typical American family. They were unique due to their long history of influence and riches, but other families had been likewise blessed.

They could uncover nothing to suggest the Garrous were unusual in any other way – and certainly nothing to suggest Louis Garrou was a werewolf.

2

After having spent the day combing through dusty books and taking notes, the pair sat on the library steps taking in the sun that shone on this chilly equinox day. Peter sat, his long legs drawn up, elbows on knees, a lollipop in his mouth as he watched the water dance in the Neptune Fountain and the traffic stream by on First Street.

"I don't get it," he said at last.

"Get what?" Angie asked as she clutched her thick cardigan closer to her.

Peter hitched a thumb behind him. "That. The fact that we've been in here for two weeks, that we've pretty much crawled up Garrou's ass and haven't learned anything about him other than he's a pampered rich boy who was given everything he's ever had, that we've learned enough about his family history that we could write a biography on it, and still we haven't found one thing weird about him. I just don't get it."

"Well, honey," Angie said, clutching her sweater even tighter as a gust of wind swirled around them, "maybe that proves the point. We said we were going to come here with an open mind to look around, see what we could find, and just take it from there. We've found nothing. Doesn't that tell us everything we need to know?"

"Yep," Peter said, still watching the cars go by before them, "it does. Thing is, I just can't believe that. I know what I saw, and I know what he really is."

I love him so much, but sometimes his stubbornness can be a real pain in the ass, Angie thought as she sighed and gently rubbed her forehead. "Honey, come on. We said we were going to follow the data. The data are non-existent. That kind of proves Garrou's not what you 'know' he is."

Peter pulled the lollipop out of his mouth with a *smack!* then finally turned to look at Angie. "Look, I know what you're saying makes sense. It makes perfect, logical sense. But this is just a feeling I have, babe. I know it's not logical, I know it's crazy, I know there's nothing proving anything, but I just feel this is the truth."

"That's insane. You know that, right? Totally insane."

Peter smiled and chuckled, then said, "Yeah, I know. It's crazy. But I'm the only one who saw this thing up close and survived, and my gut just tells me I'm right. But one thing about this makes perfect sense, though, if you think about it."

Angie lifted her brows, then cocked her head to the side. "What part?" she asked with a laugh.

"It makes sense that this would be kept hidden," he said, in between sucking on the lollipop. "It's not like he would've mentioned it in any interviews or that his parents would have reported that to anyone. This sort of thing really wouldn't be on record, would it?"

"So, wait... now you're saying the lack of proof *is* proof?"

Peter nodded and smiled, lollipop in his mouth, then said, "In this case it is."

"Honey," Angie implored, putting her hand on Peter's arm, "it's time to walk away. Seriously, this is getting unhealthy for you. You're obsessed. You need to walk away and let go."

Peter turned and took both of Angie's hands in his. "I know. I do know I need to walk away from it. Give me just one more day, okay? Just one more day, because I have something I want to look into a little more."

"Alright," said Angie, "but then after tomorrow let's just be done with this, once and for all. Agreed?"

"Agreed."

"Oh, shit. I forgot I'm leaving work early tomorrow, at around noon, for a doctor's appointment. I'll be tied up all morning in meetings, so I won't be able to come help. Do you mind?"

"Nah, that's fine. You do what you need to."

Angie thought a moment, then said, "What are you looking into? I thought we've already gone down every rabbit hole we could find."

Peter pulled the lollipop out of his mouth, then regarded its slicked, crimson head. "I really wish this was a cigarette. I guess it's helping me not smoke, but I can only stand so many of these damn things a day. Anyway... think more of a bear den that a rabbit hole."

"Huh?"

Peter tossed the unfinished lollipop into a nearby trashcan. "Something has been nagging me in the back of my mind, so I looked into all of those so-called bear attacks. The attack on Thompson's was thought to be a bear because of the description of the creature, but also because there were seven people killed in attacks on the Delmarva earlier in the summer, right?"

"Yes, that's right."

"Well, all of those attacks were from the fifth to the tenth of July, which was during—"

"The congressional recess," Angie muttered.

"Bingo," Peter said. "During the recess. Then, I found out there was a second spate of attacks, again along the Delmarva, which lasted from the seventh until the twelfth of August. Three people killed this time, in two different attacks. But then, supposedly for no known reason, all of the 'bear' attacks stopped, and there hasn't been another one since."

Angie sat looking at Peter as her mind raced with possible implications and her leg began to bounce. *This can't be. This simply cannot be! There cannot be some werewolf creature running around killing people. I refuse to believe it!*

"Surely that must be a coincidence," Angie said, the dread that had long lurked in the depth of her mind creeping further into her consciousness. "Right?"

Peter unwrapped another lollipop, then put it in his mouth. "That's one hell of a coincidence, isn't it? One more coincidence on top of all the others. How many damn coincidences are we going to accept before we just admit something's going on here?"

They sat wordlessly there for several minutes as the sun warmed their skin even as the cool breeze chilled it until Peter said, "Mmm... chocolate. Maybe I can stand this one more than the cherry. Come on, let's get back inside so I can get started on this. You look even colder than normal."

As Peter pored over newspaper articles and police reports about the summer attacks, Angie sat at the microfiche cubicle next to him, watching him but not seeing. Her mind was turned inwards, confronting her fear of the shadowy unknown that had tormented her for years. Angie felt like the thing that had always been lurking in the dark well of her mind – down too far for her to see it, yet still scrabbling and scraping around down there so she could hear it – was climbing up, and she would soon be forced to confront its hideous form. Angie wondered if she would be able to face it when she did if she could fight it if she had to. She feared her nightmares of a loathsome unfamiliar were soon about to become real.

"Okay, you want to see what I have?" Peter said an hour later, snapping Angie from her reverie. "It didn't take as long as I thought it would."

Angie shook her head and blinked, then said, "Yeah, of course."

"Okay, so... each victim was basically torn to pieces."

"Is that normal for a bear attack?" Angie asked.

"Well," Peter answered as he scratched his head, "bear attacks aren't all that common, to be honest. Not in Maryland, anyway. In Alaska, they happen more often, but those are grizzlies, and they can be pretty damn cranky."

"But not the black bears we have here?"

"If you piss off a mama bear, then yeah, she can be dangerous, but even then, the damage described in the police reports... I won't go into details but trust me. These people were ripped to shreds."

"Gross," Angie said, making a face like she just sucked a lemon.

"Yeah, very gross," said Peter, strumming his fingers on the table. "Bears don't do that. Their claws will rip you open, yeah, but these people were... well, this is overkill. If a bear doesn't eat a person, which grizzlies do sometimes, they won't destroy someone like that."

She could hear the sounds of that nightmare creature's claws in the dark as it crawled closer to the top of her mind well and could almost smell its fetid breath. She tried desperately to make it stop.

Don't come out. Don't come out. Don't come out. Don't you dare come out.

Angie thought for a moment. "Who were the victims? Anyone with any political connections?"

Peter pursed his lips and strummed his fingers louder before running his hands through his tawny hair. "Well, that's what so damned frustrating here. None of these people had anything to do with politics. They were just regular folks. Every day working people. They weren't rich, powerful, anything like that. It makes no sense."

"Well, doesn't that prove it?!" Angie said, looking around as people glanced towards the sudden outburst. "You think Thompson's death was an assassination, a hit. That Garrou killed him for political reasons. If the people killed in these earlier attacks were just regular folks, not politically connected or powerful or anything, then it couldn't have been him. That'd make no sense because why would he kill every day, run-of-the-mill people? Right?"

Peter sighed and rubbed his face with both hands, Angie noticing how tired he looked. "Yeah, I guess you're right," he whispered. "If he was going around killing people, I suppose it wouldn't be the poor, it'd be rivals, like Thompson, or other rich, powerful people." Peter slumped down in his chair and crossed his arms.

Angie patted his shoulder, then said, "So, honey... are we done now? It's been two weeks. We've learned everything we could about him and we've found nothing. I think it's time to wrap this up."

Peter nodded. "Well, I'll still come over tomorrow to finish up, but... yeah, it is. You're not available tomorrow anyway, and it's not like I have much else to do, so I'll come here. But after that, I'm done."

Angie closed her eyes a moment, as the growling and scraping sounds receded back down into the well of her mind. *Get back down there, fucker, and stay there!*

"Alright, fine," Angie said. "I'm running errands tomorrow after my appointment, so I'll be home at the regular time. We'll turn on the radio, pour some wine, dance around like straight fools, make dinner together, just like any normal Friday night. Sound good?"

"Yeah, that does sound good."

Later that night, the pair sat on the couch as they watched a movie, Angie sitting on her leg to keep it from bouncing. She wondered why she didn't feel calmer as the scraping, scampering sounds echoing from the depth of her psyche taunted her still.

CHAPTER SEVENTEEN

On a hilltop clearing in the West Virginia mountains, the old woman sat.

Her deeply wrinkled face was pinched in concentration as her closed eyes squeezed shut even tighter. She had almost a pained looked to her pale face. Her small feet dangled inches above the ground, and her body, so bent with years that she seemed to almost have collapsed into herself, leaned to one side of her rough-hewn rustic chair. The few wispy threads of thin white hair that still clung to her head swayed in the breeze. One bony hand clutched the black woolen shawl she wore as the other cradled her forehead.

She sat with a group of women encircling a crackling fire, all of whom had their eyes closed as the smoke swirled around them, the air thick with the tangy odor of burning wood. Their shadows danced all around them as the orange flames flickered in the shifting winds. The women all wore plain, black dresses, some with shawls around their shoulders like the old woman, a few with the shawls draped over their heads as a hood.

As she sat, the old woman made a groaning, grinding noise

almost like a rhythmic chant. She then spoke, her words sounding like creaking wood.

"The Dark World is growin' agin," she croaked in a heavy Appalachian accent. "Growin' stronger e'ryday. Growin' more powerful. Spreadin'. They's stretchin' out like they's reachin' out a hand to grab what they's be wantin', what they's always be wantin'. They's got a hunger that ain't gwine be filled easy." As she spoke, a group of young women sitting furthest from her wrote down her words.

A black woman sitting to her left, old and gray herself but far younger than the other, opened her eyes and said, "What is it you see, Grandmother?"

"I feel the wolf. He plans on adoin' wicked, but I kin't see what. Like he's wrapped in an evil mist."

The woman let go of her shawl and reached out towards the fire, her thin hand trembling as she did. She breathed deep from the special aromatic logs placed on the fire, moving her head from one side to the other as if trying to get a clear view of something, then again made the guttural sound as she furrowed her wrinkled brow even more.

After a moment, she said, "I kin see them."

"Where are they? Are they safe?" the black woman asked her.

"Mmmmm..." she groaned. "Yes. They's be safe. They's be home now. But they's been... they's been lookin' in library for a learnin'. They's ain't gwine find nothin'. They's gonna learn that soon 'nuff." The woman chuckled, her laugh sounding like a raspy cough.

"What can we do, Grandmother?" said another woman sitting on her right.

"We wait," she said. "We wait, and we watch. Ain't nothing else we kin do."

The woman took her hand away from her forehand and

used it to search for the head of a gnarled wooden walking stick she had leaning against the chair, patting the armrest until she found it. Though her eyes remained shut, the old woman moved her head like she was sweeping them along the circle of black-clad women.

"The Dark World is agrowin' stronger," she said, pointing her walking stick at the group of women as she spoke. "It's acomin' for us, it's acomin' for them, it's acomin for the whole dang world. It's a plannin' somthin', somethin' wicked, but I kin't tell what. But it don't matter, no how. Whatever it is, we's agot to be read for it, ready to fight when it comes. We, and they's we train. So... we watch, and we wait."

"And the two of them?" the black woman asked. "They will come?"

"I reckon they will." The old woman scanned the group seated before her with her closed eyes, then settled when pointed towards a pale-faced woman with long, red hair. "Sarah, you and your sisters keepin' an eye on them, like I asked you to?"

"Yes, Grandmother," the young woman said. "We are."

"Good," said the old woman, her voice growing weaker the longer she spoke. "They's gwine find they way to us... in time. I don' know when, I don' know how... but they's will. Then... we's gotta give 'em... the learnin' they's be needin'. Because... it's them that's... got to defeat this beast... or... none t'all."

The old woman fell silent as her head lowered to her chest and sat there, still for some minutes. The group of women also sat in silence, waiting on the old woman as the wind continued to swirl around the hilltop and the fire crackled and popped until at last, she slowly lifted her head again and turned to the black woman seated next to her.

"Naomi," she said, lifting her elbow, "I'm tired... so tired. Please help me... git to bed."

Naomi took the old woman's arm and gently helped her stand from her chair. She appeared even more bent and frail than she did sitting, and as the old woman rose from her seat, the other women stood, too. Then, leaning heavily on her walking stick she took small, shuffling steps towards a series of rough cabins in the woods some distance away from the fire as Naomi kept her steady.

She and Naomi slowly disappeared into the black night beyond the small circle of light cast by the flickering flames.

CHAPTER EIGHTEEN

1

The next day, Peter sat slouched back in his seat, legs stretched out and hands deep in his pockets as he stared at the blank microfiche screen.

He wondered why he'd bothered coming back to the Library of Congress. He and Angie had spent over two weeks in the library searching for anything that might suggest Garrou was a werewolf, or that his family had some mystery in their past, which could account for... something.

Peter wasn't even sure anymore what he'd hoped they might uncover. All they found was that Garrou had led a privileged life and benefitted from his family's wealth, which everyone in Washington already knew. They'd discovered that the Garrou family had been in America for years and powerful for generations, which, while interesting, proved irrelevant to their search.

"So why are we here?" Peter whispered to the hazy reflection of his own face in the screen. It had no wisdom to offer.

As Peter thought, he supposed it came down to his stubbornness. He believed still that Garrou was a werewolf and had so much wanted to prove it to Angie. Once he'd sunk his teeth into the idea that the answer could be found here, hidden away somewhere in the maze of books, articles, and documents, Peter just couldn't let go of that thought. Even now, having spent two weeks in fruitless searching, he'd come back for the final day just as he told Angie he would. Peter refused to give up, though he'd exhausted all his ideas and had no clue where to search.

When he and Angie had started, Peter believed they'd discover something of interest, something that could prove his point to Angie and might even suggest a way to defeat Garrou. He'd been forced to believe in werewolves since the cabin attack, yet he also questioned the details of the old legends since it wasn't a full moon that night. Turning a necklace into a silver bullet might be easy in the stories, but Peter now doubted whether that would work in real life. He'd hoped, but it appeared those hopes were shattered, and now he sat staring blankly at his reflection.

So now what? he thought. *You have all afternoon. Do you want to keep looking for something that doesn't exist? Do you want to sit here staring at yourself or do you want to do something worthwhile? Go outside, go for a walk. Visit a landmark. Whatever, just accept reality. Accept it. It's all over. As much as you don't want it to be, it is. Get used to it.*

No, thought the stubborn side of Peter. *No, it can't be. There's got to be something here, something we're missing. Somewhere in this library, in the gazillion books here, there's what I'm looking for. I just need to luck out and find the right book.*

That could take a million years, and you have one day. You promised Angie after today you were out.

So, I better get to it... but where do I look?!

As Peter argued with himself and regarded the blank screen, a shadow darkened it. Someone had approached him from behind, and an electric chill raced down his spine as Peter realized the person was standing silently at his back rather than moving on. As he turned to see who it was, Peter's heart skipped a beat and his throat closed as he saw Garrou looking down at him.

His one good eye peered at Peter from an emotionless face, while the other, milk-white dead one was now covered with an eyepatch. The puckered scar reached out from the top and bottom of the patch, looking like two writhing snakes slithering out from under it.

"It's quite an amazing history, isn't it, Mr. Brunnen?" Garrou asked.

Peter stared, wordless and confused, then swallowed hard. "H-H-History?" he said.

"Yes, history," said Garrou, as he took the chair from a neighboring microfiche cubicle and sat next to Peter, crossing his legs comfortably. "I've been told you and your girlfriend have spent weeks here looking up my family history. Isn't that correct?"

How the fuck does he know that?!

"Umm... yeah, that's true," Peter said. "And she's my fiancé now."

"Is she really?" said Garrou, smiling. "Well, isn't that just blessed news. How wonderful for the two of you."

Peter thought for a moment, then said, "How did you know we were here?"

Garrou chuckled. "Peter – may I call you Peter? – surely you understand that a man doesn't get to my position in life without having numerous ways of gathering information. Information, after all, is power. Isn't it? But of course, that's the entire reason you're here. To gather information... and, perhaps, to gain some power over me in the process?"

Peter's mind raced, not knowing how to respond, and fearing that Garrou had somehow found out why they'd spent two weeks looking into his family history.

How the fuck am I going to explain that?!

"Which is what politics is all about, right?" said Garrou with a smile. "Using information to gain power. Whoever controls information can gather all the power they want, so it's the very bedrock of American politics. I know you used to work for Sim Thompson, and I can only assume you're gathering information because of the election... although I thought I'd heard Catherine wasn't running for the Senate. Perhaps I was mistaken."

Peter nodded, his mind crackling with questions. Finally, he settled on the most obvious one, and said, "Why are you here, Congressman Garrou?"

"See?" he said, patting Peter on the shoulder. "Now there's a respectful young man, knowing how to use one's proper title. As I said, I heard you were here, looking into me, and I wanted to come by to thank you."

Peter furrowed his brow. "To thank me?"

"Yes, of course. To thank you for fighting so hard the night of the bear attack. Though Thompson and I were political rivals we were also, I always felt, friends, and so knowing that my friend came to such a grisly, horrendous death was very difficult for me to hear. I couldn't stand to think about how horrified he must have been. My heart was gladdened when I found out someone had fought for him... at the very end."

Peter sat still, staring at Garrou. He could find no words to respond as he felt the blood drain from his face and his heart pound in his chest with sudden terror. The realization that

Garrou was coyly telling him something hit Peter like a hammer blow to the head.

I never told anyone I fought off the creature. I didn't even tell the police! No one aside from me and Angie knows. So how the fuck does he know that?! Unless he really is...

Peter's eyes grew wide as he began to shudder.

Garrou then lifted a black-gloved right hand. The thumb, pointer, and middle fingers, and half the palm were stuffed to create a normal appearance, though it was clear they were missing from the way the fingers lay, stiff and unmoving.

"I'd shake your hand," he said, "but, you know... I don't really have a hand anymore, do I? So, I can't do that."

"Uhhh," Peter stammered as he tried to keep the icy chill of his growing terror under control. "Y-Y-Yeah... yeah, I'd heard about your accident. I was sorry to hear you got hurt."

"My accident," said Garrou, with a distant look in his eye. "Yes, my accident. It was rather severe, wasn't it? I do appreciate your kind sentiments, Peter."

They sat there, awkwardly saying nothing for some moments, Garrou locking his gaze on Peter. He found it almost as hard to look into Garrou's one good eye as he had his dead one, and shifted position in his seat, swallowing hard and clearing his throat. Gnawing horror crept over him like spiders crawling down his back as he felt the same seething hatred he had that day in the Rotunda. Peter wanted to flee screaming from the library. He felt the intensity of Garrou's stare boring a hole in him, like a hot drill pushing its way through his body.

"So..." Garrou said at last, "what did you learn about my family?"

"Oh, umm..." said Peter, finding it hard to focus and trying to not let his voice quiver. "Well, I found out that your ancestor, Jacques Garrou, came to Louisiana in the late 1700s. That's where the family lived until your great-grandfather moved the family to Maryland. He built a mansion on an estate near Poolesville. Your great-grandfather that is, not Jacques. Jacques lived first in New Orleans, then he bought a plantation and moved his family there. I'm not certain what happened to the plantation when the family moved here."

"We still own the plantation house and some of the land, actually. Though, obviously, it's no longer a working plantation after all these years. Now it's used for a different purpose, you see."

Peter didn't see but nodded his head anyway.

"But anyway," Garrou said, "that was a fine bit of research. Catherine would be lucky to have you on her staff... if she were actually doing anything that required researching, that is."

"Thanks," Peter said, shifting in his seat again as he wished Garrou would go away.

"And what did you find out about my family before the auspicious date of our arrival to America?"

"Well," he said, "we really didn't find anything. There wasn't much before then. Not that we're aware of, anyway."

"Oh," said Garrou, sitting forward and putting his elbows on his knees, then leaning in further towards Peter like he was about to share a delicious secret. "Well, let me tell you a little bit about the long and glorious history of the Garrou family prior to coming to America."

"Oh... O-O-Okay," Peter said.

Garrou paused, steepling his fingers under his chin as he looked away to think, and said, "Now, where should I begin? Ah, yes... we can trace our lineage all the way back to a Norman baron named Hugh d'Avranches, who was a peer of William the Conqueror's. He was given a piece of land in western England along the Welsh Marches to rule over, one in which the Saxons were apparently rather displeased with their new Norman overlords. The defeated Saxons got it in their head that rebelling against the Normans was a splendid idea, and that if they just united and worked together, they could overcome their new rulers – such a quaint notion, don't you think, Peter?"

Another hammer blow of awareness struck Peter as he recalled that just two nights before he'd had a conversation with Angie about the modern political "overlords" in America. He'd used almost the exact same wording to explain how the electorate could shake off their influence.

"I... uh," Peter mumbled, "I don't really know, I suppose."

"No?" Garrou asked. "Hmm. What a shame. Well... back to the story. Where good ol' Hugh really shone, though, was when he was tasked with the duty of conquering the Welsh. In those battles, and then in his dealings with the defeated populace afterward, he fought with such savagery and ruled with so much cruelty that the Welsh gave him a nickname. Would you like to venture a guess what it was, Peter?"

Peter shook his head, trying to swallow his fear, but found his mouth too dry. "I don't... don't know," he whispered.

Garrou smiled, then said, "They called him 'Hugh the Wolf.' The wolf, you see, because he was vicious in battle and as a ruler. He was like a wolf pack attacking its prey, tearing it to shreds. You know, that's what wolf packs do when they attack? They'll tear a bite off here and rip out some chunks there, and once their prey is on the ground, they'll rip its still-living guts out of it, tear off its flailing limbs. Of course, back in Hugh's day, sometimes people were what the wolves would attack."

Peter stared, wide-eyed and full of terror, watching Garrou as he smiled cruelly at the mention of people being torn apart by wolves. He trembled as if chilled even as a fat bead of sweat trickled down his forehead. The fear of what Garrou might do grew, and the tension of waiting, became almost too much for him to stand. Peter wanted to run, wanted to escape Garrou's menacing presence, to retreat somewhere he could be safe. His breath came in small gasps, though he tried not to let Garrou know. Peter believed he'd rejoice in being able to do this and he didn't want to give Garrou the pleasure.

Garrou sat back, tapping his chin with his fingers as if thinking. "But you know," he said, "our old boy Hugh didn't take their barb as an insult. Oh, no... in fact, he took it as a badge of honor. He used the wolf as his family crest, a great lupine head on his shield and banners to warn everyone that Hugh the Wolf had arrived, that slaughter was soon to follow. Unfortunately, he was eventually killed in battle by some random arrow. What a pity."

He's insane, Peter thought. *He's totally fucking insane!*

"For quite a while," Garrou went on, "the family didn't amount to much because apparently, we come from an illegitimate French branch of Hugh's from Normandy. He was a man driven by his appetites, after all, so that comes as little surprise. We started off as a family of bastard knights, who in time – through loyal service and a willingness to massacre the king's enemies – rose to the ranks of the ruling class, and eventually became the ranking nobility in Gevaudan all through the Middle Ages. We've long been the natural rulers over others, and, if I may be immodest, I think we still are."

"Gevaudan?" Peter asked, his voice a pinched whisper.

"Yes," said Garrou, "the Gevaudan region in France. Well, it used to be called Gevaudan, but then they changed the name of it. I believe you found that Jacques, my ancestor who first came to America, hailed from there originally. He was fortunate enough to get out just before the French Revolution because the remaining family members were all butchered during those years. Every last member of this great, noble family was rounded up and murdered by a bunch of illiterate farmers who reeked of shit. My family members all wound up with their heads on pikes. But... that's what happens when you give the peasants all the power, I suppose."

Garrou again sat as he smiled, wordlessly staring at Peter. The crushing tension and fear were almost too much for Peter to manage. He felt Garrou was taunting him, knowing the effect he had, and relished the horror he was able to elicit. Peter feared at any moment Garrou would drop the pretense and attack him, ripping him to shreds like the wolf packs he had described.

Would he do it here? he wondered. *Would he really be so insane to change into the beast here and kill me?*

"Is that the time already?!" Garrou said as he looked at his Rolex, making Peter jerk at the unexpected exclamation. "My, how the time does fly when you're engaged in stimulating conversation. Isn't that right, Peter?"

Garrou stood and stretched, then said, "Well... I need to go because we're planning an election event out in Garrett County for next week – why, you're from out that way, aren't you? Mountain Lake Park, as I recall. Correct?"

Peter's shaking had grown beyond his ability to control, and now sat quivering beneath Garrou's piercing glare like the last autumn leaf in a November rainstorm. His breaths came in ragged gulps, and though he tried to answer he couldn't form words.

"Maybe I'll swing by and see your folks while I'm there," Garrou said with a broad smile. "Stop by, let them know what a fine young man they raised. That's no easy task in this fallen world, I can tell you that. Maybe I'll even have a bite to eat."

Garrou pivoted to leave, then snapped his fingers and turned back. "I almost forgot," he said, rummaging in the breast pocket of his suitcoat. "I have a small – very small – token of my appreciation for what you did for Thompson. Ah! Here it is."

Garrou handed him a lollipop. For the second time in just a few minutes, Peter felt the blood drain from his face as his head began to swim. He took the treat from Garrou with a trembling hand.

"It's chocolate flavored," Garrou whispered. "You prefer that over the cherry if I'm not mistaken. Well, Peter, thank you for the pleasant diversion. I'm sure I'll see you again very soon."

2

For some minutes after Garrou left, Peter sat trembling, breathing heavily, his hands holding the seat of his chair as if he feared he might topple over. His head swam and his vision blurred, Peter sat with his eyes clenched tight until he was able to regain his composure. He finally took a deep breath, held it, then let it out in a long exhalation as he opened his eyes. Dumbfounded, he looked at the lollipop still pinched in his fingers.

"What the fuck?" Peter said, staring at it. With a grimace on his face, he threw it into the trash as if it were a serpent reeling back to bite him.

Peter grabbed his notebook and started writing, trying to remember everything Garrou had said. He knew Garrou was toying with him, taunting him, giving him just enough information to tell Peter he was a werewolf without saying anything provocative. Peter recognized that he still had nothing to go on, nothing he could bring to Angie; he could have recorded their entire conversation and the only thing she'd hear was Garrou's diatribe about his family history.

He tried to recall every time Garrou mentioned something he would only know if he had spies following them. Perhaps,

Peter realized, Garrou had also bugged their apartment. Maybe both. He felt very exposed at that moment, sitting there in the Library of Congress surrounded by dozens of people, any number of which could be surveilling him for Garrou. Peter paused as this occurred to him, cutting his eyes from one side and then to the other, carefully turning his head to see who might be watching him, as a paranoid, grinding fear of everyone took hold of him.

Stop it! He's fucking with your head and you're letting him. You do not want to become a paranoid conspiracy nut!

Peter put down his pen and rubbed his temples, breathing deeply to calm himself. He was amazed with what ease Garrou was able to get into his head to toy with his psyche using nothing more threatening than a conversation, a sneering smile, and a few well-placed words.

He might be totally insane, but he's also one terrifying motherfucker, werewolf or not.

"We've always been rulers over others," Peter said to himself mockingly, "and I still think we are. Fuck you, you pompous prick. Why don't you and your whole family just go back to Gevaudan...?"

Peter sat back in his seat, staring at that scribbled word on his paper. He tapped it with his pen after surrounding the word in circles, thinking back to their conversation.

"Gevaudan," he whispered. *Why did you make such a point to let me know your family came from there, Garrou? Why did you want me to know that? What is it you wanted me to find out?*

Peter thought for a few moments, then decided to use the two hours he had before the library closed to finish off his research and launched himself towards the bookcases. He found a few books about French geography and history. After using most of the time he had to pore over the books, he found they proved useless to his investigation. As time wound down on the library's open hours till there was just a half-hour left, he started flipping through a section on Gevaudan in a history book, fearing nothing would come of this final effort as well.

Peter then stopped cold when he saw the image of a revolting woodcut.

It showed a man, looking beastly and deranged, crawling on the ground like a wild animal, his clothes ripped to pieces. In his mouth, he clutched a screaming child, while other children ran from him to the safety of their panicked mother. All around him lay what remained of his victims: decapitated heads, shredded limbs, eviscerated bodies. They looked like what Peter had read about the condition of the bodies after the attacks along the Delmarva. The caption read, *Werewolf Attack, 1512.*

"What the fuck?" Peter muttered.

He flipped back to the beginning of the section and saw it was titled, "The Great French Werewolf Epidemic and the Beast of Gevaudan."

"The beast of Gevaudan," Peter whispered, excitement and fear growing within him in equal measures. After more than two weeks of fruitless searching, Peter had at last found something that might prove useful, all because Garrou *wanted* him to find it.

"Shit," he hissed as he glanced again at the clock and saw there was now less than twenty minutes before closing. Peter mumbled to himself softly as he scribbled down notes. "There were wolf-killers employed in France as early as Charlemagne in the 800s... wolf-killing was an official function of the kingdom until the late 1880s... wolf attacks, though common throughout Europe, always seemed to be far more in France... from the early medieval period into the 18th century there were several eras of 'werewolf panic'... wolf attacks multiplied and the people believed these were actually werewolves... the center of these attacks was always in the Gevaudan region."

Peter turned to the "Beast of Gevaudan" section and was again greeted by an equally brutal illustration. This colored woodcutting showed what looked like a gigantic wolf resting its front paws on a woman who lay dead on the ground as the creature ate from her torn-open belly. Behind the beast lay the body of a dead man, his head pulled off, his chest ripped open. Around them lay legs, arms, and skulls, the detritus of earlier victims.

Feeling the pressure of time running out, Peter again turned to jot down as many notes as he could, whispering as he did. "Between 1520 and 1630 there was a period of ongoing wolf attacks in Gevaudan... many of which people believed to have been werewolves... some people confessed to being in league with the devil and so were able to take wolf form... the most famous case of these werewolf attacks, the beast of Gevaudan, attacked and killed over a hundred people from 1764 to 1767."

Peter had just enough time to make copies of the woodcuts to show Angie and to return the books to their shelves before closing time. He walked out of the Library of Congress feeling excited and eager to explain everything that had happened that afternoon, from when Garrou unexpectedly showed up to their weird conversation to finding out about the Beast of Gevaudan. Peter never would have found that if Garrou hadn't pointed him in the right direction, which he felt was almost as good as a confession from the man. As he made his way back to their apartment, Peter still couldn't fathom why Garrou had wanted him to know.

Does he get some sick thrill knowing I know? Is that his way of warning us to stay away from him and his family? What's that bastard up to?

Peter was confused and couldn't come up with any answers, but he was impatient to talk to Angie because things always seemed to make more sense when he discussed them with her. He rushed home so he could start unpacking the details of this very strange afternoon with her.

"Angie! You're never going to believe..." he said as soon as he opened the door to their apartment, but then stopped, standing in the doorway. Something was terribly wrong. It was past six o'clock in the evening and she was not in the kitchen starting dinner, nor was the radio blaring as it should be. The lights were on, but the apartment was otherwise silent.

"Angie?!" he said louder. He glanced towards the small bar counter between their kitchen and living room area, and there he saw her purse and keys. She would always put them there as soon as she got home.

"What the hell?" he muttered.

Maybe she's in the bath, relaxing, or maybe napping, he thought as a vague feeling of unease crept over him. *She had a long day, so she's tired. That's all. I'm sure that's it.*

Peter closed the door behind him and took a few steps in the apartment, making his way towards the hall leading to their bedroom. As he did, Peter stopped, staring at Angie's glasses on the floor in front of the closet door. The lenses were cracked, the frames and temples crushed, looking like they'd been stomped on.

He jumped when the kitchen phone loudly rang, then rushed over to pick it up, hoping it was Angie.

"Hello?" he said.

CHAPTER NINETEEN

"Hello, Peter," Garrou said softly as he sat on his leather reading chair in the front room of his brownstone, smoking a Cuban cigar. A tumbler of Woodford Reserve sat on the table next to him.

This had so far proved to be a delightful few days for Garrou and was turning into an even better evening. The first day of autumn earlier in the week marked the beginning of his favorite season, and the muggy warmth of the city had broken on that clear, beautiful day. His legislative agenda was going well, and he'd been able to parlay his injuries into sympathy for his suffering, leading to improved poll numbers.

Garrou smiled as he thought about how he'd twisted the knife into Peter earlier, taunting and teasing him, and now he was about to enjoy the penultimate pleasure of the day. As he spoke on the phone, he stared at Angie seated before him, gagged, her hands tied behind her, her body bound tightly to a chair from the dining room. He relished the look of panic on her face as her wide-open eyes swept around, and he enjoyed her fearful shaking, the tears silently streaming from her eyes.

This was a treat so delicious Garrou wished he could eat it up.

"Garrou?" Peter said. "What do you want?"

"Oh, come now, Peter. Etiquette must be observed. My proper title is *Congressman* Garrou, after all."

There was a pause, then Peter again asked, "What do you want?"

Garrou chuckled. "Well, Peter, I enjoyed our conversation so much today I thought we should continue it. I just feel like there was an awful lot we didn't get to say, and I'd like to have a chance to. So, why don't you meet me in Baltimore, three o'clock tonight, at Fort Armistead Park? It's a lovely little spot, I'm sure you'll love it. Then we can continue our chat."

"What the fuck are you even talking about, Garrou?" Peter said. "No, I'm not meeting you in Baltimore in the middle of the night. No way. I don't have time for your bullshit right now."

"Oh... that is a pity," Garrou said. He nodded at Felix, whose hulking form stood behind Angie. He removed her gag. "Well, perhaps this will change your mind."

Garrou held the phone out to Angie. "Peter!" she screamed. "Help me! He took me and he has me—" She stopped screaming when, after another nod from Garrou, Felix touched her head, and she immediately passed out.

"You fucking son of a bitch!" Peter yelled, forcing Garrou to hold the phone receiver away from his ear. "You fucking bastard! You let her go, or I swear to God I'll—"

"You'll do nothing," Garrou said in a calm but menacing tone, "except exactly what I tell you to, Peter. You have no options here. You are not in charge. You'll do what you're told, or else your plump little fiancé here won't make it through the night alive. Is that clear?"

A short pause, in which Garrou could feel Peter's bravado

crumble as he heard his terrified gasps for breath, his voice choking up with tears. As he listened to the sound of Peter breaking down, a sound that meant the triumph of his will over that of another, his sneering smile grew broader.

"Okay, okay! I will, I'll do anything you say, but please, *please*, put her back on. Put her back on! Please?!"

Garrou laughed, a full-throated, exuberant laugh, the laugh of someone entertained by a comedy beyond all measure. He always found it delightful how quickly people's resolve cracked once they were threatened in just the right way. For some people it was to avoid pain, whereas for others it was to save a loved one from violence. Either way, eventually they always broke.

"No, sorry, Peter," he said. "I'm afraid young Miss Fontaine is indisposed at the moment and unable to come to the phone right now. You can talk to her later, I promise."

He took several long puffs from his cigar, then sipped his whiskey. "Now, like I was trying to say earlier, before I was so rudely interrupted: You will meet me tonight, in Baltimore, at three o'clock. Fort Armistead Park. You will call no one – and remember, Peter, I will know if you do, and you will not like what I do to Angie if you don't listen – and you will come alone, and unarmed. Again, I will know if you are not alone, or if you're armed, and if you choose unwisely, then Angie will suffer for your stupidity. Got it?"

"Yes," he said, sounding to Garrou like he was all but hyperventilating and choking on his tears. "Yes, yes, I under-stand. I'll be alone. I won't call anyone. I promise. Baltimore. Armistead Park. Three o'clock. Yes, I'll be there."

"Now there's a good boy," said Garrou. "Well... until I see you later tonight, have yourself a very pleasant evening. Good night, Peter."

Garrou could hear Peter screaming, "Wait-wait-wait..." as

he hung up the phone. He took several more luxurious puffs of his cigar, then blew out a long tendril of white smoke. "Well," he said to Felix, "that was entertaining, wasn't it?"

"And you believe he'll come, Mr. Garrou?" the demon asked.

"Oh, I know he'll come. He's right now terrified that I have her and what I might do to her. It's like mother always said, 'Never underestimate the persuasive power of violence.' She was certainly right about that."

"And you want me to stay out of sight tonight, correct?"

"Yes," Garrou said, to the demon who looked like a mafia thug when he wasn't chasing mice as a black cat. "You know what the plan is for tonight, what the Supreme Tribunal expects out of me. It'd be best if Peter and Angie thought I was alone. But stay close. You know... just in case."

"Yes, Mr. Garrou," said Felix. "Will do."

Garrou finished his drink and continued to smoke his cigar, thinking about what an enjoyable day it had been. He smiled as he imagined what the coming night would be like.

CHAPTER TWENTY

1

Peter crept his car up the long driveway as he approached the dark parking lot at Fort Armistead Park. The mist blowing in from the Patapsco River seemed to smother the feeble light provided by the few working lamps. As he did, Peter pivoted his head all around as if it were on ball bearings, watching for any sign of Garrou. He saw nothing as he inched the car into a parking space.

He sat, quivering, and feeling like he might vomit. Peter closed his eyes and breathed in once, held it a moment, then let it out, still feeling his throat tightening in dread anxiety. He got out of the Avalon and shone his flashlight into a thick tangle of trees, spotting a small path disappearing into the darkness of the woods. Peter shone his flashlight left and right, then turned around to look at the few cars parked by the river as they became more indistinct in the thickening fog. His entire body tingled, and his legs felt heavy as he delayed going into the black thicket ahead.

Peter sighed and whispered, "For Angie," then began carefully making his way to the woods.

He walked as if tracking game during a hunt, moving slowly, making his footfalls as quiet as possible. Despite his efforts at stealth, however, Peter's rapid, heavy breathing sounded like blaring music to him, as did his frequent involuntary swallows as his mouth turned to desert. Between his gulping breaths and the thrumming in his ears from his pulse, Peter could hear very little, and continued to shine the flashlight into the inky blackness of the woods around him and back along the trail he'd come. Peter felt like he was being watched the whole time.

"What the fuck?" he murmured when, after an eternity creeping through the woods, he came to what looked like a lost ruin from some long-forgotten civilization. To his left ran a narrow trail along the edge of the woods, while before him stone steps, overgrown with a thick tangle of weeds, were cut into a concrete structure, and beckoned him upward to another level. Peter shone the flashlight down the trail but could see nothing more than a few steps as the growing fog diffused the light. He then turned the light up the steps, then again along the path. Steeling himself, he cautiously ascended the steps.

When he reached the top, Peter could see an area of cracked and crumbling concrete through the mist. For a moment, he thought it was another parking lot until he noticed it was surrounded by the thicket of trees and was covered everywhere in a wild display of graffiti. As he shone his flashlight further along the stony area, he could make out what appeared to be a large, squat building through the haze.

"Garrou?" Peter whispered as he inched forward, the mists seeming to swallow his words just as it did the illumination from his flashlight. "Garrou? Where are you?" He heard nothing but the occasional sound of traffic passing by on the Francis Scott Key Bridge.

Peter made his way towards what he thought was a building, only to find it was a massive concrete wall that ran the length of the stone area. On it was even more graffiti, a crazy splash of colors, designs, and words. Before the wall was what looked like a small amphitheater cut into the stone, with several curved steps arrayed around a central, semicircular platform. Looking down, he could see weeds and small trees growing wildly through the many cracks in the crumbled concrete.

"Garrou?!" he said again but heard nothing. Peter inched his way along the wall, which disappeared into the mist, passing several more of those apparent amphitheaters and a few covered areas formed by concrete platforms stretching out from the top of the wall. Everything was covered in a blaze of graffiti, some just goofy pictures, some gang tags, and others, strange symbols he'd never seen before. He eventually reached the end of the wall and the stony area, seeing nothing but woods beyond.

Confused, Peter decided to go back to the small path at the steps. As he descended the stairs, careful not to slip on the slick stone, he shone the flashlight on the path before him. There he saw something he hadn't before, a large, bright red arrow painted on the trail that pointed down the path.

Peter scrambled down the remaining steps to reach the narrow footpath, then stood above the arrow and shone the light on it. The paint looked fresh like it had recently been put there for his benefit. Unable to pierce the fog with his light, Peter went forward, keeping an eye out for any additional signs.

He walked forward perhaps twenty feet, and found another red arrow, then a third after an additional twenty feet. Growing excited, Peter strode down the path to find the next arrow and saw that it turned to his right. He shone his light in that direction to discover another small set of steps going towards a curved and cobweb-infested archway, one that led under the great concrete area up above. The archway to the underground catacombs was even more covered in a bizarre splattering of graffiti than the area above. As Peter shone his light along the arched doorway, he saw over it was painted *HERE SHE IS!* in giant red letters, the paint dripping down the wall in long tendrils.

Peter, swallowing hard as his heart pounded in his chest, plunged ahead into the narrow underground corridor. As he did, the damp stench of rotting leaves and mud and other foul odors hit him hard in the face. Somewhere further into the bowels of the subterranean space, he could hear water trickling, echoing in the dark. Peter could see the ground was strewn with garbage everywhere, soda cans and plastic cups, empty packs of cigarettes, and even tattered pieces of clothing and shoes. Shining his flashlight down on the filthy ground before him, he also now saw used condoms and hypodermic needles scattered about.

Grimacing, Peter walked further into the darkness, sweeping his flashlight all around, illuminating one small circle at a time. The bizarre graffiti continued all along the walls up to the ceiling, which he saw was crumbling and covered in little pale bugs that scurried away when the light shone on them. As he reached the intersection into a larger tunnel, there was another red arrow pointing to his left. Above it was written *YOU'RE GETTING WARMER!*

Peter walked along the tunnel, careful not to slip onto the grimy floor. The echoing sounds of his own footfalls convinced Peter there was someone else in the corridor with him, so he would stop and pivot backward every few steps to shine the flashlight behind him. After what felt like years going down this tunnel, it turned to the right, at the end of which was a doorway

leading to a vast, empty hall. Above the door was painted
GETTING EVEN WARMER! Peter walked in, seeing nothing
but still more filth and graffiti, save for another doorway in the
far corner. Painted above it was three large arrows, dripping
red.

Peter crept through the doorway, seeing a set of steps that
led to a lower level. He slowly went down them, the garbage
and gang tags following along. This led to a short corridor,
which connected to a small room with another doorway in the
corner like in the hall above. *YOU FOUND HER!* was written
above it in large letters, with red, dripping arrows painted all
around the door. Next to it was painted a large smiley face.

His heart racing so hard Peter thought he might die, his
body shaking, his breath coming in ragged gulps, he slowly
peered into the doorway, dreading what he might see. All he
saw, however, was another set of stairs leading deeper into the
ground. At the bottom, Peter could see a gentle orange illuminating the dark and thought he could hear quiet groans coming
from below.

As Peter descended this second set of steps, he was
surprised to see the graffiti and garbage had stopped. Though
the concrete was tattered and worn, with cracks all along the
walls and chunks missing, this lower area looked almost clean
in comparison to that above. It also smelled pleasant, something
like burnt spices.

At the bottom, Peter saw to his left a long corridor that
went on into the distance, with a room about twenty feet down
from where he stood. The soft glow was coming from there, and
it was obvious he'd arrived where Garrou had been leading
him.

Equal parts eager and terrified, Peter jogged to the room,
only to find his way barred by a large metal gate, locked, and
chained closed. In the large room beyond, he saw it was filled

with dozens of standing candelabras with so many burning candles the space was oppressively warm and humid. The candles surrounded a giant slab of concrete the size of a car that lay in the center of the room. Dangling above this slab, standing on just her toes, Peter saw Angie, her handcuffed wrists high above her, locked in chains hanging from the arched ceiling, her head slumped forward as she moaned softly.

"Angie!" he screamed, reaching through the bars of the gate. "*Angie!! ANGIEEEEE!!!*"

Angie's head lifted at the sound of his voice. "Peter!" she groaned, her eyes wide open and wild, her skin slicked with sweat. She then began to thrash and yank on the chain as she screamed, "Help me, Peter! Please, get me out of here!!"

In a panic, Peter began pulling on the thick metal bars of the gate, which did nothing but make a loud rattling noise. He was looking around to find some other way to get to Angie when he heard Garrou's voice, soft and menacing, speaking in the darkness beyond the ring of candles.

2

"Oh, come now, kids," he said, stepping into the ring of flickering orange light cast by the many candles. As he did, Angie's eyes grew wide, and her body tensed. "You're not leaving yet, are you? We haven't even had time to chat. That's the whole reason I brought you here."

"Garrou, you sick fucker!" Peter yelled, gripping the cold metal bars of the gate like it was the congressman's throat he was crushing. "Let her go! Let her go right now! You've had your little game. Now let her the fuck go!"

"Game?!" he said, chuckling and jabbing his finger at Peter

as he spoke. "Does this look like a game to you?! Oh no, this is no game, Peter. This is deadly serious business, and you're messing with the wrong people."

"Okay, okay!" Peter said, his emotions crumbling as tears of frustration, anger, and fear welled in his eyes. "You win, Garrou. You win. You win, okay? Just please don't hurt her. We get your message."

Garrou tipped his head to one side. "Oh? And what message is that, Peter? What message is it you think I'm sending here?"

"You want us to leave you and your family alone. To stop looking into your past and not research anything about you. Okay, I got it. We'll back off."

Garrou sighed, then pinched his nose between his eyes. "It must be exhausting being wrong all the time, Peter. Seriously, how can you even stand being so stupid?"

"Then what?!" Angie screamed. "WHAT?! What do you want?! Why are you doing this to us?!"

"Ahhhhhh..." Garrou said, his index finger up. "Now that's the question, isn't it? Why am I doing this? Why have I gone through all the trouble of bringing you both here? It's certainly not to play some game like a child. Is it?"

"Why?!" Peter yelled. "Why are you doing this?! What do you want?!"

Garrou smiled, that same broad, cruel smile Peter saw while they spoke earlier in the Library of Congress. "For revenge, Peter. Revenge, cold and merciless, hateful and hard. I want you to suffer, just as I have suffered."

"I don't..." Angie said, her eyes darting between Garrou and Peter, "I don't understand. Peter, what's he talking about? Revenge for what?!"

Garrou's smile grew as a look of dawning awareness spread across Peter's blanched face.

"You see," said Garrou, turning towards Angie. "Peter was quite right, that night he told you his suspicions about me. When he told you he thought I was a werewolf? He's right. I am indeed."

Angie stared at Garrou for a moment, then said, "What? What are you talking about? That's insane."

"I know, isn't it?!" he said with a shrug, turning now towards Peter and slowly approaching him as he slipped off his eyepatch and stuffed glove. "But it's true, nonetheless. What that also means is that *you* did this to my hand, and this to my face. I am destined to be president, Peter, and to do great things for my people. You've almost ruined that for me. That's an insult that cannot go unpunished. I mean... where would my pride be if I allowed that to happen without retaliation?"

"You attacked Sim!" Peter bellowed. "You were about to kill me! What was I supposed to do?!"

"You are all prey," said Garrou, "and I'm the predator. You were supposed to die, Peter. That's what. Die."

"What the fuck are you even talking about?!" Angie shrieked. "You're insane, Garrou! You're totally fucking insane!!"

Garrou laughed, turning to stride back towards Angie. "Maybe. Quite possibly so. Perhaps even likely. That doesn't mean I'm wrong. Luckily for you, I was planning on giving a demonstration anyway..."

Oh, God, no! Please, no! No, no, no!!

Peter watched as Garrou murmured a few words, then immediately clenched, and doubled over as if he'd been punched in the gut. His face turned red like he was bearing down with all his force as his eyes clamped shut and his jaws squeezed tight. Garrou fell to his knees as he began to convulse, frothing drool streaming from his mouth and emitting a pained groan.

"Peter?!" Angie screamed, trying to back away from this spectacle but unable to. "Peter?!! What the fuck is going on?!!!"

Garrou's face was a twisted mask of agony when the groan turned into an anguished scream as a series of popping and snapping sounds, like a string of firecrackers going off, came from his body. Garrou flailed as his bones were fractured, his arms and legs breaking into unnatural shapes as they were stretched and lengthened, rippling layers of muscle added to his frame, and as his chest was expanded to twice its normal size. Garrou's transformed body burst out of the clothes he'd been wearing, shredding them to pieces.

Angie now joined her own shrieks of primal terror to Garrou's as his tortured screams grew in volume and intensity, the human tones becoming replaced with an inhuman howl. Peter, horrified yet mesmerized, stood and watched with dumbstruck amazement. He watched as Garrou's hands grew in size and length and how the fingertips ossified as they curved into long, deadly claws. He saw Garrou's body grow a covering of thick fur, his face shatter and reform as the human visage was replaced by that of a wolf, and he saw his teeth grow into a row of long, sharp fangs.

Finally, after about a minute, Garrou – or what used to be Garrou – knelt on the ground as the popping stopped and the shaking subsided. Angie still screamed, mad with horror as she tried to pull the chain out of the ceiling, the hall now filled with the stink of rotten eggs. Slowly, the wolf-Garrou stood, and Peter again felt all the mad terror and dread as he had that night in Thompson's cabin when he'd first seen the beast.

Garrou opened his eyes, the dead one a milky white, the other glowing red. He panted still, each breath tinged with the sound of a deep, menacing rumble, and stared hatefully at Peter as he approached him at the gate.

"Revenge," Garrou said in an inhuman voice, the word an enunciated growl, gravely and thick.

"PETER?!" Angie screamed. "PETER?!! *WHAT'S HAPPENING?!!!*"

"Take me!" Peter yelled, reaching out uselessly for Angie. "Garrou, take me! I did this to you, it's my fault! Take me!! Just leave her alone!! *PLEASE!!*"

Garrou growled at Peter, a sound that might have been a laugh. "Take you?" he said. "As if *you* get to decide who I take and when. I will take you, and I will take her, and your families, and your friends, too, when I want. You know what I can do... what I will do... and I'll do it when I want to. I could kill her now, right here before your eyes, you know I could. But what long torment and torture is that? A moment of sadness for you, and then... healing? Oh, no, I don't think you get off that easily. First, I want you to suffer. I want you to fear the night, to dread death at every moment, Peter. You will go insane with horror, and I will laugh. I want you to hear about your friends and family being killed, dying horribly, never knowing when the next one is going to happen, and for you to know it was me. That it's me having my revenge."

Peter stared up at the creature, looking into its glowing iris with loathing and hatred.

"And the best thing of all," growled Garrou, "is that there's nothing you can do about it. You can't call the police or go to the press. File an ethics complaint with the House leadership? No one would ever believe you. This is a secret you'll keep as your friends and family are dying all around you, and you will know I'm working my way closer to you. Then, when you're mad with torture, I'll kill her, and you still won't be able to stop me. It'll come down to you alone, and I will let you suffer long before ending it. And I will, Peter, I will. I will kill you when I choose. Because you're the prey, and I'm the predator. It's the natural order of things."

Peter stared speechless at the Garrou beast, wordless because he knew Garrou was right. There was nothing either Peter or Angie could do about what he planned, and there was no way to stop it. He couldn't report this to the police since they'd never believe a sitting congressman – and one from a distinguished family, no less – was a werewolf, and neither would the media, because no one believed in werewolves anymore.

Peter could have a video recording of Garrou transforming and people would say it was a hoax, that it was just special effects and editing. The thought of a werewolf stalking the land was too horrifying to accept. He knew people would cling to the perception of the safe world they'd created in their minds rather than accept terrifying realities.

"However," Garrou rumbled, reaching out his damaged hand to gently massage Angie's face with his talon as she cowered away in fear, "that doesn't mean you get away without some reminder of tonight."

"NO, GARROU, NOOOOOO!!" Peter screamed as he pulled on the metal bars. *"LEAVE HER ALONE!! NOOOOOOOOOOOOOOOO!!!"*

Garrou slid the tip of his pinky claw into the flesh of her soft cheek, Angie screaming as a rivulet of blood poured down her face. Then, he slowly pulled his claw downwards, slicing her cheek as he turned to look at Peter, his wolf mouth twisted into a silent snarl. When he was done, Garrou stepped back and regarded his work as Angie whimpered in pain, her cheek and neck covered in blood.

"Ahhhhhhh... now, she's beautiful. Consider that a preview of how this ends, kids. Key's on the slab." Garrou then strode away, getting down on all fours to fit through a doorway in the rear of the room.

Peter watched as Garrou's hulking form disappeared into the darkness beyond the door, then turned to Angie. Her head was slumped forward again as she wept, her body shaking in pain and exhaustion. "Angie! Angie!! I'm coming, babe, I'm coming! I'll find my way to you, I promise!!"

Peter grabbed the flashlight again and ran down the hallway to the first intersection, intent on working his way to Angie as fast as he could. Before he reached it, though, he stopped hard, throwing his arms out to push against the narrow corridor walls. He stood there, listening to his heart pound and the sound of her crying behind him, as his mind raced with fearful possibilities.

What if Garrou's waiting for me just ahead?! he thought. *What if this was all just a set up to get me running right into him so he could kill me here? Maybe this was all just a joke for him. Maybe he's waiting for me right around this corner!!* Peter felt like he could sense Garrou's presence, that he could smell the odor of sulfur wafting from the tunnel beyond as images of being torn to shreds flashed through his mind.

Fighting his urge to get to Angie as fast as he could, his body shaking, his breath coming in jagged gulps, Peter peered around the corner but saw only a short corridor leading forward. He crept down the tunnel, moving his flashlight all around and sweeping it behind him, feeling that he was being watched and followed as he had above. The tunnel led to nothing but a small, empty room with no doors in it. He returned to the long corridor.

As he made his way along its length, inching forward, his heart racing, Peter could just make out the sound of Angie crying, and considered returning to the locked gate to comfort her. Deciding the best comfort would be to free her from this nightmarish place, he pressed on instead, taking the next corridor to his left that presented itself.

With each tremulous step he took down this further long hall, the dim quiet of the underground passages pressed itself upon his ears, Angie's weeping long since lost. He timidly moved down this tunnel, glancing back and always feeling like someone was slipping up behind him, like a thousand red-glowing eyes were upon him. Peter came to another T-shaped intersection then turned to his left. After only about a dozen steps, he could faintly hear Angie's crying again echoing down the cracked walls coming from the hall ahead.

"Angie?!" he said, overwhelmed by the urge to run. "Angie! I'm coming, babe! I'm coming!!"

3

Unable to contain himself any longer, Peter discarded his fears and thoughts of bloody death, running down the hall as fast as he could. The tunnel ended with a sharp turn to the left, and as he approached, he could see the flickering glow of candles dancing on the damaged walls, coming from the room beyond.

"ANGIEEEEE!!" he yelled. "I'm coming, baby, hold on! I'm coming!!"

Peter reached the corner, and there he saw the arched, candle-lit room from behind.

"Angie!" he said, breathless as he clambered up the block of concrete. "I'm here now, baby, I'm here. We're gonna get you out of here."

"Peter..." Angie murmured. "I hurt. What... what happ... how is this... what's..."

He found the keys and unlocked the handcuffs, Angie

collapsing into his arms as soon as he did. Taking her wrists in his hands, Peter saw that they were chafed raw, bloody smears all around them. She could barely move her arms, and when – after Peter had hugged Angie, kissed her, and held her face in his hands as he looked into her eyes, asking her over and over if she was alright – they got down from the block to leave, she could only walk at a slow, painful shuffle. Peter navigated their way out of this underground maze with one hand holding the flashlight and the other wrapped around Angie, helping to support her weight.

It took the pair over an hour to work their way out. Peter got confused a few times making their way back to the surface, and Angie's every step was excruciating for her, especially the many stairs she had to walk, even with Peter helping to support her. When they finally made it back to their car, the fog was beginning to dissipate as the eastern sky was just getting touched with gentle brushstrokes of pink. Though eager to get out of this stony hell, they both stood there side by side for a while, overlooking the river, breathing deep the cool, early morning air.

They spoke not a word, but as they stood, the pair found each other's hand, their eyes meeting. Something irreversible had happened to their lives tonight in this subterranean nightmare, as if they'd passed through a door that had closed behind them forever. They both now knew their lives could never be the same again.

CHAPTER TWENTY-ONE

"Ahhhhhh... now, she's beautiful," growled Garrou, as the smell of Angie's blood lingered thick in his sensitive nostrils, driving him mad with murder lust. "Consider that a preview of how this ends, kids. Key's on the slab."

He strode away, fighting the raging beast inside him. It wanted nothing more than to pivot and shred Angie right in front of Peter's eyes, to taste her salty blood and to delight in her demolished remains. Since that would be a contravention of the plan the Supreme Tribunal forced him to accept and would displease the mages, he instead dropped to a crawl as he forced himself into the narrow corridor beyond, breaking the concrete and leaving a line of cracked walls behind him.

As Garrou pushed his way along the tunnel, thoughts of murderous destruction raced through his mind, drool flowing from his slavering jaws. He fought the Wolf for control, who ached to turn around and ambush Peter in the dark, to punish him for his insolence, to kill for the simple pleasure of it, to reduce his body to a choppy slush. Despite the painful desire to unleash violence, Garrou maintained control, whispering the words to turn back into his human form. As expected, it was taking longer than when he'd last transformed back.

He'd passed down the dark hall for about ten minutes when he heard Peter's echoing voice and the sound of running behind him.

"Angie?!" he yelled. "Angie! I'm coming, babe! I'm coming!!"

Garrou could smell his sweat, his fear, his fresh blood racing through his body, pumped by a pounding heart he could hear thumping in Peter's chest. He paused for a long, agonizing moment as he thought how he ached to slide his claws into that chest, spread the rib cage wide apart, then tear out that pounding heart. Garrou could see himself launching in face first, snapping his jaws madly, ripping and shredding his organs with his sharp teeth until Peter's blood was smeared all over his wolfen face.

No! No... must move!!

Garrou pushed himself forward, repeating the whispered words to change back into a human, but still to no avail. After a few additional minutes he found his escape route, a large shaft that led directly to the long wall on the surface. Garrou sunk his claws into the brick-lined shaft and began climbing his way upward through the darkness, his mind still screaming with the unsatisfied desire to kill. Upon reaching the top, Garrou leapt out – then froze, sniffing the air. The thick hairs on his back bristled and his heart raced as he detected the odor of fresh human blood nearby.

"Come on, Crash," he heard a whispered female voice say from one of the secluded areas below him, "I been turnin' tricks all night. I'm tired. I wanna go home."

Garrou was shrouded in mist and darkness, but he could see two forms sitting on the curved steps below, their backs to him. They talked, oblivious of the nightmares that lurked in the night around them.

"I been workin' all night too, Dee," said a gruff male voice, "but I wanna blowjob. Get your ass over here and suck me."

Garrou watched as the woman sighed then slid to her knees, the man twisting her long hair in his fist as he began to violently pump her mouth. As Garrou lowered himself from the wall and crept up on them in the foggy gloom of the night, crawling on all fours, he could hear the woman making wet, sloppy sounds in her throat, gagging and choking. Garrou could smell the change in their body chemistries, their hot fluids flowing. He could hear their hearts racing and feel their blood pumping. Their lust was palpable, though Garrou throbbed for a far different release.

"Damn, Crash," the woman said, as Garrou inched closer to them in the foggy black, "you trynna kill me with that fuckin' thing?"

"Shut up," the man said, pulling her head down to him again. "Suck it."

The woman went back to work, making a rhythmic *glurk! glurk! glurk!* sound in her throat as drool poured from Garrou's twitching mouth, his tongue lolling as he moved forward. He could almost taste their fresh, young bodies.

"What's that?" the woman said, her head suddenly popping up and looking around the man to where Garrou prowled just feet away. She couldn't see him in the misty dark and with the weeds that shrouded him.

"It ain't noth—"

"No, Crash," the woman whispered, pulling away from his grip and pivoting her head a degree to get a better view as she stood. "I think someone out there."

"What? What the fuck you talkin' 'bout?"

"I'm tellin' you," she said, her voice shaking, "there someone out there... there someone right—"

The woman stopped as her eyes grew wide and she drew in a breath to scream, though she never had the chance. Garrou leapt at her with a gigantic roar, smashing her to the ground as he sunk his claws into her shoulders and clamped his entire mouth down on her face. With a jerk, he bit the woman's head in two, her features obliterated and replaced by nothing but a slushy mash, painting the man red in her blood. Enraged by the release of such painful blood lust, Garrou initially paid the man no heed as he shrieked, kicking his legs to scramble away from him. Instead, he shredded the woman's body in a sudden frenzy, reducing her to pulp in less than a minute.

"HOLY FUCK!!" the man, covered in blood, screamed in horror as his eyes bulged out of his head, a grimace of shocked disgust carved on his face. He pushed with his legs hard to get away as he clumsily tried to stand, pulling his pants up as he did. *"DEEEEEEE!! HOLY FUCK!! WHAT THE FUCK?! MY GOD, DEEEEEEE!! HOLY FUCK!!"*

Garrou, covered in gore and shreds of the woman's torn flesh, turned on the man, growling lowly as he did. The man scampered his way to the other side of the curved steps, using them to get to his feet as Garrou approached, his taloned paw back, poised ready to strike downward. The man screamed in terror, watching the slow approach of his own death with wide-open eyes of horror – then looked down to his chest and seemed to remember he was armed.

"FUCKING DIE!!" the man howled as he pulled a semiautomatic handgun out of his chest holster, and, still screaming, squeezed the trigger until the gun was empty, the chamber locked open. Each round hit Garrou with a dull thud, then bounced off his body and skittered away with a metallic clink, as if they were no more dangerous than rubber balls. His low

growl erupted into full-throated laughter as he swept down with his upraised claws at the still-shrieking man, opening his belly with one quick slice of his talons. Still maddened with the joy of destruction, he brutalized the man's body just as he had the woman's.

Garrou paused to take in the beauty of his work, then threw his head back and let out a long, triumphant howl.

"Mr. Garrou?" a voice said behind him.

Garrou pivoted, bloody claws at the ready to strike whoever had snuck up on him. He stopped, though, when he recognized the leather-blazer-clad figure of Felix standing there, from whom he could neither hear a heart beating nor smell blood. He could detect nothing but the ubiquitous scent of burnt spices as the demon's pale gray eyes peered at him through the dark.

"Felix," he growled.

"Yes, Mr. Garrou. Are you ready to go back home now?"

"Yes..." he said, pacing like a caged animal, finding it harder to focus on his thoughts as the urge to kill lingered in his mind, "but not... yet. Not till... I turn... having trouble... doing."

"Mmm..." Felix said, nodding his head. "The gift is taking hold more and more, Mr. Garrou. You should focus, though. The sun will start to rise soon."

Garrou tried to relax, tried to direct his mind towards a picture of himself in human form as he repeated the words, but every time he tried that was interrupted by charnel house images, shredded chunks of human flesh tossed about as if in a slaughterhouse, pools of slick red blood everywhere, the delicious coppery odor filling his nose. He whispered as he tried to see himself in a tailored suit walking up the steps to the Capitol; instead, he'd catch images of limbs lying all around him as he licked blood off his claws, organs flung around haphazardly, jawless human heads lined up in a row as if they were trophy pieces.

Finally, after a quarter-hour of trying, the sudden agony in his gut told Garrou that the magic had worked. He transformed back into a human in the same excruciating, bone-breaking torture by which he'd become the Wolf earlier. Afterward, Garrou knelt naked in the cool morning air, panting, and shaking as the pain melted from his body.

"Help me," he said to Felix, who grasped his extended arm as Garrou stood.

"You did well, Mr. Garrou," Felix said. "The Supreme Tribunal will have positive things to report to the High Council. Killing these two was a good touch."

"I couldn't have stopped it by then even if I wanted to. The Wolf was too hungry for blood. I had to kill them."

"Yes," said Felix. "Shall we go now, Mr. Garrou? They're working their way up through the tunnels."

Garrou nodded, feeling crushing exhaustion like he'd never experienced before. "Yeah. Let's go back to Crisfield. I need to sleep and it's quieter there than in the city."

"Of course," Felix said, then walked the few steps to the looming concrete wall behind them. Felix traced his finger along the surface of it as hot, flashing sparks flew from his touch as if he were welding metal. When done, he'd drawn a door-sized rectangle on the wall, its edges burned black and steaming. He then tapped on it three times and drew a complicated symbol across the concrete, the stone swinging open on unseen hinges when Felix beckoned the door towards him. It showed the interior of Garrou's Crisfield home as if viewed from the threshold of the front door.

"Welcome home, Mr. Garrou," said Felix.

CHAPTER TWENTY-TWO

"I thought he was going to kill me," Angie whispered as she wept into Peter's shoulder. The pair held each other in a seated hug on the middle of their bed, as she again broke down and cried from the terror she'd survived a few hours earlier. Peter could feel her trembling in his arms as if she were chilled. "I really thought that was it. That was how I was going to die. I was so fucking scared."

Peter knew there was little he could say to calm her, having so recently suffered through a similar horror. Angie had shown him then the most important thing wasn't words but rather actions, by being there when needed and soothing for as long as he required it. She'd been there for him after the cabin attack, had held him time and again after his many nightmares, and had been his only source of strength and support during those many long days. He was determined to be her rock now.

"I know, babe, I know," Peter said, kissing her gently on top of her head as he wrapped his arms around Angie's shivering body. "It's okay, now. You're safe, babe. It's all over. You're home."

"Home?!" Angie said, lifting her head to look at Peter, her wide-open eyes wild, her face anguished. "He took me *here*. Whoever that man was, he took me, right here, out of my own home! How am I ever going to feel safe at home again?!"

In the hours since they'd left Baltimore in the early morning light, Angie had told Peter about what happened, piece by fragmented piece. She often had to pause as she spoke in little machine-gun bursts of story snippets, weeping and taking deep breaths to calm herself. The fear of what had happened was still far too fresh in her mind.

Angie had explained to Peter she'd returned to their place in the midafternoon. The door had been locked, nothing was out of place, and she could neither see nor hear anyone else in the small apartment. She'd put her purse and keys on the counter just like always, hung up her jacket in the closet, then turned to kick off her shoes.

She'd then heard a rustling noise behind her and had turned to see a squat, brutish-looking man in a black leather coat standing there, the closet door open behind him. She hadn't even had time to scream before his hand clamped on her neck like a vice, and though Angie had briefly struggled against his iron grip, she said she'd passed out within seconds. She awoke sometime later, gagged, tied to a chair, sitting in Garrou's house in Washington.

When they'd left the park, Peter had wanted to take Angie to the hospital, but she'd adamantly refused. They'd instead driven straight home to Washington. Peter had helped her up the two flights of stairs to their place, then Angie had begun to tremble again when she walked into their apartment and saw the closet. He'd wrapped her in his lanky arms and stroked her hair as he held her close, reminding her that she was safe. Before long, Angie had calmed enough for Peter to work on her sliced cheek.

The cut was as sharp and clean as if she'd been slashed by a knife, and, though not deep, Peter again had said she'd be better off going to the hospital to get stitches. She had still refused, and as he cleaned her wound and dabbed it with hydrogen peroxide-soaked cotton balls, Peter could see Angie's eyes staring unfocused on some far distant point. He knew well what that stare meant.

Now, as the late-morning sun streamed in through their bedroom window, she sat on their bed, again wrapped in his arms, with a large gauze bandage taped to her cheek. It had already become tinged with spots of dull red as blood seeped through the gossamer cloth.

"Oh, my God," she groaned as she wept harder, moaning in fear and dread. "That thug could have killed me right here, or Garrou could have killed me. He could have torn me to pieces like he did those other people, he could have—"

"Shhhhh..." Peter whispered, kissing the top of her head again. "Don't think about that, babe. Please believe me, that's not a route you want to go down. All that matters is that he didn't. He *didn't*."

Angie continued to sob into Peter's shoulder as he stroked her hair and gently rocked her. In time, her cries became quieter, replaced by sniffles which were themselves soon replaced by deep, rhythmic breathing. He looked at her and realized she'd fallen asleep once her weeping had stopped. Peter continued to hold Angie in his arms and look at her while she slept, still stroking her hair, and struck once again with how much he loved this beautiful woman.

Peter kissed Angie on the forehead as he pivoted to lay her down, then positioned himself to lie next to her with one arm draped around her, holding her close even as she slept. He awoke with a start several hours later, their room dark in the late afternoon shade, Angie still deep asleep next to him.

Careful not to disturb her, Peter got out of bed and went out to their living room area. As he passed the closet, he glanced down at her ruined glasses lying there, crumpled and smashed. He picked them up, inspecting them carefully for a moment as he puzzled over this strange abduction, then opened the closet door. Like the rest of their apartment, it was small and cramped, and was packed full of clothes hanging with various shoes scattered about the floor. The space inside was only a bit larger than the width of the door itself.

How the fuck did this guy hide in here? Peter thought as he slid some clothes along the pole from which they hung. *And how didn't she see him? Why does Garrou have gangsters working for him?!*

Peter stepped into the closet, awkwardly positioning himself in between the jackets and standing on the shoes. To make himself fit, though, Peter had to crouch hunched forward and couldn't close the door without hitting himself in the head. Even if he were to squeeze into the closet, it'd be obvious he was there as soon as someone opened it. Peter assumed he'd most likely pop out like a jack-in-the-box as soon as the door would open, so there was no hope for stealth inside it.

There's no way anyone could hide in here, not without being seen. What the fuck?!

Peter scratched his head as he stood arms akimbo, still staring at the small closet. He then went to sit and think, grabbing himself an orange-flavored lollipop from a bowl on the small counter after first picking out several chocolate ones to throw away. Peter was still lost in thought an hour later when he heard Angie limping down the hallway to where he sat. Bleary-eyed and yawning, she made her way to him, then sat on his lap and put her arm around his shoulders.

"How'd you sleep?" Peter asked. "How are you feeling?"

Angie yawned, then laid her head on his. "I'm not so tired

now. I was exhausted. I guess I didn't really sleep since I got up yesterday."

"Yeah, I fell asleep, too. I was tapped."

"I bet you were," said Angie, lifting her head to look at Peter.

"Did you..." Peter said haltingly, "did you... have any... dreams?"

"You mean nightmares?" she asked then thought for a moment. "No, I didn't. Thank God for that."

Peter let out his breath, not even realizing he'd been holding it the entire time Angie thought. "Yeah, that's definitely a good thing."

"My muscles still hurt like a bitch, though," said Angie. "First, I was tied up really tight, then I was hanging like that for hours. I ache all over. I can barely move. My face is throbbing, too."

"I bet it is," Peter said, seeing more drops of blood had seeped through the gauze while she slept, each an ugly brownish color. "Let me see your bandage. Mmhmmm... okay, we need to change this. Go sit at the counter and I'll get the things we need."

Peter gathered up the gauze, tape, anti-infection cream, and other supplies he needed from the bathroom while Angie made her way over to one of their stools at the counter. She winced as he removed the tape, her cheek around the slice a puffy, angry red. "I wish to hell you'd let me bring you to the hospital so a doctor could take a look at this. I still think you'd be better with a few stitches."

"No," Angie said. "I'm *not* going to the hospital."

"Babe, why?" Peter asked. "I don't understand why you won't go."

"Because," she said with a sigh, "I fucking refuse to explain how I got this cut. I don't want to think about how I got it. I don't want to talk about how I got it. It looks like I got cut by a knife, you said so yourself. What am I supposed to say? I was in a knife fight? I can't really say I got scratched by the cat, can I?"

"No," Peter agreed. "Not unless it was a knife-wielding cat."

"Right," Angie said. "So, the doctors would just keep asking and asking and asking me fucking questions about how I got the damn thing. I'm in no mood for that. The more I talk about how I got it the more I'll have to think about it, and I'm not ready for that."

"Okay," said Peter, "I can respect that. But you know you will have to talk about it. In time. You taught me that much."

"I know. And I will... just not today, okay?"

Peter nodded. "It will scar up and be pretty obvious. I'm not trying to change your mind; I'm just letting you know what to expect."

Angie shrugged her shoulders. "Well, then I guess I'll just be one scarred, badass bitch."

Peter chuckled and smiled. *Fuck! I love this badass bitch!!*

The pair sat in silence as Peter ministered to Angie's cheek, until she said, "He's right, you know."

Peter paused, his hands stopped midair, still looking at her cheek. "Yeah," he whispered. "I know. I've been thinking about that."

"I feel like everything has changed now," Angie said softly. "Like, how do we go back to working for Congress? What the fuck difference does any of that shit make when there are fucking werewolves in the world? Do you know what I mean?"

"Yeah," he said. "I know exactly what you mean."

"He's right," Angie said again. "We can't stop him. We can't report him. Can't go to the police or the media or the House. There's nothing we can do, and he will kill our friends, and our families, and eventually us, and there's nothing, not one *fucking* thing, we can do to stop him."

Peter stopped working on her cheek and sat on the other stool at the counter. "Well, we can't just passively live in fear, constantly looking over our shoulders, just waiting to die, can we? I don't want to live in some bunker, paranoid and terrified, just waiting for something to attack me. I refuse to live like that. That's no life at all."

"That sounds great, Peter, but what the fuck are we supposed to do?" Angie said, tears welling up in her eyes. "He's rich, powerful, a congressman, and a fucking *werewolf*. There's nothing we can do to stop him." She then slammed her fist down on the counter, gnawing her bottom lip. "This whole thing makes me so fucking angry! I could kill him right now, I'm so angry. But I don't know what to do, so then I just get fucking angrier!"

"Well," Peter said as he placed a fresh gauze over her wound, "I've been thinking about that. We need to learn about... about whatever world it is where werewolves come from. We need info."

Angie sighed. "We spent a fucking month at the Library of—"

"No," Peter said, holding up his hand, "no, I'm not talking about anything like that. It's like... remember how you were saying you had this weird feeling that there's another world, almost superimposed over ours? A weird world where strange things exist, like the thing Nate said he saw and the thing I saw? Remember?"

"Yeah. Of course I do."

"So," he said as he put the last piece of tape in place, "if these things come from some secret world that hides inside of the normal one, then there's got to be people who know about it, right? There can't be monsters and werewolves and God only knows what else running around without some people knowing about it. And if they know about it, then maybe we can learn about it from them. Maybe learn how to fight back."

Angie nodded, then said, "Okay, fine. But who are these people, and where do we find them? It's not like they're going to be in the yellow pages or anything."

Peter scratched his chin as he thought, then said, "When I was growing up, my Grandaddy would always tell stories of cunning folk that live in the woods of West Virginia, way up in the mountains. He would tell me stories of how his grand-mother would go to this, like, community of cunning folk hidden away in the hills near... where was that?... damn it, I don't remember. Wherever it was, he said she'd go there to get amulets to protect against Snarly Yaw and all the rest of those things, to get herbal medicines, and sometimes to learn about the future. I heard it was said they had some kind of mystical knowledge of a secret, hidden world."

"Soooo... like a bunch of rural witches?" Angie said.

"I guess," said Peter, getting up to make coffee, "maybe, but Grandaddy never said his grandmother was afraid of these people. He said they were good and always there to help whoever needed it."

"But what makes you think they could help us with this? Assuming they even exist, that is."

Peter stared at her a moment. "What do you mean?"

"Well, Peter," said Angie, "people tell all kinds of stories, and this one comes second-hand from an old lady who grew up in rural West Virginia. Not to be rude, but couldn't these cunning folks just be uneducated country people's rural myths?"

"Up until yesterday you thought werewolves were just myths, too."

Angie flinched, then sighed heavily. "Okay, you're right. I

need to remember we live in a new world now. So, anyway... what makes you think they'd be able to help?"

"Well, I'm thinking if they made talismans for my great-great-grandmother to protect herself back in the late 1800s, then they know something about this other world... hey, where's the spoon thingy?"

Angie tipped her head to one side. "The spoon thingy?"

"Yeah, you know, the coffee scoop."

"Oh, umm... look in the other coffee container."

"Got it," he said, holding it up like a small treasure, then put a few scoops of beans into their grinder. "So, I'm thinking we go find these people."

Angie thought for a moment. "Do you remember anything about them, like what the community is called? What the woman's name is? Where they're located? Anything for us to go on? Anything at all?"

Peter paused, then said, "No, other than she was always called 'Grandmother.' But other than that, no, I can't remember anything else."

"That's not much to go on."

"No," he sighed. "It's not much to go on at all."

They sat thinking silently for a time as Peter poured hot water over the grounds, then pushed down the plunger on the French press, their apartment filling with the odor of fresh, strong coffee. He poured two cups, bringing both to the counter where they sat.

"Cheers," he said. "You know... Mom and Dad have been dying to meet you. I know, after what happened last night, there's no way I can just go back to work on Monday like nothing happened. Why don't we take some time off work? We can go spend a little time with Mom and Dad for a bit, and while we're there, I can talk to Dad about the stories Grandaddy always told. I know he told them to my dad, too.

Oh, and maybe Mom heard some things, too. She also grew up in West Virginia. What do you think?"

Angie sipped her coffee. "Mmm... oh, that's so good. Yeah, I think that's a great idea. You're right, there's no way I can go back to work on Monday. Taking some time off would be a good idea. We struck out at the library, so why not try these cunning folks?"

Peter kissed her gently. "I'm so glad you agree."

"Speaking of parents," Angie said, "my parents have also been nagging me to meet you. After this is all over, how about we go to Alabama, so you can meet them and Nate, see where I grew up, all that? Spend a little time down there getting to know them. How would that be?"

"That sounds awesome," he said, then pressed on his belly as his stomach growled. "Damn, I'm starving. I haven't eaten... shit, since yesterday. No wonder I'm starving. You hungry?"

"I'm so hungry I could eat your face," Angie said.

"Please don't do that," he said. "I'm very fond of my mug."

Angie tried to smile, which would have been the first one Peter had seen from her since the horror in Baltimore but couldn't because of the slash on her cheek.

Grimacing from the pain, she said, "Well, I'm pretty fond of your face, too. But I don't even feel like cooking tonight. How about we just order pizza? Unless you want to cook something."

"No, I really don't... I'm on the pizza," he said, grabbing the phone. As he dialed the number and submitted their order, Peter had a brief calming sense of the normal, the mundane, the predictable. The small, daily interactions that made up a typical life, the kind of life he'd had up to that point. But he knew it was nothing other than a short pause in a devastating storm, nothing but a soothing mirage.

CHAPTER TWENTY-THREE

That night, Angie had her first nightmare.

She awoke breathless, eyes wide open in blind terror, choking on a silent scream as she clutched the sheets. As the vague image of long, white teeth and the echo of snapping jaws mixing with her own shrieks faded from her mind, Angie let out a long breath and relaxed, melting into the mattress. She lay there as her racing heart slowed, taking several long, deep breaths to soothe herself further. As she did, Angie recalled one detail from her nightmare: Garrou had ripped open her belly to feast on her organs with cruel delight, laughing at her. Angie pressed her hand to her lower abdomen as the phantom pain of his dreamt attack faded to nothing.

Angie lay there for some time as she stared at the dark ceiling of their room, taking deep breaths, blowing them out in long strings, rubbing her belly. She felt too energized after waking so abruptly to sleep as her thoughts galloped from the events of the past day – *Was that just yesterday?! It feels like years ago!* – to the horror she felt as she watched Garrou change into the beast, to the implications of this new, dread knowledge, then back to reliving her horrific experiences.

How will I ever feel safe again? Angie wondered. *He could have killed me. It would have been so easy for him to use that claw, just that one claw, to slash my throat rather than my cheek. It would have been all over for me, then. And there would have been nothing I could have done to stop him, to get away from him! Nothing!!*

She stared at the ceiling, watching as the lights from passing traffic glided along it. That helpless, trapped feeling she'd felt while chained in the concrete hell with Garrou washed over her again, a dark sense of angst and dread. It took hold of her and seeped into her bones, to her very core. A single tear slid down her slashed cheek as the deepest meaning of her new knowledge struck her, making her feel numb and overwhelmed.

If werewolves exist... then what else is out there? What other monsters are out there, crawling about the world, looking to kill us? What other horrors are possible?! God! I can't stand this!

Angie realized with numb awareness there was an existential threat that now loomed over her, one that was inchoate, shrouded in mist, one she couldn't define and barely even conceive of. The knowledge of a world in which werewolves existed, a world hidden within and yet also entwined with her own mundane one, was too horrible for her. Angie peered into the inky blackness of this strange place, feeling as if she stood on a cliff overlooking a pool of impossible depths. What lurked just under the placid stillness of the surface, what terrors roiled just below the calm, was too horrifying to consider. Yet, despite the dismay Angie felt peering into its dark depth, she peered into it, nonetheless.

She felt powerless before this shadowy threat, though she knew every moment for the rest of her life it would hold a knife to her throat. The grinding sense of helplessness she felt as she lay in the dark of their bedroom, staring with sleepless eyes at the ceiling, was born from a maddening inability to do anything about this shrouded universe of evil. Angie felt Garrou, and this world he represented, was too large, too strong, too powerful. To take up arms against it was terrible to contemplate; doing nothing and waiting to die, however, was perhaps even more terrifying.

She continued to press her abdomen as images of the dream returned to her. As she did, Angie thought of the dull fear that had hidden deep within her for years. The nightmare creature that had long prowled in her mind climbed out from the dark depth of her psyche when Garrou had transformed before her, and beholding it was even more terrifying than any imagining could be. Angie's fear of the shadowy unknown, of a nightmare monstrosity creeping in the darkness, had been set free by Garrou and the secret world he represented.

Though she'd always been able to force that vague angst back down into the well, this time it'd proven impossible to halt. The black dread in her heart had come to pass and she found the truth of this awareness overwhelming.

Angie felt powerless and weak as she imagined herself standing on a cliff, peering into the depth of that shadowy pool. She struggled as she wondered if it would be better to stand frozen with fear on the precipice, content to live in blissful ignorance until she died, or to face the anguish about what lurks below and dive in to confront it, to do battle with it.

Everything I've ever wanted, ever planned, is worthless now, isn't it? Angie asked herself as she took her hand from her belly and gently laid it on Peter, who lay on his side turned away from her, deep asleep. *How can't it be? How can I lead a normal life, now that I know this... this... this nightmare place truly exists? It's fruitless. Hell, it's almost vain to even consider it.*

Angie tried to imagine herself getting up every day and going to work like nothing was wrong, pretending there wasn't a gloom hanging over her life like a black, oily pall. She envisioned herself getting married, having kids, paying bills, living an average American life. She pictured daily life with Peter, making dinners together, going on vacations, having birthday parties for their kids, sometimes fighting then having make-up sex afterward. Angie imagined getting elected to Congress, serving as long as she could get reelected, growing old, feeling satisfied and contented as she looked back on her life.

She sneered in the dark. That now all seemed like nothing but a beautiful, silly lie, the kind of lie a person tells themselves when they can't bear to know the truth.

I don't want to be a warrior. Neither of us want to be warriors. We're not fighters, we're policy nerds. We're wonks. All I want is a normal life, with a job and a husband and a few kids. I just want to be left the fuck alone. Is that too fucking much to ask?

Angie imagined her future children. She saw them having at least two, a boy and a girl. The boy they'd name Peter, then use Nathaniel as the middle name, after her brother, and for the girl, she thought either Victoria or Elizabeth. Maybe both. Angie could imagine them now with crystal clarity, their chubby cheeks and their happy giggles, the sounds of little feet running through their home. She could see future Christmases, teaching them to ride bikes, watching with excitement the first time they plucked up the courage to jump into the pool. Angie could see herself reading to them every night, passing on to them her love for books, as Peter shared with them his passions as well – most likely horror movies.

She ached for this normal life that now seemed so impossible.

Angie placed both hands on her lower abdomen, wondering when she would begin to show, when the small life growing inside her would have a heartbeat. *Are you baby Pete or baby Vickie?* she asked her tiny human.

She'd realized her period was late just prior to beginning the fruitless search at the Library of Congress and had taken a pregnancy test then. The positive result had come as a surprise but not a shock. She had wanted to tell Peter but held off until she could see her doctor. Angie had gone there to confirm what she'd already known with the intention of telling Peter that night. Garrou, however, ruined those plans.

Angie understood now this was no longer about her, nor was it about Peter. It was about fighting for and protecting the life inside her and the life she wanted to have. As she cleaved to this belief, she could feel herself tipping forward on the cliff, the deep, dark pool below beckoning her in.

You fucker! Angie thought, snarling the words in her mind. *How fucking dare you! How dare you try to steal this from us? How dare you steal everything from us? And for what? For a sick sense of power? Revenge for something you brought on yourself?! You fucking arrogant bastard. You fucking worthless piece of shit! How dare you?!*

Closing her eyes, Angie let herself go and tipped over the cliff, plunging into the black waters beneath her.

Fine. So, there's a world where werewolves exist, and God only knows what other monsters. Fuck it. Whatever. I don't give a fuck anymore. The monster that has always lived in my mind is loose. I don't care. I don't want to be a warrior, I just want to have a normal, simple life, but so what? Who cares? If I need to kill Garrou and every other motherfucking werewolf in the country, then that's what I'll do. If gnomes and dragons and sugar plum fairies are real then I'll kill them, too. I don't care. I don't care about any of this anymore. I'm done. I'll fight as hard as I have to for the life I want.

Angie lay there in the dark feeling satisfied, as if a burden had been lifted from her, a vast load of anxiety released by choosing to dive into that dark pool. As she did, sleep drowsed her eyelids, her body growing heavy as it seemed to sink into the mattress.

She rolled towards Peter, draping her arm around him to snuggle in close as she wondered when to tell him about the baby. Angie knew this wasn't the right time. They'd soon be leaving to search for the cunning folk and was uncertain what would follow. She needed Peter sharp if they were going to free themselves from Garrou, and she knew he'd be too focused on her and the baby if he knew. If there was a fight coming, she wanted to be in it and didn't need Peter distracted by worrying about her. Better to wait until after all this was over.

Angie committed herself to her plan and the need to fight and she accepted as a given the existence of this strange, dark world of evil things. She found it easy to rest again once she did.

Deep and dreamless she slept for the remainder of the night.

CHAPTER TWENTY-FOUR

1

P eter awoke the following day eager to pack up and leave early as possible, but he first had to wait until his parents got home from church to call and make the arrangements. They were thrilled to have Peter come spend some time with them and eager to meet their future daughter in law. Peter and Angie left Washington a little after noon for the nearly four-hour drive to Mountain Lake Park, and as they made their way towards his childhood home, Peter found himself lost in a cascading series of thoughts.

I don't want to do this. I really don't want to do this. I do not want to go back home. If I didn't have to, absolutely have to, there's no way in hell I would. Not for a whole damn week, anyway. Fuck!

He wondered what it would be like spending a week in that house again after so many years and if the long shadow cast by the death of his older brother still darkened his parents' home. He imagined what it would be like sleeping in his old bedroom, now the guest room, for a week and squeezing himself into his old twin bed with Angie.

That, in turn, made him think about the many nights he spent in his room trying to ignore the closed door to Danny's bedroom. As he thought about it, Peter realized that shut door had always made him feel like he would never be enough for his parents, that his being there could never make up for Danny's loss.

Ma and Pa, I'm sorry I couldn't be enough, that I couldn't make up for your loss, but it wasn't fair to stop living just because Danny died. I'm so sorry he drowned in the lake. If I could have stopped it, I would have, but I was only a little kid, for fuck's sake. I was only five! You lost a little boy, but you still had a little one in the house. Why did you give up just because he was gone? I was still there, damn it!

Peter never saw or felt anything paranormal in the years after Danny's death. Yet, as he now sped along I-70 past Frederick, he thought they'd all been plagued by Danny's ghost, a spirit that had haunted their house by its absence rather than its presence. As Peter thought about it, he had a dawning awareness Danny had haunted him long after he'd left the house to go to college.

Lost in his own thoughts, Peter was only dimly aware when they'd driven beyond the range of their radio channel, a staticky hiss coming from the speakers now rather than music.

"Oh, hey," he said, "I guess we need to find a new station."

Angie, who had been looking out the window, turned to look at Peter, blinked her eyes, then said, "Hmm?"

"A new radio station. We've driven past the range of DC101, we need a new station."

"Oh, right," Angie said. "Okay, I'll find something."

Peter looked at her askance, worried about how she was

doing so soon after the horror in Baltimore. "How are you doing, babe? Are you okay?"

"Yeah," she said, "I'm alright. I was just thinking about... everything."

"Mmm. Yeah, we're dealing with a lot of shit now, aren't we?"

"That we are. What about you, honey? Seemed like you were gathering wool pretty well, too. What's on your mind?"

Peter sighed, then said, "I was just thinking about why I've never been back to visit my folks for longer than a day at a time since I left to go to college. Hell, even before then, I'd find every excuse I could to get out, to be somewhere, anywhere, else. That's one reason I spent so much time outside as a kid. There isn't much to do in the Park, and I was always too afraid of letting them down to get into trouble, but fuck! I *hated* being at home."

"You felt like you grew up in the shadow of your older brother, right?"

"Yeah, totally," Peter said. "He was eight when he drowned in the lake. He was out swimming with some friends one hot summer day, and then it was like an icy freeze fell on our household after he died. It's like... like he was this great unspoken after it happened, and nothing was ever the same."

"I know," Angie said, gently rubbing his shoulder. "I know it was hard for you."

"I don't think I ever told you about his room though, did I? I don't think I've shared that particular bit of this fucked up story."

"No, I don't think so. What about it?"

"It was directly across the hall from my room," Peter said, a far distant look in his eye. "Every time I went to hang out in my room – which was often – I tried to ignore the closed door to his room, the sign with his name he colored not long before he died still taped to it. That room has remained unopened and untouched since the day he died."

Angie sucked in her breath, putting her hand over her mouth. "No way! Seriously?!"

"Seriously."

"That's... pretty creepy."

"I know, right?" said Peter. "Unless they've walked in since then, which I seriously doubt, that room hasn't been opened up since 1979. It's like they've always expected him to just return home one day and go to his room as if nothing had ever happened."

"Oh, Peter," said Angie. "That's... fucked up."

Peter nodded. "All that time I spent in my room, hanging out, listening to music, doing homework, whatever, that door was there, right there. It was like a damn monument to him... almost like another gravestone. It was a constant reminder of our loss, and I always felt oppressed by it."

Angie sighed, looking out the window. "Do we have to stay an entire week? Can't we just do an overnight or something?"

"Well, I've already told them we'd be there the whole week, and I don't want to launch right into asking them about cunning folk. But to be honest, I could spend one overnight or a week, either way, sleeping in that house again even once will have me fucked up."

"Hmm," said Angie. "Okay, if you say so."

"Besides," Peter said with a chuckle, "it'll take a week for you to meet all the of the various aunts, uncles, cousins, in-laws twice removed, and other family members who live in the area. Now that you're joining the family, everyone's going to want to meet you, babe."

Angie looked at him, mouth and eyes wide open. "Are you kidding me? I'm going to be put on display for everyone to see?"

"Yeah, pretty much," said Peter. "Plan on a big family

dinner every night, just with different family members. Good news is, though, my mother's cooking is something special. You ever have rhubarb pie?"

"No, can't say I have. Is it good?"

"It is the way Mom makes it," Peter said, smiling for the first time this trip.

***

2

They chatted the remaining hours of the drive, thoughts of long dead brothers and feelings of inadequacy gone for the moment from Peter's mind. As the landscape of western Maryland turned rougher and more rural, Peter tried to take in the beautiful autumn colors, the reds, oranges, and golds clustered amongst the still green trees in the rolling hills. This had always been prime hunting time when he was a kid, a thought that made Peter think of his Granddaddy. That was a far more pleasant family memory than his earlier ones.

They had gone from a multi-lane interstate to a smaller highway, and then to a lesser regional route, and from there to a two-lane rural road. After some time of driving along wooded hills with scattered farming fields and even more scattered houses, Peter swept his arm grandly and announced, "Well, here we are. Welcome to the great metropolis of Mountain Lake Park."

Angie looked around as they drove. "Looks like a nice little town."

"It is," Peter said, nodding. "I make my childhood sound terrible, but it really wasn't. I know my parents tried, they did they best they could, but they just couldn't get over their grief. So, it wasn't perfect, but one of the best things about being a kid was growing up here. I had friends, lots of woods right by my house I could romp around in, it was safe and clean. The Park was a nice little place to grow up in."

"Looks like it."

Peter paused at a stop sign, thinking a moment. "Come on. I'll show you around a bit before we go to my parents' house."

They spent another half-hour driving around town. Peter showed off some of the parks the town offered, the Baptist church he'd gone to as a kid and that his parents still attended, houses he'd always thought the most beautiful, the high school from which he'd graduated. All these locations were bound together with stories about what happened in these different places and who used to live where and what those people are up to now. He explained how the Park was a sleeper community with many homes but few businesses, the majority of those being found in nearby Oakland.

Peter took them through that neighboring town, winding their way to the Garrett Regional Medical Center, where his father had been able to find a job rather than going down into the mines. They aimlessly wandered around between the twin towns for a while, Peter pointing out the vast acres of woods in the Broadford Recreational Area, where he and his friends would very illegally hunt squirrels when he was a boy. Angie smiled as Peter told her one story after another about his youth and the places it happened.

"I want to show you the little league fields where I started playing," Peter said. "You knew I played baseball in high school, right?"

"No, I did not! You never told me that."

"Well, I did. I wasn't bad, but I really wasn't g—"

Peter stopped talking as he took a turn onto a road and the choppy waters of a vast lake suddenly came into view.

"Peter? What is it?"

"That's the lake," he said. "Broadford Lake. That's where Danny drowned. Right down there, by that little beach."

Angie rubbed his back. "Are you okay?"

"Yeah," Peter said, sighing. "Yeah... you know what? I am. I really am. With everything we've been through the past two or so months, overcoming my brother's death from twenty years ago suddenly doesn't seem like that big a deal anymore. I'm starting to feel like this trip might turn out to be a good thing for me. Almost cathartic."

"That's wonderful to hear, honey."

"Alright... let's swing by those fields and then we'd better get to my parents' house. My butt's numb, anyway."

3

Peter took them along a road that followed the curved contours of the lake and past some run-down-looking little baseball diamonds, then made their way a short distance to a scattering of houses near a large, wooden hill. He pulled into the driveway of the last house, a small bungalow that looked like it was built in the 1930s nestled on the foot of the hill, alone and isolated on a cul-de-sac. There was a porch swing swaying in the chill breeze next to a few old-fashioned rocking chairs, and there was the odor of a wood fire pouring out of the chimney.

"Well," Peter said with a sigh, "this is it."

"It's a lovely little house," said Angie. "I love the cozy look of it. And I assume those woods back there are where you were a lot of the time?"

"Yep, I sure was. I mean, I was all over, but of course those woods were right behind the house so that's where I'd always start."

As Peter began to unload the car, he paused a moment, then looked back at the hill behind his parents' house. "You can see the lake from the top of the hill. It's only about... maybe three hundred yards away. If not for those trees over there you'd be able to see it from here. On quiet nights you can hear the water lapping against the shore. I never thought about how living so close to where Danny died must've fucked with my parents."

"Yeah," Angie said. "That makes a lot of sense."

They gathered up their bags and made their way into the house, which smelled delicious of a fresh-cooked meal. Peter's mother, short and plump, rushed over to him and squeezed him in a big hug, then, holding out her arms said, "And this must be Angie," and also wrapped her up in hug.

"Ma, yes, this is Angie, and, babe, this is my mother, Liz Brunnen, and my father, Ed."

"It's so nice to finally meet you, Mrs. Brunnen," Angie said.

"Oh, Petey, why didn't you tell us she had such a cute little accent?" Liz Brunnen said, her own West Virginia accent still thick after all these years. "And please call me Mom or Momma or Ma, just not Mrs. Brunnen. You're family, now, honey. No need for formality."

"Okay, ma'am... er, Momma."

"And look at you," his mother said. "Such a pretty girl! But what happened to your cheek, honey?"

"Oh, umm..." Angie said as she raised her hand to the bandage on her face and glanced at Peter. "I got scratched by the cat."

Peter shook hands with his father, who was an older version of his son, tall and lanky, with a tangled mop of unruly whitish-blond hair. He gently shook hands with Angie, then said, "Real good to meet the young lady that stole our Petey's heart. Glad you two could finally come visit us. It's been... how long, Petey, since you been here?"

"It's been quite a while, Pa."

"Well, I guess they keep you pretty busy in Washington," Peter's father said. "Nothin' you can do when you gotta work but work. It was a damn shame what happened to Thompson. I always liked the man myself."

"Yeah," Peter said softly. "He was definitely one of the good ones."

"Well, no need standin' around gettin' glum," said Ed. "Your momma's made us one fine dinner for tonight. Angie, I hope you like to eat, cause my wife has made enough food to feed a small army!"

The meal was just as Peter knew it would be, an overabundance of delicious, hearty foods followed up by a homemade pie. Though not the rhubarb he was hoping for, Peter was still delighted with the sweet potato pie his mother had baked instead. She assured him after dinner that a rhubarb pie would come later in the week.

As they sat there chatting over dinner, Ed and Liz telling stories about Peter when he was a boy, Angie getting to know his parents and they her, he could still see the pain etched on their faces whenever the stories veered towards Danny or even his own youth. He took note of how many times they framed their recollections by saying, *This was just before Danny died,* or *That happened not long after Danny's accident,* or similar variations. It was as if this singular event was the hinge around which the rest of their lives – and by extension, Peter's life – pivoted. He realized his parents' concept of time was based on Danny's death, like how the counting of years has always been measured by some momentous event.

There were laughs and more stories shared as the pie and coffee were served, but Peter still could see that certain emptiness in their eyes, a hollowness to their laughs. They hid it well after all these years, and Peter was likely the only person who could notice it; he was certain Angie wouldn't pick up on their sadness at all. But Peter had been watching them for years and had grown up with that shadow, so he could tell when it blackened his parents' hearts.

Peter smiled to himself as Angie loudly laughed to a story he'd heard dozens of times before. After having decided that holding on to decades-old resentments made no sense in the face of the horrifying world of which he'd become aware, Peter felt freed from Danny's oppressive ghost for the time in his life. Being in his parents' house and seeing the void in their hearts had always filled Peter with deepest melancholy tinged with a painful sense of failure for not being enough, not being able to fill that hole, of not being Danny. Now, he felt nothing at all, and decided nothing felt very good.

Later that night, after his parents had gone to bed, he and Angie sat cuddling on the couch in front of the fieldstone fireplace as Peter rolled the few remaining popping and hissing logs.

"I always liked winter because of this fireplace," he said. "I would sit here, like now, after they'd gone up to bed, and just stare into the flames, listen to the crackling, smell the wood burning. Best odor in the world, you ask me."

"I don't know about that," Angie said. "Your mother's pie smelled incredible. Does she always cook like that?"

Peter chuckled. "Yeah, pretty much. She's always been a hell of a cook. Wait till you taste her bread."

"I like them, your parents. I like them a lot."

"Well, I got the feeling they love you. By this point they probably like you more than me. No way you're getting out the family now, babe!"

Angie laughed, then rubbed her eyes. "It's been a long and day and I'm beat. You ready for bed?"

"I sure am," Peter said.

They walked up the creaking steps to the guestroom above. As they did, Peter paused in front of the wooden door across the hall, the crayon-colored letters of Danny's name discolored and dulled by a layer of gray dust. He stared at it a moment as if it were a mysterious monolith he'd never seen before, then put his hand out to open it. It hovered, trembling, above the knob for a moment, but rather than turn it to unseal the room, he instead used it to gently pat the door a few times.

No need to disturb the dead any further. I've already sent his ghost away. That's enough. I love you, Danny. Goodbye.

4

The week passed quickly and progressed just as Peter knew it would. By that Wednesday, Angie had been introduced to a dozen aunts and uncles who still lived in nearby West Virginia, together with more cousins than Peter even knew he had. These extended family members would spend the day at the Brunnen home, chatting, cooking, and gossiping, laughing loudly and often, and always taking up all the space in the small house. Peter and Angie both needed to get away from the cramped surroundings for a while, so they walked the short trail at Wooddell Park as they took in the sunny early October weather and relished the quiet, broken only by the echoing laughter of some kids at the playground there.

That evening after dinner, Angie went upstairs to take a nap and Peter suggested to his father they have their coffee on the porch. After a meandering conversation that wended aimlessly, Peter, at last, brought up the subject that had brought Angie and he back to his parents.

"Pa," Peter said as he unwrapped an orange lollipop and slipped it in his mouth, "what do you know of the cunning folk? Granddaddy told me a tale once, but... well, I don't know if I can believe it."

"Cunnin' folk?" he asked, scratching his chin as he thought. "You mean the cunnin' women, the ones that are supposed to be livin' in the woods over in West Virginia?"

"Yeah, I guess," Peter said. "I thought they were called cunning folk."

Ed sipped his coffee, then said, "No, cunnin' women. Far as I know they're almost all women."

"What do you know about them?"

He shrugged. "Well, not much, really. My grandmother told me stories, just like your Granddaddy told you. But I only know what she said, that there are people who live in the woods, up in the mountains, who are healers and can see the future and such."

"Nothing else?" Peter said, trying to keep his tone nonchalant but failing.

"No, nothin' else. Why?"

"Oh... nothing," he said, sighing and slumping back into the rocking chair. "Just, you know, trying to learn more about West Virginia so I can tell Angie about where we're from."

"Mmm," Ed grunted as he took another sip of coffee. "I don't know much... but as I recall your mother actually went there when she was a child. You should ask her."

Peter sat back up as he said, "What? Really?!"

"Yep, if I 'member correct. Hey, Liz? Can you come out here, please?"

Peter's mother came to the porch and, as his father beckoned her to sit next to him, joined Ed on the porch swing. "What do you boys need?"

"Petey was asking about them cunnin' women who live in the hills back home. I do remember correct that you said you went there when you were a little girl, right?"

"Yeah, Ed, you do. I went there."

Peter waited for his mother to explain more, leaning in on the rocking chair. After a moment of tense silence, he blurted out, "Well, where are they? Why'd you go? What happened?!"

"Jeez, Petey, hold your dang horses," Liz said. "Well, now let me think... this woulda been back in 1959, if I remember. Your Uncle Bill was down with a real bad fever that just wouldn't break. You know we was country folk, dirt poor, the drink got holda Daddy by then, so Momma made all the medicines she could. Nothing was stoppin' this fever, though. She was worried sick about Bill, thought he was done for."

She paused to think, adjusting the glasses on her nose as she did so. "We all knew 'bout them cunning women. Everyone always told stories about 'em, so Momma borrowed a car and drove all the way to Glace, which is near where they are. Your Aunt Evelyn stayed with Bill and Momma took me with her."

"Glace!" Peter said, snapping his fingers. "Now I remember. That's where Granddaddy said his mother went."

"Right, but they ain't *in* Glace, just near it somewhere in the woods beyond town," said his mother.

There was another long silence, into which Peter said, "And then...? What happened when you and Grammy went there?"

"Well," she said with a sigh, "that was forty years ago, Petey. I can't recall many details, but... I do remember we were taken to a small community in the woods. I remember a bunch of scattered cabins, people doing different jobs, and everyone was dressed real old-fashioned. There was a woman there, seemed like she was in charge. She looked like she was maybe around sixty or seventy, and everyone called her Grandmother Brigit, or just Grandmother. She gave Momma an herbal cure for Bill and something to hang over his bed. Then the fever broke the next day. That's it."

"Damn lot of good it did Bill," Peter's father said, "with the way he turned out anyway."

"Oh, now, Ed, you stop. He went through a rough patch for a good many years, but he's alright now."

As Peter's parents talked, his mind whirled with possibilities of what this new information could mean for their search. He tingled with a tantalizing sense of almost having found a way to defeat Garrou. Almost.

So, they are real. They exist, and they're not that far from here. But can they help? Will they help? Are they even still there?

"You said that was back in '59," Peter said, interrupting their debate about his Uncle Bill. "Do you know if anyone has been there recently, Ma?"

Liz nodded, then said, "Yeah, sure they have. I keep in touch with some of the girls I grew up with, and I know for a fact Agnes Waters went there just a few years ago for help when her husband took sick. She said everything was still there. It sounded just like it was when I went there."

Peter rocked in his chair, the rhythmic squeaking the only sound as silence again descending upon the porch. He stared with unseeing eyes as he thought about what this meant until his mother said, "Petey, why are you asking?"

"Just learning about West Virginia," Peter said, his eyes still unfocused as he got up, his mind galloping. "I'm going to go check on Angie. Thanks for the chat. See you."

He went up to the bedroom where Angie lay napping on his old bed, then he paused as he stood at the door looking at her. He thought she looked so peaceful lying there with one hand tucked under the pillow and the other draped over her belly that, for a moment, Peter hesitated to wake her, but after a bit he sat at the edge of her bed and gently rubbed her hair.

"Angie," he whispered.

"Mmnnfff?" she groaned.

"Angie, I'm sorry to wake you, but I found out something very important."

"Whaddya..." Angie stammered, wiping away some drool from her mouth and rubbing her eyes, "what'd you learn?"

"The cunning folk – well, cunning women – they exist. My mother was actually there when she was a girl. She met the woman in charge, she's named Grandmother Brigit. They're near Glace, Angie, and they help people who ask for it."

Angie blinked a few times, then raised herself up on an elbow as she again rubbed her eyes and yawned. "Glace? Where's that? How far is that from here?"

"It's a real small town in the hills, near the Virginia border," he said. "It's maybe about a hundred miles from here, maybe a little bit more. But they're *there*, Angie. We did it. We found them."

"Not yet we haven't," Angie said, scratching her head. "But at least now we know where to look for them."

"And we know they're real."

"Yeah," she said, plopping back down on the pillow, "now we know that."

Peter stroked her hair again, thinking about how lovely she looked, cheek scar be damned. But he was also concerned for her because it hadn't yet been a week since their nightmare in Baltimore.

"Hey," he said, Angie looking peaceful and content as his hands combed through her hair, "are you okay? You don't seem like yourself or to have the energy you used to, and I've noticed you don't have much of an appetite for breakfast. How are you managing what happened?"

Angie, eyes still closed, smiled. "I'm doing okay. Honestly, I am. I guess it's just the pressure of everything that has me so tired, that's all. But, really, I'm fine. I promise."

"Okay, babe. If you say so."

"I do," Angie said as she opened her eyes and looked at Peter. "So, now that we know about these cunning women, what are we going to do?"

"Well," said Peter, "I was thinking on Saturday when we leave, rather than going back to Washington, we head south, towards Glace. Ask around, see what we can see."

"I agree... you know, though, we might lose our jobs. There's only so long we can take a leave of absence, and we're expected back on Monday. Are you okay with that?"

Peter sighed as he leaned back to rest against the swell of Angie's hip. "No, I'm not really okay with it, but I don't know what else to do. This is something we've got to see through, and if we lose our jobs because of it, then so be it, I suppose."

"Yeah," Angie said. "I don't know what else to do, either."

"We should be able to get by until we find new jobs. But what about you? We have plans for you to run for Congress in a few years. Getting fired from a staffer job might not look good in a campaign."

"Well," said Angie, "I can't run for Congress if I'm dead, can I? I agree with you, this is something we have to do, and if we lose our jobs, then it is what it is. If we want to live free, if we want the kind of lives we choose to live, if we don't want to live in constant fear, then we've got to fight back... .and we've *got* to win this fight."

CHAPTER TWENTY-FIVE

1

As the pair made their way south along Route 32 through the Monongahela National Forest, Angie folded and re-folded the map they'd had to buy at a little gas station just over the West Virginia border. She'd been forced to become the navigator and figure out a route from the tangle of thin black, red, and blue squiggling routes.

"I thought you said you knew how to get there," she said.

"No," said Peter, his index finger raised like an academic arguing a point of minutia, "I said I knew, roughly, where Glace was. I never said I knew how to *get* to where it was."

"Well, your 'roughly' was off by about a hundred miles, mister. This two-hour trip just turned into an almost four-hour one!"

Angie knew she spoke to Peter with an angry edge to her voice she didn't intend, just as she knew the irritation she felt was misplaced. She thought about how this had happened several times during their week-long stay at Peter's parents, most of which she was able to control before she snapped. On occasion, however, she couldn't stop her raging hormones before she said something with a tone she later regretted.

She wanted so much to tell Peter, not just so he'd know why she was being randomly cranky, but also because it'd thrill him to know he would soon become a father. Angie just couldn't allow herself that small vanity, not yet anyway. Not until Garrou was dead and the threat gone from their lives, not until she'd had the chance to fight the foul creature he'd become.

Peter glanced at Angie, smiled feebly, then shrugged his shoulders. "Sorry?"

"That's okay, you big goof. Good thing your mother got up early to make us such a big breakfast."

"Of which you had hardly any, I saw."

"Yeah," Angie said, rubbing her belly, "I just wasn't hungry so early in the morning."

"Well, we should get to Glace at around eleven o'clock or so, then we can get lunch there."

"Good," Angie said, watching as they sped past the dim, thick forest surrounding them, "I'm sure I'll be starving by then."

She watched the hills grow taller and more rugged as they drove deeper into West Virginia, the towns becoming widely scattered until there was only an isolated house every few miles. Angie felt themselves ascending higher as the hills turned to mountains, climbing ever closer to the bright blue October sky above. They fell into a comfortable silence as they drove deeper into the dense forest, sunlight dying in the tangled branches above, the floor enshrouded in darkness. Despite the vivid autumn colors woven throughout the green woods, Angie felt like the forest was a shadow wrapping its black arms around them as if it wanted to drag them into its depth.

But not in an unpleasant way, Angie realized. It was almost like there was a powerful energy coursing through the woods that wanted them in it. It was as if the forest itself had a spirit. Angie sensed it wanted to wrap itself around the pair and hide them for their own protection.

The closer they got to Glace, the more Angie could feel that elusive *something*, almost like pulsing, radiating waves of energy. She'd felt it before when chained underground with Garrou, but what wafted off him felt malevolent and malicious, foul and twisted. Angie couldn't find the right words to describe what she felt coming from the forest, other than this energy felt caring.

"Can you feel it?" she asked Peter as they wound along Route 50, getting closer to Glace.

Peter glanced at Angie, then looked around, and said, "Feel what?"

"Feel that sense of... energy. Of power. It's in the air. Can't you feel it?"

He looked around again, as if he expected to see electricity arcing through the sky. "No, I can't feel anything at all."

"Oh, huh. Okay."

"What is it? What are you feeling?"

"It's hard to explain," Angie said, lapsing into silence as she thought. "It's almost like the feeling you can get just before a big thunderstorm, like there's a tingle in the air. You don't know what it is, but you can just *feel* it, nonetheless."

"Oh, okay," Peter said, nodding. "And you feel that now?"

"Yeah, I've been feeling it since we passed into the forest, and it's been getting stronger the closer we get to Glace."

"Interesting. Well, we're almost there, so we'll soon see what we can find out."

2

A few minutes after Peter said that they passed a dilapidated old sign welcoming travelers to Glace, its weather-beaten and peeling paint long since dulled. A town much smaller than even Mountain Lake Park, it was nestled on a small flat space squeezed between two mountains looming up on either side of it. Angie and Peter looked around as they continued down Route 50, noting a few side roads branching off from the main street, small houses beyond, and a smattering of businesses along the route. In less than two minutes, they realized they'd driven out of town and had to turn around.

They went back up the main street, then took a side road to the right. This led to a single lane that ran parallel to Route 50 that had small houses all along its length before it turned again to come back to the central street. Crossing over to follow the other side road, the pair found it mirrored where they had just come from, with more houses scattered along it. Peter turned the car back onto Route 50.

"Alright," Peter said, pulling into an open parking space on the main road, "let's just stop here for a while so we can talk about what we should do."

"Well, we're here now. They're close... I think that's what I can feel. Let's just go ask some people if they've heard of this Grandmother Brigit and where we can find her."

Peter nodded in agreement. "Sounds good. I think we should start—"

"Let's start here," Angie said, pointing out her window to the store they'd aimlessly parked in front of, the sign of which read *Pete's Hardware Store*. Below the name of the store was emblazoned *We Make Keys!* "I have a good feeling about this place."

Peter leaned forward to read the sign, then chuckled and said, "Okay. Works for me."

The store was small and cramped, and it smelled like old cigarettes and lacquer. Beyond the many isles packed full of hardware, a thin older man sat behind a wooden counter reading a book. As Angie and Peter made their way past his wares and straight towards where he sat, the man looked over the half-moon glasses perched on his nose at them, sighed, then laid the book down on the counter.

"Heya," the man said, tipping his faded John Deere hat at the pair, "can I help ya with somethin'?"

"Yeah," Peter said. "Are you Pete?"

"Nah," said the man, taking a moment to spit some tobacco into an empty plastic soda bottle. "Pete was my Pop. He's dead."

"Oh, I see, cause I'm Peter. I just thought... you know... that was neat... kind of..."

The man stared at Peter with unblinking blue eyes, then said, "Uh-huh. Can I help ya find somethin'?"

"We're looking for Grandmother Brigit," Angie said. "We've come a long way to meet her. We know she and her community are near here, but we don't know exactly where. Can you help us?"

The man straightened his back when he heard who they were looking for, appearing for a moment like a bristling cat. He leaned his head back to look at both of them through his glasses, and said, "There ain't no Gramma Brigit 'round here. Sorry." Then he took up his book as if they no longer existed.

With furrowed brows, Angie and Peter glanced at each other, then back at the man. "I don't understand," Peter said, "we were told she and her followers were here, near here, anyway. My Ma told me herself. She was here as a little girl."

"I don't know what to tell ya," the man said, his eyes still locked onto the pages of his book. "I guess she just told ya wrong."

The pair stood there speechless for a moment as they tried to figure out what was happening. It wasn't that the man claimed no knowledge of Grandmother Brigit that confused Angie. It seemed reasonable to her that not everyone in a town would have heard of something like the cunning women, so she thought nothing unusual about him claiming ignorance. It was the way he reacted when they asked about Grandmother and his continued icy rudeness that disturbed Angie.

"I think ya kids better go now," the man said to his book. "I'm gonna be closing for my lunch break real soon."

Peter sighed, then pivoted around towards the door. Angie shrugged her shoulders and shook her head in disbelief, then, as she walked out of the store, turned back to the man.

"Thanks anyway for your time," she said, then pointed at his book. "And, by the way, Hood's not hiding in the house, he *is* the house. Enjoy your lunch."

As the door slowly closed behind Angie and Peter, they heard the man at the counter say, "*Shit!*" as he slammed his book down.

"Well," said Peter, "that was all kinds of weird, wasn't it?"

"Yeah, it sure was. His reaction was bizarre. I wonder what he's got against Grandmother Brigit."

"I don't know. Maybe he asked her for help, and she refused him, so now he's angry at her about it?"

"Could be anything, I guess," Angie said as she shook her head, then looked at the squat, brick building next to the hardware store and saw it was a bank. "Let's try here."

Peter looked at the sign. "Premier Bank. Why a bank?"

"Well, I figure everyone will do their banking at the same place in a small town like this, so they likely know everyone here. They'd have to know about a group like the cunning women, maybe even sold the land to them. Plus, added bonus: It's right here."

"Okay," Peter said, "that's good enough reason as any I guess."

They walked into the bank through a pair of stout wooden doors that opened with a sonorous creak. The old bank interior was of marble and gold-painted lettering and wrought iron details, something that was once likely the pride of this small town. The lobby was empty, with an office to one side, the door open ajar labeled *Bank Manager*, and just one teller on duty, a mousy little woman with gallinaceous features.

"She looks like a chicken," Peter whispered to Angie as they approached the counter.

"I know," she said, trying to suppress a laugh.

"Does that make her a motherclucker?"

Angie giggled and bit her lip, not wanting to laugh in the woman's face now that they had arrived.

"Can I help you?" said the teller.

"Hi, yes," Angie said. "This might sound a little odd, but... my fiancé and I are here looking for a group of people who live somewhere in the woods nearby. We understand that they're led by a woman named Grandmother Brigit. Do you know where we might be able to find them?"

"Grandmother... Brigit?" the twitchy woman chirped. "No, I don't know anything about Grandmother Brigit."

"Is there anyone else here who might?" Peter asked. "A loan manager, maybe? Someone who deals with mortgages and things like that?"

"No, I'm sorry, but there's no one else here who knows anything about that."

"Would the manager—" Angie started to ask until the door to the bank manager's office closed with a loud bang that echoed like and explosion throughout the marble interior.

"Now, if you will please excuse me," the teller said as she locked her cash drawer and placed a *Closed* placard in front of her work area, "I need to go to lunch. Thank you." The woman scurried away to the rear of the bank and beyond their sight.

Angie and Peter turned to look at each other. "What the fuck is going on here?" Peter said. "Why is everyone acting like this?"

"I don't know," said Angie, as she put her hand to her head and closed her eyes. "Listen, we need to get some lunch. I'm so hungry now I'm a little dizzy and I feel like I might throw up."

"Shit, you look pale. Did you eat anything at all?"

"I ate a few bites of toast at breakfast and that bag of Combos we got at the gas station," Angie said as they went back out to the car, Peter helping to keep her steady, "but other than that, no."

Peter opened the car door and helped Angie get in, her dizziness abating as she sat. When he got in the car, he said, "Well, looks like our food options are limited. I saw a guy with a trailer and a roadside grill up here a bit..."

"You mean Joe's Special Burgers?" Angie said, pointing ahead to where a large, bearded man with a dirty apron cooked meat on a grill by the road a hundred yards in front of them. "No thanks. Roadside burger places seem a little hinky to me."

"Yeah, very hinky. Okay, so the only restaurant in town I saw was Buck's Chuck Wagon, back that way," he said as he hitched his thumb over his shoulder.

"Let's go."

Peter turned the car around and drove the short distance to the edge of town, then pulled into the restaurant's gravel parking lot. Angie's wave of nausea and dizziness had passed, but she'd learned that when this happens it'd come back worse if she didn't soon get some food in her. She'd discovered that the hard way one day while trying to work through lunch after having skipped breakfast.

They walked into a small diner that had a few patrons sitting at a long lunch counter, plus some tables and a line of booths along the windows looking out on Route 50. The décor of the place appeared to have not been updated since the mid-70s, with grimy orange and white linoleum tiles flecked with brown, and garish lemon-lime wallpaper.

"Charming," Peter said to Angie as they took it all in. "C'mon, let's go sit in a booth."

The booths were all covered in a dull orange fake leather that had become worn and cracked, and when the waitress came over to get their drink order, Angie asked for some crackers to keep the vomiting at bay. She came back right away with their sodas and Angie's crackers, then took their lunch orders.

"Alrighty," the young woman said, "we'll get that right out to y'alls."

"Hey, one quick thing before you go," Peter said.

"Yes?" she said with a smile. "What kin I get you?"

"We've come here looking for Grandmother Brigit. We were told she and her people live near here, in the woods around here. Maybe up in the hills. Do you know anything about that?"

As soon as Peter asked his question the woman's smile faded. She looked over her shoulder at the customers sitting at the counter and the man serving them, then said in a harsh whisper, "I don't know nothing about that." She then turned to disappear back to the kitchen.

Peter sighed as he ran both hands through his sand-colored hair. "And once again we strikeout. I'm definitely getting the feeling no one in this town *wants* us to find Grandmother and her followers."

"Me too. But I can't figure out why."

Their burgers and fries were brought out soon thereafter, which Angie saw included the waitress wordlessly leaving their bill on the table. She didn't have time to think about that, though, as she launched into her burger, quickly devouring everything on her plate.

"Wow," Peter said when he realized she was already done eating. "I guess you were famished."

"Yeah," said Angie, holding up the bill, "and since it doesn't seem like pie is an option I wanted to fill up."

"Well, I'm about done, anyway," Peter said as he wiped his mouth and put the napkin on a half-eaten hamburger. "Let's get out of here."

They paid the bill, and as they did, Angie noticed the man working the register looking at them suspiciously, and some of the patrons cutting their eyes towards the couple. She suspected the waitress had told others what they were looking for while they ate. Now, everyone in the restaurant – perhaps everyone in town, by this point – was watching them as if Angie and Peter were unwanted, ill-intentioned interlopers.

3

They returned to the car, and Angie said, "This is a weird day."

Peter again sighed as he ran his hands through his hair in frustration. "*Fuuuuuck!* I'm about ready to pop this is so fucking irritating."

"I hear you there. I'm annoyed and confused, and I don't know what comes next."

Now what the fuck are we going to do? We're here, we're right *here*, for fuck's sake! We're so close, and yet no one claims to know anything."

"Which you know is complete bullshit," Angie said. "I thought the guy in the hardware store was just being a jerk, but now I realize it's everyone in town. They don't want us asking around about Grandmother Brigit."

"But why? What are they hiding?"

"I wish I knew," Angie said as she put her head back to stare at the car ceiling and think. "I sure wish I knew that."

As Angie sat there, wondering why the people in town were acting as they were and thinking about what to do next, she saw movement to her right out of the corner of her eye. She glanced that way, and as she did a sudden sizzling chill of terror raced down her spine as she saw the plain-faced redheaded woman walking steadily towards the car, her unblinking eyes fixed on Angie.

"Peter!" she yelled, slapping his thigh but unable to tear her eyes away from the woman. "Peter, Peter, Peter! That's her, that's the woman who was following me!!"

He looked up to see the black-clad woman quickly approaching them. "What?! What the fuck?! How... what?!"

"Peter," Angie croaked, a dread fear grasping her throat and making it hard to speak, "get us... out."

The woman was almost at the car.

"PETER!" Angie now shrieked, a raw, animalistic panic overtaking her, "GET US OUT OF HERE!!"

"I'm trying!" he said, as he fumbled getting the keys out of his pocket.

It was too late. The woman was upon them.

The red-haired woman walked to the car, standing by Angie's window for a moment, her pale green eyes staring down at her. She then bent down to look into the car, peering first at Peter, then back to Angie. Then, the woman tapped on Angie's window. With her jagged breath catching in her throat and her hand trembling, Angie rolled it down.

"Y-Y-Yes?" Angie whispered.

"Grandmother Brigit has been expecting you," the woman said, "and I'm to show you the way." She then got into the back seat of the car without being invited.

"You're... you're from Grandmother Brigit?" Angie asked.

"Yes," she said. "My name is Sarah. Now, Peter—"

"How do you know my name?!"

"As I said, Grandmother has been expecting you, and she knew you'd soon be coming. She knows who you are. Now, please take a left on this road here, Hollywood Glace Road, and take it for about ten miles. I will tell you when to turn."

Peter shook his head as if trying to shake off sleep, then did as she told him. As they pulled onto the road and began the drive to wherever Sarah was leading them, Angie turned to look at her. Though she already knew the answer, she asked, "Have you been following me?"

"My sisters and I have been, yes."

"Why?"

"Because Grandmother Brigit asked us to," Sarah said, then lapsed into silence as she stared out the window.

CHAPTER TWENTY-SIX

1

The trio drove in silence to wherever Sarah was leading them, Peter and Angie stealing glances at one another as they did. He kept looking into the rear-view mirror at this odd woman in the back seat of his car, who placidly watched the autumn-painted forest scroll past. It was as if getting into a stranger's car and leading them to Grandmother Brigit was a normal occurrence for her. As he did, Peter could now see Sarah had pale freckles splashed across her plain face, and she smelled vaguely of campfire and the woods.

After about ten minutes of driving, Sarah leaned forward and, as she pointed, said, "Okay, Peter. There is a turn coming up to our right just after that fallen tree, do you see it?"

"That dirt road there?"

"Yes. Follow that for a few more miles – but take it slow. The road is a little rough."

Peter decided Sarah had a knack for understatement after just a few minutes of crawling along the road because "rough" didn't quite capture how deeply rutted and uneven it was. He crept the car ahead, weaving a way forward to avoid the deepest cuts and gouges in the surface, trying not to get the car stuck. He'd then veer back when large stones that looked sharp enough the shred the tires reared out of the packed soil.

They drove for perhaps a mile, steadily climbing higher up the mountain, before the road switched back to continue creeping upwards, then switched directions back again. As they did, Peter looked down the steep cliff at the very edge of the road to see the thickly wooded hillside sweeping up to meet them. He glanced at Angie and saw she was gripping her seat and gritting her teeth as she bounced her leg, a look of angst etched on her face.

"Peter, be careful," she whispered.

"I am, babe. Believe me, I am."

There's no shoulder and no guide rails, so we could slip right off this damn mountain, he thought as he picked his way around the rough road. *But the woods are so dense we'd probably just tip over and roll a few times before one of the trees caught us. So, we wouldn't go down the hill, just be trapped in a car stuck in the woods. Stories like this always end with, "... and their bodies were found in the vehicle come spring." Wonderful.*

Peter started to sweat despite the chill and gripped the steering wheel like it was his life as the tension of the past week, of this bizarre day, of this nerve-wracking drive wore on him. It felt like the growing pressure had been crushing and grinding him to a powder. He thought about what awaited them at the end of this road and the hopes both he and Angie had for what came next, though he feared those hopes might be forlorn. Yet, nonetheless, he steadily climbed towards the mountain top.

2

They continued to follow the rutted dirt road, switching back and forth several more times as they ascended the mountain. Though the sun shone on this cool October day, little of that light made it through the tangled canopy above, leaving the road obscured in twilight dark. Peter felt like he had to focus all his attention on the road to make sure they didn't slip off the side, almost as if he were driving through a snowstorm. His eyes darted back and forth from the road, to checking out the windows, back to the road, to the mirrors, to the road, and so on. As he did, Peter caught flashes of Sarah calmly watching their progress out the window.

She's either incredibly chill by nature or on drugs. Right now, I'm betting on drugs.

After twenty minutes of working their way along the switchback, Sarah leaned forward again. "The turn is coming up very soon. It will be to the left."

Peter slowed the car even more, peering forward through the gloom. "I don't see anything; all I see are trees. I can't see another road. Where is it?"

"Right there," Sarah said pointing, and as Peter crept the car ahead, he could now see a small opening in the solid curtain of leaves, a narrow trail leading off into the darkness beyond it.

"You want us to take the car in there? Right into the forest?! We won't get stuck?"

"No, it'll be fine," said Sarah. "It's not big, but the ground is firm."

Peter sighed as he closed his eyes and had a flashback to the night he went to meet Garrou in Baltimore. He'd wanted to be anywhere else in the world at that moment and had dreaded the thought of plunging into those woods hidden in the misty darkness. His heart pounded and his breath had come in gulps, but he'd known there was nothing else he could do. That same sense of trapped helplessness poured over him now.

He looked at Angie, who smiled weakly at him. "We don't have any other choice," she said as if she could read his mind.

"No, I guess we don't." He lifted his foot off the brake and inched the car onto the tight opening in the trees.

The trail lazily inclined upward, taking them closer to the mountain top. It cut through the woods with such little space that branches slid along the Avalon's side with screeching squeals as the rear-view mirrors were knocked out of place by tree trunks. Peter felt like the trees themselves were scraping bony fingers down the car as they passed by in a bid to grab hold of them. Though driving along a woodland path that was just wide enough for a car to pass through, Peter was relieved to see there was no precipitous drop off at the edge of the track.

They crept along this tiny trail for half an hour until Peter could see a bright patch of sun just ahead. The path ended in a small, grassy clearing in the woods, from which Peter could see no way forward.

"What the hell?" Peter whispered.

Is this a trap? Have we just made a terrible mistake? Could she be some crazy woman who heard us asking around town and lured us up here to kill us? What have we done?!

"We're here," said Sarah cheerily as she got out of the car and walked towards the woods ahead.

"We're here?" Angie said, glancing at Peter before getting out of the car to follow Sarah. "Where's here?!"

Peter got out, the tension and angst that had crushed him earlier now seeming to melt away as he stood in the clearing, the sun shining on his sweat-slicked skin, the breeze that whispered through the treetops chilling him deliciously. He stood there a moment and breathed in the verdant odor of pine, fallen leaves, and the living earth. Peter realized he could hear dainty tinkling sounds and saw there were dozens of little wind chimes and bells hanging from branches all around the clearing. This small space in the forest felt mystical and mystifying.

Sarah paused at the edge of the woods and waited for Peter and Angie to join her there. Once they both arrived, she pulled back a branch with a tangle of golden leaves as if it were a drape, revealing a small footpath leading up the final length of the mountain.

"Grandmother Brigit is awaiting your arrival," she said.

Peter and Angie looked at each other, then grasped hands as they walked forward into the shadowy path, Sarah following behind them. After just a few minutes of walking up the steep incline, the pair panted breathlessly as they emerged from the thicket of wild woods onto a large, flat clearing at the peak of the mountain.

"Welcome to Red Mountain," said Sarah.

3

Peter stood there catching his breath, amazed by what he saw. There were numerous rough-hewn cabins and larger buildings arrayed in grid patterns scattered in clusters throughout the clearing, and beyond he could see several crop fields. Most of these were now nothing but freshly turned over dirt, though a few still clung to their late-season produce. Scurrying around everywhere, he could see women dressed like Sarah, in simple, anchoritic black dresses, woolen shawls tossed over their shoulders against the chill breeze running across the hilltop. Some were hauling water out of a large well, others tending to the fields, still others sitting in groups as they read from books, talked, or sat silently with their eyes closed.

Mixed in amongst these Peter saw men and women in modern clothing.

"Whoa," Angie said, looking around. "I can feel it, Peter. I can feel that power I was able to sense earlier. This is the source of it. Can you still not feel anything?"

Peter looked at Angie, then shook his head. "No, not energy. I just feel... quiet. It's the calmest I've felt in quite a while."

"This is Grandmother Brigit's community?" Angie said to Sarah. "This is where you live?"

"Yes, I live here now with my sisters."

Peter, pointing to some of the normally dressed people, said, "Who are they?"

"Well," Sarah said over her shoulder as she began walking towards a cluster of buildings, "I think that's something for Grandmother Brigit to explain. She's waiting for us at the Meeting House."

Still holding hands, Peter and Angie followed Sarah as she walked past the fields, the well, and several of the larger buildings. In one of these, he saw some of the modern-clothed people entering, and as the door opened, Peter thought he caught a glimpse of what looked like a library. Through a thicket of woods, he could see a hissing and crackling bonfire in a clearing surrounded by some of the black-clad women, who were standing there, hands linked, in a circle around it.

His attention was drawn away from the fire as they approached a large, long building, just as ungainly and rough-hewn as the cabins surrounding it. On the narrow porch of this building sat a cluster of women surrounding a chair that Peter at first thought had a lumpy black cloak bunched and balled up on it. Not until they got closer did he realize there was a small woman seated there, a black shawl across her shoulders and another over her head as a hood. Her humped back arched so far it looked to Peter like her head, which hung low, had become too heavy for her small body. The wrinkles on her pale face were etched like a web of deep crevasses, and she was easily the oldest person he'd ever seen.

My God! Peter thought. *She looks frail enough for the breeze to just blow her away!*

When they were still several paces away, the woman pivoted her head from a conversation with a younger woman and, in a West Virginia-accented voice that, to Peter, sounded like a gasping rasp of sandpaper, exclaimed, "Ah... here's they is now. Peter and his Angel."

Though until very recently, this ancient little woman somehow knowing Peter had thought of Angela as his Angel would have made him question how that was possible, he now accepted such things as the reality of his new life. Peter watched as her head turned and swayed but her eyes remained clamped shut, her brows furrowed, as if she were working out some difficult problem.

"I's is Brigit Connor," she said, extending a thin and knobby hand that Peter carefully shook, fearful he might snap it in half like a dry twig. "But 'eryone here call me Gramma Brigit, o' just Gramma. I's so glad you two got 'round to finding your way to us."

"We've come a very long way to find you, Grandmother," said Angie, a broad smile on her face as she let out a long, weary sigh. "It hasn't been easy getting here."

"I know that, Angel, I know that," said Grandmother Brigit, clapping Angie's hand between her own. "I's bin watching you two for a long spell now – oh, and pay them town folk no mind, they's protective of us here. They don't like strangers snoopin' 'round, askin' questions 'bout us none, but they's just lookin' out for us. They meant you no insult. Come sit and chat with an old woman awhile, won'chya? Girls, let these two sit there, please."

Two young women with bright, flame-like red hair got off the rustic-cut loveseat they were sitting on, then joined Sarah on the porch. When they turned to stand on either side of her, Peter realized Sarah was one of a set of triplets.

"Why have you been watching us?" Peter asked as he and Angie sat.

Grandmother Brigit turned her head towards him, her eyes still unopened. "Because that's what we do, Peter. We keep an eye on the Dark World so we can fight against it and protect thems that are threatened by it. We take in the survivors and teach them how to fight back."

As she said this, Grandmother Brigit pointed her trembling hand towards the long building Peter had seen earlier, from which some of the people in modern clothes were coming and going.

"Survivors? I don't understand," he said.

"There's always some who get touched by the Dark World but ain't taken by it. Their lives are forever changed because now they know it's real. They can't just go on pretendin' it ain't so, and they's usually filled with anger and rage. They can't go back to the life they once had because of what the Dark World done to them, so they come here and learn how to fight against it."

Peter and Angie looked at each other. The inability to return to their normal lives had been a specter haunting their recent conversations, and that glance silently shared their fears this unwelcomed fate awaited them at the end of their journey.

"What's the Dark World, Grandmother?" said Angie.

Grandmother Brigit brought a bony hand to her forehead as she made a low keening sound before she answered, a sound that wordlessly spoke long stories of sadness and pain, agony and regret. "The Dark World... it ain't nuthin' but evil. It's all evil. When the Good Lord cast Satan and his demons down into Hell, they created the Dark World to get revenge against us humans. To torment us, to torture us. To drive us mad and to make us do all nature of sinful and evil acts. All them tales you told you'self ain't true; all them monsters you all thought was just stories... they's all real. All of 'em. Demons, ghosts, blood-sucking vampires—"

"And werewolves," Angie whispered.

Grandmother Brigit nodded her head. "Oh, yeah. Beasts like that are real, all too real. You both know that now, dun'chya?"

"Yeah, we know all about that," Peter said distantly, as a memory of the rancid fear that he'd felt at Thompson's cabin and then again in Baltimore soured his turning stomach. He glanced over at Angie to see a far-distant look on her face and a gentle touch to her belly.

She must feel that fear, too. I hate feeling sick everything I think about what happened to us. Fucking Garrou! I hate the motherfucker!

"Which is why you're here," Grandmother Brigit said with a knowing nod. "You come here lookin' for help. You want to find a way to fight, to beat the beast that hunts you."

"Yes," Peter said, no longer able to contain himself as a confused babble of words poured out of him, "we need your help, Grandmother. We're in trouble, and... we don't know... we'd hoped you could... we have to save our..."

"It's a'right, child, it's a'right," she said, waving her hand to calm him. "Dun'chya worry none. You come to the right place, now. You young'uns wasted your time at that fancy lib'ry, but that's a'right. That was the bridge you all had to cross over to get here, and this here is where you need to be. We'll teach you all we can about the Dark World, about the people in it, how to fight back against this beast. You gwine need stay with us awhile, but this here's the place fer you to be fer now."

"People?" Angie said, her attention drawn back to the conversation from wherever her mind had been lingering. "There are *people* in this evil world? Not just... creatures?"

Grandmother Brigit chuckled, a croaking, coughing laugh. "Oh yes, child. The Dark World wouldn't be able to reach us if people didn't work with it, want to be a part of it. Sometimes, they's the wors' monsters of 'em all. There's plenty of people working right 'long side the demons, helpin' them to torture the rest of us."

"Why? Why would anyone want to be a part of something like that?!"

"Same reasons as always, child. Power, wealth, just because they like hurtin' other people. Because they's evil, pure and simple."

Peter turned to Angie, and said, "Sound like anyone we know?"

"Yeah, it does. I guess I thought he was alone, like, this random monster. I just never thought there was a whole damn network of people around him."

"Mmmhmm..." Grandmother Brigit groaned. "They's all around us, e'rywhere. You two should know better than most that the only thing people with power want is more power."

Peter looked at the ground and thought about some of the elected officials he'd met while working as a congressional staffer. A few were there because they honestly wanted to serve the nation and avoided the snares that line the Capitol's corridors, whereas many had arrived in Washington with noble intentions only to become media darlings and get sucked into the trap of fame, power, and wealth. There were also a great many who – aside from not being werewolves – were very much like Garrou with their self-assured, smug superiority and their contemptuous loathing for the average person.

"This is a lot bigger than we thought it was," he said.

"So it is to most folk who come to us," said Grandmother Brigit. "They's twisted up by what happen'd to them, heartbroken, feelin' lost. Like you two did after what happen'd in Baltimore last week."

A thought occurred to Peter that hit him like a slap across the face and filled him with a sudden flash of crimson anger. "Can you see the future? Did you know what was going to happen to us?!"

"There ain't no future," she said. "The future ain't writ yet. That's like tryin' to read a book that ain't done, ain't nothin' but blank pages. Naw, it ain't writ none, but it is suggested. We can see diff'rent images, all shadowy like, of what might happen, but no one on the Good Lord's green earth knows what *will* happen."

Peter nodded, the flare of anger fading to nothing as quickly as it had sparked in his mind.

"So now what happens, Grandmother?" Angie asked.

"Now, you both have a mess of work and learnin' to do," Grandmother Brigit said, "but that's fer later. Fer right now, Naomi here will walk you to your cabin, show you 'round a spell. We's gwine talk more later."

4

An elegant, almost regal-looking thin-waisted black woman with shots of gray hair streaking her temples who'd been sitting next to Grandmother Brigit stood, then motioned to Peter and Angie to walk with her.

"If you would follow me, please?" Naomi said with a smile as she pulled her black woolen shawl up around her shoulders and walked down one of the grassy aisles between buildings. "I'm glad you're here, at last. We've all been watching and waiting, eagerly anticipating your arrival. We're so glad you're safe."

"Thank you, Naomi," Peter said, then quickly added, "Oh, I'm sorry; should we call you Grandmother, too?"

She chuckled, and said, "No, that's an important title. There has always been a grandmother and there always will be one, but it's not me."

They walked back in the direction Peter and Angie had come, and when they approached the large building they had passed earlier, Naomi said, "This is the library. We have a large collection of books about how to defeat the evil ones, but also several dozen different grimoires, or books of black magic."

Peter shook his head at those unexpected last few words. "Wait, why would you have those here?"

"Because we know the only way to defeat your enemy is to know them completely, so to do that we read their own words. This allows us to understand them, to get inside their heads. You'll also find a copy of the Red Book, something every community of cunning folk must have. It contains thousands of years' worth of our collected knowledge and wisdom."

"Naomi," Angie said, "I'm still a little confused about who all of you are, exactly. Until Peter mentioned cunning women to me last week, I've never heard of such a thing before."

"Mmm... yes," she said. "Well, you know, that's just one of the names for us. We've been called soothsayers and curse-lifters, folk healers, the good walkers, and even the wise old women – and those are just the European names for us. There are cunning women all around the world, from every culture, of course. But what *are* we? That's an interesting question, Angie."

The trio walked in silence for a moment as Naomi thought, and then she said, "The easiest way to think about us is we're healers, in every sense of the word. Back in the days before modern medicine, when someone took ill, they were brought to us. We had the knowledge of healing herbs – and we still do – we knew how to make poultices, salves, and tonics. Most folks don't need that from us anymore, not here in America, anyway, though some poor people still come to us for that. Not only are we easier to get to but they also know and trust us... "

How hard is it to get to their doctor's if getting up here is easier for people?! Peter thought, suppressing the giggle that question brought up for him.

"But we also heal in different ways. Like you heard Grandmother Brigit say, we are some of just the handful of people on the planet who know about the Dark World – or the Atrocissimus, as it's formally known – without being part of it. We're gifted with Second Sight, we can watch people from afar and protect them as much as we can, and even have an idea of what the future might be, like you heard Grandmother explain. We know how to make talismans and charms using things from the natural world – like wood from certain trees and just the right kind if flowers – that the unnatural world despises."

"So," said Angie, "are you like... white witches?"

Naomi stopped walking, then turned to look directly into Angie's now wide-open eyes. "Child, I know you didn't mean any insult by saying that, so I'm not offended, but I will kindly ask you to never, *ever* refer to us as witches, white or otherwise."

"I'm so sorry, Naomi," Angie said, seeming to shrink in Naomi's withering gaze. "I meant no disrespect."

"I know you didn't, Angie," she said softly, smiling now as she put her arm around Angie's shoulder to continue walking. "But it's very important for you to know that witches and wizards are the servants of the Dark World, people who are league with Hell itself. They're altogether evil, unredeemable, and in return for all nature of obscene atrocities, they've been given great supernatural power by the demons. We, on the other hand, have been accorded these talents by God, gifts freely given that we've had since birth."

"So," said Peter, "how does that work? How did you know to come here? Is this the only one?"

"Oh, there are places like this all over the country, and thousands all over the world," Naomi said. "We're not even the only one in West Virginia. There's another one out in the western part of the state, near the border with Kentucky. Every state has at least one, some have dozens, but they're all hidden away, far from prying eyes."

Naomi paused in front of a non-descript rough-hewn cabin that canted slightly towards the right. "As I said, all of us cunning folk were born with these gifts, and from a very young age we knew things, we saw things, we could sense things others couldn't. Then, in our teen years, we were drawn here or to some other place like this. Some heeded the call and came right away, some fought it, some simply refused to accept the reality of it and insisted on living their own lives the way they wanted, thinking they could demand things be a certain way and control..."

She paused, one arm wrapped around her waist while her other hand lay gently on her chin, her thoughts far away for a moment. Her attention brought back to Peter and Angie, Naomi sighed, smiled, then said, "But no matter. One way or another, we all found ourselves coming home to a place like this eventually. At any rate... we are here at your cabin."

Naomi opened the wooden door to reveal a small, one-room cabin with a writing desk, two rustic chairs, a fireplace, and two beds on the far side of the room. Their bags were already waiting for them on the beds.

"This is where you'll be staying while you're here with us. All the meals are served communally in the dining hall, and you'll hear a bell rung when it's time to eat. I'll send one of the triplets over when it's time to show you the way. Tomorrow you'll start your training. I'm so glad you're here and I'll see you later at dinner."

Wordless and as if in a daze, Peter and Angie wandered to the beds then sat on the edge, looking at each other. Peter thought about the bizarre day they'd had, and what lay awaiting them now that they'd arrived here to, as Naomi said, start their training. It occurred to Peter he had no idea what exactly that meant, but he let go of that thought until tomorrow.

Peter and Angie grasped each other's hands, smiled weakly then nodded, their silence communicating everything that needed to be said.

CHAPTER TWENTY-SEVEN

1

The next day, Angie found the training to be far from what she was expecting.

She'd had a series of images running through her mind – which she jokingly thought of as the *Awesome Eighties Movie Montage Scene* – in which she and Peter were taught to fight with enchanted swords, of running for miles and learning how to do backflips while throwing symbol-etched shuriken, maybe even clambering up high ropes while the elders yelled at them from below to go faster, dig deeper.

The instruction offered on Red Mountain proved to be far less awesome and montage-worthy than all that. After breakfast, Angie and Peter had been given a reading list of books by one of the triplets together with instructions to meet with Grandmother Brigit in the afternoon to discuss the assigned passages.

Angie was appalled by what she read in the hand-written vellum pages of the books, in which she learned the bloody details about how people gain magic powers from the Dark World, some of the evils that lurk in the shadowy places of the world, and of the single-minded obsession demons have with tormenting humans. Both Angie and Peter had blank faces and vacant stares when they met with Grandmother Brigit inside the Meeting Hall later that cool, rainy day.

"That was..." Angie said, groping to find the right words, "just... so horrifying. I just can't believe... babies? They sacrifice *babies* to the demons?!"

They sat in a corner of the Meeting Hall clustered together as other elder women likewise met with survivors giving them instruction on the Dark World. As Angie glanced around the softly-speaking groups, she wondered if they, too, were as disgusted by what they had learned about the evil slithering unseen all around them as she had been – or had they already been introduced to it in the most personal ways possible?

"They do," Grandmother Brigit answered in a crackling croak. "Babies, young'uns, ol' people, they don' care. They bleed some, burn some, drown some, whatever the demon tells 'em to do, theys gwine do."

"And all this," said Peter, "all this evil and murder and torment. It's just for power?"

Grandmother Brigit nodded. "Yup. People always done anythin' fer power, an' they's always will, I'm 'fraid."

Angie struggled to find the words to express how disturbing she found all this. After a few moments of gaped-mouth staring at Grandmother Brigit as her lips moved soundlessly, she instead lowered her eyes to the rough hardwood floor.

"But," Grandmother Brigit said as she raised a bony, shaking finger, "you all got's to remember that it ain't just the big coven you need to watch fer. There's small ones out there spread 'round all over the place, doing their evil with no connection t'others, and there's even some folk out there actin' all on they own, like they's a lone coven. They ain't got the power the big coven do, but they's just as deadly as it is because they sacrifice young'uns and babies and e'ryone just the same."

Angie grimaced and rubbed her belly without being aware of it. She thought of a passage she'd read in one of the books describing how children were often sacrificed by first having parts of their bodies cut off, torturing them during long mutilation rituals for the pieces to be used in potions and spells before offering their bloody death to a demon. Even worse was the section on babies being cut out of a still-living mother to likewise be mutilated and dismembered so their body parts could be used in foul concoctions; the book explained that the increased suffering led to a more powerful black magic. But even worse than all that for Angie was the triumphant, celebratory way in which it'd been written by the wizard the grimoire had belonged to.

"But the evil ones in the big coven ain't dangerous just 'cause o' the sacrifices they make. They's e'rywhere, in the go'ernment, business, schools... they's a lot o' the television and movie people. They's e'rywhere. It's them you got to look out fer, too, because they's the ones you kin't see coming fer you."

"With some of the people I've met working in Congress," quipped Peter, "hearing they might be a bunch of Satanists doesn't surprise me much."

"But truth is," said Grandmother Brigit, "despite all their power and wealth, they's the slaves of the demons just like the demons are Satan's slaves. Slaves is what the demons that rule over the Dark World want to make all of us. They want us all to be *his* slaves."

I'm no slave, Angie thought, *and neither will my baby be.*

"This is a hidden world o' horror that wraps itself 'round this one, the way two diff'rent kinds o' ivies will grow 'round each other up a tree in the woods. And they gots all sorts o' horrors to use against us, things you once thought were foolish, childish notions, but ones not even your worst nightmares can make up. These creatures sneak 'bout in the dark, always lookin' for ways to make death and destruction."

"Like werewolves," Angie said.

"Mhmm," Grandmother Brigit groaned, "like werewolves. They's just one o' the tools the demons use to torment people."

"So how do we stop him?" she asked. "How do we stop Garrou from coming after us? How do we kill him?"

"It ain't as easy as all them stories make it out to be. See, thing is, the folklore about 'em is all wrong. The big coven is always secret and hidden, so people over the years tried to figure things out about werewolves to explain what was happ'nin', and that folklore is what come down to us. You know he don't need no full moon to turn into the beast, it don't catch, and he ain't in'ersted in eatin' people, just in killin' 'em. He kills just fer the pleasure of it, to praise Satan. No, he's in the big coven, and must be high rankin' in the group where he worships, which means he been chosen by the demon to be a weapon on earth. So, as time goes on, he's just gwine get stronger and stronger, more diff'cult to kill."

Angie and Peter glanced at each other, brows raised and eyes wide open.

"*More* difficult to kill?" Peter asked. "I put an ax in his head and it hardly did anything but blind one eye and give him a scar. How much harder can it be to kill him? What does that mean?"

"That means no silver bullet is gonna kill a werewolf who come into his full power," Grandmother Brigit said with a bitter laugh, "but no kind o' bullet is gonna work, neither. See, as time goes on, the demon spirit will take 'im over more and more, and before long, bullets will just bounce off 'im. At some point, he'll get stuck in werewolf form and be like that forever."

"How will we know if he's gotten there?" Angie asked.

"You don't. Not till you try to shoot 'im, anyway."

Peter sighed and rubbed his face. "So, what are our options, Grandmother?"

"You can burn 'im, but that ain't gwine be easy," she said. "You can always kill 'im when he ain't the beast, but that ain't gwine be easy, either, what with 'im bein' a congressman and such."

"And we'd go to Federal prison for the rest of our lives," Angie added.

"Yup," Grandmother Brigit said, "there's that, too. The best thing to use 'gainst a werewolf that has become that strong is holy water. It don't kill 'em, but it burn 'em like acid with a pain that's unbearable. The wound ain't never gwine heal, neither. You splash 'im with enough holy water and there ain't no way he'll be able to stand up 'gainst you. He'll run right outta there with his tail 'tween his legs like a beat dog."

"But it won't kill him?" Peter asked. Angie knew how badly he wanted to kill Garrou for what he'd done to them, and she surmised the reason for his question by the hard look on his face.

"No, it won't do that. He might die later from the pain or from an infection, but even though it'll hurt 'im because o' the demonic spirit in 'im, it don't kill a werewolf the way it would a demon."

"So, what's to stop him from coming after us later?" Angie asked. "If we don't put him down right away, won't he just come back later to finish us off?"

Grandmother Brigit nodded. "He might, but we's gwine fix you all up before you go with things that'll help with that, don't you worry none. But that's fer later, not now. Fer now, we's gwine talk more about some of the other nightmare creatures that are walking 'round the Dark World..."

As that first afternoon wore on, Angie found herself learning more about things she once never thought possible that she now had to embrace as the daily details of her new life.

2

The proceeding weeks followed a similar pattern: Angie and Peter were given long passages to read from some of the many old, leather-bound books the cunning women had in their library, then they'd meet with Grandmother Brigit, Naomi, or one of the other elder women in the community to discuss the readings. Lately, they'd also been meeting with one of the women individually and on this sunny October afternoon, Angie strolled arm in arm with Naomi along a path that ran around the edge of the autumn-clad clearing as they chatted.

"Angie, we've been talking for quite a while now and I've gotten to know you well, so let me ask you this: When you first came to this mountain, you felt something, didn't you? I'm willing to bet you actually felt it even before you came to the mountain, perhaps even before you reached Glace. Am I correct?"

Angie looked askance at her a moment, then chuckled and smiled. "Yes, I did."

"And it was like..." Naomi said as she waved her arm, trying to find the right word, "an energy, like pulses of radiating power. Correct?"

"Yes," Angie answered as she nodded. "I felt it grow stronger the closer we got to Glace, and then when I got here it was like... almost crackling with energy."

"Oh," Naomi said, snickering. "Crackling? This is a good

word for it. And, let me further guess that Peter didn't feel anything. Right?"

"You are once again correct. He had no idea what I was talking about – well, at least as far as feeling the energy goes. He said he felt calm and relaxed here."

"Ah, I see," Naomi said, as if this all made perfect sense to her. Angie did not share in that comprehension.

"Naomi, why are you asking me all this? What does it mean?"

She thought a moment before answering. "There's a reason we cunning folk are almost all women. Women have a unique... sense, perhaps you'd call it, or maybe even spirit. It's been called intuition before, but that doesn't quite capture it. Whatever you call it, it means we have a different connection to all of creation than men do. We're inexorably linked to the phases of the moon due to our own cycles, and to creation itself because we continue the work of creation in our wombs. We connect with the earth and the entire universe beyond in ways men can't."

"Umm... okay. I don't quite follow, Naomi."

"You felt something when you came here, Angie, because you have a greater sense of that connection than even the average woman does, and this will be vitally important for what is to come next."

Angie furrowed her brow and tipped her head to the side. "Are you saying I'm a cunning woman?"

"No, I'm not saying that, because if you were, you would've known it long ago and you'd be living in a community like this in Alabama. But I am saying you have a mystical connection to all of creation that you will need to tap into as the trial you're about to begin unfolds."

"I don't understand. How can I use a connection to creation for what we're about to do?"

Naomi patted Angie's hand, then said, "As you go forward to face the beast, you're going to be challenged and troubled. This is no easy task you and Peter are setting out to do. The answers you need may not always be readily available when you need them, so you're going to need to learn how to quiet your mind and open your soul to what creation is telling you, and most importantly, to trust that you *know* what to do. More than anything else you must learn to trust yourself."

Angie fell quiet as she thought about what Naomi said. She'd always felt far more comfortable trusting facts and data, information she could learn from a book, numbers she could crunch and run through analytics until they offered up some gem of knowledge. She had long ago put aside any faith in the *I know it just because* mentality; not only did she personally feel uncomfortable with it, but Angie knew she'd never be viewed as a serious professional if she didn't have a battery of data to back up her opinions. She decided trusting her feelings rather than her knowledge would not be easy for her.

"And this is the perfect time for you to learn how to connect to the song of creation and all life," said Naomi as she stopped their stroll and pointed to Angie's abdomen, "what with you creating life inside you even now."

Busted! Angie's voice screamed inside her head as she dropped her eyes to the ground for a moment, then covered her face with a hand as she giggled.

"I should have known you all would figure that out," she said between her laughter. "I assume Grandmother Brigit knows, too."

"All the cunning women here knew it as soon as you came to the mountain," said Naomi with a broad smile. "We could sense the life growing inside you. Plus, it doesn't hurt you never eat much at breakfast and then gorge yourself come lunch."

"Yeah..." Angie said, shrugging. "I feel nauseous in the

morning. Luckily, I don't get sick, but I sure do feel like I want to."

"Well," Naomi said as she took a small bundle out of a pouch she had hanging from her belt, "perhaps this will help with your morning sickness."

"What's this?" Angie asked as she took it, opening the thick wax paper it was wrapped in. She saw it was a bundle of loose, chopped herbs of various colors, the odor of which was spicy and delicious.

"That's ginger, and peppermint, and few other medicinal herbs thrown in for good measure. Boil up a little bit of this every morning in a tea and it'll help settle your stomach."

"I will, thank you."

"I take it you haven't told Peter yet. May I ask why?"

Angie sighed deeply and rubbed her forehead before answering. "Well... I found out the same day Garrou took me. I was going to tell Peter that night after he got back from work, but I never had the chance. It was obvious after that night my life would never be the same again, but also that there'd be no way we could live anything even approaching a normal life until Garrou was dead. So, I decided I couldn't afford to have Peter distracted or worried about me if we were to kill this beast. I'll tell him when this is all over. He'll be thrilled to know he's going to be a father."

Naomi nodded solemnly and smiled. "Yes, of course... of course."

"So," Angie said, "can you teach me to open myself up to creation, to trust my intuition?"

"I can indeed," said Naomi as she gestured toward a fallen tree for them to sit on during the lesson.

"This is going to be hard for me, Naomi, but I'm willing to try.

"Well, being willing to try is always the most important

step in learning anything new. It takes many years of dedicated practice to master this skill, but I can teach you enough before you leave to use for the fight you have coming up."

Angie spent the rest of that day the same way she spent her remaining time on Red Mountain: Reading, discussing the readings with elder women, and meeting with Naomi to learn how to connect with all creation and trust the knowledge she gained. By the end of her nearly month spent amongst the cunning women, Angie was beginning to feel as if she and Peter had a good chance of succeeding.

<hr/>

3

The fiery colors that burned throughout the surrounding woodlands when they'd arrived had muted to the dull browns and maroons of late October, and the trees were now all but winter denuded. In their time amongst the cunning women, Angie and Peter had learned much of the demonic workings of the Dark World, of the people involved in it, and everything they could about werewolves. They were eager to descend from the mountain and bring the fight to Garrou, and now once again sat with Grandmother Brigit in the Meeting Hall for their final lesson.

"I do wish you all could stay and learn 'erything there is to know," she said in her crackling voice as they ended for the day. "I'm proud o' how much you two ha'learned, but there's still so much more you need to know about the Dark World."

"I wish we could do that, too," Angie answered, "but we've already been here almost a month. We need to get going if we have any chance of stopping Garrou."

"And then there's the matter of our jobs and apartments

and bills," Peter added. "One way or another we need to see about them."

What jobs? Angie asked herself, believing they would both return to Washington to find themselves jobless, evicted, and their professional reputations ruined. She'd hardly thought of their lives off the mountain since they'd arrived, and both had known this was a possible outcome of disappearing for a month, the consequences of which they'd willingly accepted. *Whatever, it doesn't matter. I'll work at McDonald's if I have to. There's just no way we could live with the threat of Garrou hanging over our heads. Fuck it.*

Angie wondered if their friends and families were worried about them. This had been the longest she'd gone without contacting Nate or her parents since coming to Washington, and though she did let them know she'd be unreachable for a while, she feared they might be quite concerned by now. This, she felt, was just another sad reality of the hard road they'd been forced to take. Any hurt feelings could be patched up later, Angie thought, after Garrou was dead.

"I know all that, I know that," said Grandmother Brigit, waving away their objections. "But I still wish you could stay longer. We've prepared you as much as we can for the fight you got coming up, but there's 'bout two-three years' worth of training you still need."

"Despite that... do you think we're ready?" Peter asked.

"Ready as you can be, in terms o' learnin', anyway. But you ain't quite ready to leave us just yet."

"Not quite ready?" asked Angie. What else is there?"

"We's got a ceremony people gots to go through before they can leave the mountain. It's a pur'fication and protection ritual."

The pair sat speechless a moment, then Peter said, "Protection ritual? What is it? What's it to protect us against?"

Grandmother Brigit shrugged. "To protect you 'gainst the Dark Work, o' course. We'll talk about the details of it tonight after supper, so you all know what's coming, but don't you fret yourself 'bout it none. You 'member a while back you asked what was to stop G'rrou from comin' after you if you all hurt 'im with holy water?"

Angie and Peter nodded in unison.

"Well... this is what will stop 'im."

CHAPTER TWENTY-EIGHT

1

Garrou sat in his Crisfield home smoking a cigar as he watched the crabbers sail in and out of the Chesapeake, the late October sky gray with low-hanging clouds that threatened rain. He loved the dark, choppy dark waters this time of year, the salty sea air, the squawking gulls, and especially the view his house afforded him overlooking it all.

He always found the steady, regular flow of crabbers coming and going to be somehow relaxing, soothing. It was particularly so at moments like this when he sat in such a silent rage he wanted to tear people to bloody shreds.

Where are they? Where the fuck are they?!

2

It had been two weeks since he'd lost track of Peter and Angie, and in that time his mood had spread like a black thundercloud creeping in on a summer afternoon. After he'd terrorized the pair in Baltimore, Garrou had enjoyed a spectacular week as he'd watched his likeability poll numbers climb, as the press continued to paint him as a brave survivor overcoming his injuries, and as he gathered together more votes for a bill he had authored. He'd barely thought of Peter and Angie at all that week, and during the brief moments he did, Garrou would smile as he imaged their fear.

That Saturday, he'd worked the phones from his house overlooking the Chesapeake Bay to negotiate with a few representatives who relished playing the obstructionist to see what he'd have to give in return for their support. Late in the evening it had occurred to him he should take a peek at the young couple's suffering and ordered the sacrifice he'd need.

It was almost midnight by the time Garrou knelt in his subbasement sacrarium, scarlet in the smeared blood of a scragglylooking boy from one of the coven foster homes who now lay dead, crumpled on the floor before the altar. He stared, mute and confused, as the mixture in his scrying bowl turned pitch black, glowed, and unfolded to reveal nothing but an inky blackness.

"What... the fuck?" he said to himself.

Perplexed, his mind had raced to find an explanation. He glanced at the corpse lying on his floor, watching to see if there was any movement coming from the ashen gray body.

Nope, he'd thought. *He's all the way dead, so it can't be that. Unless... Could they be... Why now? That makes no sense.*

Garrou knew the Dark Eye couldn't perceive any who were on consecrated ground, and even though he could guess the reason for his inability to pierce the veil hiding Peter and Angie, the timing of it had confused him. If it were a few hours later on Sunday morning, it would have made perfect sense, or perhaps even earlier in the day when they were possibly at a wedding or some other event, but at midnight on a Saturday? Garrou, no less puzzled the longer he looked into the basin of black liquid, had scratched his chin at that unanswerable question.

"Where are you?" he had whispered, before closing the spell and going to bed.

The vexing question of where they might be hiding had receded into the back of his mind with the following days' demands, though it was never too far from his thoughts. By midweek, Garrou was back in his sacrarium, the blood of another sacrifice dripping down from the sigils on his body, only to find the scrying bowl again revealing nothing, a darkness so profound he could see his own confused face in the black reflection.

"What... the... *fuck?!*" he'd yelled into the scrying bowl as if it were a longtime friend that had betrayed his trust.

The following Friday, Garrou had been on the cusp of a long weekend, and he'd arranged enough sacrifices to scry several times a day if needed. He was determined to find them, to listen in on their conversations, to learn where they'd been hiding. By Sunday evening, his altar was covered in a thick layer of congealed maroon blood and the Chesapeake had a dozen new reanimated corpses trolling its depths, yet the scrying bowl had continued to show him unfettered nothingness.

What the fuck are you two up to? he thought, seething with a slow-burning rage. *Where are you hiding? Do you think you can camp in a church forever? You can't, and when you step foot outside of it again, I'll fucking rip you to pieces. Fine, you want to play a game with me? Then I'll just have to play it my way.*

Garrou had decided to abandon scrying in favor of a more

aggressive way of gathering information. It had been some years since he'd had the pleasure of watching a demon torture someone, and he looked forward to it since there are no entities in all creation more talented at the artful application of pain than demons. The accomplishments of every human practitioner throughout history paled to uttermost insignificance in comparison to the demons' fiendish abilities. Felix was especially skilled at eliciting pain and breaking not only the bodies of his victims but their minds and even their souls as well.

It was always a delight for Garrou to watch a true master ply their craft.

He'd spent several days of the previous week questioning Angie's friends, Malcolm and Freddie, as Felix caused pain like nothing that could otherwise be experienced in this life. Always pragmatic, Garrou appreciated the fact demon torturers didn't need restraints, nor cumbersome machines, nor even to touch their victim if they didn't want to. Felix had bound them both in the sacrarium through his awesome powers, then used those same abilities to induce sensations of bones being snapped and crushed, of skin being slowly flayed from their bodies, of being set aflame.

"Now, gentlemen," Garrou had said over their agonized shrieks and pleas for mercy, "I need some assistance with a little problem that's come up. Felix... would you, please, for a moment?"

The demon nodded, and the men's pain had immediately ceased, as did their screaming. They stood there held by implacable, unseen bonds, their skin dripping sweat, quivering from the diminishing agony. Their heads hung low as their heavy breathing returned to normal.

"There, now isn't that better? Screaming does so interfere with a decent conversation, don't you think?"

"Whaaa..." Malcolm had mumbled through a shattered

mouth, his teeth broken from clenching his jaw so tightly, "Wha' d'ya wan'?"

"I want to know where your friend, Angie Fontaine, has gotten to, together with her fiancé, Peter Brunnen. I was hoping you might be able to help me locate them both. It's really quite important I do so."

"I don'... I don' know. She took... leave o' absence... beginnin' o' month... that's all... all I know..."

"Oh, come now," Garrou had said, grabbing Malcolm's hair and holding up his head to look into his bleeding eyes, "I know how staffers talk, and I'm quite certain there's been gossip about where she might have gone to. Two staff members don't just vanish from Congress without other staffers talking about them. So, what have you heard?"

"Nothin'... I shwear, I've heard nothin' 'bout it."

"Nothing? Not a word?"

"Nothin'... I shwear."

"Not even a whisper?"

"No... nothin' at all."

"I don't entirely believe you," said Garrou, getting close enough to Malcolm he could smell the man's blood. "I think you're holding out on me."

"I schwear, I schwear," Malcolm had said, tears welling in his eyes, "I don' know an'thin'."

"Hmm," Garrou had grunted, dropping Malcolm's head to approach Freddie. "This one here. He's your boyfriend?"

Malcolm nodded.

"And would you say you love him?"

Malcolm again nodded. "Yeah, I do."

"Good," Garrou had said as he nodded to Felix. "Love conquers all, doesn't it?"

Freddie had immediately thrown his head back and screamed, his mouth opening so wide his jaw snapped and his eyes bulged out of his head. His entire body tensed with the unbearable agony of demonic torment as his shrieks of pain were joined by Malcolm's for pity and reason and for an end to this nightmare, all of which were ignored for days.

Despite the unending anguish, however, Malcolm still claimed to have no idea where Angie and Peter were.

Though the results of the questioning proved to be disappointing, the physical torture then transitioned to the most entertaining part for Garrou as Felix worked on shattering their minds. He would gently take one of their faces in his hands as if to kiss the man, then stare into his eyes. In the man's mind, he suffered torments irrespective of time or space, being lost in the demon's will for centuries, for eons, perhaps forever. By the time the interrogation was done, each man was a bulging-eyed, drooling, gibbering shadow of the person who had entered the sacrarium, each with a twisted smile on his face so wide his curled lips were cracked and bleeding.

"I looked into their minds, Mr. Garrou," Felix had said after breaking them. "I don't believe they know a thing. I don't think they could be hiding it if they did, not that well."

"Fine," Garrou had said with a discontented sigh. "When I come back on Saturday, we'll start with the next one."

"What do you want me to do with these two?" said Felix, waving his hand at the slavering, babbling, shattered things that were once Malcolm and Freddie.

"Well... you might as well paint the altar red with them. No use wasting good blood."

3

Now Garrou sat in the sunroom, watching the sky contemplate rain and the crabbing ships slid in and out of the bay as confusion fueled his smoldering rage. He'd always been a problem solver and enjoyed finding solutions; when answers eluded him Garrou would become angered, the irritation motivating him to work even harder. Lurking just beneath that quiet fury, though, was another feeling, an uncomfortable sense to which he was far less accustomed that felt like a shard of ice inching closer to his heart with every passing day.

Fear.

Garrou had felt fear during his life, though it was something from which his privilege had largely shielded him. But despite his wealth and connections, he'd felt dread when he almost got caught lighting a crack house on fire during his agoge, or when Peter smashed the ax into his face. Having to stand before the Supreme Tribunal had initially kicked off something close to panic.

But these were mere *moments* of fear, pure animalistic responses to something in his environment that could potentially threaten him. Once the moment had passed, Garrou carried on, feeling as invincible and indomitable as ever. The fear he felt now, as he waited for Felix to return with his quarry and smoked his cigar, drumming his fingers on the arm of his chair, was something very different to him.

This was no singular, punctuated moment. It was a deep-rooted angst, an existential loathing that threatened to upset Garrou's carefully crafted paradigm one icy inch at a time. As he sat there watching the crabbers and trying to enjoy his cigar, his mind kept drifting off to thoughts of how the Supreme Tribunal might react if they found out – *Don't you mean when they find out?* a puckish voice in his head countered, one he tried to shove into the abyss of his mind – that he'd lost track of Peter and Angie.

They never ordered me to keep track of them, a calm, reasonable version of his voice said in his mind.

They're not the in the habit of giving obvious orders, are they? countered that maddening puckish voice again. *Nor have they ever proven to be overly forgiving in the past.*

Peter and Angie are just... gone! People disappear all the time.

They don't disappear so far that the Dark Eye can't see them. What, do you think they moved into a fucking church?!

But I haven't done anything wrong!

What do they care? You got your face mutilated in an ax attack and you lost half your hand, and they called you to kneel before them like you were some fucking beggar caught stealing scraps of bread from their table. You didn't do anything wrong then, either, and they still threatened you.

Garrou stopped drumming his fingers and slammed his fist hard down upon the arm of the chair. He then sighed, opening and squeezing his hand as he stared out beyond the horizon, his mind lost in question and doubt. He felt much like that fellow in the old story with a sword dangling over his head kept aloft by one thin thread.

How would they do it? Any way they want to! They could do it at anytime, anywhere. They could order me to appear before them again, and if I refuse, they'd just send some demons to drag me there, kicking and screaming, so all the fucking gifts in the world wouldn't do me a damn bit of good. They could order Felix to kill me in my sleep, or someone close to me I'd never suspect, or some random killer trying to look good to them – hell, I could even be on someone's agoge list. What the fuck?! I have got to find out where they are!

He put his aching hand over his mouth as he continued to ruminate on these dreadful thoughts until his reveries were interrupted a few minutes later when he heard Felix arrive with their next guest.

"Mr. Garrou?" Felix said as he closed the closet door behind him. "I got him."

Garrou went into the living room to see Felix standing there as he dragged in an unconscious man whose eyes were bloated shut and black, his nose crushed, his mostly toothless mouth agape and his jaw hanging at an unnatural angle as red-tinged saliva drooled out of it. The beaten man, who'd been attacked so savagely blood was coming out of his ears, was now barely recognizable as Rick Johnston.

Garrou stared at Rick a moment, then looked at Felix, lips pursed, brows raised high.

The demon shrugged. "It's been a long time since I got into a scrap with a human, and this one put up a fight. I might have gotten a little carried away in the moment."

"A little carried away?!" Garrou said, squatting next to Rick's face to get a better look at the man. Rick's breathing was labored and raspy, and as his chest heaved to take in air, Garrou could hear a rhythmic crunching sound coming from it. He prodded Rick's head and his skull shifted, feeling under Garrou's fingers like a cracked hardboiled egg. "Well, this one's useless. He's just about dead."

"Sorry, Mr. Garrou."

I'm going to get incinerated by the Supreme Tribunal as a traitor and my familiar gets his rocks off beating to death people we need to question. Fucking great.

Garrou nodded. "It's fine. We have a list of people we can work through yet. But in the future do try and not kill anyone prematurely, okay?"

"Yes, Mr. Garrou. What do you want me to do with this one?"

Garrou looked again at the pulp of Rick's face, a sizable

pool of blood gathering under his broken body on the hard-wood floor. "Looks like he's already all but bled out, so maybe your colleagues in the Void would appreciate a new volunteer. They'll have him all patched up in no time, don't you think?"

Felix smiled. "That they will, Mr. Garrou."

Garrou puffed his cigar as he watched Felix drag Rick back to the closet door, then tap in the black magic to turn it into a portal. When Felix opened the door, Garrou was thrilled as always to see the cold, inky blackness of space with nothing but a few pin-prick stars in the background together with the cloudy sweep of a yellow-green-looking nebula. Felix lifted Rick and threw him into the Void, his body floating away as if in the current of some unseen stream. As he closed the door, a far-off roar could be heard, but then as the door clicked close, there was again nothing but the sounds coming from the bay.

"Do get rid of the blood, Felix," said Garrou. "This floor is oak."

"Yes, Mr. Garrou."

Garrou returned to his seat in the sunroom and his thoughts. After some time lost in his mind, he chuckled humorlessly.

I'm afraid it's time to raise the stakes, Peter. I did warn you this would happen. Granted, I didn't think it'd happen like this, but I did tell you exactly what would happen, what to expect. You can't act like you didn't know how this was going to end. Alright, then... now I know who to tell Felix to grab next.

CHAPTER TWENTY-NINE

1

Despite the late morning sun pouring in through the cabin windows, Peter had built up a large fire to keep them warm. As it snapped, popped, and hissed loudly in the fireplace, the flickering orange flames took away some of the chill they felt while wearing the plain, loose-fitting white robes they were asked to put on for the upcoming ritual.

I feel like a reject from the boys' choir, he thought as he scratched his bearded chin. *I hope this is worth it.*

The thin fabric did nothing to protect them from the cold, and though the folds of fabric were held tight by a simple rope belt, the cool air reached their naked flesh underneath from the open back slit that reached down to the waist held closed with two fabric ties. They sat on their beds while they waited for the ceremony to begin and chatted, discussing what came next.

"So," Peter said to Angie, who sat on the other bed dressed in a similar white robe, "what do you think about my idea?"

"Well, it makes sense," she answered. "I know what Grandmother said about using the holy water, but I agree we should also blast him to pieces with guns. We should at least try. Maybe between the two, we'll be able to put him down."

"Exactly. I mean, while I like the idea of burning his smug face off with acid – especially if it's painful and never heals – I don't want him just to suffer for the rest of his life, I want his life ended."

"Right. Okay, so... what is the plan for—" Angie said until she was interrupted by three firm knocks on the cabin door.

Peter stood and opened it, and there he saw Naomi holding before her a large white candle inscribed with a variety of symbols.

"It is time, Peter and Angie," she said.

Angie joined Peter at the doorway and, taking each other's hand, they walked together out of the cabin. There, standing in two long lines beyond Naomi, Peter saw the cunning women flanking either side of the path leading to the Meeting Hall. Each woman held a small white candle, the flame of which was sheltered from the breeze with a hand while they sang a gentle, lilting song, sweet yet somehow also melancholic. Peter concentrated on the words of the song as Naomi slowly led them closer to the Meeting Hall, but he couldn't make them out.

"That's not English they're singing in, is it?" he whispered to Angie, leaning his head close to hers.

"No," she answered. "I think... it's Latin."

Latin? That is not something I expected to hear being sung here!

Proceeding at a slow, somber pace, it took them some minutes to arrive at the Meeting Hall, which Peter saw was now decorated in autumnal wreaths and garlands made of oak boughs, evergreens, and ivy. Naomi walked through the open door and strode to the center of the hall, Peter and Angie following.

There, Peter saw that the inside of the Meeting Hall was arrayed with hundreds of candles, their yellow glow diffused by the low-hanging smoke lazily drifting up from many spicy-smelling incense burners. At the head of the hall sat Grandmother Brigit in a throne-like seat, her tiny, bent body looking even smaller in the oversized wooden chair. As he swept his eyes along the interior, Peter could see it was likewise decorated with garlands made from the surrounding woodlands.

As Peter and Angie followed Naomi to the center of the hall, the cunning women that had provided the cordon for them to walk through now entered the Meeting Hall as well. The women walked all the way around along the walls of the hall until they formed a ring, still holding their candles and singing their sweet-sounding canticle. Peter saw all the chairs had been removed and now only two tables covered in cushions were there instead, with an elder woman standing next to each one.

"Who come here seekin' th'armor o' the Light?" asked Grandmother Brigit in her raspy voice, raising it above the still-singing women.

"Peter and Angie come here seeking the armor of the Light," said Naomi on their behalf.

"And is they ready to do battle with the Dark World?"

"They are ready to do battle with the Dark World."

She nodded to Naomi, and said, "Then let they come fo'ward."

Naomi returned the nod, then pivoted to address the couple. "Peter and Angie, do you promise to be without fear in the face of the Evil Ones, to have courage so you might be a beacon of light in a world of darkness, to speak the truth in all things, and do no wrong?"

"We do."

"Now, step forward and be seen," Naomi said, then moved aside to join the line of gently singing cunning women.

"Peter an' Angie," said Grandmother Brigit, "this here is a ritual of purifyin' and protectin', as old as old can git. You all will git the armor of the Light put onto your bodies fer all time, armor that we also wear," she paused, pulling up the black sleeve of her dress to show a faded blueish blotch that was once a tattoo encircling her wrist. "Emblems, powerful and with great meanin', will be tattooed onto your bodies, and these symbols will help protect you in that fight that lies ahead and from the Dark World where'er you all go. The ink fer these tattoos you're 'bout to receive are made with pure water from our well, cinders from the fire, holy oil, and protective herbs. Peter and Angie, do you all un'erstand what I've said?"

Both nodded and said, "Yes."

"But," Grandmother Brigit went on, raising a shaking finger, "ain't nobody got to do nothin' because we all gots free will. If you don't want these tattoos, then you ain't got to git 'em. So, Peter and Angie, do you *choose* to put on the armor of the Light we's offerin' you here today and to go into battle 'gainst the Dark World wearin' it?"

The pair, still holding hands, looked at each other wordlessly for a moment, then nodded. "We do," they said in unison.

"A'right then. Martha... Abigail. You all may begin."

At her words, the singing stopped as the cunning women blew out their candles and joined Martha and Abigail as they knelt in silent prayer. After a moment of silence, the two elder women arose and gestured for Peter and Angie to each lay on a table. Once the couple positioned themselves on the cushioned tables, the elder women's assistants untied the rear slit of their robes, exposing their backs, and the cunning women began to softly sing another song, one with honeyed, mesmerizing tones like the one before it.

Peter tried to get comfortable and closed his eyes in anticipation of what he was about to endure. As Abigail's assistant stretched the skin of his back taut and the elder woman began murmuring prayers, he felt the ink-tipped needle begin to be repeatedly tapped into his flesh. He at first felt no pain at all, just a strange tingling that radiated outward in sizzling ripples with every tap. But as the hours dragged on and the tapping continued, Peter's back started to scream in discomfort. He opened his eyes at one point to see Angie grimacing as Martha struck the tattooing rake with her stick, the steady, monotonous tapping sounding like a metronome gone wild.

Tap-tap-tap-tap-tap! went both women's striking sticks for hour after long hour, the sunlight slowly diminishing to a dull gray, then to complete dark, until all the light in the Meeting Hall came from the many candles scattered throughout it. Peter had lost any sense of the passage of time, his entire world reduced to the stinging pain of his back, the tapping sticks, the murmured prayers, and the spicy smelling incense.

Tap-tap-tap-tap-tap-tap-tap-tap!

At one point several hours into the process, as the elder woman's tattooing rake drilled like a jackhammer into the flesh just on top of his spine, Peter cursed her in his head and regretted his decision to get the tattoos, until he opened his eyes and realized the cunning women still surrounded them, kneeling on the rough wooden floor, praying, and singing their mystical sounding canticles. Their humble dedication to his fight made Peter feel like a whiny child for complaining, and he promised himself to be as tough as they were.

Tap-tap-tap-tap-tap-tap-tap-tap-tap-tap!

After many hours of getting tattooed with what he thought was a large circle on his back, Abigail and her assistant moved to his wrists and ankles, then some hours after that, the very top of his chest and back where it transitioned into his neck. He glanced over at Angie and saw that Martha was tattooing her in the same spot as her assistant stretched out her skin and wiped up the blood.

Tap-tap-tap-tap-tap-tap-tap-tap-tap-tap-tap-tap-tap-tap!

After more hours than Peter could guess, the tapping finally ended. His body ached and his flesh felt like it was on fire, but the process was done at last as Abigail and her assistant helped Peter get off the table and to his feet, just as Martha and her assistant did for Angie. When they once again stood, the cunning women, at last, stopped singing and likewise stood up.

"Peter an' Angie," Grandmother Brigit croaked as she was assisted off the chair and gently guided by a cunning woman towards the couple, "you all now wear the armor of the Light. It will protect you in this fight you got coming up, but you gots to 'member that like any other armor, it can still be pierced by somethin' powerful enough. But we got one final thing to do, yet..."

As she spoke, of one the elder women brought Grandmother Brigit a copper basin filled with water. She dipped her fingers into it, then flicked some first onto Angie, then Peter, and then back again. After she had repeated this several times, the elder woman handed Angie the basin.

"This here is holy water," Grandmother Brigit announced. "The tattoos will pr'tect you all, but they's can only do so much on they own, so now this holy water gonna pur'fy you, too. Drink it and be fully ready to face the evil ones o' the Dark World."

Angie glanced at Peter, raised the copper basin to her lips and drank half the remaining water, then smiled and passed it to him, her green eyes open wide. He also drank the holy water, finishing it and feeling a pleasant tingle ripple throughout his body as it went down inside him. Peter smiled as it felt like an exhilarating cold breeze tickling him from the inside, one that was both invigorating and exciting.

"This here ceremony done," declared Grandmother Brigit as loudly as her raspy voice would allow. She then raised her right hand to the sky and said, "An' now, by the power o' God... go to war and bring death to the Evil Ones o' the world."

<hr />

2

Early the next morning as darkness still clung to the land, Peter and Angie sat after getting their bags packed and ready to go, as he drank some coffee, and she sipped an herbal tea she'd recently started making. The ceremony had lasted until past midnight; their skin burned and their muscles ached after over twelve hours of having tattoos tapped into their bodies. When they'd returned to the cabin, the couple had collapsed into bed rather than talk about what had happened or what came next for them.

"How do you feel?" Peter asked, devouring some fruit, nuts, and cheese the cunning women had given them the day before to eat after being forced to fast for so many hours because of the tattoos.

"Terrible, thanks," answered Angie. "My whole body hurts and the skin on my back is on fire. I can only imagine how sore the ladies are that gave us these. They were on their feet for twelve hours straight."

"Or the other cunning women, who were on their knees that whole time singing and praying. I'll tell you what, these women are tough."

"That they are," Angie said, raising her wrist to the candle to carefully inspect it. "I didn't get a good look at these at all last night. What'd we even get tattooed with, anyway?"

Peter likewise brought a wrist near the candle so he could get a better look at the tattoos he was given. There, amongst the red, irritated skin, he saw a band of symbols had been tattooed in one unbroken ring all the way around his wrist, the looped and swirling ligatures connecting the emblems making it difficult to pick out individual ones. But as he looked closer, Peter thought he could make out a P and an X overlayed, perhaps some Greek letters curling around each other, and maybe an A with a cross woven through it. Peter checked and saw the pattern followed on his other wrist and his ankles as well.

"Wow," he said, "these are pretty complex. Oh, hey, can you check to see what's on my back?"

Peter took off his shirt and turned as Angie picked up the candlestick, putting the flame close to his raw flesh so she could get a good look. He could feel its heat on his already scorching skin.

"Whoa," she exclaimed, "now this is *really* complex!"

"What? What is it?"

"It's... umm," Angie said, then paused. "It's... like, two concentric circles... with words going all around between the two. Alpha... omega... otheos? I don't know what that is... then three other words. Then there's a large triangle in the center, with a six-pointed star inside that... and then another, regular star inside *that*... then a circle in the center of the star. Plus, lots of other symbols and such. I don't know, it's super complex."

"I can't really picture that in my mind."

"Here," she said, putting down the candle and turning as she lifted her shirt, "see if it's the same as mine."

Peter raised her shirt the rest of the way and saw that there were little ink and blood drops marking the fabric in a circular shape and heard a soft peeling sound as the cloth pulled away from her skin.

"What is it?" Angie asked. "Is it the same as yours?"

"It's a... giant smiley face!"

"A what?!"

"Yeah, a big, goofy smiley face. With its tongue out."

"What?! Are you messing with me?"

"Yes," Peter said, laughing at his own joke. "I totally am. It's the same as mine."

Peter traced the raised black lines of the fresh tattoo, following first the line of the large circle on Angie's back and then the smaller one. He looked at it carefully, seeing there was far more intricate detail than Angie had at first described to him. There were many additional signs and symbols woven into the design, and geometric shapes that somehow gave the tattoo a rolling, flowing quality to it. Peter traced the figures without blinking for a moment, lost in its beauty and power until Angie spoke.

"It's pretty amazing, isn't it?" she asked.

"Yeah," Peter answered, shaking his head. "It really is. The skin on your back looks so angry though."

Angie nodded. "Yeah, so does yours. I never really intended to get a tattoo, and certainly not on my back. That hurt."

Peter looked now at the tattoo going around the base of Angie's neck and saw it was a long line of lettering. He gently traced the letters with his fingertip.

"Oooo!" Angie exclaimed as she quivered and giggled. "That gives me the shivers."

"Oops, sorry. I'm trying to make out what the letters say."

After a pause, Angie said, "Can you tell what it says?"

"Well, I think it's in Latin. I can't tell where it begins or ends, like it's just a ring of words. But... let's see... oh, I know this word: Contra. Umm... nequitiam et insidias diaboli esto...

not certain how to pronounce this... praesidium? Imperet illi deus... uhh... supplices deprecamur... tuque... princeps militia... umm, caelestis... yeah, I don't know. I bet Mr. Haag, the language teacher at my high school, is rolling in his grave right now."

"Did you feel like your collar bone was going to break?" she asked.

"I think it did, actually," Peter answered with a chuckle.

He now faced Angie, having worked his way around the tattoo collaring her neck. They looked into each other's eyes a moment and smiled, then Peter leaned down to kiss his fiancé. They gently hugged, careful not to squeeze the other's tender backs too hard.

"I can't wait to begin my life with you," Angie said. "To *really* begin my life with you, free of fear and worry and dread, once this is all over. I love you so much."

"I love you too, babe."

Angie cupped Peter's hairy face in her hands, then said, "Are you going to shave this off once all this is done?"

"No, I don't think so. It's kind of – if you will pardon the pun – grown on me this past month."

"Good. I've come to like it, myself."

Peter sighed as he scratched his hairy chin and sat back down. "We need to talk about what the plan is. I don't know if we ever thought we'd actually get to this point, but here we are. Grandmother warned us about the Dark Eye, so we need to have everything planned out and fixed in our minds before we walk off this mountain."

"I know we do. Problem is, other than splashing him with holy water and shooting him, we don't have even the beginning of a plan."

"Exactly."

The pair sat in silence for a moment as they thought about

the problem before them. Peter felt the fatigue of a twelve-hour tattoo session and fast combined with a night of poor sleep crushing down on him, making it hard to think clearly. He tried to piece together their options but found gathering the different threads of thought to weave together into a coherent fabric challenging.

"So, the main problem as I see it," Angie said after a minute of silence, "is that everything is too random, too chaotic. He can attack us anytime he wants, anywhere he wants, and we'll never know where or when he might suddenly appear. We can't go anywhere without feeling like we're going to set off a booby trap. Not at night, anyway."

Peter looked at her. "At night? Why at night? He doesn't need the full moon to change."

"No, but do you remember all those attacks you found out about while we were researching him? Every single attack happened at nighttime. I'm guessing that he only attacks at night because that way he can use the cover of darkness to sneak up on people, and to keep a giant, hairy beast a secret from the modern world."

"Hmm..." Peter intoned, leaning back in his chair, and stroking his sandy beard as he thought. "That's a great point. Your beauty is matched only by your brains, m'dear."

"I know," Angie said with a wink.

"Okay so whatever we do, during the night we'll have to hunker down and—" Peter stopped speaking and stared blankly at the far wall.

As the silence stretched out, Angie said, "What? We'll have to what?!"

"Sorry... something just occurred to me. 'Hunker' made me think of bunker. What we need is a bunker, a fort, almost, where we can go and draw him to us. We can load up on weapons, ammo, water, food, whatever we need. Then, when he comes to us, we can blast him to pieces."

"Okay... okay," Angie said, nodding and bouncing her leg in excitement, "I like this idea. I like it a lot. Do you have any place in mind?"

Peter thought, and even in the dimness of his fatigue-enshrouded mind, there was only one place that made sense to consider.

"The cabin," Peter answered after a moment with a grin that grew into a wide smile. "It's perfect. It's secluded, so he'll feel safe enough to attack, but it's in enough of a clearing that we'll see him coming. It's small, but that's good because then there's less area for us to defend. We can go to my parents' house, grab my guns, and ask Pa to borrow some of his."

"That sounds great. And if I remember the windows have wooden shutters on the outside, right? We can close them up and force him to come through the front door."

"Right," said Peter, finishing the last of his coffee. "Okay, so the question is: How do we get Garrou to come to us? How can we guarantee that he'll attack us in the cabin rather than just waiting us out?"

The pair thought in silence for a few moments. This time, Peter's mind refused to work at all, fatigue making it seize up like an engine running devoid of oil. He tried to think, he tried to picture alternatives, but all his mind could conjure up as a vast blackness and an urge to go back to sleep.

I'm so tired. So very tired...

The quiet went on until Angie said, "We piss him off. We make him so angry, so filled with rage, that there's no way he'll be able to help himself. He'll *have* to come to us, and then we have him. We have him."

"Okay... how do we do that?"

"I have an idea," Angie said, smiling wickedly.

CHAPTER THIRTY

1

They discussed their plan of attack until the rising sun scorched the eastern sky orange, working out as many little details as they could, hoping they weren't missing any openings. Angie relied on her analytical thinking because she knew one overlooked point, one bit of minutia that slipped past their attention could ruin their entire carefully crafted plan and leave them dead, nothing but bloody, mangled masses of twisted flesh. That was something she'd much rather avoid.

As the pair went through their plan, they made a list of things they would need to grab from Peter's parents' house, including the guns, ammunition, tools, some planks of wood, and various other things. One item on that list would require him to break the seal and go into Danny's room to look for.

"How do you feel about that?" Angie asked.

"Not good, really," Peter answered, "but there's not much I can do about it. I just hope my parents don't freak out too much about me going into Danny's room."

"And if they do?"

Peter shrugged. "I guess as long as I'm alive they can forgive me later. Nothing else we can do."

"Right," Angie answered. She thought for a moment, then asked, "Wait, what if he spies on us on the drive to your parents' or once we're there? What if he sees us taking the guns?"

Peter stroked his beard. "Well, we already know not to talk about the plan at all once we're off the mountain, and I guess if he sees us grabbing guns, he'll assume we're trying to protect ourselves. Hell, he might even assume we're coming after him, but without the details, it won't matter."

"Okay, sounds good," Angie said as she swung her backpack into her shoulders, grimacing as it settled onto her back. "Are you ready?"

Peter grabbed a bag in each hand, then nodded. "Yep. Let's go."

Angie opened the door to a cold, crisp morning, the frost-covered grass shimmering like strands of white gold in the clear morning sunshine. They skipped the path leading throughout the community and instead cut across the field to get straight to the woods. The frosty grass crunched as they made their way towards the path leading back to their car, and the chilled air felt fresh and invigorating as it filled their lungs.

As they approached the trail leading down the mountain, Angie saw from across the clearing several black-clad figures waiting there for them. Once closer, she could make out Naomi standing there, arm-in-arm with Grandmother Brigit, a thick woolen cloak hanging from her frail shoulders to protect her from the morning breeze.

"Good morning, Grandmother Brigit... Naomi," Angie said, nodding to the other elder women standing there.

"Mo'ning," said Grandmother Brigit, her raspy voice

cutting through the morning quiet. "We wanted to see you all before you left and git'chya on your way."

"Thank you for getting up to see us off," Peter said, "but you really didn't need to just for us."

"Yes, we did, actually," answered Naomi, handing something to Grandmother Brigit. "There are a few things you need yet from us, things that will be important in the fight you have ahead of you."

"These here herbs ward off werewolves," Grandmother Brigit said, handing Angie a bundle of dried plants gathered together, their stems bound with a piece of twine. "Hang this on the door o' whate'er house you staying at. It's made o' Wolf's Bane, mostly, with a few other pr'tective herbs mixed in, and them beasts can't stand the sight of it."

When she had finished speaking, one of the other elder women handed Grandmother Brigit a large Mason jar full of water, which she then passed on to Peter. "And this here is the holy water I said we'd give you. That's enough to put G'rrou in such pain ain't no way he gwine be able to fight back. But 'member, it ain't gwine kill 'im. Just hurt 'im real bad."

"Yeah," Peter said, glancing at Angie, "we'll remember that."

"Thank you, Grandmother Brigit," Angie added. "Thank you all so much for everything. Good-bye."

Grandmother Brigit nodded as she leaned on her gnarled walking stick, her eyes clamped shut like always and her brows knitted together.

"Good-bye, children," she said. "Now, go with God as you go to war."

"Good-bye," Naomi said, "and good luck."

After their good-byes and thank yous and well-wishes were done, Angie and Peter continued walking towards the edge of the forest and the trail beyond, ready to leave this strange, mystical place and return to the real world, prepared to fight for their lives, to kill or be killed. But, just before entering the forest, they heard Grandmother Brigit's hoarse voice calling them.

"Peter!" she cried out. "You come back to us when you ready. When you and your Angel are ready... come back to learn e'erything we can teach you."

The pair stared at her a moment as the wind gently whispered through the naked trees, until Angie said, "We will, Grandmother. We promise."

<hr />

2

The pair clambered down the steep slope in silence, careful not to slip on any of the frosty rocks. Being just a few degrees warmer down from the mountain top, the frost had disappeared by the time they reached their car, which was covered in a month's worth of fallen, wet leaves. After loading the car with their luggage as the bells and windchimes in the trees tinkled gently in the constant breeze, they were ready to leave at last.

"Hey, do you mind driving?" Peter asked. "I'm so tired I can hardly keep my eyes open."

"Yeah, I'm alright to drive. Stay up until we get back to Glace, but then you can nap if you want. I might need you to take over at some point because I didn't sleep well, either."

"You got it," Peter said as he yawned and got into the passenger's seat.

The clearing wasn't large enough for Angie to turn the car around in, so instead, she had to do a series of three-point-turns to orient it. Once in the right direction, she inched downward along the narrow path that wound its way through the trees, the grasping branches again making screeching sounds as the car passed by. They crept along this trail for half an hour until finally making their way to the dirt road; as Angie navigated her way down the mountain between the sheer cliff, the gouges, and the sharp rocks, she experienced a whole different kind of anxiety than she had being the passenger on the way up.

After twenty minutes of switchbacks and a few slips on the muddy road, they at last made it all the way down to Route 50 and Glace a few miles beyond.

"Okay," Peter said, "are you good from here?"

"Yeah, I am. I'll wake you if I need you to take over, okay?"

"Gotcha," Peter murmured as he put his seat back, snoring loudly within the minute.

Angie drove in silence as she made her way northwards back through Glace towards Maryland, alone with her thoughts as she reflected on her experience at Red Mountain. Training with the cunning women this past month had been so monumental, so significant, she recognized this would be the hinge around which the rest of her life pivoted – even more so than finding out about the existence of werewolves. Learning of the nameless terrors that prowled through the world and the shadowy malevolence of the Atrocissimus had been an unpleasant shock for Angie, but the more the cunning women taught her the more she trusted in her own knowledge. She'd felt her mystical connection to all creation growing, and as it did, Angie believed they would be able to overcome evil.

Give it a name, she thought. *Naming something reduces the fear of it. The shadowy evil in this case has a name, and it's Garrou. Louis P. Garrou.*

She wondered if he were watching them even now. Her eyes furtively glanced around the car as if trying to spot a well-concealed camera without making her watchers know she was aware of their presence, but then sniggered at her own silliness.

Angie knew the Dark Eye didn't require any cameras, and all the careful searching in the world would never reveal whether she was being spied upon or not.

Smiling, she thought about how annoyed Garrou must be if he were watching at that moment. All he'd see is her driving down a random road, Peter sleeping next to her, the only sound the constant drone of the wheels on asphalt and the hacking noise of Peter's snores. Angie tried to picture Garrou watching them, seeing the look of anger and dismay spread across his smug face as he realized all his effort had been in vain. She so much wanted to raise her middle finger in an act of silent defiance, but since that might somehow betray their plan and tip him off about their newly acquired awareness, Angie resisted the temptation.

Her mind now turned to thoughts about their plan, running through it once again and trying to find holes in it, holes that could get them both killed. Though filled with confidence thanks to the cunning women, the thought of taking on a werewolf – one who had almost "come into his full power," as Grandmother Brigit put it – still scared Angie. She'd learned too much about the Atrocissimus and werewolves for her to not be afraid.

We might not both make it out of this alive. You do know that, right?

Yeah, I know. I just haven't wanted to think about it.

Well, listen, this shit's about to get real, so you'd better think about it.

I don't want to. I don't want to think about going through all this just to have to live without Peter.

Too bad. You need to.

Angie sighed, acquiescing to the coldly logical, demanding voice in her head. She glanced over at Peter, who was stretched out in the passenger seat, arms crossed, mouth wide open as he slept with a small thread of drool leaking out. Not the sexiest look, but Angie loved him with a fire and a passion that burned hot inside her nonetheless, one that made the thought of living without him intolerable to even consider.

She had a sudden image flash into her mind, one of Peter again stretched out with his mouth wide open, but rather than sleeping in the car he was on the floor of the cabin, blood pouring out of a gaping wound in his neck, a thin, crimson bead of it sliding down his cheek. It was like a bursting spark in uttermost darkness, so intense that she flinched away from it for a second. She looked back over at her fiancé, seeing him again sleeping in the car.

Don't you dare get yourself killed, you big goof.

Touching, but you still haven't really thought about it, have you?

No.

You need to.

I don't want to.

Quit being sentimental and think about it.

Fine! So, let's see... if that happens, I'll be a twenty-five-year-old, unmarried pregnant woman, almost certainly unemployed, with my professional reputation in DC ruined. Oh, and don't forget about homeless! So... I guess I'd have to move back down to Alabama to move back in with Mom and Dad. I'm sure Dad would hire me as a paralegal, and then I suppose I'd follow in his footsteps and get my law degree, practicing small-town law with him. I'd live with them until me and the baby could get a place on our own, and then I'd tell little Petey or Vickey stories about their daddy, the wolf-killer.

Angie felt tears welling up which she angrily wiped away, willing her eyes to dry as she clenched her jaw tight. She told herself she didn't have time for tears and believed thinking about such a heartbreaking end to their story only invited failure. Having appeased the insistent voice in her head she pushed thoughts of Peter's death out of her mind and turned on the radio. Though at this point in the drive Angie only got a few weak signals that were full of static, the garbled music fading to white noise helped her keep the thoughts and images of Peter's death out of her mind.

She finally found a radio station with a strong signal playing music she liked, so Angie continued on until about the halfway point. By then, fatigue had begun to settle on her like a heavy weight and made her eyelids flicker as she ached for sleep. Angie pulled over, then shook Peter awake.

"Wha..." he groaned after the third time she called his name.

"Honey, wake up," Angie said. "I need you to take over driving, okay?"

He sat up and glanced around looking dazed, his wide-open eyes unfocused and bleary. "Where... ugh, my mouth is dry... where are we?"

"I've been driving for about two hours, so I guess we're almost half of the way there. But I'm about nodding off and don't want to crash the car."

"No," he said, rubbing the sleep out of his eyes, "no, crashing wouldn't do at all, will it? Okay, let's switch places."

Angie settled into the passenger seat, putting her glasses into the center console, and trying to get comfortable. She at first thought a nap might elude her as her mind went to turning over their plan once again as soon as she closed her eyes, but she soon drifted down into the delicious blackness of sleep.

———

3

"Angie," Peter said, gently rubbing her shoulder. "We're here. We're in Mountain Lake Park."

Peter had pulled her out of a lovely dream, and though the details were already disappearing from her memory like snow melting in the hot sun, Angie could recall it was about her and Peter and their toddler child playing together on a seaside beach while some building burned to cinders behind them. She arose in her seat, pulling it back up into the normal position as she looked around and saw they had just arrived in town, still a few blocks distance away from Peter's parents' house. The bright sun of earlier had been replaced with angry gray clouds.

"I'm starving," Angie said, a headache matching her upset stomach. "I need to get something to eat. Soon."

"Well, don't worry. I'm sure my mother will either be cooking something for lunch or have a ton of food in the fridge."

She nodded, rubbing her stomach, and hoping she could make it there without throwing up. Although the spicy tea Naomi had given her worked well against the morning sickness, Angie hadn't yet eaten anything all day. As the nauseous feeling rolled her stomach and her throat grew tight, she was regretting the foolish decision of skipping food for so long.

"Look," Peter said as he handed Angie a folded newspaper that highlighted a short article about Garrou. "I stopped at a gas station while you napped and picked the paper up. Read the article about him."

She read through it quickly, her eyes widening when she settled on the third paragraph of the story. Angie turned to look at Peter.

"This means he's going to be tied up all day Saturday on the Delmarva," she said, "and there's no way he would miss and big election event like this."

"I know, it's perfect! So... Friday," Peter said as he nodded, letting the silence fill in the blanks where his words would normally be.

They pulled into the short driveway of the Brunnen house a few minutes later and were relieved to see Ed's gigantic Ford F-350 parked outside. The plan required them to borrow that, too, and if he were out somewhere, they'd have to wait for him before they could begin to discuss grabbing the things they needed. Neither of them wanted to wait to bring the war to Garrou any longer than they had to.

"Hey, make sure to keep your sleeves down while we're here," Peter said before turning off the engine, rolling down and buttoning the checkered sleeves of his shirt. "My parents hate tattoos and will blow a gasket if they saw we have some. I'd also rather avoid having to explain why we have matching tattoos all over the place and where we got them."

"Right, okay."

They got out of the car, Peter stretching and rubbing his bottom, Angie making her way straight for the front door and the food that lay beyond it. Halfway across the lawn, however, she stopped abruptly as a strange tingle crept all over her body. She looked at the front door and the festive autumn wreath hanging on it, feeling a vague sense of dread wash over her about what they'd find in the house. As she stood there trying to decipher the meaning of this, Angie became aware of something – or more precisely, the absence of something.

"There's no fire going," she said, sniffing the chilly air as Peter joined her there. "Your father doesn't have a fire going. Didn't you say he always gets a fire lit on days like this?"

"Yeah, he does," Peter answered, concern carved onto his face as he looked up at the chimney. "There's no smoke."

Their eyes locked onto each other's for a moment, communicating volumes in the silence, then both walked forward towards the door. Peter put his hand on the doorknob, pausing for half a second before turning it, then opened the door. It swung inside with a moaning creak that to Angie sounded like a groan of pain. They stood in the doorway peering into the dark house and heard the noise they feared the most.

Nothing at all.

No fire crackled and popped from the fireplace. Peter's mother could not be heard in the kitchen cooking, there were no sounds of sports blaring from the television, and his father wasn't yelling instructions to the players. The house was silent, cool, and dark, looking to Angie far too much like a crypt for her liking.

Angie's heart began to race in her chest and her throat grow tighter, catching her breath, and in the tomb-like silence of the house, she could hear her blood thrumming through her ears. The sense of some nameless fear, shadowy and inchoate, grew more insistent as her tingles intensified.

"Mom?" Peter yelled out from the porch, listening carefully, and leaning into the house a bit as he did. "Dad? Where are you? Are you in here?!"

His calls echoed unanswered throughout the empty house.

Peter stared into the gloomy home, his head turned slightly as he did. As the couple stood on the porch, like two unwanted guests hoping for admittance to a party, Angie's body continued to tingle in hot ripples. Naomi had taught her to listen to the song of creation and to rely on her unrecognized knowledge, but she hadn't had time to teach her how to puzzle out what things meant. Though still ignorant of the details, Angie knew this sense was a warning and meant... *something*.

After half a minute of hearing nothing but silence, Peter ran his hands through his hair and took a step into the house. He stopped as Angie's hand suddenly shot out and grabbed his wrist.

"Don't," she whispered. "What if there's something in there, waiting for us?"

"Do you sense something?" he answered in a likewise whisper. "Is there something in here?"

Angie paused, then shrugged. "I don't know. I still can't tell yet. All I know is that something happened here, and something either *is* here or *was* here. I just can't tell the difference, yet."

"Okay," Peter said, looking back at the car. "Let's get the Wolf's Bane and the holy water. That way, if it's Garrou or his familiar, we'll be prepared."

"But won't that... you know..." Angie answered, trying to communicate more with her nonverbals than her words.

Peter clenched his eyes and sighed heavily as he again ran his hands through his hair. "Maybe, but I don't know what else to do at this point. Do you?"

Angie did not and shook her head in answer. Peter then trotted back to their car and got what they needed, handing Angie the herbs when he returned to the porch and unscrewed the lid from the holy water, careful not to spill any.

Angie held the herbs out from her body, as a vampire hunter might clutch a crucifix, and Peter raised the jar near his shoulder, ready to fling the contents if needed. He looked to Angie like he was wielding a sword, an image that made her smirk from the humor of it. Although there was nothing she found funny about their situation, she couldn't help having the urge to laugh like a lunatic even as her dread continued to grow, swelling until Angie felt like she would choke on her own gasps for air.

The couple shared one final look at each other, then nodded, a cold fear coursing through Angie's body seemingly in place of her blood, chilling her and making her tremble. Peter stepped in slowly, quietly, walking as Angie imagined he would while stalking through the forest during a hunt. She followed him in, taking similar careful steps, being very mindful of each move forward, allowing her footfalls to make no sound at all. Despite her careful walking, she was dismayed to discover in the obdurate silence how loudly the old wooden floor creaked.

Working together, the couple moved forward, looking to Angie like the strangest military fire team, armed only with a jar of water and dried herbs rather than guns. She again struggled not to laugh, the absurdity of their situation smashing head-on into her growing angst. As Peter opened the closet door in the living room and they cleared it, together with the kitchen, laundry room, and the basement. The tension was so great, Angie felt like she might go mad, fearing her emotions would pour out then in gales of raucous laughter as she tore her face bloody to make the insanity of their existence stop.

They crept upstairs after confirming there was no one on the ground floor, the steps again squeaking and groaning like obnoxious claxons, which Angie felt would alert anyone upstairs to their presence. As they did, the humor of their situation Angie had found earlier evaporated, and all that remained was a fear that danced on the border with panic. Her desire to laugh was replaced with a need to scream her throat raw as they inched their way along the narrow hallway, clearing first Peter's parents' bedroom, then his old room, and then finally Danny's. Dust-covered and full of stilted air and memories, Angie wasn't at all surprised when, after checking the closet, Peter got out of there as quickly as he could.

Joining him downstairs, she found him pacing in the living room, fighting back tears.

"They're gone!" Peter cried, the anguished tone in his voice blending with panic and rage as he paced in a tight arc, his emotion growing with every pivot. "They're gone, and he's taken them, babe. He said he'd do it and he did it. He's got them and he's going to kill them. He said he would. The fucker said he would!"

Angie stopped his pacing by throwing herself into Peter with a hug, wrapping her arms around him as she said, "You don't know that, hon. You don't. Not with certainty."

"No, I do. I do know that. My dad's truck is outside, his hunting gear is in the closet, and you sensed there'd been something here. There had been, and it was when his demon came here to get them. I know it."

A tear scrolled its way down Angie's cheek regardless of her attempts to stop it. Despite her encouraging words, she knew Peter was right. Angie had known before she'd even entered the house and would have realized it if she'd been better at decoding these vague senses of hers.

"You'd better call your parents," said Peter after a moment, and Angie could see the muscles in his jaw clenching as he kept his emotions in check. "You know... just to make sure."

Angie nodded, then walked into the kitchen to call her folks, but first, she munched some saltine crackers to quell her queasy stomach. She was able to get hold of her mother, and for perhaps the first time in her life, Angie was pleased to listen to her berate her for taking so long to contact them. Her mother told Angie she was worried sick, and her father was worried sick, and even Nate was worried sick about her. She reminded Angie it was nearly a month ago that she said she'd be difficult to get hold of for a while, but a month is quite a bit more than just a while. Angie smiled at the reassuring voice of her mother but watched with sadness as Peter hung the Wolf's Bane bundle on the front door, then sat on the couch, covering his face as he did. She knew at that moment with inexplicable certainty he'd never hear his mother's voice again.

She wanted so much to tell her mother to pack up and go stay at the beach house they had on the gulf coast, for her parents to get Nate and go there immediately and tell no one where they were – but then she wondered to what end? If it had been Garrou's familiar who'd kidnapped Angie from her own apartment using black magic to gain entry, as Grandmother Brigit had told them, then what good would telling her mother to hide do? Assuming she listened to Angie without pushback, which she knew was unlikely with her mother, Garrou would just use his magic to find them and take them.

No. She decided the best way to protect her parents, Peter, and their baby was to kill Garrou and end the foul stain of his evil once and for all.

After just a few minutes, Angie was able to get off the phone and joined Peter on the couch, who sat staring into the cold fireplace. She sat next to him, rubbing his back, saying nothing. She knew there was nothing to say in a moment like this.

"They are gone, aren't they?" he said numbly after a few moments.

"Yes," Angie whispered, trusting the voice from within her own wisdom that answered the question for her. "He took them and they're... gone."

She watched as Peter squeezed his eyes shut tight and struggled with his grief, his anger, his fatigue, stopping himself from crying, balling his hands up into tight, shaking fists. Angie would normally have encouraged him to cry if he needed to, to talk about what he was feeling, to vent all his negative emotions. Now, she instead let him have this moment to steel himself, understanding from her own experiences where the iron will to control his emotions came from.

After a moment, Peter's fist stopped shaking and his jaw unclenched. He sniffled once, sighed, then said, "It's cold in here. I'll get a fire started."

As he began to load the fireplace with scraps of papers and the kindling, Angie asked, "So now what do we do?"

Without pausing his task or even looking back at Angie, Peter answered, "I'm fucking exhausted. Between last night and the drive and now all this shit, I'm too tired to... you know. Not today. We need to rest today. I say we stay here today and just relax, then spend the night here. We can get up early, load up what we need tomorrow morning, and then we can go about our business. Sound good?"

"Yeah," she said. "That sounds very good."

Angie leaned back into the couch, and as the heat of the growing fire reached out to warm her chilled skin, she also felt deep-seated fatigue her brief nap had left unsatisfied. The thought of spending the day relaxing in the Brunnen's empty house before unleashing the first steps of the plan tomorrow sounded like the perfect idea.

The thought of killing Garrou sounded even better, bringing a fierce smile to Angie's face as she watched the crackling flames grow.

CHAPTER THIRTY-ONE

After passing a restful day and sleeping well, the pair awoke early the following morning to begin loading Ed Brunnen's truck with everything they needed. Angie had a long drive ahead of her and both were eager the get their plan started.

They first went out to the garage, where Peter grabbed a few boards and cut them to the size he needed while Angie took the hammer, nails, and a few other things, then loaded them in the truck. Working together, she and Peter then took his father's small jon boat and loaded it into the oversized bed of the pickup truck after first removing its registration stickers. They then transferred their bags to the Ford as well, Angie tossing in her emptied backpack so she could use it later.

In the house, Angie and Peter removed every shotgun and handgun, together with all the boxes of ammunition. They had debated whether they should bring the hunting rifles as well, but Peter thought the shotguns allowed them more firepower quickly, with the ability to chamber new rounds as fast as they could use the pump action. In the narrow confines of the cabin the shotguns, together with pistols, seemed the best option.

They brought out the last batch of guns to the truck and Peter put a handgun on the pile of weapons then snapped his fingers and said, "Oops, I almost forgot."

He ran back towards the house, Angie following. She waited for him in the living room as he rummaged through Danny's bedroom, allowing him some privacy as he did so. After about fifteen minutes he came down, holding the item in his hand like it was a lump of gold.

"Oh, wow," Angie said, taking it. "That is realistic. It's so light, but it looks real."

"Yeah, I know. Danny had a few of these realistic ones and I guess he would have developed it into a collection... had he lived."

"Does it still work after all these years?"

"It sure does," Peter answered, squeezing a button to make it whir. "I put in new batteries while I was upstairs. There's a little electric motor in it so all you'll have to do is press it once. No need to keep pumping."

Angie nodded. "Good. Let's hope I don't need it."

"Amen to that. I'll get it filled up for you."

As they walked outside, Peter grabbed the bundle of herbs from the door and transferred that to the truck as well, then filled the item they both hoped Angie wouldn't need to use. The truck was fully loaded and ready to go, so once the item had been filled, they were at last ready to set their plan in motion.

The couple held each other in silence for a moment as the clear morning sun shone down upon them, words failing to convey the depth of meaning that looking into each other's eyes eloquently did. They hugged and then kissed.

"You be careful," Peter said, swiping away some of Angie's

hair that had fallen into her face, "and remember to watch your speed. You're not going to want to get pulled over with that small arsenal of guns you have in the truck."

"I know. I will be. You be careful too, okay?"

"I will. I'll call you as soon as I see him, and then you can call me once you're back on the road after it's done."

"You're sure he'll be there?"

"Well... he takes a group of people there for dinner every Friday night Congress is in session, and he has that big campaign event tomorrow, so I don't see why tonight would be any different. I'll be waiting for you at the rendezvous point once you're done, okay?"

"Got it," Angie said, then giggled. "Damn, we sound like we're planning the invasion of Europe or something."

Peter chuckled. "I know, but honestly, that's kind of how I feel. Like this is a military operation of some sort."

"Yeah... okay, I'm going to hit the gas station on the way out of town, then we can get on the road."

"Okay. I'll take the lead while we're on the interstate because if there are any speed traps, they'll get me first, which is good since I don't have any guns with me. I'll be able to stay with you all the way until Frederick."

Angie nodded, as the pair again hugged. She wanted to get their plan in motion, rid themselves of Garrou and his threat, be free to live their lives without his obnoxious intrusion, but at that moment in time, she ached to stay right there in Peter's arms, to let the universe collapse into nothing but their embrace, to just feel his body and his warmth and his touch. She wanted everything else to fade away into oblivion and let existence mean nothing but her embrace of Peter. Judging from his clutching reluctance to let her go, Angie assumed Peter felt just the same.

But wanting was irrelevant when there was a job to do, and they sadly let go of each other to begin their plan.

What was it his Granddaddy always used to say? No way through it but to do it.

"All right," she said, "Let's get going. I'll see you later tonight."

They separated into their different vehicles, Angie having a flicker of amusement as she noted the irony of having to pull herself into the huge truck while Peter ducked down to get into the Avalon. Her mirth quickly evaporated, though, as she thought about the day ahead of her, setting her jaw and leaving her with nothing but a single-minded focus on completing her part of the plan.

Their little two-vehicle convoy drove to a gas station on the edge of Mountain Lake Park, where Angie filled the tanks with all the gasoline she would need and got a few bags of Combos for herself to munch on. She gave Peter a thumbs up once she was settled back into the truck cab, and in just a few minutes they were on Route 135, beginning her six-hour voyage across Maryland.

As she drove behind Peter, humming and singing along to the radio, Angie rubbed the small bump in her belly, the one she'd just noticed that morning as she looked at herself in the bathroom full-length mirror. She'd feared Peter might notice, putting her intention to participate in jeopardy, but eliminated that concern with some well-placed, baggy sweatpants. Angie spoke to her distended abdomen as if it were a child strapped in a car seat inside the truck with her as she cruised along the interstate and had already started to refer to their unborn child as Bubbins.

"Okay, Bubbins," she said, patting her bump, "We just got on Route 68, which is also Route 40, and then in a little while after that it turns into I-70... I know, Bubbins, I know. It's all a little confusing, but you'll get used to it in time."

She thought about their baby, their little Bubbins, their future Petey or Vicky. She wanted the baby to have a normal life. She wanted their Bubbins to grow up in a stable household, to join Boy Scouts or Girl Scouts, to play Little League softball or baseball, to learn how to hunt and fish, to develop a love of books and reading. She wanted their Bubbins to have friends and go to the prom and just be an average kid.

But the more Angie thought about it the less likely that seemed.

We can't keep what we know from Bubbins. That wouldn't be fair. And we'll have to teach Bubbins what we know to keep him or her safe. They'll want to get revenge on us after what we're about to do, so they'll most likely hunt us the rest of our lives. Bubbins won't have a normal life, it's just that simple. We're going to have to raise our child with complete knowledge of the covens and to grow up to be a witch hunter and demon killer.

Yeah... I'm okay with that.

The drive continued uneventfully, Peter honking and waving when they reached Frederick as he diverted to take I-270 to Washington while she continued driving along I-70. She felt a brief pang of envy, as at this point Peter was only about an hour away from his destination whereas she still had another three hours yet to go in her drive. She glanced at the digital dashboard clock and saw it was just a few minutes past eleven, then shrugged.

Oh well, she thought as she popped a few more Combos into her mouth. *He'll have to sit in front of the restaurant for hours. I'll get off in a little bit and stop for lunch, maybe rest a while.*

Which is just what she did. Since the sun didn't go down

until around quarter-past six this time of year, Angie had many hours before her, so she opted to stop at a family restaurant and enjoy a long, relaxing lunch. If she had to eat alone, she would have preferred to have had a beat-up, dog-eared copy of one of her favorite softcover horror books with her, but being alone with her thoughts wasn't so bad, either.

As she sat there waiting for her lunch to arrive, Angie couldn't help but notice a young couple around her age, one with a chubby little toddler and an even chubbier infant. She stole glances at them as the couple entertained their kids, the father coloring a placemat with the toddler while the mother read a book to the infant, feeling a flash of anger that something so prosaic, so typical, yet so precious in a person's life had been stolen from her. She put the anger away, down in the well where the monster had once lived, promising herself she would let her rage fly loose later that night. After swallowing her anger, Angie was able to enjoy her restful lunch break.

After stretching her lunch out for an hour, Angie continued driving as she wended her way across Maryland, her thoughts focused on what awaited her at the end of her drive. She enjoyed the views afforded her of the various massive cargo ships from atop the Chesapeake Bay Bridge, then felt an unrelenting urge to press on to her goal as she sped south along the Delmarva. A few hours later, she was pulling into the outskirts of Crisfield.

She slowed down to look around, orienting herself to the town. Angie passed numerous roads that branched off from the main strip leading into Crisfield, chain restaurants and stores scattered all along its length. She could tell those roads led to various developments and clusters of houses, but those were irrelevant to her. There were a few things she needed to find first before settling in for her long wait, none of which were to be found following those roads.

Angie wandered around for about half an hour, managing in that time to find some piers that thrust out into Daugherty Creek, but ones that were positioned on the wrong side of town, too far from her goal – a goal that she still hadn't found yet. The long hours of driving in the truck started to wear on Angie as she sat in the pier parking lot, holding her head in her hand, and wondering how to proceed. If she couldn't find Garrou's house their entire plan would fall to pieces, and everything up to this point would have been a waste of time.

She roughly knew where Garrou's house was. Angie had come across an article about him and his slick, modern home in an architectural magazine when she and Peter had been researching him the month prior in the Library of Congress. There'd been a picture of Garrou on the cover with the steel and glass monstrosity behind him, an expanse of unobstructed water beyond. The article had described the house as being perched on the edge of town, on the water, near the confluence of Daugherty Creek and the bay. That vague description encompassed most of Crisfield, leaving her with few options.

She didn't have an address for him, so Angie couldn't find it that way, nor did she want to bring attention to herself by asking anyone from town where Garrou lived. The realization this was the glaring hole in their plan she'd been trying to find hit Angie like a brick falling on her skull as she now rubbed her forehead, knitting her brow together savagely.

Fuck! Now what am I going to do? I can't drive around here all day just hoping I stumble onto his house. I still need to find the fucking boat launch and be in place by sundown... so now what?!

As she rubbed her head in frustration, Angie thought about the tingling sense of unlearned awareness she'd felt the day before when she and Peter had arrived at his parents' house. She'd known something had happened there, and that the

Brunnen's home had been visited by evil. Angie hadn't been told this, nor did she deduce it from clues; she just *knew*.

She closed her eyes and took a deep breath, calming and settling herself like Naomi had taught her, then took another deep breath and let the air out in a long, whistling string. Angie sat like that for perhaps a minute, breathing slowly, until her eyes snapped open, and she put the idling truck in gear. Nothing had looked different as she turned back onto Maryland Avenue to drive into town, she didn't have a whispering, echoey voice guiding her, nor was she being visited by a ghostly image of Grandmother Brigit pointing the way.

Despite the lack of theatrics, Angie again just *knew* where to go.

She drove with the casual confidence of one familiar with a town, following the avenue past more stores, a bank, a church, and though Angie had never seen any of these buildings before, she'd known exactly where they'd be. She turned at an intersection in the Crisfield downtown area, following it past a large marina, the many long piers looking like branches on the nude trees now that all the boats had been removed for the winter. Angie paused a moment at the intersection where she knew to turn left, feeling her tingling sense change into something different, more threatening, something like a rippling series of uncomfortable heat prickles blistering her skin.

I'm getting close, Angie thought. *I can sense it. I can feel the evil coming off his place, even from here.*

She turned and found herself driving down a desolate road as a salty, muddy odor assaulted her nose. The road had become strangely rural with one turn, a few spread out houses dotting it along the way, the slow-moving waters of the creek to her right and a vast expanse of marshy wetland opposite that. Angie didn't even want to think about what skeletons Garrou might literally have hidden in that bog.

Angie crept down the road, noting every grand house she passed had a vast private lawn and a long pier stretching out into the black water creek. After about half a mile the road pivoted towards the choppy waters, then carried on perhaps another five hundred feet until it turned sharply again to the left, hugging the shore of the creek as it did. Angie, however, could only glimpse a part of the course it took along the creek; she had stopped in what would otherwise be a cul-de-sac, if not for the road carrying on through it with two squat posts on either side. Between the posts, a chain dangled loosely as it swayed in the breeze, blocking her way forward. On one post was a sign stating *No Trespassing* while on its twin was one that declared *Private Property*.

Subtle, Garrou. Real subtle, Angie thought as she peered down the shore road as far as she could see. About a half-mile away, she could spot the sunlight gleaming off steel and glass, twinkling through the marshy reeds.

"Bingo," she said. Some seagulls croaked nearby as if joining Angie in celebration.

The heat prickles dancing all along her spine intensified, warning Angie she was close, so very close to indescribable evil as she turned around in the quasi cul-de-sac. She returned along the long, lonely road from which she had come, then turned again, driving past the marina once more.

Rather than turning back to return downtown, however, her mystic awareness told her where to find the final thing she needed, so instead, Angie passed the middle school, then turned to take another country road for about a mile, the huge swampy area now to her right. There, after passing some woods and fields and a few isolated houses, Angie found what she already knew would be there: A secluded boat launch, one tucked away right where she needed it to be.

She pulled the truck into the small parking lot in which

there was only one other pickup, orienting herself so her face couldn't be seen from the road or anyone returning from the creek. Angie looked at the glowing green numbers on the dashboard clock and saw it was a few minutes past four. That gave her an hour until she planned to go.

"And now," Angie announced to the empty truck, rubbing her belly, "we wait."

CHAPTER THIRTY-TWO

1

P eter was angry. As he took point in their drive across
Maryland, he had many long hours to gnaw on his wrath,
a slow-burning rage that grew steadily as the miles sped past
and his thoughts lingered on Garrou.

Though his anger had been rising for months he'd kept it a
well-hidden secret from Angie. Peter knew if she found out
how furious he was, Angie would fear his actions might be
based on emotion, driven by rage, and could take matters into
her own hands somehow. They'd created a workable plan, and
the last thing he needed was for Angie to do something
preemptively thinking she was protecting him. Despite the ire
that had been building within him over the past several weeks,
he'd stuffed and swallowed it, showing nothing but his normal,
well-tempered self to Angie.

It hadn't been easy to play it cool and appear calm. It had
often felt like a visceral pressure building up inside Peter over
these many weeks, especially after what happened with his

parents. He'd wanted to scream, to smash things, to rant and rave, to bring bloody vengeance down upon the people that had done this to him and Angie and his parents and all the other innocent victims. He ached to lash out and tear down the entire twisted system that supported such evil and used people as disposable pawns.

Instead, he'd locked away his fury deep inside him, sequestered alone in the dark far from the light of reason. In the hidden blackness of his mind, Peter's anger had begun to entwine around a murderous hatred, like two noxious, pale vines rising together, weaving themselves to join as one.

As Peter cruised along I-70, he thought about the many different reasons he hated Garrou. He had long despised everything the pampered, privileged autocrat represented, and that was when he only knew the congressman as an undeserving scion of a powerful family; he'd always loathed anyone who'd earned their position through family connections and backhanded dealing rather than their own merit, a bias he'd inherited from his blue-collar upbringing.

Garrou, in his mind, was the classic example of someone who'd had riches and success heaped upon them not because of what they did but rather who they were. Up until recently, that had proven adequate reason to detest Garrou, but his mounting anger had given Peter additional justification to abhor him. Now that Peter knew the man for the monster he truly was, his animosity had grown like blossoms after a warm spring rain.

As he drove, Peter clenched his jaw and squeezed the steering wheel tight, wringing it, as he thought about what Garrou had done to Angie. The obnoxious impotence Peter had felt when he realized there was nothing he could do but play Garrou's twisted game, and to stand by as he took Angie, terrorized her, scarred her. All they'd wanted was to be left alone to live their lives, but because of the consequences of

Garrou's own actions, he'd dragged them into this new world. Peter ached to return the violence he'd brought to them, only magnified tenfold, offered up unmercifully.

Peter's anger had also been stoked by the frayed remnants of his own idealism, of which not much remained after discovering the dark truth of the world. In researching Garrou he'd learned more about the death of Senator Wilkes, something that had always been described as a "tragic accident" when it'd been reported earlier in the year. After Garrou had revealed himself, Peter realized the senator's death had been no accident, it'd been a political assassination to create opportunity, just as Thompson's attack had been to eliminate a rival. The few persisting threads of idealism still in Peter made him appalled by that and disgusted at the thought of an American politician using violence to seize power.

Peter's tattered idealism was also offended at the thought of Garrou seizing the White House. The worst kept secret in Washington at the time was that he planned to run for president, a thought Peter found horrific now that he knew Garrou's true nature. It angered him to think that one so foul, so evil, so consumed with power and domination and cruel control should ever sit in the Oval Office.

More than anything else, Peter's hate-tinged anger was fueled by Garrou having stolen from them the life they'd planned to live. He and Angie had spoken a great deal before her kidnapping about where they wanted their shared life to go. They'd planned to continue making contacts in Washington, get married, move to Alabama so Angie could run for Congress, have kids; they'd planned to live a delightfully predictable, normal life. A safe life.

Glancing in the rear-view mirror to snatch a quick look at Angie, Peter thought about how the life they would now be forced to live was going to be anything but normal. They'd have to disappear somewhere after killing Garrou, and he envisioned them winding up in a secluded compound somewhere surrounded by weapons like a family of fringe survivalists. The only difference would be rather than hiding from the government, they'd forever have to worry about being hunted down by a vengeful coven or tormented by demons, and rather than guns he and Angie would fight with holy water, herbs, and protective seals. This was not the kind of life he'd wanted to live, and it was all because of Garrou.

You've taken away everything from us, Garrou, he thought as he grimaced and ground his teeth. *Now let's see how much we can steal from you.*

Peter's rage and hatred had swelled far beyond just Garrou. It had swollen to encompass the entire Coven Universal, all the smaller covens, the lone wolf Satanists, and everyone involved in their evil. His anger reached out to include the demons themselves and all the other foul creatures he'd learned about while with the cunning women, his resentment and loathing multiplied from the infuriating sense of powerlessness facing such entities. Peter decided he'd have to learn more about defeating all these evil creatures.

His blood lust for everyone – and every foul creature – involved in the Atrocissimus had grown ever since their stay with the cunning women. On their first night on Red Mountain, Peter had violent dreams of vengeance and retribution, which had gone on unabated every night since. In these dreams, Peter saw himself as punishment personified, the living hammer of God; he hunted magic users and killed them, tracked down coven houses and burned them to the ground as the evil ones inside tried to escape, he bled those who wantonly disposed of human life. As he dreamt, Peter imagined himself destroying vampires and werewolves, killing devils, banishing ghosts.

He knew these were nothing but dread fantasies, as Peter reminded himself every morning, his anger and hatred no less diminished by having these violent dreams. Yet despite their ephemeral nature, he'd float away into other such dreams the following night.

Peter had become so immersed in his own foul mood and dark thoughts that he was surprised when a sign for the approaching interchange between I-270 and I-70 loomed up ahead. Shaking his head to return to reality and taking a sip of his now-cold coffee, he was pleased so much of the drive had passed him in a blur but now focused carefully on the road ahead, nonetheless. Peter honked and waved when they reached Frederick as Angie continued along I-70 towards Crisfield while he diverted to Washington.

"Bye, babe," Peter whispered to himself as he sped down the off-ramp, watching the truck grow further away from him. "Please be careful. Please, whatever else you do, be careful."

Peter took another sip of his cold coffee as he picked up I-270, then cranked up the radio now that he was back within range of DC 101 again. He'd given too much thought to Garrou and revenge and instead wanted to focus on the task awaiting him in Washington. Their plan required he and Angie to simultaneously move different pieces of the puzzle in place, and while her job was dangerous for very specific reasons – so dangerous that he'd planned to take it until she pointed out the other role for tonight would be far more effective if Peter did it – what he was about to do later in the evening was terrifying in its own way.

As he sped towards Washington, Peter turned over his portion of the plan in his mind once again, visualizing his task, thinking about what he might say. Everything hinged on Garrou being there at the restaurant, as Peter had told Angie he would be. However, despite his confidence when speaking to her earlier, there was a nagging doubt tickling the back of his mind, fearful that, tonight of all nights, he'd unexpectedly change his routine.

What will we do then? What if he doesn't show? He has that event tomorrow on the Delmarva, maybe he'll head out there tonight and we'll miss the chance we have. Then what? Shit, I don't fucking know. No, stop! I can't obsess about all the possibilities. If something goes awry, we'll figure it out later. I'll wait until seven o'clock, and if he's not there by then, I'll call Angie. Not much else we can do about it.

The remaining drive passed quickly, and Peter once again found himself in Washington. The trees had been full of dark green leaves when he and Angie had left to see his parents in late September; now, just days before November, the trees were winter-naked and skeletal. A chill wind whipped through the streets as the denuded trees swayed in the breeze, as if they, too, were part of a coven and had assembled to celebrate their sacrifice. Peter pushed that image out of his head.

"Stop it," he said to the empty car, flinching at the sound of his own voice. "You keep thinking like that and I guarantee you'll fail tonight."

Peter glanced at the dashboard clock only to see it was not yet noon, which gave him around five hours to kill before he needed to be in place. He didn't want to be spotted in town by anyone who might know him – he didn't want to explain where he'd been for the past month, and he thought it safer to assume everyone was in the Coven – so he changed course and headed towards neighboring Silver Spring.

Once there, Peter considered going through a drive-thru to get some lunch, but the queasy, rolling feeling in his stomach suggested that would be foolish. Instead, he drove to the most secluded spot he could find in Meadowbrook Park, and though separated from downtown Washington by just a few miles, he felt certain no one he knew would see him. There Peter waited impatiently for the afternoon to pass by as he again thought about how his part of their plan might play out.

2

After waiting for what felt like an eternity, Peter's patience had run out by four o'clock, and he decided it was time to move. He wondered how things were going for Angie and hoped she was well as he pulled out of the park, turning onto Route 410. Peter was slowed by the Friday afternoon traffic as he turned onto 16th Street and entered the city proper, making him happy he'd decided to move out early.

Though only about a ten-mile drive straight down 16th Street, it took Peter nearly an hour to get in place with the tangled traffic and bad luck getting stoplights. He finally reached the correct block, where he then turned right, and at the next intersection right again onto 15th Street. Finding no parking spots with a good view available, Peter went around the block again, then again, and then three more times before he was able to slip into an opening at the end of the block down from the Old Ebbitt Grill. From there, he could keep watch on the entrance to see if Garrou would arrive while also being far back enough he couldn't be spotted.

Peter sighed as he checked the time, seeing it was only three minutes past five. He strummed his fingers on the steering wheel, wishing for the first time in several months he had a cigarette. The thought of sucking in sweet menthol taste while he sat there waiting, blowing out clouds of white fumes as he watched the blue smoke curl up from his cigarette became overwhelmingly enticing. He didn't even have a lollipop to use as a replacement, having given them up while with the cunning women since his supply had run out after a few days. Peter padded his jacket and rifled through his glove compartment in the forlorn hope he'd find one there. He didn't.

"Fuck," he muttered, the phantom taste of a burning cigarette driving him mad as the hour inched by.

He continued to obsess about a cigarette, the sunlight diminishing on towards dusk. At six o'clock, his attention was grabbed by the sudden appearance of a limo driving past him, then stopping in the street just at the Old Ebbitt's doors. Thoughts of smoking evaporated from Peter's mind as he sat up and watched carefully, eager to find out who was about to get out of the car.

"Be Garrou, be Garrou, be Garrou," Peter whispered as he clenched a fist, unaware he was doing either. "Come on, please be Garrou."

The limo remained unmoving for some seconds with its blinkers on, other cars backing up behind it or going around, Peter's heart beginning to pound as he waited to see who was arriving for dinner. The rear doors opened, and Peter watched as a woman he knew to be a major political donor got out of the back, followed by a congressman he recognized but didn't know much about. He was followed by two other donors and a senator.

Peter had a wave of nausea wash over him and felt like vomiting as the senator closed the rear door behind her. The disappointment was palpable, and he had a flash of panic as he thought perhaps Garrou won't come out tonight – until the front passenger door opened, and there he saw Garrou, with his coiffed blondish hair and his dimpled tie, exiting the limo.

I bet you think you're a real man of the people now, don't you, because you rode up with your driver. I can only imagine what a big deal you made about sitting up front so your rich friends could have the back to themselves. You're quite the martyr, aren't you? Fuck you, you pampered piece of shit.

He watched as the group, laughing and talking, walked into the restaurant appearing to Peter as if they believed the world existed solely for their pleasure. He picked up his new Motorola to call Angie after they entered the Old Ebbitt Grill.

"Hello?" she answered, her voice sounding distant.

"He just arrived at the restaurant with a large party," Peter said. "You're good to go."

"Got it. As soon as it gets dark, I'm on it."

"Okay. Bye,"

And so, it begins, Peter thought to himself as he let out a long breath, the tension and worry melting from his body as he did. That sense of relaxed calm didn't last long, however, as twenty minutes passed, then thirty minutes, then forty, and still he hadn't heard anything from Angie. The time stretched on and on, and Peter's mind whirled as he sat in the dark, picturing a variety of outcomes to explain the silence. They were each more horrendous than the next for her.

As Peter sat bouncing his leg and cradling his head, his mobile phone rang an hour after calling Angie.

"Hello?" he answered.

"It's done," Angie said. "You're up."

"Got it," said Peter. "Bye."

He was just about to disconnect the call when he heard Angie say, "Wait!" He listened to what she said about what had occurred during her part of the plan with great interest, a broad smile spreading across his face as she did.

"Fuck, I love you!" Peter announced when she finished. "You are one badass bitch, my love."

"Yeah, I know," Angie said with a giggle. "Now why don't you go fuck up Garrou's night?"

"I'm on it. Love you"

Peter sat in his car a moment longer, smiling savagely as he thought how he could use what Angie told him to their advantage. His anger raged within him, but rather than the sense of maddening impotence he'd had before, this cold fury felt energizing and empowering. Peter felt like this wrath was guiding and focusing him on the task before him as he got out of the car to put the second piece of their plan in motion.

He was still smiling as he walked into the Old Ebbitt.

CHAPTER THIRTY-THREE

1

Angie sat in the truck for the intervening hour watching the shadows slowly stretch as the afternoon grew towards evening, strumming her fingers against the steering wheel, checking the glowing digital numbers every few minutes. At five o'clock she was preparing to begin her part of the plan by tying her hair into a tight bun, then putting on a ball cap and a pair of sunglasses, when she saw the owner of the other truck approaching the boat launch in a canoe. The man never took note of her as he got his boat out of the water; fifteen minutes later she had the launch all to herself.

"Time to roll," she declared to the empty truck cab.

Angie put a puffy coat that smelled vaguely like Peter's mother on over the sweatshirt she was wearing to further disguise her appearance, then filled her backpack with everything she needed to get the plan initiated. After slipping its hefty weight onto her shoulders, she hauled the light aluminum jon boat out of the truck and dragged it to the water's edge, then slowly positioned herself in it, careful not to fall over into the cold water.

Don't fall in, for the love of God, whatever you do, don't fall in. You used to do this all the time as a kid with Dad. It's like riding a bike, right? It'll all come back to me. Right? Maybe. Just, please, don't fall in the water!

She nestled herself in the boat as she adjusted to its rocking, then shoved off into the languid creek. Once a little distance from the shore, Angie started up the small trolling motor and turned herself away from the launch and the road behind it, obscuring her appearance even more. To the casual observer, she would look like an unidentifiable person in a jon boat taking in a late-day jaunt along the creek.

She settled in for the slow-moving cruise and waited for Peter's call. As she did, the snail's pace offered by the trolling motor afforded Angie a perfect view of the swampy marsh surrounding Garrou's home, which she now turned to look at. Although she could still only see glints of the setting sun reflecting off the house from her location in the creek, Angie realized his home was almost impossibly private. The closest neighbor was about a mile away, separated from his affairs by the chain barring access to his lane and the many acres of swampy bog. His home was surrounded by wetlands on three sides and the creek on the fourth, and it was clear to Angie Garrou used this privacy for foul deeds inside that house.

Angie continued to make her way along the creek, appearing to wander yet actually tacking ever closer to his home. She wanted to be in position for when Peter called but didn't want to make it obvious she was headed in that direction should she be spotted before the sun went down. At one point, she fought the lazy current pulling her into the bay and turned the boat towards the shoreline, when a flash of light reflecting off the glass made Angie aware she could now see Garrou's house.

There she saw what appeared to be a steel-framed rectangle, the spaces between beams filled with giant floor-to-ceiling panes of glass highlighted with brick portions that together made up the outer walls, and a smaller, similar-looking rectangle on top of it with a deck protruding all the way around it. Angie assumed this is what passed for the second story in modern architecture. The roof canted off bizarrely at various unusual angles. If not for the many shades pulled down behind the windows, anyone could have watched whatever went on inside that house.

"Which you certainly don't want, do you, Garrou?" Angie asked the modern-style house with a grimace.

The new Motorola mobile phone she and Peter had just gotten rang a moment later, the electronic beeps harsh and strange on the quiet waters.

"Hello?"

"He just arrived at the restaurant with a large party," Peter said, his words sounding shrill and echoey. "You're good to go."

"Got it. As soon as it gets dark, I'm on it."

"Okay. Bye," said Peter, before disconnecting.

Angie checked her watch and saw it was just a few minutes past six. The sun would go down in about fifteen minutes, with full darkness following not long after that. She licked her dry lips and felt her heart begin to race as darkness enveloped her, the only sounds being the cries of seagulls above her and the water gently lapping against the jon boat. As the world around her slowly faded to blackness, Angie thought about what trials the next hour would bring her.

2

Once full darkness had fallen, Angie turned the boat and slowly made a direct line towards Garrou's house, guided by a light shining on his private pier. She approached it, cutting off the humming motor some yards away so she could float the final distance, wanting to be as silent as possible. After lashing the vessel to the dock, Angie remained in the boat a moment and looked around, trying to see if there was anyone at his compound. Illuminated by only the lamp rising above Garrou's pier and two small lights at his front door, the dark revealed none of its secrets.

Angie swallowed, her parched throat clicking as she did. She desperately needed to get to that house and wanted to clamber up the dock and go right to work, but their plan would fall to pieces if someone spotted her trespassing on the congressman's private property – to say nothing about her future after she was arrested. The heat prickle-like sensations had been warning her since even before she launched the jon boat, so Angie knew there was great demonic evil here, but at that moment, she was more concerned about human servants that might call the police on her.

Angie closed her eyes, again taking several deep breaths and letting them out, slowing down her thoughts so she could achieve a calm focus, a silent mind. In that silence, she could hear all creation singing to her, and just as she had earlier, Angie opened her eyes, knowing everything she needed to. With a firm resolve, she set to work knowing there was no one else on the property, and further knowing the house was unlocked with no alarm system.

She climbed up the dock ladder, knelt to get the gun Peter had given her out of the backpack and slipped it into the pocket of the oversized coat she was wearing, then swung the heavy pack onto her shoulders. Although Angie knew there was no one else there and was aware of what evil lurked inside the house, she still felt it wise to proceed with caution, so she carefully made her way forward.

Mindful of every step, Angie worked her way to the front door. Her heightened awareness told her the demonic evil bound to Garrou was nearby. As she stood with her hand poised over the doorknob, Angie glanced to her side and realized there was a cat sitting there licking its paws, paying her no mind in typical feline manner. She smiled, then opened the door, which swung in with a whisper.

Her heart racing, her breathing coming in shaky gulps, Angie paused on the threshold for a moment as she peered into the inky blackness of the house. She could feel the evil, the loathing, the bitter hatred, and anger that emanated from the darkness like it was a foul odor, and it almost overwhelmed her. But rather than turning to flee in the face of this overpowering malevolence, Angie instead clenched her jaw and steeled herself as she walked into Garrou's home.

The house was as cold as it was dark, but also stuffy, as if it'd been closed up for several weeks, and smelled pleasantly of burnt spices, almost like incense. She shuffled a few tentative steps into Garrou's home, feeling on the walls for a switch. Finding one, she flipped on the lights to reveal an interior appointed in a slick modern style, matching the overall design aesthetic of the house. Angie paused to take it all in as she slipped off her backpack, thinking "design" was the perfect word: Every detail, every color, every pillow that appeared lazily tossed had been put there by careful design for effect. The house felt lifeless and sterile to Angie, like a movie set dressed as a home.

Whatever else it is, it's time to get to work.

She'd entered into a large, open concept living room-kitchen area, with a hall leading off to her right and other rooms to her left. Angie took a few steps down the hall and opened a door, one that revealed stairs leading downward into the further dark. Coming from the blackness below Angie could sense an even more intense wave of the evil she'd felt when she first opened the front door. She guessed this is where Garrou had his altar set up and sacrificed his victims, as she had learned from the cunning women he would. To avenge all those murdered down there – who she realized no doubt also included Peter's parents – Angie decided to give it special attention.

She strode back to her backpack, and there took out the two gasoline tanks she'd filled earlier that morning before beginning her trek to Crisfield. Angie opened the first one, then brought it back to the steps leading to the basement and poured the stinking fluid down the stairs. Angie dumped the gas down into the basement for a moment, letting it splash and flow down the polished wooden steps, then backed up, leaving a trail leading to the living room. There, she poured some gas all over the perfectly appointed furniture, then used the empty tank to smash out a few of the tall windows, venting the anger she'd stuffed at lunch and cackling happily as she did so.

Angie tossed the empty gas can into the middle of the room and was about to get the second one when she noticed a framed picture on the wall. It caught her attention because it was a symbol much like the one she and Peter had tattooed on their backs. As she stared at it, though, Angie realized it was strikingly different as it incorporated many of the demonic sigils they'd learned about. Angie assumed this was a picture of a similar Satanic protective symbol.

For reasons Angie couldn't explain, she thought this might be a good thing to steal, but as she took the picture off the wall, several things all happened at once. The prickly tingles Angie had been experiencing the entire time she'd been near Garrou's house now shrieked down her spine so intensely she arched her back even as the odor of burning incense enveloped her and she heard a sound like a large piece of cloth unfurling. She whirled around and saw the thuggish-looking man she'd seen before with Garrou, the one she now knew was his demonic familiar.

He glared at Angie, his lip curled in a silent snarl, then began to slowly approach her as he said in a growl, "I don't know who you are, but those seals you have tattooed on you can't shield you from us forever. Eventually, they'll wear off, the light will dim, and when they do, we will know you, and we will get you..."

Angie, chilled by fear and a nauseating sense of loathsome hatred, froze for a moment, her face carved into an expression of shock, horror, and dread. Even though she knew about the familiar, even though she'd been instructed that he'd take the form of some common animal, even though she was prepared to meet him here, Angie still felt almost overpowered by sensing his evil and his gnawing hatred. It was only when he was a few feet away that Angie could make herself move again, stepping backward as he continued to pace towards her.

"... and when we do... oh, little girl, when we do, how we will torment you, how we will torture you. Oooooh, the things we will do to you are indescribable, unimaginable... and I assure you, you *will* suffer deliciously."

Angie pulled the gun out of her pocket with a shaking hand, leveling it at the demon. He paused, looked at the gun, then laughed so much and so long he couldn't speak for nearly a minute.

"Oh, my, little girl," the demon said, still chuckling as he did, "believe me when I tell you those tattoos will protect you against me far better than that thing will."

"Oh, yeah?" Angie said, her courage returning to her, riding an angry wave of her own hatred for the demons and black magic and Garrou. "Let's find out, shall we?"

She pointed the barrel at the demon's human face and pressed the trigger of Danny's old, realistic-looking water gun and held it, just as Peter had shown her. The electric motor whirred to life, and as it did, a long stream of holy water squirted out of it, splashing the demon all across his cheeks and eyes.

As the water sprayed across the demon, he let out a high-pitched shriek, a scream, a wail of pain, agony, and fear, inhuman and unnatural, like no cry that could ever be made on Earth. Black, oily smoke roiled and twisted from the spots on his face where the holy water had hit as he stood, screeching in unending agony, his body affixed in place and shaking wildly.

The smoke curled into a pillar around and above the demon as more of his flesh crisped, blackened, and then turned into this dark, whirling vapor. Angie watched, her eyes open wide and a ferocious smile on her face, as the demon continued to screech in pain and dissolve into nothing but the curling pillar of writhing smoke. Then, with a final choked exhalation, the smoke dissipated away, and the demon with it.

I just killed my first demon, she thought, the smile still on her face. *I could get used to this!*

Angie stood unmoving in Garrou's living room for a moment as she thought about a life of killing demons, water pistol still extended, eyes wide open, until the pungent odor of gasoline assailing her nostrils snapped her back. With a quick shake of the head to clear her mind, Angie returned to her backpack and swapped out the framed picture for the second can of gas, then continued dousing Garrou's living room with it, trailing some into the kitchen. Finally, she ran to the top of the stairs, leaving a trail of gasoline to connect back with the puddles already in the living room.

Satisfied, she left the gas can there, then grabbed her backpack and rushed out the door. Angie stood with her back against the wall next to the entrance as she reached into her pack and retrieved a safety flare, then took off the cap and struck the ignitor. Mesmerized for a moment by the sparkling white flames, Angie pivoted like a soldier in a war movie, tossed the flare into Garrou's house, and turned to run as fast as she could while it was still midair.

She'd managed to put some distance between she and the house before the flare landed, igniting the gasoline fumes. They lit with a *whoosh!* as flames raced throughout the house, blowing out most of the windows on the ground floor. Glass peppered Angie as she ran towards the dock, most of which bounced off the puffy jacket she wore, though a few shards sliced her exposed neck and left her with hot scratches all along it.

Angie ran straight for the boat, not wanting to linger once Garrou's entire property was bathed in a bright yellow-orange flickering light, her long shadow a black void racing ahead of her to the dock. She knew the firefighters and police would soon converge on this spot, and she needed to be gone long before that happened. Angie felt dangerously exposed until she'd managed to climb back down into the jon boat, then, as she unlashed it from the pier, she took a moment to look at what she'd done.

Garrou's carefully designed masterpiece of modern architecture was now nothing but one roaring flame, all the windows shattered, the steel beams beginning to glow cherry red. She smiled as the light danced in her eyes, the heat warming her face even from this distance. The thick black smoke pouring up from the burning house made Angie think of the demon she'd destroyed, adding an even greater sense of accomplishment to this evening.

And so, it begins, she thought suddenly, not certain whether she meant the plan she and Peter had concocted or their peripatetic life living on the fringe of society as demon-killers. Regardless, Angie did know it was past time to go.

She pushed away from the dock as she started up the trolling motor, feeling at first even more exposed and vulnerable on the water than she had while running back to the dock. After just a few minutes, Angie heard the wail of approaching sirens; she stuck close to the marsh so she could hide in the shadows as she inched her way back. After an eternity navigating through the dark, Angie returned to the boat launch, looking around to make sure she was alone once she got there.

Angie beached the jon boat, got out, then turned it around and pushed it back into the creek with the trolling motor on. The cold water numbed her feet as she did so, but Angie was too excited to care. She rushed back to the truck, tossed the pack into the cab as she climbed up into it, then paused to calm herself before starting the engine; it wouldn't do for her to race out of the parking lot, drawing attention to herself and maybe getting a speeding ticket. Once again relaxed, Angie started the truck and pulled out, retracing her course back into town. As she pulled onto Richardson Avenue to get out of Crisfield, Angie dialed Peter's new number.

"Hello?" he answered, the connection again sounding echoey.

"It's done," she said tersely. "You're up."

"Got it," he responded. "Bye."

"Wait!" Angie said quickly before he hung up, then went on to explain what had happened with the familiar as well as taking the demonic seal picture from Garrou's wall.

"Fuck, I love you!" Peter said once she was done. "You are one bad ass bitch, my love."

"Yeah, I know," she answered giggling. "Now why don't you go fuck up Garrou's night?"

"I'm on it. Love you"

As Angie drove out of Crisfield to meet Peter at the rendezvous point, she passed several police cars and fire engines racing in the opposite direction, their red and blue lights flashing brightly. Glancing in her rear-view mirror, Angie could see the orange glow of the inferno she'd created, then sighed and smiled.

It had been a long day, she was dead tired, and still had a lengthy drive ahead of her. Nonetheless, Angie couldn't recall ever feeling more satisfied in her entire life.

CHAPTER THIRTY-FOUR

Garrou had just finished his steak and was leaning back into the soft cushioning of the corner booth his party sat in, savoring the aftertaste of his meal, and enjoying the light buzz he had going after his third glass of wine. The only thing that would have made this dinner better is if he could be smoking a cigar at that moment.

While not technically a business dinner, Garrou nonetheless used the gathering as a chance to do some business; he'd invited this group of colleagues together to help him achieve his goals, using food, drink, and camaraderie as a way to help make that happen. His guests had as always been carefully selected to offer him as much benefit as possible, and he had specific aspirations for what he wanted to get from each of them. One of those goals for the evening was to convince Senator Barclay to give him her support, an ally that would be crucial if he were to win her state's many electoral college votes.

"I respect where you're coming from, Ellen," Garrou said to the Senator as the remainder of the table debated some political point. "Your state hasn't supported my party in a presidential election since... what... the Seventies, maybe? Maybe longer? I understand we're not popular there and that I'm even less so, and that coming out to endorse me might prove difficult for you, but you know I will never forget my friends once I have the Oval Office."

As Garrou said that he glanced out the window overlooking 15th Street at the Ionic colonnade of the Treasury Building there, though what he saw in his mind's eye was what lay just beyond it. As Garrou sat in the Old Ebbitt Grill having dinner, he was just a tenth of a mile away from the White House, close enough to walk there in a minute, so close to the seat of American political authority he could almost feel the power and prestige emanating from the building itself. Achieving access to that building as its honored occupant was his obsession, his destiny, it was his duty – it was also the loadstone hanging from his neck, the onerous weight the High Council had laid upon his shoulders.

He couldn't even contemplate failure as that would mean his own violent death. Garrou needed to not only win the White House but to crush his opponent, to leave no question of his overwhelming victory, no chance for clever legal maneuvering. To do that he would need allies of all political colors.

"Lou," Senator Barclay intoned, "I'm just not convinced. Look, it's a guarantee you'll win the Senate seat in a few days, obviously, so welcome aboard. But I'm not convinced someone who will be in the Senate for just a few weeks has any business announcing a run for the presidency."

"I've already served in the House for several years, let's not forget that. Lots of congressmen have been president."

"Yes, but you wouldn't be running for president as a congressman, you'd be using the stature of the Senate to propel you forward. I'm sorry, but I just don't think that's right. It just strikes me as... dangerously ambitious."

"Oh, but I am ambitious," Garrou said with a charming smile. "Aren't we all, though? Honestly, isn't that why we all got into politics, so we could get the power we needed to accomplish the goals we feel are most important... for the people, of course."

"I'm not ambitious," she countered, taking a large gulp of expensive white wine. "I just want to do what's best for my constituents. I just want to serve the people."

"Of course, you do. Don't we all?"

The Senator put her empty wine glass down, then thought for a moment and looked askance at Garrou. "You said earlier if I endorsed you, you wouldn't forget your friends. What exactly did you mean by that?"

"Ah," Garrou said quietly, leaning close in to speak as if conspiring with Barclay. "Well, not only am I talking about future legislative initiatives of yours I'd support, but... I'm sure you know Mr. Donovan and Miss Cartwright here are well known and, dare I say, rather generous donors to politicians who offer something they can support."

"Yes, I know all about them, but we've never agreed on enough points for either one of them to offer me any generous support."

"So, I've brokered an agreement on your behalf that if you support me, they will—" he started to say, then left his sentence dangling and unfinished as he glanced over towards the window again. Rather than looking at the Treasury Department looming outside, he saw Peter standing there in the restaurant, smiling and beckoning Garrou to come join him.

Barclay waited a moment, then said, "What? They will what?!"

Garrou shook his head and blinked, then smiled as he said, "You know what? I think they should be the ones to tell you the good news. If you will excuse me, though, I see someone from my staff I need to chat with."

He buttoned the coat of his double-breasted suit jacket as he got up, then strode across the restaurant to where Peter stood waiting, hands clasped at his waist. Garrou paused in front of him for a moment, trying to read the look on his face and failing. After a moment of uncharacteristic uncertainty, he motioned to the bar and said, "Hello, Peter. Can I buy you a drink?"

"Sure," Peter answered. "But I'll just have a Coke. I have a long drive ahead of me yet tonight."

The two men found a quiet spot at the end of the bar and sat as Garrou ordered himself a whiskey and Peter the Coke. They said nothing as the bartender got their drink orders, staring forward yet looking at each other in the mirrors backing the bar. He had an uneasy sense Peter was trying to stare him down, the way boxers might do before a fight. He sensed there was something disturbingly different about Peter, an aura of confidence Garrou hadn't seen earlier, and he shifted in his seat as Peter's mirrored eyes continued to bore into his own. Once their drinks arrived, Garrou took his and lifted it once.

"Cheers," he said, sipping the expensive bourbon. Peter said nothing in response, instead staring ahead and drinking his soda.

The pair sat like that for several minutes, neither saying anything but instead staring at the other's reflection, sipping their drinks as if the tension wasn't growing palpable. As the ongoing awkward silence stretched on, Garrou finally turned to Peter and said, "So, let's just cut to the chase, shall we. I have a dinner party I need to get back to. Why are you here, Peter? I'd assumed you and Angie had run far away, gone for good."

"Well, Garrou... I guess you can add that to the long list of things you're wrong about,"

Although Peter's insult struck him like a stinging slap across his cheek, Garrou chuckled instead of giving vent to his anger, very much aware he was in public, still within sight of the table of donors and future allies.

He slapped Peter on the shoulder as he laughed and said, "Good one, Peter. I always did like your sense of humor. Where have you and your lovely fiancé been? I've been searching all over for you."

Peter turned to Garrou at last, looking at him with a puzzling smirk on his face. "Oh, I'm sure you have, you cancerous mass. But where we've been is none of your business."

What the fuck is going on here? Garrou wondered. *This is not the same sniveling little whelp I saw in Baltimore. Where were they? What happened while he was gone? What's gotten into him?*

"Peter," Garrou said, beginning to get up, "if I want to be insulted, I can just go back to the House floor and get slighted by people far better at it than you. So, if you have nothing intelligent to say, I'm going to go order my dessert."

"Sit down," Peter responded. "I have a very important piece of information you're going to want to know."

Garrou paused, still turning over in his mind what had happened and trying to figure out why Peter was so very different. He sighed and shrugged, trying hard to look casual, then sat back down on his stool.

"Okay, fine. You have my attention. Now, please, what do you want?"

Peter smiled, then wagged his fingers to motion Garrou to come closer to him. He leaned in slightly, but Peter again motioned him to come even closer. When he did, Peter leaned in to speak right into Garrou's ear, and whispered, "While you were here eating dinner, Angie was in Crisfield... and burned your house to the ground."

Garrou remained unmoved for a moment as a ball of flaming rage erupted inside him, and he squeezed his hands into tight fists as they hung at his side. His anger was multiplied by being in public, having no recourse to express his fury, not even to threaten Peter. Garrou looked up at him, who was broadly smiling, a look of profound pride carved on his grinning face. He ached to shred that face off Peter's skull.

"Aww," Peter said in a taunting, mocking tone. "That makes you mad, doesn't it? Will it help any if I told you that not only is your house now just a pile of twisted metal but while Angie was there – you remember Angie, right? Lovely girl, super smart, has a scar on her cheek – she also killed your little pet. It's amazing what holy water will do to those things, isn't it?"

Peter laughed loudly as Garrou choked on his unexpressed – and inexpressible – fury. His jaw clenched until his teeth hurt and his eyes felt like they were bulging out from his sockets as his hands began to tremble. The chatter and laughing in the crowded restaurant echoed in his head, and he suddenly felt like the entire place was pointing at him, laughing, mocking him for this affront. He glanced at the table from which he'd come, and there he saw Senator Barclay beaming as she shook hands with the two mega-donors.

Stay calm, stay calm, whatever you do, stay calm. Get yourself under control. You can't even afford to look upset here, with all these eyes watching you, and you can't fuck up getting Barclay on your side. Play it cool, man!

"If you actually did this thing," Garrou said coldly, "it would have been incredibly unwise of you. All I need to do is call the police and tell them the crazy man who burned down my house is sitting with me at the restaurant, and they'll come to arrest you, then later they'll get Angie. Then, when you're in prison, my... colleagues... would get you in time. You would pay for this beyond your wildest nightmares – *if* you actually did this, which I don't believe you have the balls to."

Peter ignored his barb and still had that obnoxious smile stretched across his face as he took a swig of his soda and nodded. "Oh, yeah, we did this, all right. Doused your house with gas and lit that bitch up like Fourth of July fireworks. *Whoosh!* I'm going to bet you lost something real important in that fire, didn't you? Maybe something like... oh, I don't know... an altar? And, yeah, your familiar is quite dead. Angie said it shrieked and screamed in agony as it dissolved into black smoke. Isn't that just delightful?!"

Garrou, struggling to maintain his composure and not kill Peter in this very public place, took his Nokia out of his breast pocket and said, "That's it. I'm calling the police."

"You can do that, sure you can, but I didn't tell you what Angie took from your place. You'll definitely want to hear about that first. Trust me."

Garrou paused, his finger hovering above the keypad, sneering as he looked at Peter. His stomach rolled and he had a wave of nausea wash over him as his mind raced with the possibilities of what she might have stolen from him, something no doubt incriminating or embarrassing that would ruin his chances of becoming president. Being taunted by Peter about everything made his rage grow even more, which was further amplified by being so publicly exposed. This favorite restaurant of his was beginning to feel like a trap.

"What'd she take?" he asked, trying to appear indifferent.

"A picture you had on the wall, the one of a Satanic protection seal. If you call the police, we'll admit to everything, but we'll also let the whole world know who you really are."

"That's nothing but a piece of fine art, you idiot," Garrou lied, laughing as he waved his hand dismissively. "It means nothing and proves less."

Peter shrugged. "Maybe. But everyone knows you plan to run for president. Ask yourself how will that play out with the voters? You'll be like Gary Hart, only rather than a picture of a staffer on your lap you'll go down over a picture on your wall. It's really quite hilarious, isn't it?"

Garrou clenched his jaw again, gritting his teeth as he admitted to himself Peter was right. Even the mere suggestion that he had a connection to Satanism would ruin his chances of being a contender in the primaries let alone winning the election, and he knew the press would eat this story up like maggots on a fresh corpse. He knew there'd be nothing Emma Oscuro or any of his fellow Coven members in the media could do for him with a story like that. His chances of becoming president would be finished, as would be his life.

"This must be such a trying time for you, Garrou," Peter said, another wide smile on his face. "You probably want to go wild and get all wolfy on me, don't you? Do all those things I just *know* you're thinking of right now. Such a shame we're here in public... and you having a party of bigwigs over there. How annoying that must be for you."

Garrou shook with restrained fury as he made fists so tight his fingernails cut into his palms. He looked over his shoulder at the table, where he saw his party enjoying their desserts and after-dinner conversation as Barclay caught sight of him looking. The senator laughed as she lifted another glass of white wine with one hand and beckoned him to return with her other.

"What do you want?" Garrou hissed, his anger drawing his

throat tight. "You came here tonight to do more than just to piss me off. So, what is it? Why are you here?"

It was now Peter who sneered at Garrou, his lip curling in apparent disgust before answering in a harsh whisper. "What I want, is to kill you. You started this and we're going to finish it. But thing is, I know what a coward you are. Without your black magic and your little demon plaything, you're *nothing*. So, I'm going to make it easy for you and tell you where we're going to be..."

Peter grabbed a small beverage napkin and took a pen out of his pocket, then scribbled an address on it before sliding it over to Garrou. "That's the address for my family's cabin. That's where Angie and I are going to be waiting for you. You can't miss it. There's a giant stone at the end of the dirt road leading back to it, painted white, big black letters that say 'Brunnen.' If you think you're strong enough to come get us, then by all means, please do try. But I don't think you will, Garrou, because you're really just a coward and a weakling. You're nothing, and you always will be."

Garrou held the napkin in his hand at arm's length and looked at it as if it were serpent poised to strike him, then crumpled it in his fist.

He smiled at Peter, then softly said, "Your parents suffered greatly. I really want you to know that. Their screams lasted for days and days, and by the time we were done with them, they'd scratched their own eyeballs out of their faces to make the tormenting visions stop. They were nothing but slavering, babbling husks of the people they once were. I did that to them, but that's nothing compared to what I'm going to do to Angie and you when—"

Garrou ended his monolog abruptly as Peter got up off his stool and said, "You're boring, and you talk too damn much.

Thanks for the Coke, but I need to get going. I hope to see you soon, but I seriously doubt I will, coward."

With mouth agape and eyes wide open, Garrou watched as Peter took two steps away from him then abruptly pivoted back. "Oh, just as a reminder, we're going to have the picture there with us. Maybe we'll send it to the press, maybe we won't, who knows? Maybe we'll just piss all over it as we laugh at you. You never can tell. Okay... bye!"

Garrou watched in shocked amazement as Peter strolled out of the restaurant, turning to continue down the street past the window. He turned back to the bar after first glancing around to see who might have heard their exchange, looking down into the amber depths of his whiskey, dumbfounded by what had just happened. He remained there a minute longer as he tried to wrap his mind around everything that occurred. Garrou finished the rest of his drink, straightened his tie after standing, then walked back to the table with a large smile on his face.

"I'm so sorry for the interruption, friends," Garrou announced as he took his spot in the booth again. "But you know how it is. Our business never really ends, does it?"

Garrou listened to the details of what Barclay and the two donors had been discussing with a smile on his placid face that was as false and lifeless as a mask. He nodded and made terse comments as needed to make it appear he was paying attention when in actuality his mind raced to find an explanation for Peter's radically different attitude. As he did, his emotions raged inside him. Garrou was confused and reeling, feeling like a fighter who'd been punched too many times in the face, dizzy, teetering back on his heels.

Garrou didn't know where Peter and Angie had been for a month or what made him suddenly become so bold. He didn't understand what had made them decide to attack him first, to taunt him with what they'd done, and then challenge him to come find them. He couldn't grasp any of these things.

The only thing he knew for certain was he needed to get to that cabin as quickly as possible and kill them before things spiraled out of control.

CHAPTER THIRTY-FIVE

1

Peter had already been waiting a few hours at the Frederick I-70 rest stop the pair were using as their rendezvous point when Angie arrived later that night. She pulled the truck in next to the Avalon, and though she looked drawn and exhausted, Peter had never recalled finding her more beautiful as they embraced. They remained wrapped in each other's arms for some time, Peter unwilling to let go of her.

"How was it confronting Garrou?" Angie asked finally, pulling back to look up at Peter. "Seeing him face-to-face again, speaking to him?"

Peter thought for a moment, then said, "You know, I went in there with this big smile on my face feeling so powerful after what you told me. I toyed with him and pissed him off so much I thought his head was going to explode!"

"I wish I could have seen that," Angie said, giggling.

"Yeah, it was terrific... I mean, my knees might have gotten a little wobbly as I walked back to the car, but still, it was awesome. I got him all roiled up and then told him right where we'd be. He'll definitely come as soon as he can."

"Good. The sooner he comes the sooner we can kill him."

Peter nodded in agreement. "Mhm. We definitely know we have tonight and all day tomorrow, but as soon as the sun goes down, we'll need to be on guard. Just in case."

"Okay... did you get the food?"

"Just what we'll need for tomorrow," Peter answered. "I figure once we get there one of us can run into Dellslow to get a week's worth of food and water."

"Well, let's quit talking about it and get to it. I'm so exhausted I'm going to zonk out as soon as we hit the highway, though."

True to her word, Angie fell asleep almost immediately, leaving Peter alone with his thoughts during the two-hour drive to Dellslow and the cabin just beyond. Although the only thing they wanted to do on arrival was go to bed, they decided it'd be better to bring in everything to have more time the next day to prepare. They carried in their bags together with the guns, the tools, and boards they'd grabbed, plus a few other things, then made certain to hang the Wolf's Bane bundle on the door. They both then fell into a deep slumber, sleeping well into the morning.

Once up the following day, the pair made breakfast together outside at the fire pit. Peter tried to remember the last time they made a meal together, and he couldn't recall; he knew it had to have been before Angie's abduction, but the details slipped his mind. Regardless, it felt good to again be doing something together they so enjoyed, even if it was just scrambled eggs and bacon fried over an open fire.

As they sat around the fire in the morning chill, eating their breakfast, Peter had a sense of this being a special moment, a punctuated point in their lives, one they would remember forever. It seemed to resonate somehow as if the air itself vibrated. Sitting there in the woods eating a simple meal, he felt like they were on the precipice of something magnificent, something life-altering. Peter rationally knew it could also be life-ending, but he chose to not even consider that option, and instead focused on how this would be the last normal day of their lives.

"It feels... *heavy* out here today," Angie whispered, "Feels like something big is going to happen."

"Yeah," Peter answered softly, "I was just thinking the same thing."

"It feels kind of like graduation, maybe, where your life is about to go around a big corner and you're not certain what's waiting for you on the other side."

"But you hope it's something awesome."

Angie nodded her head in agreement as she chewed on some bacon.

"Angie... why are we whispering?"

She shrugged as she breathed in the cold morning mist, looking around at the bare trees, then said. "I don't know. It just felt... quiet out here. Solemn. It felt like a moment where we should be quiet, too."

"Well," Peter said as he stood and stretched, his normal speaking voice sounding like an explosion in the silent forest, "I'm afraid quiet time is over. We have work to do."

2

After breakfast, the pair loaded all the shotguns and pistols they brought, arranging them against the walls in the kitchen area under the loft, leaving the boxes of ammunition within easy reach together with the Mason jar of holy water. Angie volunteered to drive into town to get supplies while Peter, now armed, stayed behind to lock the wooden shutters closed and then, using the boards he'd cut at his parents', nail them to the windowsills over the shutters.

He tugged on each one afterward, feeling very confident these would at the least slow down Garrou. Peter was in the process of using the remaining boards and nails to make something else when Angie returned from her supply run.

"Look what I made," he said, holding up a board through which he'd pounded a dozen nails. "I've made a trap."

"Hey, I know where you got that idea from," said Angie.

"Yeah... knives would've looked cool but that's really impractical. I figure we'll put it right in front of the door. That way, if he bursts through, he'll hopefully slow down a little once he steps on this."

"Sounds good. Help me get this stuff unloaded, okay?"

After getting all their food and water stored, the pair felt the press of time crushing down upon them as the afternoon seemed to melt away in their hands. They spent that time digging a shallow ditch around the cabin, into which they pounded many sharpened stakes. The rocky soil of the campsite made it a miserable job and prevented it from being as deep as they'd hoped, but both felt a bit more secure by the time they'd finished. They retreated to the safety of the cabin immediately after pounding in the last stake just as the sun set and darkness crept upon the forest, Peter securing a padlock into the heavy-duty hasp he'd added to the door earlier. He placed the nail trap in front of the door, yanked on the lock a few times, then grunted.

"Do you think that will stop him?" Angie asked, her voice dulled by fatigue.

Peter sat down heavily, head in his dirty, blistered hands. He leaned the shotgun he now always had with him against the wall. "I don't know, to be honest. With the way I saw him burst through that door at Thompson's... I just don't know."

They sat there in exhausted silence for some minutes, both starving yet neither having the energy to open the cans of stew they planned to have for dinner and put the pot on the wood-burning stove. As the dark outside deepened and the orange glow of the lanterns illuminating the cabin grew stronger, Peter's and Angie's flickering shadows looked like two dancers wrapped in black gossamer cloth.

"How long do you think it'll take?" Angie murmured.

"I don't know. Soon. Probably not tonight, but... soon."

3

That first night in the cabin, one of the pair would sleep for two hours while the other kept watch, as they had agreed earlier when crafting their plan. Peter volunteered to go first, though he struggled to stay awake, and his aching muscles screamed for rest. He spent most of that time pacing back and forth in the small space to remain alert, pausing at each window to peer out the decorative pine tree-shaped holes cut into each wooden shutter, then turning back to pace again. Peter would look out the window each time, only to see nothing lurking in the silver-moonlighted forest.

The next night was the full moon, and Peter couldn't help but wonder if Garrou would show up then in a nod to the dramatic. He thought Garrou would like the image of his wolf form bathed in the soft white light of the moon, something completely consistent with his flair for the dramatic. Despite that, however, Garrou did not, nor did he the night after, nor the night after that. He failed to make an appearance the entire intervening week.

It proved to be a long, difficult week for Peter and Angie. After passing through the protracted overnight hours of the first few days, the pair would rejoice with the rising of the sun each morning and the chance to get out of the cabin. They'd gather water at the nearby lake, cook their food at the firepit, take sponge baths as best they could, and enjoy breathing air that wasn't stifling and still.

But they were soon jumping at every snap in the forest, every rustle in the thick underbrush, afraid they were about to be attacked. Though their rational minds told them Garrou would never come for them during the day, their animal minds quickly developed an overwhelming paranoia, feeling unsafe and exposed everywhere except in the cabin.

Making matters worse, a cold rain moved in on Wednesday that lasted off and on for the remainder of the week, so their days were soon as long and monotonous as the dark hours of the night. The pair only went outside to gather water and clean the buckets they used for their waste, which, until they were emptied each day, made the cabin reek with the foul odor of human excrement.

Sleep deprived, dirty, and surrounded by the constant stink of their own filth, Peter and Angie were by the end of the week on edge and irritable. Now, on the day before Halloween, they'd had a terse conversation about their limited options and what they might do. They were running low on food and would need to risk a trip into town, but they were running lower on cash. They both feared that, despite the provoking and taunting, Garrou might not come at all, that he might instead wait them out and pick them off at his leisure. They felt trapped, confused, unsure what to do; with their exhausted minds, they lacked the capacity to figure out another plan.

But another plan wouldn't be needed because that night, as the rain pounded outside and the clouds blocked even a hint of moonlight, the Wolf finally arrived.

CHAPTER THIRTY-SIX

A ngie sat up, awake and alone, a shotgun cradled in her arms as she stared out into the darkness a bit before midnight. A dreadful fatigue weighed heavily on her, and she looked forward to her watch being over in a few minutes, though, as uncomfortable as she was, Angie wondered if she'd even be able to sleep. She could never recall a time she'd ever been so filthy her whole body itched, and she found the foul odors wafting off her indescribable. The only thing challenging her own stink was that of the waste bucket, filling the cabin with a revolting stench.

"This place smells like a fucking outhouse," she whispered to herself, choking a little as she could almost taste the aroma.

Angie stood and was just about to wake Peter when an electric burn sizzled down her spine so unexpectedly, she arched her back and cried out. She rushed first to look out one window, then the one opposite it, and then finally peered out the window next to the front door. Though Angie spotted nothing, she didn't need to see to know what was happening.

"Peter!" she yelled, shaking him hard. "Get up, now! He's here!"

Peter sat up, then grabbed the shotgun lying next to him and put the Colt 1911 back into the holster at his side as he leapt up to one of the windows. "Where is he?!"

"I don't know, I can't see him yet. But I know he's out there. I can *feel* him."

Peter looked at Angie for a moment, then simply nodded his understanding. He opened the Mason jar, standing with it raised in his right hand, the shotgun resting against his left shoulder. Angie took her place next to him, shotgun at the ready.

They stood like that for some moments, the tension in Angie's body rising, her muscles growing tight and quivering with building pressure. She tried to listen but heard nothing besides the rain rattling on the roof. Angie had expected Garrou to come crashing through the door as soon as she sensed him, but this pause had the pair glancing at each other, brows furrowed. She shrugged at Peter.

"What's he doing?" Peter whispered at last.

"I don't know. I think he's... watching. Waiting. Thinking."

CHAPTER THIRTY-SEVEN

G arrou had approached quietly, a job made easier by the wet ground and the sound of rain pelting against everything. He'd crept up to around fifty yards away from the cabin, then inched his way around to get a better view. He wanted to get a good look at the place, so he'd know what he was getting himself into.

Garrou could see it was a tiny log cabin, most likely one-room, only one door in the front with a window flanking it, a lone window on either side of the cabin. He saw the windows were covered and locked, with reinforcing boards nailed over the shutters. Garrou knew he could tear them off the wall, shutters and boards together, but the window was narrow; he feared losing the element of surprise. Though he could smash through the window, he knew it was too slim for him to enter the cabin, nor could he burst through the walls because of the thick log construction making them up.

Garrou continued to surveil the cabin as he crouched behind a tree, where he saw the door was of a rustic plank board construction. Though the boards were no doubt thick –

perhaps even double-layered – with additional boards in a Z-pattern for more stability, he could easily smash through it. He also saw there was what looked like a wide trench dug all the way around the cabin with many sharpened sticks protruding at crazy angles along it. Garrou saw there was an opening in the trench but that it had been left offset from the front door, making it impossible for the average assailant to hit the door at a run.

The Wolf, however, was anything but average.

Very clever, you little bastard – kill blood tear death – but I can just run and leap headfirst into your – blood death kill – cabin and rip both of you to shreds before – kill rip shred destroy blood kill tear rend kill rip kill – you even know what happened.

Garrou shuddered for a moment, fighting against the wild impulses of the Wolf. This had been the first time he'd transformed since Baltimore, and he felt it taking over more of his thoughts, more of his mind, more of himself. Garrou estimated he only had around a dozen times he could become the Wolf again before losing himself forever to its savage, primal nature. He knew he needed to make tonight count.

So, get ready – rip rend blood kill tear – to die – death tear kill destroy kill – you little fucker – kill kill killkillkill!

Garrou slunk away through the dripping underbrush, taking his time to move as stealthily as possible, until he'd positioned himself facing the front door. He could cover the fifty yards in seconds, then come smashing into the cabin, teeth snapping and claws flailing, rending both to shreds in a flash, painting the walls crimson with their gore. The cabin was so small they'd have nowhere to run, and after just a brief explosion of bloody violence, Garrou would finally have his vengeance.

They were his. Garrou licked his maw in anticipation of tasting their hot, salty blood.

He slowly stood from the underbrush as the rain fell harder, allowing himself for the moment to be consumed utterly by the Wolf, reveling it its rage, its power, its unrestrained brutality. His vision narrowed, his heart beat faster as his muscles tensed, getting ready to explode. He filled his lungs, growling with every intake of breath. The Wolf was ready.

Garrou sprinted towards the cabin door with all his strength.

Kill kill kill kiiiiiiill...

CHAPTER THIRTY-EIGHT

A shrieking chill again ripped down Angie's spine as she quivered violently and cried out. She then raised her shotgun to the door and screamed, *"HERE HE COMES!!"*

CHAPTER THIRTY-NINE

It took Garrou mere seconds to cover the distance between his spot in the woods and the cabin, but just before he got ready to make the leaping jump into the door, something happened that made time slow down and take on a stretched out, elastic nature.

As he took his last step before leaping, a bundle of something hanging from the front door exploded into a brilliant white light with strands of ethereal violet flames bursting out like raging snakes, flooding Garrou and the entire woods in the illumination. The light was so bright it struck him like a hammer to the face, searing Garrou's eyes even as it made a loud, rumbling sound that felt like needles in his sensitive ears and made his heart feel like it was about to burst apart.

He tried to stop running but because he was on the slick ground, Garrou was unable to get purchase as time slowed down for him and he watched himself slip and fall in a lengthy, drawn-out view. Unable to stop himself, his claws tearing up chunks of muddy soil and stones, he slid helplessly into the shallow ditch as he snapped off several stakes, then hit the door with a dull thud.

There, crumpled up at the threshold, Garrou could now see the bundle was a batch of Wolf's Bane threaded together with several other herbs, all of which were repugnant to the Wolf. He scrambled to his feet as quickly as he could, then sprinted back from where he'd started. The light and rumble diminished after he'd retreated, plunging the forest once more into inky black silence.

Garrou crouched again as he peered at the cabin, confused, and feeling the icy chill of fear begin to creep over him. It was obvious that, wherever they'd disappeared to for a month, it was a place where they could learn about Wolf's Bane and get a bundle of it, then be told to hang it from the door. He squatted at a large oak tree as he tried to think of alternatives, the screaming, furious voice of the Wolf making that difficult. It just wanted to rend and rip and tear, and Garrou raked his claws deep into the oak trunk as he struggled with his bloodlust.

When Garrou realized he was shredding the tree, he looked at the deep gouges he'd left in the trunk as an idea occurred to him, his glowing eye following it upward to the dark sky above. From there, he looked from treetop to treetop, working his way back to the cabin itself. Ever the problem solver, Garrou figured that if he couldn't get in through the door, that the walls were too thick and the windows too narrow, there was still one option open to him.

Kill kill kill – fine – rend rip tear destroy – I guess I'll just – blood death kill – get in some other way – kill kill KILL!

CHAPTER FORTY

Inside the cabin, Angie and Peter stood together, ready to face Garrou this one final time. She had expected him to smash through the door at any second; instead, Angie heard the sound of something hitting the door and making it shudder once, then silence again.

"What was that?" Peter whispered, his throat thick with fear.

Angie shook her head, her breathing shallow, the shotgun in her hand rattling as she began to quiver. "I don't know."

Her whole body tingled, and she felt overwhelmed by her extra senses, but Angie was even more so because she had no idea how to interpret what these meant. Her throat reflexively swallowed though her mouth was dry as her mind raced with possibilities, all of which were horrifying and bloody.

Angie and Peter stood, terrified and confused, in the orange glow of the cabin for long minutes that felt like infinity, the only sound the driving rain outside and their own rapid breathing. Her arms had grown sore from remaining in position, though she was unwilling to lower her gun for fear of being caught unawares. Angie glanced over at Peter, who looked pale and terrified, the jar of holy water shaking in his tremulous hand.

Angie looked around, her eyes darting everywhere like she was a trapped animal. She hoped against hope she might see or hear something from outside that could give them a clue what Garrou was up to, but between the rattling rain and the black night, she learned nothing.

Eyes wide open and searching, heart-pounding, breath coming in gulps, Angie had no idea what to do or what their options were – until she suddenly arched her back and yelled in shocked surprise.

"HE—" was all she had time to yell before there was a loud crashing sound on the roof, followed by the sound of heavy footfalls above. Turning her eyes upward, Angie could see the beams bending even as she heard wood creaking until there was a crashing sound like an explosion as a hairy, clawed hand smashed its way through the roof.

"HE'S COMING THROUGH THE ROOF!" Peter screamed. "GET READY!!"

After punching his left hand through it, Garrou ripped a chunk of wood off the roof, and in the gaping hole, Angie could see his glowing, malevolent red eye peering down upon them, the reek of the cabin challenged for a moment by his sulfuric odor. Garrou's eye lingered upon them, then he roared so loudly the cabin shook.

Angie watched with growing horror as Garrou seemed to somehow become even more bestial, as if possessed by a rage they'd never seen before as he smashed and tore off chunks of the roof, ripping open a hole that slowly grew big enough for him to fit through.

"HE'S COMING, HE'S COMING!" Peter yelled, glancing

370

down at the nail trap, and pointing. *"HE'S GOING TO LAND ON IT, GET READY!!"*

After only a minute of frenzied pounding, punching, and tearing, Garrou had opened the hole enough for him to get in. He leapt down into the cabin, where he missed the nail trap by inches, then roared angrily.

CHAPTER FORTY-ONE

G arrou had gotten a good look at Peter and Angie before the Wolf took over to shred the hole open and had seen they were well armed and prepared to fight. He'd always found that level of hopeful naivety to be almost charming.

He dropped down into the cabin with a crash, prepared to launch immediately into a savage attack and kill these two irksome fools as quickly as possible, but the moment his feet touched the wooden plank flooring, the entire cabin was flooded with another searing white light, this time coming from Angie and Peter themselves. It looked to Garrou as if their bodies had turned into nothing but pure luminescence, the shocking white light joined with a shrill keening sound.

The light emanated from them hot and searing like they were two brilliant stars, burning Garrou's eye so much he roared in pain and turned his face away. He could see almost nothing of the cabin, and he couldn't even tell them apart as their lights had merged into one. Rather than the deliberate, graceful attack Garrou had planned on making, he instead was forced to just lash out at them in rage, pain, and desperation.

CHAPTER FORTY-TWO

Peter and Angie had been training for this moment for weeks and thinking about it for months. Confronting this beast had been Peter's obsession of late, it was his one passion, his preoccupation. It had become his sole focus, swelling until it was his only reason for existing; even the time he spent with Angie had lately been about getting to this point.

They'd made elaborate preparations to kill Garrou and had both paused their lives and careers and aspirations to end him. Now was their chance to finish it.

But, as the gigantic werewolf creature fell to the floor and seemed even larger in the small confines of the cabin, Peter realized there was no way to prepare for the horror Garrou's raging wolf form created. When he'd last seen him like this in Baltimore it was terrifying, but the fear had been mitigated by Garrou speaking reasonably and remaining calm. Now he was a massive, raging beast with teeth like knives and his long talons bared.

Peter felt like a gazelle or zebra on the savannah clutched in the iron jaw of a lioness, desperate to escape but unable to surmount its obdurate fate. Garrou roared at Peter and Angie and filled for a moment with an overwhelming terror, they both flinched and recoiled at the thunderous sound of his cry.

Peter lurched backward in a reflexive reaction to his fear, forgetting he was holding aloft the open jar of holy water. He spilled almost all of the remaining precious fluid behind them when he jerked back, horrified by the sound of splashing. He stood mesmerized for a moment, looking with dismay at the almost empty Mason jar, his mouth wide open, his eyes even more so.

CHAPTER FORTY-THREE

Although the scorching light largely blinded Garrou, still, he could smell his prey, the changing scents as their body chemistry altered, the fear itself that now wafted off them. Over the annoying sound of the light, he could still hear their racing heartbeats and their labored breathing. If he were able to look at them, Garrou knew he'd see two people appearing like hunted animals that now realized their pathetic lives were over.

How delightful.

He had only to press his assault, sloppy as it may be, and in time they'd run out of bullets. He had only to keep up the attack and await the inevitable.

CHAPTER FORTY-FOUR

"KILL HIM!!" Angie shrieked as she began unloading her shotgun into the flailing Garrou, snapping Peter back to the fight at hand.

She pumped new rounds into the chamber as fast as she could and shot straight into Garrou's face. The shotgun blasts seemed only to obscure his vision. His attacks were uncontrolled swings as if he were blinded by the shots, slashes that were often so wild they gouged into the walls or became blunted by the overhanging loft, under which they stood. A flurry of scattered shotgun pellets dropped harmlessly to the floor after every shot Angie took; frustration and fear animated Peter when he realized the guns were having no effect.

"WILL YOU FUCKING DIE!!" Peter screamed as he stepped forward and flung the remaining holy water directly into Garrou's face.

As soon as it touched him, he screamed in agony as steam poured up in long, twisting tendrils from his cheeks and mouth and brow with a loud *hisssssssss!* Garrou stopped his flailing when the water hit him to clutch his face, stumbling back a few steps as he shrieked in a symphony of torment – halting just before he put his foot down on the nail trap.

As Garrou stood, screaming, and shaking in anguish, Peter watched the skin melt off his face and chest just as if he'd been doused with acid. Thick chunks of his hirsute flesh slid from his body, landing on the floor with a bloody, wet *splosh!* Garrou's skin flowed from him like a stream of melted red wax as Peter looked over at Angie, who met his shocked gaze with her own for a second.

They then smiled as both raised their shotguns together, blasting away at him as fast as they could work the pump actions.

CHAPTER FORTY-FIVE

G arrou's entire world had devolved into nothing but a
universe of pain, his haughty confidence of a moment
earlier now as ruined as his face.

He'd been warned long ago of the dangers of holy water,
but in all his years as the Wolf, he'd never been concerned
about it. Garrou knew from experience he was more likely to be
confronted by guns, but since most people didn't arm themselves with vials of holy water – not even the occasional priest
he took special delight in shredding – this had never been
something he had to think about.

Now, with his face and neck feeling as if they were on fire,
Garrou understood the danger of this sacred weapon as a
nauseating dread crushed down upon him. The brilliant light
still shone from Angie and Peter's bodies, obscuring his vision,
and making it impossible to deliver a clean attack, yet the
growing panic he felt made him want to end this fight immediately.

His legs felt weak as fear mixed with his pain and fury.
Though the guns had no effect on him, he was finding it hard to

stand steadfast as his legs shook and wanted to give way, and he stepped back a little with every blast before lurching forward again to swipe at the keening light.

Mad with wrath blended with panic, Garrou launched himself forward with a desperate need to kill these two at last.

CHAPTER FORTY-SIX

P eter and Angie took advantage of the brief pause in his
attack Garrou's pain had allowed them, though it proved
useless. They unleashed a constant barrage of shotgun blasts
directly into his face and chest as fast as they could, switching
out their spent guns for preloaded ones. Peter's ears rang
painfully from the battle-like cacophony while the air was thick
with smoke and the pungent smell of gunpowder, but the
pellets just bounced off his body like they were spitballs.

Garrou attacked them again with even more primal rage
after just a short respite, his slashes and swings wild. Peter saw
their shotgun blasts had him wavering and on his heels, yet still
he came back attacking furiously.

At one point he managed to grab hold of Angie's shotgun,
and Peter felt an icy terror race down his spine as he feared
Garrou would pull her to him, but instead he just bent the
barrel to make the gun inoperable. At another, Peter realized
too late that a downward slash was coming straight for his
face. If not for the fact Garrou's claws were deflected by the
loft, ripping out a ragged chunk of wood, Peter knew he

would have been killed by that swipe; as it was, it left a painful, bloody slice running from his forehead down his cheek all the way to his jaw, missing his eyeball by a hair's breadth.

"PETER!" Angie screamed, *"I'M ALMOST OUT OF LOADED GUNS!!"*

Peter looked over at Angie, where he saw she had one final preloaded shotgun plus two revolvers. He then glanced at his own stash and was horrified when he realized he was down to the ten-gauge loaded with deer slugs and the 1911 strapped to his leg. They still had several boxes full of ammunition but because Garrou had attacked so savagely they had been unable to take time to reload.

Peter pulled the trigger on the twenty-gauge he was using – only to have nothing happen at all. His gun was empty, and he was now down to his last shotgun.

Peter grabbed the ten-gauge and stepped towards Garrou, figuring if he was going to die anyway, he'd do his best to take Garrou out with him. As he did, several things that would forever change his life happened almost at once.

He shot a slug directly at the center of the beast's chest, the giant shotgun roaring and recoiling painfully into his shoulder. Though the slug bounced off Garrou's furry body and fell to the floor, Peter was surprised to see him take a step back, as if knocked off balance by the impact.

Peter pumped a new shell into the chamber as he stepped forward, and the shotgun again roared to life, Garrou stumbling backward once more.

Another blast from the massive gun and Garrou again stepped back – until he paused, roaring and trembling, immobilized by pain.

Peter watched as, with great effort and growling, Garrou lifted one paw-like foot, and then the other. He was shocked when he looked down and saw blood pouring out of the soles of Garrou's feet, the nails of the trap behind him smeared red.

He stood stunned for a moment as he realized what this meant.

Peter shrieked to Angie, *"HIS LEGS AND FEET, THEY'RE VULNERABLE! SHOOT HIS LEGS, SHOOT HIS LEGS, SHOOT HIS LEEEEEEGS!!"*

He unloaded the last two deer slugs into Garrou's legs, splattering blood and fur on the floor beneath him. He obviously had some amount of protection on his extremities because Peter knew such a point-blank blast would otherwise have blown Garrou's lower legs into bloody stumps, but it was still gratifying to see this nightmare creature bleed.

Peter dropped the shotgun and took the Colt 1911 out of his side holster, shooting Garrou once in the legs with the fat round, then again pulled the trigger.

Only to have nothing happen.

He glanced down at the pistol to see a single brass casing jammed in the gun slide, a gentle whisp of smoke rising from the blocked and useless chamber.

But before he could clear the casing so he could empty the clip into Garrou, he looked up to see the beast moving towards him, a giant clawed paw raised to strike him down.

CHAPTER FORTY-SEVEN

Angie had tossed her shotgun aside when she'd shot the last shell at Garrou and had pivoted back with her final preloaded gun only to see Peter stepping closer and blocking her from shooting, too. He blasted Garrou with three quick shots from a gun that roared like a cannon and that seemed to knock the beast back with every hit.

She couldn't understand at first why Garrou paused but looked down to see a puddle of dark red blood streaming from his feet even as she heard Peter scream, *"HIS LEGS AND FEET, THEY'RE VULNERABLE! SHOOT HIS LEGS, SHOOT HIS LEGS, SHOOT HIS LEEEEEGS!!"*

Angie brought the shotgun up to her shoulder and was moving forward when she glanced over at Peter, knowing before it happened that his gun was about to jam, leaving him exposed to the enraged monster before them.

Without thought or hesitation, Angie grit her teeth as she stepped in front of Peter and began shooting, unloading the first shell directly into Garrou's legs, spattering thick scarlet ribbons of blood on the log wall behind him. She pumped to reload, knowing Peter had cleared his gun jam by then and stood beside her, also shooting at Garrou, riddling him with bullets. Angie shot repeatedly, screaming her hatred, anger, and triumph out over the roars of the guns until she had unloaded all five shells, shredding Garrou's shins and feet.

All while he was being attacked, Garrou was backpedaling, roaring furiously and swiping with his long claws as if blind. After stepping forward to empty her shotgun, Garrou swiped towards Angie one final time.

Angie stood there confused as she felt suddenly nauseous and weak, then dropped the shotgun with a loud *clunk!*

CHAPTER FORTY-EIGHT

I*'m about to die*, Peter thought, surprised to find a cool sense of calm wash over him as he prepared to be killed.

Rather than dying, however, he watched as Angie stepped in between him and Garrou, blasting into the beast's legs and ripping open his shins. Her action snapped Peter's attention back to his uninterrupted life, and he cleared the gun jam with a swipe of his finger. He joined Angie in the barrage aimed at Garrou's vulnerable extremities, who recoiled in pain from every blast, his flailing arms looking as much to keep himself from falling as they were deliberate attacks.

Garrou's entire body was shaking after they'd emptied both their weapons into him, Angie dropping her shotgun to the floor. As she did, Peter watched Garrou leap up into the hole he'd ripped in the roof, his shredded legs doing little to help him and showering down a rain of blood to the floor beneath. He growled as he clambered his way up and finally pulled himself out to the roof.

Peter stood motionless, staring up at the hole, unwilling at first to believe they'd won. But when he heard Garrou's groaning growl diminish as he ran away, a cry of joy and triumph burst out of Peter.

"We did it!" he yelled, a broad smile on his face. "We did it, Angie! We beat him!!"

He turned now to look at Angie, and it was then he heard the choking, rasping sounds she was making and saw her hands were clutching her neck.

"Angie..." he asked, the smile fading as an irrational panic gripping his heart and a wave of cold swept over him like a frigid winter's wind. "ANGIE?!"

She slowly turned towards Peter, and that's when he saw her face was pale, her eyes wide open with shock as her mouth worked silently, gasping for air. He looked at her hands clenching her neck, and it was then Peter realized they were covered in bright red blood, a torrent of it pouring down her neck and chest in a steady stream.

"*ANGIE!!*" Peter yelled as he rushed to her, catching her in his arms just as she collapsed forward. "NO! No, no, please don't die, no, NO... *NO!!*"

He lowered Angie to the floor, her bulging green eyes staring into his own with a look of fear, confusion, and dread as she reached out a red-covered hand to Peter, smearing his face with her blood.

"Angie, no – please, oh God, no!" Peter said, taking her hands in his, holding them close to his heart. She made gurgling sounds as her mouth still worked and tried to speak, gulping air, her blood appearing almost vibrant against her pale white skin. He looked at her wound and saw Garrou had slashed open a vein in her neck, blood pouring out of it and pooling on the rough wooden floor beneath her. He pressed his hand on her wound in a useless attempt to stem the flow of her blood as he clenched his jaw, trying to make her survive by force of will. "No, no, no, no-no-no, please no!"

"Bay-bay-bay," she said in between her slowing breaths. "Bay... bay... bay..."

"No, no, you're not going to die, Angie," Peter screamed, as he kicked the nail trap out of the way, unlocked the padlock and opened the door, then picked her up and rushed out into the damp night, his tears falling like the rain. "You're not going to die; you're *not going to die!* Don't leave me... please don't leave me!"

Peter carried her out to the truck as best he could. He knew Garrou might still be around, but he had to get her to the hospital. He heard Angie let out a long, low sigh not long after he got her inside the Ford but refused to acknowledge what that meant, holding her bloody hand all the way to Morgantown and telling her everything was going to be alright; the doctors were going to fix her up, that she was going to make it.

She did not.

CHAPTER FORTY-NINE

1

G arrou limped away from the cabin in an agony like nothing he'd ever felt before.

Every timid step he took sent explosions of pain tearing up his feet and legs which were barely able to support his weight, while his face felt like it was a raging fire. Each step was a new torture, another excruciating burst of searing anguish. He turned when he smelled Peter's odor outside the cabin as he made a dash carrying something, the brilliant glow emanating from his body now gone. Rather than renew his attack, Garrou just slinked away further into the woods. He couldn't tell how bad the damage was and feared what he would find once he transformed into his human shape.

He painfully made his way to his car, murmuring the words to change back all the while through his labored and ragged breathing. Garrou knew he wouldn't change anytime soon, though, so he was stuck in the dark, wet woods until he could. After struggling for an hour to reach his car, he eased himself down the side of it to sit on the wet ground and rest his screaming feet. Garrou tentatively touched his face but then pulled his clawed hand away as soon as he did, feeling ripples of sensitive skin and raw, exposed flesh, together with a fresh burst of blistering pain.

He sat there for many long hours, leaning against the car as he repeated the words to change back like they were a mantra, suffering through the inexpressible pain of his wounds. Finally, just as the eastern sky turned a brilliant orange, Garrou returned to his human form; it was the first time the pain of transforming was not the most excruciating thing he felt.

Garrou lay on the cold, wet ground for some minutes, breathing heavily and staring up at the brightening sky. He finally sat up and looked at his damaged legs. His shins and feet looked shredded, peppered with many dozens of little holes, each of which had a dull red line of congealed blood trailing out of it. Scattered all around his lower legs and feet were several larger holes that had torn out great chunks of flesh, thick tendrils of ruined tissue dangling from them. Garrou knew his legs would have been blown off if not for the limited protection he had due to the Gift.

He struggled to get off the ground, using the car to pull himself up. Once on his human feet, Garrou's pain became amplified, with every tender step accompanied by a harsh groan as he hobbled around to get his bag of clothes out of the car. He intentionally cast his eyes to the ground as he opened the rear door lest he catch a view of himself reflected in the mirrored window. He knew he'd have to look at himself soon, but he just wasn't ready yet.

Garrou soon realized there'd be no way he could get himself fully dressed, so instead, just opted to put on his silk boxers and a hooded sweatshirt. After dressing as much as he could, Garrou got in the car, started the engine, and turned the heat all the way up, then put on his hood and crossed his arms. He sat there shivering with his eyes closed, gently rocking back and forth in his seat.

Please, please, please, please, please, he thought repeatedly as his shaking subsided and his cold skin grew warmer. Finally, after ten minutes of mute denial, Garrou took down his hood and looked into the rearview mirror, twisting it straight at his face.

And was horrified by what he saw.

The left side of his face was gone. He looked like he'd been flayed alive, his skin blasted away to reveal the tissue beneath, moist and glistening in the morning light. Garrou cried out in disgust as he looked and saw his tanned flesh replaced with bloody red meat, through which poked the exposed bright white of his cheekbone and ocular orbit. His cheek had melted away exposing his teeth and tongue, making it look like he had an insane, crooked half-smile. His one good eye seemed to bulge out of his socket maniacally.

Garrou's skin had curled away from his injury and looked like a crisp piece of burnt paper, threads of flesh hanging down from his smoldering gash. The holy water had mostly splashed on his face, with some splattering on his neck and chest as well. Everywhere it hit him looked raw and ruined, and it burned with unceasing fervor as the wound still sizzled softly after all these hours.

He stared at himself in shocked horror, his eyes open wide open, the one good eye appearing like a bloated blue spot staring out from his pulpy, destroyed face. Garrou stared, unwilling to believe this disgusting visage was his new reality until he pivoted in his seat to roll down the window and vomit.

Garrou was terrified, confused, and felt trapped for the first time in his life. He covered his head with the hood again to shield himself from even a glimpse of his face, then grabbed the

Nokia to call his mother. She was the only person who would have any idea what to do next.

"Yes?" she answered after the first ring, surprising Garrou to find her up so early on a Sunday morning.

"M'ther!" he lisped sloppily, red-tinged drool pouring from his mouth. He hated how pitiful and weak he sounded, but he was incapable of speaking any other way due to the pain. "I nee'... yur help!"

He explained everything that had happened to him, going back to seeing Peter in the Rotunda to scrying on the pair, to being called before the Supreme Tribunal and Baltimore, to their disappearance, burning down his house, losing Felix, and coming to West Virginia to finally end them. Garrou told his mother about his wounds, especially the holy water burns on his face, and the unbearable pain he was suffering.

"I see," Mariette said with a sad sigh. "Come to Raven Hill Manor immediately. Make certain you're not seen by anyone. I will make up an herbal tincture for you that will ease your pain."

Garrou grunted in response, then put the car in drive and slowly pulled out of the sheltered spot near a dirt road where he'd hidden the car. Operating the pedals with his ravaged bare feet was agonizing, but once Garrou got on the interstate he put the car on cruise control for the three-hour drive to Poolesville, dulling the pain somewhat.

He arrived exhausted to his mother's palatial mansion, dizzy with pain. Garrou struggled up the marble stairs to reach the front door, but once he did, he was assisted into the sun-washed breakfast room by two of his mother's servants who all but carried him to his chair. There, at a table set with coffee for two, sat his mother, rigid and regal-looking as ever. She stared blankly at him with her icy eyes.

"Good mornin', M'ther," he slurred at her from under his

hood, keeping his head turned away and peering out at her from the covering in shame and disgust as if he was a Biblical leper. "I think I migh' miss brunch t'day."

Mariette continued to hold him in her cold gaze a moment, until she softly said, "Remove your hood. Let me see your wound."

Garrou slowly pulled the hood down, revealing to his mother not just his damaged and hideous face but also his failure. Mariette hardly reacted when he did, offering him nothing but a small twitch in her eyes.

"In that glass," she said, pointing in front of Garrou, "is an herbal mixture of my own making. Drink it. It will take away all your pains."

Garrou reached out for the dark green liquid with a hand that trembled from the unceasing torture of his injuries. He took a sip, careful to keep it on the good side of his mouth lest the tincture leak out of his open cheek, then flinched as its bitter taste hit the back of his throat. Despite the revolting flavor, however, Garrou felt an immediate reduction to the burning pain in his face and the throbbing in his legs. Excited by this sweet relief, he pressed his hand over his cheek so he could finish the concoction in several large gulps.

He sat with his head back and his eyes closed as he felt the potion working through his body, the searing heat of his pain diminishing until it was at last gone. Garrou let out a long, relieved breath, rejoicing in the feeling of wellness once again. He opened his eyes to look at his mother who sat there motionless, appraising him with a look like a full moon on a frigid winter's night.

"Th'nk you," he said.

Mariette nodded and said, "Of course."

"Can you heal me?"

Mariette thought for a moment before speaking. "I've never

personally seen the effects of holy water on the Wolf before, but I was taught the wound would never heal. However... I believe I can take care of it. There may be a large scar on your face, though."

"Anything is b'tter th'n th's," Garrou said, finding it more difficult to speak than before despite the disappearance of his pain.

"So, please do tell me again how someone of your power and capabilities was bested by two idiots with guns."

"It wasn't th' guns," Garrou countered, the words coming haltingly as his tongue tingled and drool flowed from his gaping cheek. "It was th' holy w'ter. I don't know... where they learn'd abou' tha'... but they did."

"And what of the injuries to your legs? Those were from guns, were they not?"

"Th't wa'... wa'... jus' d'mb... lu – lu – lu..." Garrou sputtered, suddenly unable to speak at all. The difficulty talking with such a grievous wound to his mouth had finally silenced him, and Garrou felt frustrated beyond all measure by that. He sighed, then reached for a glass of water.

And found he was unable to move his arm.

"Louis?" his mother said, a thin crease forming between her eyes as she sat forward. "Whatever is the matter with you? You were saying something about luck, I believe."

Garrou attempted to speak again, but now could only make inarticulate clicking and grunting noises. He tried turning his head but to no avail. His body was paralyzed, only his eyes moving, racing around the room, trying to communicate his need to his mother, trying to get the servants' attention. But they all just waited and remained impassive.

What the fuck what the fuck what the fuck?! Garrou screamed in the silence of his own mind. *What's happening to me?! Am I having a stroke?! Mother, help me! Please, Mother, HELP ME!!*

"My tincture," Mariette said as she stood, her voice weighed down with heavy sadness, "is a powerful one. Now that it's taken effect you wouldn't be able to move at all for days, other than your eyes."

Horrified, Garrou realized what was happening. In his mind, he said the words to transform into the Wolf, even though he knew that was useless; the words had to be said out loud, made manifest in the world, for the black magic to have effect. Paralyzed and powerless to take action, his heart pounded in his chest and his breathing raced as he watched his mother approach him down the long table.

"You'll still breathe, of course, and your heart will beat, but otherwise, you are utterly immobile." Mariette spoke to Garrou but didn't look at him; instead, her gaze fell above him, a distant look in her eyes.

He watched his mother stalk closer and closer to him, a look of pleading confusion in his eyes. Garrou began to make a sound in his throat like bursts of muffled screams as he saw her pause to open a napkin-wrapped bundle on the table, which, as the cloth fell to the floor, proved to be her ceremonial dagger.

Mother, please, no, don't do this. Don't do this to me. Please!

"The High Council... well, they see everything, Louis. They know everything. They're forever watching us, especially those of us highly placed. Those of us to whom much power and authority have been granted. They are insistent and... demanding."

Mariette continued to slowly pace her way towards him, razor-sharp athame in her hand, flashing in the bright morning sunlight. Garrou tried to force his legs to move, to power his arms by the strength of his will, to make his lips move so he might transform – anything at all so that he could escape. But everything was useless.

He was trapped.

All he could do was watch as his mother walked up to the chair he was imprisoned in and step around behind him, gently stroking his hair like she did when he was a child.

"They know what you did, Louis," she whispered, her voice breaking as she choked on her words. "They watched as you failed in your attempt to kill those two. They watched as the holy water seared your skin and you fled. They... they told me of your failure and warned me that the family... the family would no longer be held in esteem if your actions were not... dealt with. That the family would lose our protections and be expelled from the Coven if you were not punished, and that... that I must do it as an act of obeisance... and send proof of the deed."

Mariette continued to stroke his hair while she spoke, until her hand abruptly gripped some of his golden strands, pulling it hard as she placed the blade to his throat.

"What else am I to do, Louis?" she said with a tone of desperation. "I'm sorry, but... there is no power without sacrifice, and no sacrifice without pain."

2

With a harsh yank, Mariette jerked Garrou's head back to expose his throat and pulled the blade across his flesh, cutting short the stifled cry he was making. Her dagger opened his neck with an easy slice, blood squirting out all over the table and pouring down his chest in a steady stream. She pushed the blade back, then pulled again as she began sawing off her son's head.

Mariette didn't look down as she did this, instead staring straight ahead with a blank look in her eyes as his hot blood splashed all over her hand. She sliced deeper into his neck, sawing the athame through his spine, pulling up on his head as she did. Mariette finally cut through the remaining bits of muscle and skin, pulling Garrou's head from his body with a disgusted grunt.

She stood there unmoving for a moment staring forward with unseeing eyes. As a single tear trickled down Mariette's pale cheek, the athame slipped from her bloody fingers to clang onto the floor.

"Hail Satan," Mariette whispered.

EPILOGUE

1

A gentle snow fell outside Peter's cold, empty apartment as Christmas carols from the neighbor's could be heard through the thin walls. He did not share in the joy of the season.

He sat cross-legged on the floor, staring out the window at the snow, an eviction notice and the loaded Colt 1911 in front of him. Peter moved only enough to chain smoke cigarettes, the ashtray full of pungent gray dust and crushed butts. The heat had been turned off to his apartment a few days earlier, but he sat there barely aware his fingers were as numb as his emotions had been since Angie's death. He had already been sitting there for hours, watching the fluffy snow fall to the ground; rather than seeing the wintery picture outside, he was instead lost in a maelstrom of his own thoughts and memories.

2

He'd taken her that night to the hospital in Morgantown, clutching her hand and telling her everything would be alright, stuffing down the whispering voice of reason that told him she was already dead. Peter burst into the emergency room carrying Angie and screaming for help, his clothes smeared red with her blood while his own ran down his face from the wound he'd received. The medical staff took her back to a trauma bay while Peter was directed to the waiting room, where he sat, anticipating some medical miracle.

After an hour of staring blankly at the patterns on the linoleum floor, a disappointed-looking doctor told him the news. They'd revived Angie's heart a few times, the doctor explained, but each time afterward she'd crashed again, her weak heart no longer able to sustain life. The last time she'd flatlined, there was nothing they could do to bring her back.

"While you're here," the doctor said after delivering the news, "why not let me stitch up that gash you have? It looks pretty bad."

Peter raised a hand to his face only to pull it back again after having his injury burst into flames at the touch. He'd been so preoccupied with Angie he had forgotten about his own wound, the physical pain numbed by his emotional anguish. While sitting in a bay as the doctor stitched his cut, a Deputy Finley arrived from the county sheriff's office to question Peter about Angie's death.

After offering his condolences, Finley said, "So, Mr. Brunner... can you tell me what happened to your fiancé?"

Peter turned to look at Finley, though his blood-shot, distant eyes peered through him for unmeasurable miles beyond the deputy.

"It was a bear," he murmured after an awkward half-minute of mutely staring at Deputy Finley. "It must have been a rabid bear."

"A bear?"

Peter nodded, tears welling up in his eyes.

"Yeah," Finley said as he jotted down something on a note pad. "There were a bunch of bear attacks over in Maryland this past summer."

———

3

Peter was allowed to leave the hospital early that morning, with a reminder Finley would be contacting him if he had any additional questions. He got into the truck, where he saw the passenger seat stained a maroonish-brown from Angie's blood. The full weight of everything that had just happened – not just Angie's death, but defeating Garrou, the disappearance of his parents, his ruined future, everything – came crashing down on him like a grievous weight. Peter cried, sobbing loudly as he punched the truck cab ceiling until his hand hurt, then, drained of emotion and energy, slept for several hours sitting in the truck.

When he returned later that day to the apartment he'd shared with Angie, Peter paused in the open doorway for some minutes. It was exactly as they'd left it weeks earlier and disquieting how normal it felt. Too normal for him to be comfortable, as he expected Angie to walk out from the bedroom at any moment.

But she won't, will she? She's dead.

He walked into their apartment, overwhelmed for a moment by her sweet lilac odor. He'd never noticed before how much the place smelled of her perfume, her own distinct scent, and his eyes welled up again as he thought of the many times he'd been awash in that fragrance. Peter picked up a shirt Angie had carelessly flung on their couch and smothered his face in it, breathing in memories of her as he drowned in her odor.

"I have to stop this," Peter said, his voice sounding like a thunderclap in the quiet apartment as he wiped his eyes. "If I keep up like this, I'm going to be nothing but a blubbering mess. I'll drive myself insane."

He reverently laid the shirt back on the couch, appearing for a moment like he believed it were a relic.

Peter sat, his ears ringing in the painful silence of the apartment. He turned on CNN for some background noise, then put his head back to think. He closed his eyes and felt himself drifting off the sleep, when the voice of Bernard Shaw on the television suddenly made Peter's head snap up, his attention riveted to the news.

"And this announcement just coming in from the office of United State Congressman Louis P. Garrou: The congressman dead after an apparent heart attack last night in his Washington home. Garrou, who was poised to become the next Senator representing Maryland, had recently suffered a tragedy when his home burned to the ground..."

Peter was no longer listening to the news story, having melted into a gale of laughter that echoed throughout the apartment, a full-throated one that bordered on the insane.

"Of course, they would do that," Peter said in between his riotous laughs. "Of course, they would! They'll paint him as some kind of fucking all-American hero, the defender of life, liberty, and pursuit of happiness, mom and apple pie, and all that other bullshit. Of course, why wouldn't they?!"

Peter thought for a moment as his laughing quieted, then walked into the kitchen where he and Angie had made so many meals together, danced and laughed – and occasionally had sex on the table – to get the phone. When he did, he saw the red light blinking on their answering machine, of which he noted there were many. He'd check those in time, but first he had to call Angie's parents.

That call was as heartbreaking as he feared it would be. Peter tried to maintain his composure when Angie's mother answered the phone but found that an impossible goal. He became choked up as soon as he heard her voice and wept after he told her of Angie's death. Her mother screamed and cried until her father took the phone, demanding to know what was happening. Peter told him they were in the woods camping when she was attacked by a rabid bear.

After ending the call and again getting his crying under control, Peter listened to the many messages they had on their answering machine. They'd missed numerous calls from friends checking in, wondering where they were, as well as an increasing chorus of messages from their credit cards, utilities, and other creditors demanding missed payments. There were a few messages from Angie's landlord, each growing more agitated in tone, as he wondered where his rent was and the consequences if she didn't pay. Peter smiled wryly when he heard almost identical calls from the offices of their separate congressional employers, first reminding them they'd need to file additional paperwork if they needed more time off, then checking on their wellbeing, and then finally terminating them.

"Well, we both knew that was coming, didn't we?"

As he sat there thinking about what came next for him, Peter realized they'd missed over a month's worth of mail. He went to the lobby to check their small box and found it stuffed full of envelopes, much of which proved to be worthless junk mail. Mixed in amongst the things that'd go right into the garbage, however, there were a few items of great importance, like the several overdraft notices Peter had received from his bank, as well as a notice from the phone company of a looming shut off date.

"Great," he muttered to himself as he re-read the notice. "Thing just keep getting better and better, don't they?"

4

By the time he had returned back from Angie's funeral in Alabama, he was out of tears.

Once Angie's body was released by the morgue, her father made all the arrangements to have her transported from Maryland back to her hometown. Her father also offered to pay for Peter's plane tickets, a proposal he happily accepted.

The few days he spent in Alabama were a blur, and on the return flight only three things stood out in his memory: The constant warm rain, that the town Angie's family lived in was gorgeous, and that Peter would have loved having this kind, warm family as his in laws. He knew he would have been very happy living down there with them, making his life with Angie in Alabama.

But that, too, had been stolen from him.

There were several important messages waiting for him when he returned to their apartment. The first was from Deputy Finley, who said there would be no charges filed against him since this clearly was the result of an animal attack; the ruined roof and the deep claw gouges in the walls attested to that, as did the many inhuman tracks left in the mud outside. The second was from a Maryland state police investigator following up on the missing person's report Peter had filed earlier about his parents. Finally, there was a message from

Angie's landlord saying he was going to begin the eviction process.

Peter picked up the phone to call the state police investigator only to be greeted with silence. He hung up and tried again, and again heard implacable nothingness.

"Fuck you," he said to the empty apartment as he dialed the number on his mobile phone, some of the anger he'd felt before the fight with Garrou returning to him. "Fuck you, and fuck you, and *especially* fuck you."

That night he lay sleepless in bed, staring at the ceiling and watching the lights from passing cars slide across it as he thought about his future, feeling like all the paths open to him were blocked by brick walls. Peter had been having trouble sleeping since Angie's death, the difficulty getting to sleep growing with every passing night. After some hours of lying there, trying to capture sleep, Peter had just started to drift off when he heard a phone ringing.

"Shit," Peter said groggily as he grabbed his mobile off the nightstand and answered it, only to hear the phone ring again. Confused, he looked at the Motorola a moment until he realized the ringing was coming from the kitchen.

As the phone continued to ring, he walked down the hall to the kitchen, then stood there in the dark watching as the disconnected phone rang again, then rang one final time before the answering machine picked up. His stomach leapt a moment when he heard Angie's voice on the machine, only to have his heart almost stop when he heard Garrou's voice speaking to him.

"Hiya, Peter," the voice said. "I bet you never thought you'd hear from me again, right? After all, I am dead, thanks to you."

"No, no, no, no," Peter said, backing away from the phone, squeezing his hands tight against his head. "This isn't real. This can't be happening."

Peter felt like vomiting when he heard the voice on the machine laugh as if they were having a normal conversation.

"After everything you've been through, and you think *this* can't be real. Seriously? But anyway... I just wanted to let you know those fancy little tattoos you have on your body, they're not going to work forever, Peter. All armor rusts, boy, and eventually the light from those seals you have on you will fade away to nothing. And when they do... oh, when they do, it's beyond description what the demons will do to you. You don't have the power to stop them."

"Fuck you!" Peter screamed at the phone. "FUCK YOU!"

"Come on, Peter. You can do better than that, can't you? That's just so... sophomoric. Moronic. Surely someone who came up with the plan to kill an all-but-fully empowered werewolf could be more creative than 'fuck you,' right?"

Peter stared speechless at the phone, feeling like he was losing his hold on reality as he squeezed his head harder.

"But then again," the Garrou voice said, "it wasn't really you who planned it, was it? It was Angie. She always was the brains of the operation. And the beauty. Hell, she burned down my house and killed my demon, so she was pretty much the brawn and the balls of it, too. Matter of fact... you were always just a worthless hanger-on, weren't you?"

Peter wanted to scream that these insults weren't true, that their love was shared equally, but he decided not to give into the temptation and let whatever this thing was feel like it had won.

"Speaking of Angie," the voice whispered, "want to know something? I have her here with me, in Hell. Turns out your darlin' little Angel was anything but, Peter. Seems like she was quite the naughty little girl before you two met. Oh... but she never told you that, did she? She never told you all those wicked things she did when she was younger, with the boys in the neighborhood, with the entire high school football team, with her father and his friends..."

"NO!" Peter roared, unable to restrain himself. "No, that's a lie, I know it is!"

"Would you like to speak to her, Peter? I have her right here."

There was a moment of silence as Peter truly thought he might go mad, then his breath stopped when he heard Angie's voice on the line.

"Peter!" her voice cried out in anguish. "Peter!! Why did you let me die? Why didn't you protect me?! I died for you, why didn't you?! Why didn't you stop him! I *died* for you!!"

"Angie, I... I..." Peter said haltingly, then shook his head. "No... no, you're not Angie. This isn't real. You're not Angie and that isn't Garrou."

"You want to see her again, Peter?" the Garrou voice asked, sounding deeper than before and more malevolent. "You can, you know. You just need to die too, like she did for you. Quit being a fucking coward and just end it, just fucking kill yourself. You want to die, I know you do, so just fucking do it!"

"No," Peter whispered, calm now that he understood what this ruse was about. "No, I'm not going to kill myself. Fuck off."

"JUST FUCKING DIE!" the thing with Garrou's voice shrieked as it turned into a demonic roar, *"JUST FUCKING DO IT AND KILL YOURSELF, YOU FUCKING COWARD! JUST FUCKING DO IT!!"*

Peter rushed forward to pull the phone cable out of the wall and unplug the answering machine, though the voice continued to scream at him through it. He bound them together with their own cords, opened the nearest window, and threw them out into the night. The demonic Garrou voice screeched at him all the way down to the lawn below.

5

The next day, Peter packed up his belongings from the apartment, then stopped at the business office to inform the landlord of Angie's death. He said he was still owed two month's rent whether she was dead or not and wanted to know who to contact to get his money. Peter wrote out her father's name and contact information, comforted by bloody images of stabbing the landlord to death with his pen.

He returned to his own apartment, frowning as he noticed the distinct absence of Angie's scent. Peter lamented for a moment not taking a shirt or two of hers, but thought it was perhaps for the best he hadn't.

Peter took a pack of cigarettes out from the carton he'd picked up on his way to his apartment, then lit one, breathing the smoke in deeply as he checked the messages on his own machine. He felt trepidatious about hearing the demonic-Garrou voice at any moment, or even worse, the Angie voice, but he made it through without being so ambushed. He called the newspaper to put in an ad for furniture he needed to sell, then turned on the television as he started going through the few boxes he'd brought back from Angie's. Peter brought a box back to his bedroom as he half-listened to an episode of *Seinfeld* he'd already seen several times.

He pulled out a few things from the box and put them where they belonged, a crushing sadness bearing down upon him. As he pulled out a few more items, Peter saw something impossible at the bottom of the box. With a trembling hand, he pulled out the Colt 1911, which he knew should still be in West Virginia. He checked the clip and saw it was loaded, as the canned laugh track on the show swelled in the background.

"Oh, no!" he heard Jerry Seinfeld whine, going off script. "George, look what Peter just found."

Stunned, Peter padded into the living room, where he saw Seinfeld and George looking at the camera as they held identical copies of the gun in their hands.

"Jerry, what do you think he'll do with that?"

"I don't know, George, but if he had any balls at all he'd do this," he said, then slipped the gun into his open mouth and pulled the trigger, thick chunks of blood and brains splattering on the gray wall behind him to uproarious laughter. "See, Peter? Isn't that easy?"

"Or you could do this," George added, placing the gun under his chin, blowing off the top of his bald head, to even more laughs. "Either way, just fucking do it. You'll get to see Angie again."

"And we all know how much you miss her, don't we?"

At that moment, a television version of Angie dressed like Elaine walked through Seinfeld's apartment door to applause from the unseen audience. Like the other two, she spoke to Peter through the television screen.

"Peter," she cooed, stalking closer to the camera. "I know you miss me, I know you want to see me again. But the only way you get to do that is by killing yourself. Don't you *want* to see me?"

So close to the supposed camera that Angie's face took up almost the entire screen, she pouted like a child. After the incident with the phone Peter knew not to engage with these demonic mirages, so instead he stared mutely at her image on television. She then leaned in as she cupped her hand around her mouth.

"Hey, Peter," the Angie thing whispered. "Want to know a secret? I was pregnant when you let me die..."

No, Peter screamed to himself. *No, that's a lie. I know it is.*

They lie about everything, and they're lying now. It's just another trick.

"You didn't just allow me to be killed, but you also allowed our baby to die because you were too weak to protect us. So, quit being a little pussy and just fucking do it, Peter. Just kill yourself."

A flash of static as the channel changed, and Peter suddenly saw himself on the television as if there were a camera in his apartment. He reflexively glanced up to the corner of the room only to see what he already knew he would. Nothing at all, no camera, though his movements on the screen matched his in real life.

Until, that is, the television version of him turned his head to look into the nonexistent camera, an insane smile on his face. Peter stared at his doppelganger for a moment as its smile grew wider, until it brought the gun up to its temple and pulled the trigger, a geyser of blood splattering the wall behind it red. It fell to the floor with a thud as a laugh track and applause played.

Peter, his eyes wide open, his body trembling as if chilled to the bone, stood watching as what appeared to be his corpse bled out on the carpet. He then grabbed the remote to turn off the television and tossed the 1911 onto the couch as he walked into the kitchen. There he lit a cigarette and took several deep drags before calling the newspaper back to add the television to the ad for things he was selling.

———

6

Over the next several weeks, Peter's life continued to get worse by every possible measure as the unrelenting pressure of the demons to kill himself drove him to desperation.

His heart always ached for Angie, and Peter caught himself drifting off more often to pleasant memories of their brief time together. When he wasn't thinking about her throughout the day, he dreamt of her by night during the brief snatches of sleep he was able to get. His life seemed empty and worthless without her in it.

Though intellectually Peter knew he should try to find employment he didn't have the energy, so instead he spent his days sitting in his apartment smoking and staring blankly at the walls. His apartment became more barren over those weeks as he sold his possessions to have some cash, and though he had enough for a little food he never had enough for rent or other bills.

Peter got rid of any device the demons could hijack to torment him. He no longer had a house phone or his mobile – not that he could afford to pay for them – and had sold his television and radios. He discovered the need to keep the car stereo off when he drove his father's truck out to the Frederick rest stop to get the Avalon back, having been enticed by the siren song of Angie's voice urging him to veer into oncoming traffic and kill himself.

They're nothing if not consistent, Peter thought as he drove there in silence.

Now, in mind-December, Peter sat in his cold apartment watching the snow fall as he wondered if the demons weren't right. He'd stood up and fought against Garrou, he'd done the right thing, struggled against true evil and had accomplished something meaningful, just as he'd always wanted.

For his reward, he'd been forced to suffer. Angie had been

killed, his parents were dead, his career ruined, his future fore-closed upon. He was sleep deprived and emaciated. He had almost no money, little food, his utilities were being discon-nected, and with the eviction notice he'd just received, Peter would soon be homeless in the winter with nowhere to go. The only possessions left to him were his car, clothes, and his smokes.

And the Colt 1911. That he still had.

Peter butted out the cigarette he was smoking and looked down at the gun. He'd lately been questioning what was real, but as he picked it up and felt the heft of the blued metal pistol, he was reminded how very real the gun was.

He pulled the gun slide back then let it go with a loud click that echoed in his vacant apartment. Peter stared at the falling snow as he slipped the gun barrel into his mouth, tasting the almost sweet oil on it, the gun metal feeling cold against his lips and tongue.

Watching the snow fall wouldn't be such a terrible way to die, he thought.

But despite his broken heart, Peter just couldn't bring himself to do it no matter how many times he groaned as he tried to pull the trigger. He tossed the gun away with a scream, anger and hatred pushing aside his tortured sadness, thoughts of what brought him here racing through his head.

"This is because of them," he growled to himself, pounding the floor. "The demons, the coven, all of them, those fuckers. Garrou killed her, but it was them, all of them! They did this to her. They did it to me, to my parents, to everyone else. Fuck them! I won't die because of them!!"

Peter then stood, shaking his fists, and turning as if he saw himself surrounded by an unseen mob.

"Do you hear me?!" he yelled, stabbing his finger. "Do you fucking hear me, you bastards?! I won't kill myself! Fuck you all. I'm going to fight, and I won't ever stop fighting. I

FUCKING REFUSE TO DIE FOR YOU!! *DO YOU FUCKERS HERE ME?!"*

He knew then where he had to go.

Peter ran into his bedroom to grab a bag, then randomly tossed some clothes into it. He slipped in his cigarettes and the gun, took his apartment key off his key ring, and left it on the small kitchen bar counter, then walked away. Peter drove to the nearest gas station where he used the last of his cash to fill the tank, and finally began the four-hour drive to West Virginia.

The going was slow due to the roads, and Peter feared he might run out of gas before he reached Glace. He was running on fumes by the time he reached the neither plowed nor treated dirt road stretching up the mountain, and though the Avalon slid several times on the slick road, Peter somehow made it up to the concealed trail. Making his way along the snow-covered track was even more difficult, but he eventually reached the woodland clearing just as the car ran out of gas and sputtered to a stop.

He stepped out of the car and paused a moment to again breathe in the mountain air and listen to the wind whispering through the pines, the many bells tinkling with every breeze. Peter grabbed his bag then made his way up the steep trail, slipping several times in the snow and barking his knee against the rocks jutting up through it.

Eventually, gasping for breath, his knees throbbing in pain, Peter made it to the cunning women's community – only to find Naomi flanked by two other elder women waiting for him there. Their black woolen cloaks flapped in the unobstructed wind.

"Naomi," Peter whispered as he took a few hesitant steps towards her, "I need help, Naomi. May I please speak to Grandmother Brigit?"

Naomi glanced to the ground, then looked at him and said, "She died two weeks ago, Peter. I'm Grandmother now."

Exhausted and broken, feeling like a sailor alone and adrift far out to sea for too long who has at last spotted a friendly ship, Peter fell to his knees on the snowy ground. Putting his hands together as if in prayer, he looked up at Grandmother Naomi with painful desperation in his eyes.

"Teach me," he said. "Teach me everything you all know. Teach me what I need to learn so I can bring the war to them, so I can slaughter them and make them pay for what they've done. Please, Grandmother, please. I'm begging you. Teach me."

Naomi smiled and bent to gently pull Peter up off his knees, then invited him to join their little community of survivors with a welcoming sweep of her arm.

THE END

Dear reader,

We hope you enjoyed reading *All-American Werewolf*. Please take a moment to leave a review, even if it's a short one. Your opinion is important to us.

Discover more books by Antonio Ricardo Scozze at https://www.nextchapter.pub/authors/antonio-ricardo-scozze

Want to know when one of our books is free or discounted? Join the newsletter at http://eepurl.com/bqqB3H

Best regards,

Antonio Ricardo Scozze and the Next Chapter Team

ABOUT THE AUTHOR

Extraordinarily little is known about Antonio Ricardo Scozze, the mysterious writer who appears to have knowledge of an esoteric world of horrors that is intertwined with our own. All that is known about him for certain is that he lives and writes in a small community called San Michele Vittoroso, and that all his writing is an attempt to pull back the veil on these hidden eldritch terrors.

All-American Werewolf
ISBN: 978-4-86751-241-8

Published by
Next Chapter
1-60-20 Minami-Otsuka
170-0005 Toshima-Ku, Tokyo
+818035793528

15th October 2021